WHAT
HAPPENED
ON
BEALE
STREET

BOOKS BY MARY ELLIS

SECRETS OF THE SOUTH MYSTERIES
Midnight on the Mississippi
What Happened on Beale Street

CIVIL WAR HEROINES
The Quaker and the Rebel
The Lady and the Officer

THE NEW BEGINNINGS SERIES
Living in Harmony
Love Comes to Paradise
A Little Bit of Charm

THE WAYNE COUNTY SERIES
Abigail's New Hope
A Marriage for Meghan

THE MILLER FAMILY SERIES
A Widow's Hope
Never Far from Home
The Way to a Man's Heart

STANDALONES
Sarah's Christmas Miracle
An Amish Family Reunion
A Plain Man
The Last Heiress

WHAT
HAPPENED
ON
BEALE
STREET

MARY ELLIS

HARVEST HOUSE PUBLISHERS
EUGENE, OREGON

WHAT HAPPENED ON BEALE STREET
Copyright © 2016 by Mary Ellis
Published by Harvest House Publishers
Eugene, Oregon 97402
www.harvesthousepublishers.com

Library of Congress Cataloging-in-Publication Data
    Ellis, Mary, author.
    What happened on Beale Street / Mary Ellis.
        pages ; cm. -- (Secrets of the South mysteries ; book 2)
    ISBN 978-0-7369-6171-4 (softcover)
    ISBN 978-0-7369-6172-1 (eBook)
    I. Title.
    PS3626.E36W48 2016
    813'.6--dc23

                                               2015027110

ACKNOWLEDGMENTS

Thanks to Dale Canter, retired Chief of Police for the cities of Maple Heights, Moreland Hills, and Richfield, Ohio, for assistance with police procedures. Without your professional help, my story would be even more fictional than it already is.

Thanks to the helpful guides at the Mississippi Blues Trail Museum and lovely Peabody Hotel in downtown Memphis. Your hospitality is legendary. Although my tale about the Carlton jewels is purely a figment of my imagination, I found inspiration walking the halls and hanging out in your gorgeous lobby. Love those ducks!

Thanks to Memphis writer pals Johnnie Alexander and Patricia Bradley for your help, and also the Wayne County Writers' Guild, especially Ruth, Bobbie, Christina, Darrell, Cyndi, and Kira, for brainstorming the subplot with me.

Thanks to my dear friends Pete and Donna Taylor, and my husband, Ken, who allowed me to experience the city of Memphis in all its glory. Researching with friends and family is so much more fun.

Thanks to my agent, Mary Sue Seymour; my lovely proofreader, Joycelyn Sullivan; my editor, Kim Moore; and the wonderful staff at Harvest House Publishers. Where would I be without your hard work?

ONE

New Orleans

*N*icki Price opened one eye to find an irate face looming over her in the dark room.

"Why do you pay a phone bill if you refuse to answer the thing?" Her roommate slapped the phone down on Nicki's solar plexus, none too gently.

"I do pick up when people call during daylight hours." Letting her cell fall to the floor, Nicki turned over and snuggled deeper under her covers.

Chloe Galen plopped down on the edge of the bed. "Nic, you're a partner in a big-time PI agency. You need to be ready for adventure twenty-four-seven."

"Spoken like a true artist-in-residence, who paints solely when the creative impulse strikes but under no circumstances before noon. Besides, Price Investigations is not a big-time agency. I work for my cousin for chump change." Nicki tried to bump Chloe off the bed with her hip. "Isn't it the middle of the night? Why are you still up?"

"Because whenever I doze off, your stupid phone wakes me up. How can you stand the theme song from a TV Western for a ringtone? If you don't answer the next time it rings, I'm coming back with a bucket of cold water." Chloe picked the phone from the rug and handed it to her friend just as it began its annoying tune again as though on cue.

Nicki sat upright and kicked the tangled covers to the foot of her bed. "Hello?" she demanded crossly. "Whoever you are, do you have any idea what time it is?"

"Nicki?" A familiar voice on the other end sounded distant. "It's Danny Andre."

"Danny. I would recognize your Barry White imitation underwater." Nicki changed her tone as every trace of sleepiness vanished. "How are you? *Where* are you? I heard you moved to the big city to seek fame and fortune. I have major news too—a new job, cool apartment, and a real live *fee-ahn-say*." She couldn't help grinning as she said that last bit.

"That's great, Nic. I'm happy for you," he said. But the subsequent moments of silence didn't convey much enthusiasm.

Nicki's smile vanished from her face. "Hey, what's going on? I don't hear anything from you for months, and then you call in the middle of the night?"

"Sorry about that. I keep forgetting normal people keep normal hours."

"Forget about normal. What's wrong, Danny?"

"Anything I can do?" Chloe whispered. She was lingering in the doorway.

Nicki shook her head as she dug through her nightstand for pen and paper.

"Remember our promise that we'd be able to tell each other anything? I didn't know who else to call since my sister has had enough of me lately. This might send Isabelle around the bend." His laugh sounded hollow.

The fact that her childhood best friend resurrected a playground pledge sent a chill through Nicki's veins. "Of course I remember. Nothing has changed, so spill your guts. What did you do? Knock over the Natchez Savings and Loan? Why not hide out in New Orleans? Providing you dress like a tourist, no one will find you in the French Quarter."

Her jest fell short of its mark, while the sound of his labored breathing tied Nicki's gut into knots. "Danny, please say something. You're scaring me."

"Then that makes two of us. I'm in real trouble, Nicki. I got myself into a mess."

She closed her eyes, trying to rectify his pleas with her best friend from the sixth grade until their high school graduation. Danny Andre was the sweetest guy she knew. Everyone liked him, from their Sunday school teacher to the surly old man who kept every ball that landed in his yard. Even her mother liked him, despite insulting every other male that crossed the Price threshold. Danny was more diplomatic than a Swiss banker and twice as generous.

"How much trouble can someone get into playing a saxophone in a Memphis orchestra?" she asked.

"I play in blues clubs where I pick up gigs and fill in for regulars. My job is a far cry from the New York Philharmonic."

"*What*? Your granny told you to stay out of the bars when you left town." Nicki waited for a sarcastic retort, but she heard the sound of muffled sobs instead. "Sorry. No more bad jokes. Tell me what I can do to help."

"Could you come to Memphis? Maybe bring your cousin and that new fiancé of yours? Bring some of his friends too. The more the merrier."

Unfortunately, she hesitated a second too long. "Sure. Hunter and I will drive up as soon as he's done testifying in court. Shouldn't be more than a few days. I would love to see Memphis as soon as he can break away. I'll check if Nate can—"

"I'm sorry, Nic. How stupid of me to think you could drop everything and hightail it upriver. We ain't in the seventh grade anymore. Let's get together when things calm down for Hunter. I'll call you."

"Wait, Danny! Give me your address and I'll come this weekend even if Hunter can't. I'm not too busy for my friend—"

But he had already hung up.

"What's wrong with him?" asked Chloe.

Nicki turned to face her future sister-in-law. "I have no idea. I'm obviously terrible at crisis intervention. If somebody was out on the ledge contemplating suicide, I'd probably ask them to wait till after my pedicure." She put her face in her hands and groaned.

"Give yourself a break. It's hard to be Johnny-on-the-spot at two o'clock in the morning." Chloe walked over to the bed and bent to give her friend a hug. "Who is this Danny person? Does my brother have something to worry about? I know for a fact Hunter is crazy about you, 'crazy' being the operative word."

Because trying to get back to sleep would be a fruitless endeavor, Nicki got out of bed, slipped into her robe, and then padded to the coffeemaker in the kitchen. "Danny Andre was the only person in high school who didn't think me weird during a weird period of my life."

"An old boyfriend from your misguided youth rears his head?" Chloe perched on a tall kitchen stool.

"Not a boyfriend, just a friend. Danny is in trouble, but I was too busy explaining how great things were for me to help him."

Chloe's expression softened. "What kind of trouble? IRS liens, problem with the musicians' union, advice for the love-lorn? Hunter could help with the first, Nate the second, and I'm your girl for the third."

Nicki released an exasperated sigh. "I have no idea. He hung up too fast. I need to get to Memphis ASAP. Danny wouldn't have called unless it was serious." As soon as she swallowed a mouthful of reheated coffee, she punched in his number. The call went straight to voice mail.

"Do you know where he lives in Memphis?"

"Nope."

"Yet you're going to jump on a plane."

"Yep. He and Christine Hall were my closest friends. Danny refused to ask someone to our prom so we could go as a pack of nerds. Now that Christine is dead, I need to step up to the plate." Nicki poured coffee into a travel mug.

"What about your job?"

"PI work isn't like being a bank teller, Chloe. Nate and I have to wait for clients to hire us."

"Do you plan on telling my brother where you're going?"

Nicki stopped fussing with sugar packets. "Of course I will, but I don't want to call him until the sun is up. One of us should get a decent night's sleep. Until then I'll take a shower and pack a bag. The more I replay the conversation with Danny, the more I think I shouldn't waste time."

With that she walked back to her room and into the bathroom, curtailing Chloe's questions. Steam soon enveloped her in a moist cocoon, but Nicki found no solace. The fear in Danny's voice echoed in her ears. Why had she been so blithe, so careless with his request? It wasn't as if he pestered her with one demand after another.

By the time she was dressed and had dried her hair into a mane of curls, the love of her life had arrived. Hunter Galen was sipping coffee at the table when she walked back into the kitchen.

"Rumor has it you and I are going to Memphis. It's one of my favorite cities—birthplace of the blues and home of the tastiest barbecue in the South." Hunter smacked his lips and reached for her hand. "Good morning, my love."

Nicki threw her arms around him while scowling at her room-mate over his shoulder. Chloe simply shrugged and offered her an adorable smile.

"What are you doing here, sweet man?" Nicki kissed the top of Hunter's head, his hair still damp from a shower. "You have a big day ahead of you. Your busybody sister must have forgotten you have to testify in court or bad people will get away with murder."

Chloe placed a cup of coffee on the table and slunk from the room.

"I couldn't sleep anyway." Hunter tightened his arms around her waist. "What's up with your friend? Is this the knight who rescued you from a snake-infested island? Nate said the guy swam out from shore to carry you back in a pirogue."

"You already called my cousin?"

"Yes, on my way here. I needed to know about any rascal who would invite you to visit at two a.m."

"I'm going to slap your sister silly," Nicki fumed.

"I'd pay a dollar to watch, but first tell me the story about snake island." Hunter kneaded her back with his long fingers.

"Nate and his pals stranded me in the middle of a swamp without a pole or oars. I couldn't use my hands for paddles because gators live in that water. My cousin planned to return when the moon rose. Danny heard about their prank at the Dairy Queen and rescued me first. But he certainly didn't swim. He paddled out in another pirogue and towed mine back. My, how stories change with each retelling."

"I would love to meet so brave a hero."

Nicki buried her face into Hunter's starched shirt, trying to forget the panic in Danny's voice. "I can count on one hand the times Danny asked me for anything. Today he gave me a chance to even the score, and what did I do? Rambled on about how great life is ever since I found true love. How could I be so self-centered?"

"Chloe said he woke you up from a dead sleep."

"If you heard how scared he sounded, Hunter, you wouldn't make excuses for me."

"I would make excuses for you even strapped to a rack beneath a pendulum blade."

Nicki pulled away. "Something bad has happened. I need to go to Memphis but haven't decided whether to drive or fly."

"I'll ask the DA to petition the court for a continuance and book us on the next flight." Finishing his coffee, Hunter got to his feet.

"No, sweet man. Thank you, but you don't want to annoy the judge. Besides I'm a licensed PI, equipped to swim through whatever snake-infested waters Memphis has." Nicki reached for her shoulder holster and Beretta from the shelf above the stove.

"Have you ever been to Memphis, Nicolette? Have you spent time in the clubs and smoky after-hours dives where musicians congregate?"

"No, but Danny was a former choir boy at First Baptist Church of Natchez. I doubt he would hang out in those places." She placed a bottle of water into her bag.

"People change. I'm sure singing gospel on Sunday mornings didn't cause whatever trouble he's in."

Nicki pivoted to face him. "You need to be in court. I'll do what I can and come back before you miss me."

Hunter lifted her chin with one finger. "Humor me by asking Nate to go with you. Memphis is no place for a brand-new detective, male or female. Before I leave for court, I'll arrange your flight, hotel, and have a rental car waiting at the airport. Please, *cherie*?"

Nicki grinned. "But Nate was the one who stranded me on that island, remember?"

"I remember. Rest assured that history won't repeat itself in the Mississippi delta. And if you'll be in Memphis for a while, I'll fly up once I'm done testifying. I know some special places you will like."

"You have a deal, Galen. Call the airlines while I finish packing. Then I'll enjoy pressing Nate's buzzer until he drags himself out of bed."

⮑

However, when Nicki arrived at her cousin's apartment, the door was ajar. Drawing her weapon, she crept inside, fully prepared for mayhem. But by the time her eyes adjusted to the dark, she heard the sound of water running in the bathroom and someone humming the Mississippi State fight song.

She inched her way to Nate's bedroom, where a half dozen shirts and pairs of trousers had been strewn across the unmade bed. "Nate?" she called from the hallway. "It's Nicki. Why is your door wide open?"

Her new business partner emerged from the bathroom dressed in jeans and a sport shirt. "Because Hunter called and said you were on your way. Give me another ten minutes and we can be off." Nate took his gun from the nightstand drawer along with an extra clip of ammunition.

"You'll come to Memphis without begging or bribery?" Nicki remained where she stood, not wishing to invade his private space.

"Sure, why not? We don't have any cases at the moment, and your well-heeled fiancé insists on paying our expenses no matter how long we're gone. And that's just two of my reasons." Nate placed his shirts and pants into a suitcase and then dumped everything else on top unceremoniously.

"I'm not sure why Hunter wants to help Danny. He doesn't know him."

"Because he doesn't want you driving your car or staying in a cheap motel in a bad neighborhood. And, frankly, I don't either or I wouldn't be taking expense money from him. Danny was my friend too, Nic, and Natchez boys stick together." Nate zipped up the case and then said, "Are you ready? Hunter said he booked us on a nine o'clock flight."

Nicki blinked, confused. Because Danny hadn't played sports in school, the two barely knew each other. "Wait a minute. Did Hunter tell you to act like this dynamic duo thing was your idea? So I wouldn't get my feathers ruffled?"

"Don't overthink this, Nic. An expense-paid trip to somewhere I haven't been sounds like a vacation."

She sighed but decided to give in gracefully. "Okay, but let's leave before Hunter hires a private bodyguard for me." Turning, she pulled her case out the door.

I'm in real trouble, Nicki. I got myself into a mess. Each time Danny's words replayed through her mind, the uncomfortable feeling in her gut turned downright ominous.

TWO

Memphis

*N*ate pressed the button to lower the window once they reached Riverside Drive. Moist, humid air wafted inside, negating the car's air-conditioning. He would be hard-pressed not to behave like a tourist because, at the moment, that's what he was. Before setting up his office in New Orleans, he'd spent little time in cities. The small town outside Natchez where he grew up didn't appear on maps beyond the county level. Even the town where he went to college, Starkville, paled in comparison to Memphis, especially when students went home for summer vacation.

This sprawling metropolis at the junction of Tennessee, Louisiana, and Arkansas attracted the brightest and best from one end of Old Man River to the other. Memphis had inspired countless stories, songs, poems, and young men's dreams from B.B. King to Mark Twain to small-town boys like Nate. He hoped Danny Andre's visions of fame and fortune hadn't led him down an alley of no return. Nicki, who had barely said a word since their plane landed, stared at a coal barge as though she didn't see the identical sight in Louisiana on a regular basis.

"Are you all right, cousin?" he asked, turning off the radio.

A shrug served as her reply.

"According to the GPS, we're almost to the hotel booked by Mr. Deep Pockets." The bait Nate dangled generated no quick retort. Usually, Nicki jumped to defend Hunter against even the most minor disparagement, but not this time. "I'm hoping this place throws in a free breakfast buffet like the chains along the interstate. Don't you just love those cool waffle machines with little jars of marmalade?" He grabbed her knee and shook it, a knee covered by a long, ladylike skirt.

"Fancy places don't offer free breakfasts, but maybe you'll find a fruit basket in your room or a bowl of nuts in the lobby." Nicki spoke with straight-up sincerity, not with her usual sassy tone.

"Take it easy, kid. Things will be fine. Andre was probably over-reacting about his car getting towed or his cat running away. A quick trip to the impound lot or the county pound and his world will look rosy again."

"You can't be serious." Nicki turned her focus to a street sign. "Hey, we just passed Beale Street, where most of the blues clubs are." She punched the redial button on her phone for the twentieth time since the airport.

"Yes, but we need something to narrow our search. Danny still isn't picking up?" Nate waited at the traffic light, unsure whether right turns on red were legal in Tennessee. A blare from a car horn answered that particular question.

"No. It just rings and rings. No voice mail, no answering machine."

"Who else could we call? Does he have family in town?"

Nicki pulled her address book from her purse. "Danny will kill me if I call his sister and worry her over nothing. They lived together for a while when he first moved to Memphis. He sort of drove her crazy with typical guy stuff, like socks all over the apartment and cleaning his fishing tackle with Izzy's good hand towels."

"Women can be such neat freaks. Did I ever meet her? Izzy Andre sounds like a Cajun slushy."

"How could you not have met her? Our high school wasn't that big. She went by the name Isabelle and would be around your age."

Nate turned down a side street to drop Nicki off under the hotel's covered porte cochere, thinking about Isabelle Andre.

Oh, he remembered Danny's sister all right, but their acquaintance had been limited to him admiring her from afar. Queen Isabelle would have crossed the street to avoid bumping into him or any other sports jock. She was supermodel pretty, with waist-length black hair, green eyes, and porcelain skin that indicated Creole blood from long-forgotten ancestors. She thought most male classmates were destined to cut her grass or clean the skimmers of her future pool. Female peers were either competition to be bested or so unworthy they deserved only pity. Somehow Nicki had avoided either category. His cousin seemed to truly like the woman, and from what he could gather, the feeling was mutual. The last he heard, Izzy had married her college sweetheart upon his admission into some expensive law school. The fact she was now living in Memphis struck him as odd.

"Why don't you hop out here and get us checked in?" said Nate, shaking off the past. "I'll park in the garage and carry our bags to the lobby."

"Hang on a minute." A moment later Nicki spoke into the mouthpiece. "Hey, Izzy, it's Nicolette Price from Natchez. I got a bizarre call from your brother that spooked me. Danny may be in hot water and he's not picking up. Anyway, I happen to be in Memphis, so please call me with his address. I plan to drop by to punch him in the nose for scaring me in the middle of the night." Nicki recited her number, ended the call, and thumped her head on the dashboard. "I hate it when I ramble on like that. Izzy already has my number, and I sounded like a total moron."

"No more so than usual." Nate reached behind her to open the door. "This boy is salivating for something to eat. Is it too early for sweet-and-tangy baby back ribs?"

Nicki produced a frightful face but got out of the car. Ten minutes later, dragging her suitcase and his, Nate walked into the grand lobby of the Carlton Hotel. "Grand" did not do the place justice. He let his gaze scan the interior from the marble floor up to the ornate, chandeliered ceiling the way someone would admire a famous masterpiece. Dark hardwood panels were polished to a high gloss, sparkling étagères displayed memorabilia from decades long ago, and recessed spotlights illuminated portraits of those responsible for the hotel's illustrious past.

Nate approached the central courtyard, in which a fountain rose from a marble pond, complete with resident fish. Bistro tables and chairs awaited those wishing a late night snack, along with sofas and chairs grouped for intimate conversations. A wide mezzanine with access to second-floor rooms encircled the lobby, giving the lobby a European ambiance. Everything and everyone in the hotel spoke of old money and exquisite taste.

"Not like you to admire something unconnected to pro sports." Nicki poked his side with her purse.

"When your fiancé calls ahead, he certainly spares no expense. I'm hoping the front desk didn't book us into the honeymoon suite."

"Ha, almost. The guy kept calling me *Mrs.* Price and clucked his tongue when I said adjoining rooms wouldn't be necessary. Apparently, he never heard of cousins or siblings traveling together. Elevators are this way. I can't wait to take off these heels."

After Nicki had swiped her keycard in a door on the seventh floor, Nate preceded her into a room that could only have been eclipsed by the presidential suite. "Holy cow. Look at the space in here. Why don't I sleep on the sofa and save Hunter some dough?" He pointed at an overstuffed couch in an alcove.

Nicki plopped down on the bed. "Nothing doing. If we're still here next Friday, Hunter's flying up to take me out to the best spots in town. He'll bunk in your room."

"What, no third suite?" Nate teased.

Nicki giggled. "He suggested that, but I said no way. He can save his money for our wedding. I don't even want to know what this place costs."

"Try Danny's number again." Nate gazed on the Mississippi River from her window.

As Nicki reached for her purse, her phone burst into the theme song for *Rawhide*. "Hello? Hey, Izzy, thanks for calling me back."

Eager to check out his room, Nate headed to the door to give her some privacy.

"Slow down. I can't understand what you're saying." Nicki scrambled off the bed. "You're in his apartment right now?"

Nate let go of his bag and circled the four-poster bed so he could gauge her expression. "What's going on?" he asked. Nicki had paled to the color of milk.

She motioned to the pen and pad on the antique desk. "Okay, take a deep breath and give us Danny's address. Nate came to town with me." Nicki began scribbling the moment he handed her the pen. "We're on our way. In the meantime, don't touch anything and try not to worry."

Nate clamped a hand on her wrist to get her attention. "Tell her to hold on. Talk to me, cousin."

"Hold on a second, Izzy." Nicki covered the mouthpiece with her palm. "After she listened to my message, she went straight to Danny's apartment. I guess I freaked her out. The place is a wreck. Overturned furniture, the coffee table smashed, and somebody punched a hole through a wall. And…and there's blood on the kitchen floor, lots of it."

Nate steadied her with a firm hand. He'd never seen her so

flustered. "Follow standard procedure. Tell her to call the police and that we're on our way."

Nicki did as instructed and then thrust the address at him with trembling fingers. "Good thing we have GPS. I have no idea where this is."

He tucked her phone into her purse. "Did Izzy say how much blood? Like from a broken nose or like someone bled out?"

"I don't know. Stop asking stupid questions." Nicki burst into tears.

"Sorry. As soon as you change shoes, we can go." Nate pointed at the ridiculous high heels Chloe undoubtedly told her to wear.

"Good idea." Nicki dug her sneakers from her suitcase and threw the offending shoes across the room. "But I'm taking my gun and don't try to stop me."

"I wouldn't dream of it."

A few minutes later Nate closed the door to her luxury suite behind him. While they hurried down the hall, he slipped the clip into his weapon and tucked it into his shoulder holster. By the time the elevator door opened, all thoughts of a relaxing vacation had vanished like mist on the river at sunrise.

It took ten minutes to reach Danny Andre's last known address. In that short period of time, they moved from the world of luxury getaways and top-tier corporate expense accounts to a jungle of abandoned warehouses, tenement apartments, and decayed early twentieth-century houses. Thugs with nowhere to go and nothing but trouble to get into lingered on street corners and in doorways of abandoned homes. At least, Nate hoped no human inhabitants dwelled within.

"We're here." Nate disconnected the GPS and shoved it beneath the seat.

Nicki remained still with her eyes clenched shut, but her moving lips revealed she was praying.

"Don't worry about those men, Nic. We're both packing, and I know you're a crack shot."

"You think I'm worried for myself, Nate? I'm hoping this is all a horrible mistake. Maybe Danny left three pounds of ground meat on the counter to defrost and rats got into it. Men can be so thoughtless at times. Soon he'll come home from a friend's house and wonder what all the commotion is about."

Only his cousin could dream up such a scenario. But, frankly, there wasn't half the amount of commotion Nate expected at Danny's residence. Only one police cruiser was parked at the curb, and he didn't see a forensic van or an unmarked sedan belonging to a detective. "Are you sure you're ready for this?"

Nicki met his eyes and nodded. "He's my friend, but I'm also a professional investigator."

"Even seasoned veterans sit out cases that hit close to home. There's no shame in staying here while I go inside." He tried to sound as nonjudgmental as possible.

With a snort Nicki jumped out of the car. "We know nothing at this point, so stop babying me."

Nate had to hurry to keep up with her. If any street thugs had evil thoughts, they would have had a hard time catching them. Unfortunately, without a working elevator, three flights of dirty concrete steps separated them from Danny's floor. Halfway down the hallway, a uniformed cop leaned against a doorjamb, smoking a cigarette.

"Man, doesn't that guy know this building is a firetrap?" Nate muttered.

Nicki had reached the open doorway. Stepping in front of her to enter the apartment first, Nate was initially surprised by the threadbare, spare furnishings in the drab living room. His bachelor status, along with zero decorating abilities, guaranteed his New Orleans townhouse would never be featured in a magazine, but Danny's apartment was the saddest representation of human existence he'd ever seen. Although neither dirty nor cluttered, nothing within view could have come from anywhere other than curbside discards. A pang of sorrow filled his gut, despite the fact he barely knew the man.

"Hello?" he called. "Private investigators Nate and Nicolette Price from New Orleans."

A cop stuck his head around the corner. "You're a long way from home, Mr. and Mrs. Price. Be careful you don't contaminate my crime scene."

Snapping out of her fog, Nicki squatted down to evaluate the contents of the smashed coffee table.

"For the record, my partner and I are cousins, not spouses. Any sign of struggle in the other rooms?" Nate pulled on gloves and tossed a pair to Nicki.

"Somebody rummaged through the dresser drawers, and then we have this in here." Officer Flynn, according to his badge, pointed at a nasty pool of dried blood.

"What is that officer at the door doing that he let two sightseers wander into a crime scene?" A second cop glared up from where she marked blood spatter for the forensic team. Her name badge indicated a surname of Ryan.

"I got a call from Danny Andre. He's my friend." Nicki stepped into the cramped kitchen and gasped. Despite her previous assurance to the contrary, the sight of this particular blood caused her to stagger.

"Hey! I'll tell you the same thing I told the guy's sister. Go sit in our squad car downstairs until I have time to take your statement. I won't have people fainting or puking into potential evidence before the techs get here." Officer Ryan's tone conveyed no sympathy.

Nate stepped between the two women. Looking at Nicki, he

said, "If Izzy is here, why don't you find out what she knows while I do the same up here?" When she started to protest, he cut her off. "Think for a moment. Izzy is probably scared to death and could use a friend."

"I'll be downstairs when you're ready for my statement about the phone call." She glanced at the blood spray on the refrigerator and the coffee carafe smashed against the wall, and then she slowly backed from the room.

Officer Flynn opened his notebook. "How do you know Mr. Andre?"

Nate's gaze landed on what looked like a bicuspid molar. He hoped the bloody tooth belonged to Danny's adversary.

"We were all friends in high school. He called Nicki last night and asked her to come to Memphis because he was in some kind of trouble."

"What kind of trouble?" Flynn's brows knit into a straight line.

"He didn't say and apparently regretted making the request afterward."

"What request is that?" Officer Ryan resumed marking blood droplets.

"For Miss Price to come to Memphis." Nate spoke slowly and succinctly.

"Was Andre a user—crack, meth, pills? Know what his drug of choice happened to be?"

"He wasn't a user, to my knowledge. Why would you draw such an assumption? Were drugs found inside the apartment?" Nate bit his inner cheek to keep his voice level.

"Not so far, but did you happen to notice the neighborhood on your way over? Only dopers, hookers, and ex-felons who can't figure out a new career path live here." Officer Flynn examined the streaky window glass.

"And those whose take-home pay won't buy a three-bedroom ranch out in the suburbs with a white picket fence."

Flynn pulled off his gloves. "That where you live in Orleans Parish? Maybe in the Garden District, home of blue-blooded dinosaurs and the bleeding heart, artsy types?"

"Actually, I live in the warehouse district—artsy, but a notch above this, socioeconomically speaking. How about you, Flynn? Where do you hang your hat after work?"

"Back to your corners, both of you." Officer Ryan got to her feet. "I'm not sure why you're still here, Mr. Price. You've had a look around. Perhaps your friend will call and clear this up. Leave your number in case we hear anything."

Nate held out his card. "We're staying at the Carlton while in town."

"*The Carlton*? Talk to me again about socioeconomics," Flynn all but snarled.

Nate left his card on the counter and strode from the apartment. To rein in his temper, he took his time on the three flights of steps down. Sparring with the police wouldn't help Nicki or Danny. As he approached a car by the curb, he spotted Nicki and a woman deep in conversation. He knocked on the window to get their attention.

"How ya feelin', Nicki?" he asked when they both got out. "And you must be Izzy Andre. I'm Nate Price. Pleased to meet you." He stuck out his hand toward the tall, leggy brunette.

The woman blinked and stared as she shook hands. "I'm fine, thank you, Mr. Price. I believe we met in high school. You're Nicki's new boss?"

"That's me. Somebody has to teach this greenhorn the ropes." Unfortunately, his response would have been more appropriate at a hometown reunion instead of their present circumstances.

"Danny mentioned Nicki was pursuing her dream of becoming an investigator." She placed her hands on her slim hips.

"Well, Izzy, we're here to help any way we can."

"Only my closest friends call me Izzy. I don't really know you, Mr. Price."

Unfortunately, the Mississippi River was too far away to throw himself into. "I beg your pardon, Miss Andre. I got used to hearing Nicki—" Nate shook off the pointless rationalization. "I stand corrected, ma'am."

"What did you learn upstairs? The police shooed me out when the sight of so much blood made me queasy."

"Understandable. I saw obvious signs of a struggle but not of forced entry. Danny apparently let whoever he got into a fight with into the apartment. They're also looking for evidence of drug use."

Isabelle glanced at Nicki as though for confirmation. "Go on."

"Somebody rummaged through his drawers, but it could have been Danny earlier today. Maybe he was looking for a particular garment. Although there's a bit of blood, the amount wouldn't indicate a loss of life." Nate stuck his hands in his pockets.

"Is that it, Mr. Price?" Isabelle's voice rose with intensity.

"For now, ma'am. The police will run the blood samples against their databases. They also bagged his razor from the drawer to determine his blood type in case Danny isn't in the system."

"We'll know more after forensic techs process the apartment." Nicki interjected, wrapping her arm around her friend.

"I will wait by the phone until I hear from my brother." Isabelle faltered, unsteady on her feet. "Or until I receive an update from the police department."

Nate bristled for the second time in fifteen minutes. "I didn't say Nicki and I were finished. We intend to find him, Miss Andre."

Isabelle pulled away from Nicki. "How can you help? You

didn't know my brother very well. Danny didn't use drugs, and he wouldn't tear apart a drawer to find a piece of clothing, not even on his wedding day. And as far as *being in the system*?" Her tone became brittle. "He's not because he is the sweetest, gentlest man on earth. Nicki, I hope you'll stay for as long as you can, but there's no reason for you to remain, Mr. Price. I'm sorry you made a pointless trip to Memphis."

THREE

To say that Nate and Izzy hadn't hit it off during their initial introduction would be an understatement of epic proportions, but what did Nate expect? Her cousin was always so happy-go-lucky, so casual with everyone he met. Whether young or old, male or female, Nate treated everyone as if they were future friends instead of commensurate with their acquaintance. Nicki remembered running into one of their former teachers while at the mall in Natchez. Nate called the woman "Carol" instead of "Mrs. Bennett" like everyone else. The woman's three grandchildren nearly doubled over with laughter, but Nate never realized his faux pas.

Izzy had always been sensitive about overfamiliarity. Maybe a deportment class or book had taught her the maxim: "People will only respect you if you're respectable." So she treated people courteously and demanded nothing less in return. She didn't know Nate, and apparently she didn't remember him from high school. And considering the day's frightening chain of events, she wasn't at her best.

Nicki felt that Nate shouldn't have gotten his nose out of joint. Not every woman on earth would find his shaggy blond hair, tanned and trim physique, and boyish charm appealing. It was bound to happen eventually. She just wished it hadn't been today. What if Nate dropped her at the hotel and headed back to the airport? What would she say to Hunter? She knew very well he didn't want her in Memphis alone.

Fortunately, by the time they got back to her suite Nate seemed to have recovered his dignity. "Hand me my bag. I want to find my room and get unpacked."

"Does this mean you're staying?" Nicki asked, unable to stop herself.

"Of course I'll stay until we find your friend. Nothing has changed." Nate leaned on the doorjamb. "Did you think the Ice Queen would run me out of town?"

"She's been known to have that effect on people." Nicki walked around the bed to retrieve his bag.

"I'm sure that's true, but I'm here for you, Nic. I know you'll want to call Hunter and catch your breath for an hour or two, but call me when you're ready to get something to eat. Neither one of us had any lunch today."

Nicki shuffled her feet on the plush carpeting. "I would rather not leave the hotel in case the police call here instead of our cell phones."

"Agreed. That's why I had the lobby coffee shop in mind. I'm sure they have barbecue on the menu, but don't take too long. There's no basket of fruit like you promised." Nate offered her his signature wink before closing the door.

Alone in her room, Nicki took a few minutes to scrub her face and hands and let her tears fall. *So much blood...so much of Danny's blood.* Maybe she wasn't cut out for her chosen vocation after all. She'd worked so hard to get this job with Price Investigations, but the sights and smells in that apartment almost caused her to become physically ill.

Signs of a struggle. No forced entry. Blood spatter inconsistent with arterial spray. All the jargon heard on television took on new meaning when it referred to someone you loved. And Nicki loved Danny Andre as a friend. He was the kindest person she had ever met, just how Izzy described. Poor Izzy had no idea what to do with herself. She couldn't remain at Danny's apartment, and she couldn't come with them after verbally thrashing Nate, and she didn't want to go home alone. Nicki decided she wouldn't be able to relax until she was assured that Izzy was all right.

Izzy picked up on the first ring. "Hello, Nicki. Have you heard from Danny?"

"No, but I tried several more times. Why doesn't he have an answering machine?"

"He had one, but he hocked it."

"Any close friends? I hope that wasn't his blood we saw. It will probably be hours before the police process the apartment and come up with leads, so why don't you grab a bite to eat with Nate and me? Just something casual here in the hotel."

"Thanks, but I need to stay by the phone."

"You have a cell that can go with you. Anyway, you need to keep your strength up, girl."

There was a moment's hesitation before Izzy spoke. "I couldn't face your partner after being so awful. Please pass my apologies to Mr. Price. I haven't been sleeping well for the past few weeks."

"Hey, at least you didn't try to run him down with your car." Nicki tried to smooth her friend's discomfort with a joke.

"Sounds like a story you'll share another time. I'm going to heat a frozen meal and check Danny's recent Facebook posts."

"By tomorrow Nate and I will have a battle plan for tracking him down. Are you sure you don't want to stay here with me?"

"No thanks, Nicki. Please tell your cousin what I said, and I'll be in touch." Izzy disconnected before Nicki could begin her next round of arguments.

A few minutes later, Nate handled the apology delivered through an intermediary rather well. "It's fine. Her reaction was to be expected, really. Miss Andre is under a lot of stress. Look, they have a table ready for us." He nudged her toward a booth on the right.

Nicki glanced around the less fancy of the two restaurants in the hotel, which was anything but unfancy. The lush opulence of the lobby and her suite was evident in the coffee shop as well, but at least they had ribs on the menu.

"Good grief. Check out these prices," Nate whispered under his breath. "Let's sneak out when the hostess turns her back. They must have a Joe's Rib House within walking distance."

"Nothing doing," she hissed back. "You promised we would stay inside the Carlton until we heard something. Besides, Hunter's paying for our meals here, and he made me promise we would eat someplace nice when I called him with an update."

Nate crossed his arms. "This trip is no longer a fun getaway. We may be in Memphis a while."

"I know, but I'm too tired to walk anywhere right now. Please, Nate?"

"Sure, Nic. It's fine with me." He patted her hand. "I'm just trying not to drain Hunter's bank account. He'll need money for a villa in the south of France for his bride."

"Maybe we'll go abroad for our honeymoon, but I don't want to live anywhere but New Orleans." Nicki's eyes unexpectedly flooded with tears.

"Glad to hear it. Now I know where to go for holiday meals for the rest of my life." Nate squeezed her fingers. "Pick out something so we can order as soon as the waiter arrives. And no lollygagging during the meal. I want to listen to the police scanner when we're done to hear about anything going down in this town."

Nowhere near as hungry as she should be, Nicki selected a broiled chicken breast with herbed rice and a house salad. The food arrived within a reasonable time and tasted as delicious as she expected it would. After dinner, Nicki headed back to her room, where she stripped off her wrinkled outfit and stepped into a hot, soothing shower. She needed to wash away the afternoon's *bad miasma,* as her Mamaw would call it. Although she hadn't touched anything connected to the crime scene, Nicki tried to wash away the memory of Danny's depressing apartment.

Why didn't I stay in contact with him? Why haven't I been a better friend? She wasn't arrogant enough to think she could have changed what happened, but once she was under her covers, shame over her complacency kept her tossing and turning.

Hours later, after finally drifting into a fitful doze, the annoying ringtone of her cell brought her fully awake. Pawing at her nightstand in the dark, Nicki located the phone. "Hello?" She pulled up the covers for protection from the unknown.

"Nicki, it's Izzy…"

"Did you hear from the police?" she asked. At first all she heard were choked gasps and stifled sobs.

"Yes, I just hung up with…Officer Ryan. They found a…body…someplace downriver. They gave me an address."

"Is it your brother?" Nicki felt the chicken and rice churning in her stomach, along with two glasses of sweet tea.

"They won't say for sure. They want me to come to where they are. Whoever they found has no identification…on his person." Izzy made small mewing sounds. "Will you meet me? I don't want to be alone."

"I'll do you one better. Nate and I will pick you up. Give me five minutes to get dressed—"

"No, Nicki. Your hotel is right next to the river. All you need to do is head down Third Street, which turns into Route 61. Write down the address and I'll meet you there."

"If that's what you prefer. Is it okay if I bring Nate?" She was already shrugging off her nightgown.

"Of course. He's your partner as well as your cousin, and I'm sure he's very good at what he does." A raspy cough punctuated her sentence. "Please hurry, Nicki. I don't think I can face this alone."

Nicki repeated the address back to her and said goodbye. She was already sobbing as hard as Danny's sister. The body the police found could be some hapless hobo who fell from a railroad overpass, or possibly a delta angler who had enjoyed too many cold ones while fishing that afternoon. Or it could be someone from so far upriver identification wouldn't be possible for days.

But somehow, just like Izzy Andre, Nicki knew exactly who it would be.

FOUR

*I*t was a good thing that little traffic remained on city streets during the early morning hours. And that Memphis's finest men and women in blue were busy with more serious crime than speeders. From the time Nicki called, waking him from a pleasant dream of bygone success on the gridiron, Nate hadn't slowed down. He got dressed, grabbed his wallet and car keys, and walked out the door.

His cousin met him at the elevator with a face devoid of makeup and hair that looked like a haystack after a windstorm. Nicki didn't say much as they climbed into the rental car, except for repeating the address provided by Isabelle. Nate tried to fill the car's dead air space with comforting words such as "It might not be Danny," and "Plenty of people go missing on any given weekend in the city," and "That body could have floated down from Iowa for all we know." When none of them elicited a response, Nate concentrated on closing the distance between the hotel and their intended destination as quickly as possible.

When they reached a small community park, they had no trouble locating the crime scene. The only cars present were two squad cars and the van from the crime lab. Techs were just climbing from the vehicle as Nate shifted the car into park. Nicki sat motionless, staring at the river cloaked in a blanket of fog. Flashlight beams bounced erratically as officers cordoned off the area with yellow tape.

"I don't see Miss Andre's car. Doesn't she drive a Prius?" asked Nate, remembering the car at Danny's apartment.

Nicki pivoted on her seat as a car crept toward them. "This must be her now."

When the vehicle pulled into the adjacent space, it indeed was a dark green Prius. Isabelle climbed out, looking far less imposing than she had earlier.

"I'm so happy to see you," she said as Nicki jumped out of the rental car.

The two women hugged while Nate watched like an uninvited interloper. Then he approached them cautiously. "Why don't you two wait here while I check out the situation?"

Isabelle pulled from Nicki's embrace. "Thank you for coming, Mr. Price. The officer who called said I might need to confirm identification."

"I understand, but let me speak with the police first."

"We'll wait here." Nicki slipped a supportive arm around her friend.

But Nate got no farther than the yellow tape stretched between plastic cones. "That's far enough, Mr. New Orleans." Stepping from the fog, Officer Flynn was so close Nate could smell cigarette smoke on his clothes and coffee on his breath.

"Good morning. I would have thought you'd be off duty by now." Nate mustered his most cordial tone.

"Just my luck to catch this at the end of my shift. What are you doin' here? Nobody called an out-of-town PI."

"You called Miss Andre, and she called us. Besides, as I said earlier, I knew Danny from high school, so I can make the identification and spare Isabelle the trauma."

"Nobody's looking at anything until the medical examiner gets here for a prelim. Nobody's trashing my crime scene."

"You're sure a crime has been committed?" Nate felt his proverbial hackles start to rise.

"Considering my stiff looks younger than thirty, I doubt he dropped dead of old age." Flynn pulled a cigarette from a new pack. "The county ME is on her way. Why don't you stay in your vehicle with Miss Andre until we need her."

Because the request hadn't been a question, Nate swallowed his reply. Nicki was now inside Isabelle's car, so he waited in the rental. The windows on the Prius began to steam up as the women talked and ran the heater against the damp air. About an hour later, as the first streaks of dawn appeared in the sky, the ME arrived carrying a quart-sized travel mug. Soon the riverbank sprang to life. Nate watched as two men in suits ducked under the tape without hesitation. He hoped the detectives wouldn't resent their private-for-hire counterparts as much as the uniformed cops apparently did.

"Good morning," he called out, approaching the crime scene.

Both detectives peered up from squatting positions. One frowned at the interruption, while the other slicked a hand through his hair and straightened to his feet. "Say, don't I know you?" His thick accent pegged him from the hills rather than coastal areas.

Nate smiled with recognition. "Chip Marino, the best wide receiver ever to play for the Bulldogs."

"Nate Price. Or are my bloodshot eyes playing tricks on me? You must be the PI sticking his nose in police business." He stretched out his gloved hand and then seemed to rethink the gesture.

Nate pretended not to notice. "That would be me. Are we still in the city's jurisdiction?"

"Yep, for another quarter mile or so. Otherwise, he would be the sheriff's problem." Marino hooked a thumb at the covered corpse and motioned for Nate to move away from the technicians. "You living in Memphis now? Can't believe I haven't run into you before today."

They walked to a thicket of briars close to the riverbank. "No. This is my first time in Memphis. My cousin and I came to help out a high school friend, Danny Andre. But by the time we got to his apartment, something bad had happened and the police were there."

"So that's how you crawled under Officer Flynn's skin."

"Danny's sister asked us to come to his apartment. Then the police called her a couple hours ago saying they found a body. We're here to see if it's her brother."

"Man, I can't believe they didn't have her come to the coroner's office." Detective Marino opened a leather portfolio and jotted down some notes. "So you think our stiff might be this Danny Andre you went to high school with?"

"Maybe. His sister, Isabelle, is waiting with my partner to make positive ID. Officer Flynn doesn't believe I'm capable of facial recognition."

"Probably a good idea since she saw him more recently. So this Isabelle Andre and your PI partner from New Orleans are also in the parking lot at 5:00 a.m.? This is turning into a three-ring circus." He chuckled with amusement.

Nate failed to see the humor, but he tempered his irritation. He needed a friendly face in law enforcement. "My partner and I are both originally from Natchez, same as Danny and Isabelle. We're here to find out what happened, whether there was foul play or not. And we'd appreciate a leg up. Not all my professional brothers appreciate those on the hourly dole." He gestured toward Flynn.

"You got that right. I'll give you whatever heads-up I can, but nobody gets close to the body until the ME releases the crime scene. Then you, the sister, and your partner can have a look." While the two men watched, techs tented the area to protect it against a light drizzle. "Are you sure Miss Andre wouldn't rather view the body at the morgue? That's where this guy's headed next."

Nate gazed at the river and shook his head. "She's here now. The river probably washed away any blood, so he won't look that much different cleaned up."

"Yeah, along with any evidence too," Marino muttered. "Okay, since they called at the crack of dawn and asked her to come down here, you may as well get this over with. Give us a few more minutes and I'll wave you over."

The detective went back to work, leaving Nate to choose a spot to wait midway between the women and the crime scene. With Nicki trying to comfort Isabelle, he didn't want to crowd their space, especially not after yesterday's dressing down. Despite his assertion her comments had rolled off his thick hide, Isabelle's disrespect had stung more than he thought possible. You would think by the time people reached their thirties, *anyone* from their old hometown would be a welcome sight, even if he hadn't met her high standards in the past. So Nate watched traffic on the river instead. Fishermen with small outboards hugged the shore, while tugboats pushing low-riding barges maintained their course in the shipping lane.

Detective Marino returned twenty minutes later, saying the initial medical examination was complete. "You can bring Miss Andre over for a look-see, Nate. The ME has released the body for transport."

Nate walked back to the parking lot, but Nicki jumped out before he reached the car.

"Is it Danny?" she asked, her face ashen.

Nate stopped in his tracks. "I don't know. I didn't get a look at him. The detective wants Miss Andre to make the ID."

Nicki ducked her head inside the car. A few moments later, Isabelle emerged from the backseat looking pale and drained. The two women walked to the riverbank hand-in-hand, like schoolgirls who had been sentenced to a lifetime of detention.

Officer Flynn lifted the yellow plastic tape for them as Nate's former college teammate stepped forward. "Hi, I'm Detective Charles Marino. Are you sure you want to do this here, Miss Andre?"

Isabelle tightened her grip on Nicki's hand and nodded. "Let's get this over with."

Marino slowly raised the sheet covering the body. The corpse, stiff and bluish, hadn't been in the water long enough to bloat or decompose. The man's fingers were rigid, his clothing fully intact, his hair plastered to his skull as though gelled, while his eyes stared lifelessly at the heavy clouds overhead.

The man looked cold, underfed, and exactly like the Danny Andre Nate remembered from Natchez. Despite the fact ten years had elapsed, there was no doubt in his mind whatsoever as to the identity of the dead man.

Both Nicki and Isabelle gasped simultaneously. Isabelle staggered against Nicki, who also seemed ready to faint. Marino reached out a hand to steady Isabelle. "Take it easy, Miss Andre. Are you sure this is your brother?"

Isabelle took several great gulps of air. "Yes...that's Danny. What happened? Was he shot? Did someone kill him and then just...just throw him in the river?" Her voice edged toward hysteria.

"We'll know more after the autopsy, ma'am. You have the department's deepest condolences, along with mine personally." Marino glanced at Nicki. "You must be Nate's partner. Why don't you take

Miss Andre back to your car? Allow me a couple of minutes with Nate, and then y'all can go home or wherever you're staying."

Nate swallowed hard against a bad taste in his mouth. Marino's voice had become sticky sweet, and his gaze never left Isabelle. Certainly Chip, the former campus lady-killer, wasn't flirting at a crime scene. "Maybe you should wait until her brother is buried before you turn on the charm," he said after Nicki and Isabelle were beyond earshot.

"Was I that obvious? I must be losing my touch, but you can't blame a guy for trying. That chick is gorgeous even at five a.m." Marino pulled on his goatee.

"Last I heard she was married. Sorry about that. What can you tell me at this point?"

"What about your partner from back home? She ain't bad looking."

"She's engaged and about to set the wedding date. I believe we were talking about Danny." Nate pointed to where the techs were shifting the body onto a gurney for transport.

Marino grinned sheepishly. "Well, for starters the guy wasn't shot, but he had plenty of bruises and contusions on the face and torso consistent with the struggle in his apartment. Nothing that would have been fatal, though. The ME noted some puncture wounds in his upper arm, along with hemorrhaging in the eyes. Both point the fickle finger of death at drug overdose. Looks like your old pal OD'd. That's where I would put my money." The detective closed his portfolio as though he'd already wrapped up the case.

Nate pinched the bridge of his nose. "That can't be. Danny was no druggie. The guy was straight as an arrow."

"Yeah, and he loved his mama and went to church every Sunday. That's what they all say."

"I would stake my reputation that if Danny OD'd, somebody else was holding the needle."

Marino studied him curiously. "You're awfully sure about a guy you haven't seen in a decade."

"True enough, but Nicki saw him within the last year and talked to him on the phone. People just don't change their stripes that fast."

"You were at his apartment. Nobody but crackheads, meth-lovers, and hardcore junkies live in that neighborhood, along with your garden-variety alcoholics."

Nate's annoyance notched up a level. He recalled Mississippi State's favorite wide receiver downing plenty of postgame beers despite the coach's policy to bench any player caught drinking. Marino had frequently jeopardized a four-year athletic scholarship to indulge in his beverage of choice. "Danny was a stand-in musician, a sax player who didn't have a regular gig because he was still new in town."

Marino's laughter turned snide. "Come on, man. Don't you know how musicians stay awake on day jobs and then play all night for whatever's in the tip jar?"

"Maybe some take drugs, Chip, but not Danny. Did you see any signs of long-term abuse?"

"I didn't get up close and personal in the rain on the riverbank. Let's wait until the ME issues her report regarding cause of death. Then we'll know whether it was accidental, foul play, or suicide from jumping off the bridge. But hey, since this guy was a friend of an old college teammate, I will dot my *i*'s and cross my *t*'s on this one." Marino handed Nate his card and slapped him on the back. "Good seeing you, Nate. We are definitely going out for beers and barbecue before you head back to the Big Easy."

Nate expressed his appreciation without asking the obvious

question. *If I wasn't a personal friend, would you do a sloppy job and then shove the file into a drawer?*

Back in the parking lot, his cousin was ready to pounce. "What did that detective tell you?" asked Nicki.

Nate repeated Marino's sparse observations and conjecture. When he explained how he knew the guy, he emphasized the detective's assurance that a thorough investigation would be made.

"He had better do his job." Nicki's sorrow was rapidly mutating into anger.

"And we will see that he does." Nate slipped an arm around her shoulders. "I'm sorry about your friend, Nic. I prayed all the way here it wouldn't be Danny."

Her face contorted with misery. She opened her mouth to speak, but no words issued forth.

While he tried to comfort his cousin, Isabelle climbed from the car. "Thank you, Mr. Price. And please believe me when I say that detective is wrong. Danny was dead set against drugs. I don't know how or why, but someone murdered him. I'll pay you whatever your agency charges. Just find my brother's killer." She fixed her serious, sad eyes on him.

"I agree with you, Miss Andre. Why don't we get out of the rain to talk about this?" Nate opened her car door. "Right now you don't have to hire anyone. If it's ruled a homicide, the case will be assigned to a Memphis detective."

"I don't want this swept under some rug because of snap conclusions about Danny. If you're an investigator, then hiring you is what I need to do." In keeping with her high school moniker, Ice Queen Isabelle climbed into her car and drove away without another word to either of them.

FIVE

*N*ate was only semi-conscious when he picked up his phone. With a painful crick in his neck, he gawked around the luxury accommodations. Slowly details of the last several hours brought him to full alert. He hit the answer button. "Price Investigations."

"That you, Nate?" asked a male voice. "Chip Marino from Memphis Homicide. If Nicolette Price really does work for you, I suggest you get down here and put a leash on her. I would estimate she's one snide comment away from being arrested."

"*What?* Why on earth would you arrest my cousin?" Nate stood up so fast his chair fell over backward. He'd fallen asleep at the antique desk in his swanky room while searching databases for possible drug arrests for Daniel Andre.

"Whoa," said Marino. "Not me. But the security guards at the Shelby County offices take stalkers very seriously, especially those issuing thinly veiled threats."

"Where are you? Where's Nicki?" Nate slipped on his loafers and ran a comb through his tangled hair.

"Coroner's Office on Poplar Avenue. Your cousin has been camped outside the ME's door demanding to talk to whoever is in charge. She's insisting the Andre case be given top priority to anyone coming in or out of the office."

"Have security kick her out. She has no business on a restricted floor."

"No joke, old buddy. Officers have already removed her from the premises. That crazy woman isn't to come within twenty feet of this investigation or she will be arrested. She's making quite a nuisance of herself."

Nate ran his hand over his face as he tried to piece together the story. "It's barely after noon. We just saw you this morning. Neither of us slept much last night. She must have sneaked out after we got back to the hotel."

"That's what I figured. She's been here since the office opened. The coroner called me an hour ago complaining about her after your partner dropped my name. Dr. Blackwood told her she would get to Mr. Andre later today but had higher priority cases first. Well, that just set off the crazy woman. The doc only took time to talk to Nicki out of courtesy to me. Otherwise, some pushy PI from Louisiana wouldn't get much airtime here in Tennessee if you catch my drift." Marino's dry laugh contained little amusement.

"What do you mean, 'out of courtesy to me'?"

"I've been itchin' to get to that part. Your cousin told the ME and the security guards that she was working the case with Memphis Homicide. Man, was I reassigned to someone else and nobody bothered to tell me? I already have a partner—not as cute as Nicki, but a whole lot saner."

"I'm sorry, Chip. Nicki's still a greenhorn. She's had her license less than a year, but she's already mastered the bull-in-a-china-shop method of investigation."

This time the detective's chuckle sounded genuine. "I wouldn't have called if Nicki stayed on the sidewalk where she was ordered to remain. But according to security cameras, she's lurking between parked cars in the county's underground garage. Miss Greenhorn somehow figured out which vehicle belongs to Doc

Blackwood. I hope Nicki ain't packin' heat, because I let it slip that she *ain't* my partner in crime-solving."

It took less than twenty seconds for the visual to run through Nate's mind: his cousin jumping up next to the ME's van and spouting demands with her holstered Beretta 92 in plain sight. With Nicki's wild hair and overly enthusiastic persona, the coroner would press a button on her pager and every cop within a five-block radius would converge on his clueless cousin. "I'll be right there. Please don't let anybody shoot her. And, Chip, I owe you one," he added before ending the call.

Nate didn't bother to brush his teeth or change his wrinkled shirt. He hurried down to the lobby and then out the doors to his car. He reached the office of the medical examiner on Poplar Avenue in under ten minutes, a testimony to his one-time aspiration to become a NASCAR driver. Nate spotted the sign for "Authorized Parking" and drove down the ramp into a subterranean garage. He hoped the sound of gunfire wouldn't soon punctuate the early afternoon somnolence.

With great relief Nate spotted his former MSU teammate talking to his partner while she leaned against a late model sedan. Nicki was listening with crossed arms and a defensive, hipshot stance as Marino gestured wildly with his hands. If Nate was a betting man, twenty bucks said the guy was reliving his glory days on the football field.

Nate stopped near a vacant spot and rolled down his window. "Is this streetwalker bothering you, Detective? I'd be happy to take her off your hands and spare you the paperwork down at county lockup."

Marino hooted while Nicki scowled. "Nate! Thank goodness you're here. I was trying to impress on the detective the need for speed in this investigation. While we sit on our thumbs, crucial evidence can literally be swept up with last night's litter on Beale Street."

"So glad to see you, old buddy. My supply of polite conversation was running dry." Marino straightened to his impressive six feet two height. "If you have this situation under control and your cousin isn't planning any more attacks on county workers or elected officials, I gotta get back to work, even though the *need for speed* never dawned on us numbskulls in homicide."

"Yeah, I got this. Thanks again."

Nate waited until Marino sauntered away before focusing his full attention on his newest employee. "Get in the car before I kill you in full view of the security cameras."

"We're being watched?" Nicki peered up and around, zeroing in on a unit mounted to a steel beam thirty feet away. "Is there no privacy left in America?"

"You know there isn't. And those of us on the right side of the law don't have a problem with that." She had barely closed her door when Nate peeled up the ramp.

"Hey! I don't have my seat belt buckled," she complained.

"That minor infraction is the least of your problems, Nicki. What in the world were you thinking?" Nate gave her no time to answer. "Badgering a high-ranking official, not to mention an overworked doctor, irritating off-duty cops, and lying about working with Detective Marino? I should fire you! You don't even deserve last week's paycheck." Nate slammed on the brakes at a red light. "And how on earth did you get there? We rented one car and I've got it."

"I took a taxi from the hotel," said Nicki, now meek as a lamb.

"That's it? I just asked you a pack of questions, and you chose *that one* to answer?" Nate, on the other hand, roared like a lion.

"If you would just calm down, boss—"

"Oh, you recognize the fact that you have one? Because it sure didn't appear to Detective Marino you are under anyone's supervision."

"Detective Marino," she said contemptuously. "That guy showed up today chomping on a glazed donut. What a cliché." She looked at the urban landscape along the way instead of at him.

Nate sucked in a breath and held it. He needed to calm down because throttling his cousin would be hard to explain at the next family reunion. Aunt Rose had a temper equal to his. "What Detective Marino chooses for his morning meal is neither my concern nor yours. I suggest you start talking, or so help me I'll drive straight to the airport and drop you off. If you take a taxi back to the hotel, you'll find your clothes already on their way back to New Orleans in care of Hunter Galen. It's time that guy finds out what a stubborn, bull-headed woman you are."

Pulling into the queue for valet parking for the Carlton, Nate relaxed his grip on the steering wheel. "What do you have to say for yourself?"

Nicki looked green around the gills. She opened her mouth and gasped as though she were choking on a chicken bone.

Nate slapped her in between the shoulders. "What's wrong with you? Did a cough drop go down the wrong pipe?"

She shook her head as a floodgate of tears opened.

"All right, forget what I said about telling Hunter. Every man deserves his fate with the woman of his dreams." Nate waved off the valet and pulled back into traffic. At the end of Third Street he turned onto Riverside Drive and headed to the park while Nicki continued to weep. They might as well have this out without a scene inside the hotel. He pulled into a spot with a lovely, if unappreciated, view.

"Consider this a meeting of Price Investigation partners. Nothing discussed will leave the confines of this car. Now tell me what's gotten into you. You can't behave like that if you're a PI."

Nicki pulled out a wad of tissues from her purse, but drying her eyes was a futile exercise. "I lost it when I saw Danny's body lying on the riverbank," she said, while tears continued to stream down her face. "All cold and…and wet…and…utterly alone. He looked like one of those rubber corpses used in haunted house displays instead of…instead of a talented young man who had people who loved…loved him."

Her tears hampered speech for several more minutes. Nate waited patiently, caught between sympathy and annoyance over her reckless actions.

"I hated how the forensic techs treated him…like he was just another lowlife who happened to wash ashore that day."

"You thought the forensic team behaved disrespectfully?"

Nicki sighed as she stared at ships on the river. "No, I guess not. But they saw marks on his arm and jumped to the junkie conclusion. '*Okay, boys, let's wrap up our work here.*'" She looked at him with red eyes. "Danny delivered meals to shut-ins, cut old people's grass on Saturdays, and hauled their trash to the curb. Do those things sound like the actions of a crackhead?"

Nate patted her hand. "No, Nic. They don't. I'm sure Dr. Blackwood will do a thorough job despite your initial impression."

"Maybe, but did you see your pal Chip in action? That sleazebag was more interested in ogling Izzy than evaluating the crime scene."

"So you figured insulting the guy and threatening to call the governor if Danny's autopsy wasn't moved up the list would be helpful? You lied to law enforcement about working in Memphis as what…a Sherlock Holmes consultant?"

"I know Danny was murdered, Nate. This was no accidental overdose. He made the wrong person angry and nobody cares but me and Izzy." Nicki dropped her face into her hands.

Nate waited until she cried herself dry. "That's where you're wrong. I care, and believe it or not, Detective Marino cares or he wouldn't have called me. You were five minutes away from being arrested for trespassing, stalking, intimidation of an elected official, and maybe even a federal weapons charge. Did you take your gun into the county offices?"

Dabbing her nose, she shook her head. "I locked it in the safe in my room, and it's a good thing I did. If Marino had wasted another minute of my time about MSU's chances for the SBC championship, I may have winged him in his arm or leg."

Nate fought back a smile. "He was trying to distract you until I got there."

Nicki leaned her head against the headrest. "I'm sorry. I know I overstepped my bounds, being that we're from New Orleans and all. I promise to use better judgment from this point on."

"It's not just that we're from out of state. You seem to have forgotten the chain of command in an investigation. As private detectives, we have no jurisdiction and no access whatsoever on a murder case. If we expect to be kept in the loop, then we need to maintain a good relationship with Memphis police."

She looked at him from the corner of her eye. "Should I apologize to Dr. Blackwood or maybe those security guards? If necessary, I'll even grovel to Chip Marino."

He released an exaggerated sigh. "No, that won't be enough. On the phone Marino told me he doesn't want you to come within twenty feet of him or this investigation. His chummy talk about the Bulldogs was only to calm down a crazy woman—his description, not mine."

"So you're firing me after all." She shrugged. "I might as well have winged the guy."

"I'm not firing you. Consider this a probation period. If you want to stay in Memphis and help with the case, you have to stay out of Marino's way. I'll do the footwork like the gumshoe I am while you take care of things behind the scenes."

"Sounds like house arrest at the Carlton." A ghost of a smile lifted the corners of her mouth.

"Yes, but it's a rather snazzy place for incarceration. If you prefer to go home, that's fine too. You could clean out filing cabinets of closed cases while I'm gone."

Nicki grabbed his elbow. "Please don't send me home, Nate. I'll wear an ankle monitor or a dog collar or a ball and chain attached to the desk in my suite, but I don't want to leave until Danny's killer is caught."

"Relax. You can stay." He carefully extracted her long nails from his arm. "But you'll keep your distance from Detective Marino. And you'll operate under my direction the entire time you're in Tennessee. Understood?"

She nodded her head.

"Say it, Nic. I know you don't lie, so I want verbal agreement to come from your mouth."

"I will tell you if I leave the premises, maintain strict curfew, and be super nice to everyone in the hotel." Her expression betrayed the return of her spunk.

Nate straightened the lapels of his sport coat. "That's a little better. Now let's go get something to eat. I'm starving. It'll be hours before the ME comes to a decision anyway."

"Thanks," she whispered. "I know I blew it back there, but it hurt seeing Danny like that. I didn't realize how much I missed him until today. I want to do right by him, for Izzy's sake and my own."

"Danny was lucky to have you for a friend." He kept his eyes on traffic because his own emotions were close to the surface. "We'll take things one step at a time, but I'll make sure Mr. Joe Football leaves no stones unturned on this one."

The two of them ate pulled pork sandwiches, Memphis style, and split an order of fries. When they finished their second glass of iced tea, they waddled back to the car and drove the short distance to the hotel. "Why don't you catch up on email and then get some sleep, Nic. You look like you got hit by a bus."

"Really? Because that's the look I was after." She lifted her hair from the back of her neck while they waited for the old-fashioned elevator. "Since I seem to have some time on my hands, I think I'll crawl under the covers and stay there." Once they reached the seventh floor, she turned and looked at him with her luminous brown eyes. "Nate, will you call me the *moment* you hear from Detective Marino, night or day, regardless of the hour?"

"You won't contact him or anyone else on the case?"

"I gave you my word during our company meeting today."

"Okay, but we probably won't hear anything until tomorrow or the next day. This is a big city—lots of murders. Go to bed." He headed in the opposite direction.

Inside his room, the view of the cityscape wasn't as impressive as hers was of the Mississippi. For the next hour he studied online newspaper archives for gang activity and drug busts in the metro area until he couldn't keep his eyes open. He'd just crawled under the covers of the antique reproduction bed when his phone rang, jarring him fully awake.

"Hey, old buddy."

Nate yawned widely before saying tiredly, "How ya doing, Chip? I take it the ME has reached a conclusion."

"Man, I was just enjoying a burger and ESPN when my captain called. Maybe Doc Blackwood was more rattled by Miss Greenhorn than she let on. She finished her autopsy before leaving the office today. The Danny Andre case is now officially a murder investigation."

Nate bolted out of bed. "Are you the lead detective? What can you tell me?"

"Was there any doubt?" Marino swaggered. "Like we figured, Andre died of a heroin overdose. But he had three times what would have been a lethal level in his blood and no old needle marks. As in zero. Usually the adventurous sort doesn't start out experimenting with smack mainlined into a vein. They snort a little of this, smoke a little of that. But the physical condition of the body indicated no prior use."

"That's what my partner believed to be the case."

Marino was silent a moment. "You'd be wise, old buddy, not to bring up your partner. I trust that you warned her to keep her distance."

"Yeah, she's confined to the Carlton until her fiancé gets here. He's coming next weekend to show her the city's sights."

"Man, give that guy my sympathy. Anyway, I was just faxed the ME's conclusions after her autopsy. Andre must have rubbed somebody the wrong way. She says he had the tar beat out of him, consistent with the struggle at his apartment. There's also bruising around his neck and throat, indicating some kind of choke hold. Either while under restraint, or after he was unconscious, some-one apparently injected a lethal dose of heroin. Can't say whether still in the apartment or right before they threw him in, but the guy was dead before he hit the water. Body in river less than eight hours, consistent with the time frame of Andre's phone call. We'll interview his neighbors and canvass the street in the morning. Right now, I am done for the day."

"Thanks, Chip. I appreciate you keeping me in the loop."

"No problem. What are old friends for?"

Nate hung up, feeling some of the same guilt Nicki had mentioned.

What are old friends for? That's probably what Danny was think-ing when he called Nicki yesterday.

SIX

*I*sabelle couldn't remember a less productive Sunday open house since earning her real estate license. Of the five couples who stopped by to tour the four-bedroom, two-bathroom Colonial on a double lot in Germantown, three clearly hadn't been preapproved for financing. This was no starter house, available with a minimum down payment. Two of the couples had never owned a home before, while the third admitted to having a condo until the bank foreclosed several years ago. Isabelle patiently listened to their woes about job loss, high medical bills for a live-in parent, and special dietary needs for a sick child, but she wouldn't be the one approving the mortgage. Unfortunately, none of their problems would change a loan officer's mind.

Isabelle suspected the other couples were simply nosy neighbors because they spent a lot of time studying utility bills. People wanted to know how much their biggest investment was worth in a shaky market. Everyone consumed the three dozen oatmeal cookies she had baked from scratch and drank the pitchers of sweet-tart lemonade with plenty of compliments, but if her luck didn't improve soon, Isabelle would have trouble meeting her own bills.

As she turned onto the tree-lined street of her development,

Isabelle forgot about the cookies, spilled lemonade, and lack of sales. All she wanted to do was kick off her high heels and peel off her linen suit. Why on earth had she bought something that wrinkled at the mere mention of humidity?

Inside her living room, she turned up the AC, scratched her cat beneath his chin, and headed for the kitchen. With an icy bottle of water pressed to her neck, Isabelle hit the button on the answering machine. Of the four calls indicated, two were from her broker and one was from Nicki. But it was the last message that turned her palms clammy.

"Hey, pretty lady, hope you're missin' me as much as I'm missing you. Can't think about nothing else but us hooking up. If you're regrettin' how we left things, give me a call. You'll find me ready, willing, and able to wipe the slate clean."

Isabelle shakily pressed the button to replay the message, noting he left no name or number. *Like I'm supposed to automatically know who he is and how to reach him.*

Unfortunately, she knew exactly who it was.

She hurried around the condo shutting window blinds and making sure doors were locked. Then she sat in the dark studying the parked cars on the street before heading to the bathroom for a long shower. But even hot water couldn't wash away her anxiety. Despite the pleasant tone and friendly affectation, the man who left the message wasn't her friend.

For several hours after she was in bed she listened to the air-conditioning cycle off and on, flinching with every loud muffler or squeal of brakes. Finally, she fell into a deep, dreamless sleep. A body could grow so weary that even potential mayhem couldn't keep the eyes open. The next morning, she awoke to twisted sheets and a warm ball of fur curled up in the crook of her knees.

"Good morning, Mr. Chester. Will it be salmon pâté or chicken giblets for breakfast?"

An arched spine and loud purr provided an ambiguous response.

Isabelle padded to the pantry, where she kept stacks of canned cat food but halted before making a selection. An odd splash of color had caught the corner of her eye. Running to the sliding glass doors, she threw back the sheers. Dark red paint had been splashed across her chaise lounge and glass-topped accent table. Droplets speckled the flower boxes along the railing, and a large pool had collected between the chairs.

Isabelle carefully opened the slider and stepped onto the balcony without giving Chester access to his favorite perch. The last thing she needed was paint on his paws. Outside, a coppery stench assailed her nostrils, triggering a gag reflex. *Not paint, blood. At least a quart if not more.* Isabelle staggered, her fingers smearing a semi-dry blotch on the rail. She jerked back her hand, transferring blood onto her cotton nightgown.

"Oh, mercy!" She fled inside and held her hand under the kitchen faucet until long after the residue was gone. Two, three minutes spun out as she forced her mind to work. With trembling fingers she hit the speed dial button for Nicki, grateful they had programed it while waiting in the car.

"Hey, Izzy, what's up? I was going to call you later." Nicki sounded sleepy but cheerful.

"Thought I'd beat you to the punch. How did you and Nate spend Sunday?" she asked, suddenly reluctant to come to the point.

"We found a church close to the hotel. Then Nate spent the day trying to track down a copy of the preliminary autopsy report. As for me, I talked to Hunter and my mother and searched the Internet for recent crimes in Danny's neighborhood. How about you?"

"Could you come over? Something bad has happened."

Nicki hesitated. "What kind of bad? If this is something to do with Danny, I have to send Nate. I've been…removed from the investigation. It's a story I'll save for later."

Isabelle continued to scrub her hands under hot water. "Not Nate. I want you, Nicki. Believe it or not, this has nothing to do with Danny. Please hurry."

"I'll be there as quickly as I can. Give me your address."

Half an hour later a woman Isabelle had seen little of since high school came to her rescue for the second time in less than a week. Over the years she had gained perspective on Danny's best friend. Despite her current circumstances, it was hard not to trust a person her brother described solely with superlatives.

Isabelle pressed the button for the downstairs entrance and waited in her doorway, using the jamb for support.

Nicki brushed past her into the condo. "Have you heard the ME's decision? Is that what has you freaked? Nate was probably—"

"No. I haven't heard anything about that, but there's something you need to see." Isabelle cut her off and led the way into the living room, where the open curtains allowed full view of the ghastly sight.

"Good grief! Is that blood?" Nicki carefully opened the slider and stepped onto the balcony, her freckled complexion draining of color. She dipped one finger into a pool and brought it to her nose. "The smell and consistency are right. Call the police."

"I already did. They should be here any minute." Isabelle twisted her scarf into knots.

Nicki held up her palms as though to ward off evil spirits. "I told you on the phone that Nate suspended me while we're in Memphis because of what happened at the ME's office. Sorry, Izzy, but I lost my cool about the hasty OD conclusion. I was almost arrested for interfering in police business, obstruction…who knows what else."

Isabelle remained inside, unable to get near the grisly scene. "Whatever happened earlier, I assure you this isn't connected."

Nicki wiped her fingertip on a tissue. "How do you know? If this is blood, and I'm pretty sure it is, Danny's killer may be after you now."

"Germantown PD." A voice at the door accompanied by knocking startled both women.

"Uh-oh." Looking stricken, Nicki ran back into the living room and crouched next to the armoire. "The cops can't find me here! I was supposed to tell Nate before leaving the hotel."

"Is the guy your partner or your jailer? Go hide in the bathroom while I talk to them, but keep the door open so you can listen. I don't want to repeat my story twice."

Isabelle waited until Nicki disappeared down the hall. Then she walked to the front door and invited the two uniformed cops into her home. After brief introductions, she pointed them in the right direction. She remained in the living room while they examined and photographed the balcony. When they were finished, Isabelle explained in detail her one disastrous date, followed by subsequent encounters with a man who insisted they were soul mates. Each time she recounted the bizarre details of dinner and a movie with a whacko, she felt more desperate. What kind of woman agreed to go out with someone she met while showing a house?

"Tell us about the other run-ins you've had with him," said one officer.

Isabelle described Tony Markham attending open houses no matter what the price range of the listing, of hanging out at her favorite coffee shop, and of walking into her neighborhood store while she'd been shopping, as well as his repeated calls to give him "one more chance to show they would be perfect together."

The police offered each of the same rationalizations she'd told herself.

"How do you know he wasn't interested in buying a house?"

Lots of people stop at Starbucks on their way home from work. It could have been just a coincidence.

Maybe your grocery story was running the best sales that week.

All she could do was shrug and state with conviction, "I know he's stalking me. He didn't like it when I refused to go out on a second date, and now he won't leave me alone."

"Whose blood do you think that is?" asked the female cop, her expression more sympathetic. "Are any of your pets missing?"

Isabelle picked up Chester and clutched him to her chest. "No, this is my only pet. I don't know whose blood it is. Can't you run tests to find that out?"

The male cop didn't appear convinced by her gut feelings. "Yeah, we'll run DNA on the sample and check for matches in the database. Because there's no body, it's probably animal blood, maybe from a slaughterhouse. Without evidence at the scene pointing to this Tony Markham, this could be simple vandalism or teenage mischief. There's no sign anyone was inside your condo, and if you didn't see this bad date outside your building..." He let his words trail off.

"I didn't stay up all night watching the street," she said. Isabelle was growing sorrier by the minute that she called them.

"We understand, Miss Andre. We'll check with the building super to see if there've been similar incidents. It may be a group of kids with too much time on their hands."

"What am I supposed to do in the meantime?" She gestured toward the balcony.

"I would wear rubber gloves when you clean that up. Maybe you could ask your neighbors to keep an eye open. Neighborhood watches are good deterrents to this type of crime. Like I said, we'll talk to building management and call you if we get a lead." The pair was already heading to the door.

Once they were gone, Nicki crept up behind her. "Good

thing I didn't stick around for introductions. That heavy-set cop and Detective Marino are probably pals. From what I overheard, they're cut from the same cloth."

Isabelle's reaction wasn't what Nicki had expected. She laughed and rolled her eyes. "Okay, what do we do next? I don't care if Nate fired you. You're still my PI."

"Well, I suppose I can help since this is Germantown and not Memphis." Pulling her digital camera from her bag, Nicki relaxed for the first time since walking into the condo. "First, I'll take pictures of the damage and then we'll clean up the mess. You're sure the police took samples of the blood?"

Izzy nodded. "One had a little kit in his pocket that he used."

"Why don't you find us gloves, a bucket, bleach, and rags that we can throw in the trash?"

While Izzy gathered supplies, Nicki photographed the crime scene. Even if the blood wasn't human, only a sicko could wreak such havoc. In her opinion, sending a message with blood wasn't the handiwork of a spurned suitor. This spoke of intense rage.

By the time Izzy returned with what they needed to decontaminate the balcony, Nicki was starting to disagree with her conclusion. And when they had finished scrubbing, she was downright convinced this had something to do with Danny.

"I need to head back to the hotel before Nate notices that the car is gone. But before I leave I want you to write down Tony Markham's phone number and his address."

"I have his number but don't know where he lives." Izzy dug an address book out of her purse. "Our relationship never got that far."

"Okay. Just tell me everything you remember about the guy, no matter how obscure."

"He told me he worked in a bank but never mentioned which branch or his job description. He's fond of cats but doesn't like dogs. He said he got bit by a Doberman when he was a child." Izzy was quiet a moment while filling a kettle with water. "He loves Chinese food, and his favorite way to spend a weekend is watching movies on the couch." Two bright spots appeared on her cheeks as she glanced down at the floor.

"What, Izzy? Don't be embarrassed. Tell me what came to mind. You never know what might help."

"After I went out with him and things didn't go well, it got me thinking. A few days before our date, I'd stopped for takeout on my way home from work, moo goo gai pan. And during that same week I'd stayed home with a cold. I was curled up on the couch watching Hallmark Channel movies the entire day. Think about it, Nicki. He could have been spying on me for weeks. He probably saw my cat because I sit on the balcony with Chester."

"Write all of this down along with every date you can remember. Start keeping a log in case we file a formal complaint against this guy."

"What if it wasn't him? What if the damage really was done by bratty kids like the police suggested?"

"For now the log is for us. But you must be prepared." She smiled encouragingly at her friend. "And...there's something else I need to ask. Would you mind giving me a key to Danny's apartment? Nate wants to take a look around."

"Maybe you should tell me about the coroner's report." Izzy braced both hands on the counter behind her.

"It was as we suspected...no accidental overdose. The case is now officially a homicide. It appears that someone restrained him and maybe someone else injected a lot of heroin. If it was one guy, he would have to be very strong."

Izzy's eyes turned glassy, but her voice remained level. "Heroin? In that case Nate should check into Danny's roommate."

Nicki's chin jerked up. "What roommate? I saw only one bedroom in that tiny apartment."

Izzy grunted her disapproval. "Danny took in a former junkie off the streets. The guy had been sleeping on his couch for weeks. You didn't see his stuff because he probably doesn't own much. The homeless are always stealing from one another." She shrugged her shoulders. "I told Danny it was a bad idea, but he insisted the guy had nowhere else to go. Danny said this friend had gotten clean and sober, and he was determined to help him stay that way."

Nicki pulled a notebook from her purse. "Okay, profiles part two. Write down everything you remember about this former addict. Start with his name and how he met Danny."

A half hour and two cups of tea later, Nicki left with the key to Danny's apartment and a solid lead to give to Nate. After the day she'd had Saturday, this was a better way to start off Monday. Fortunately, she was able to return the rental car to its assigned spot without Nate knowing she'd left the Carlton. Thank goodness her cousin was a night owl, while she had always been a morning person. On the one hand she resented his restrictions, yet on the other hand driving out to Germantown had felt wildly exciting. Rather like riding your bike to the edge of town when your mother expressly warned you to stay on your block.

While Nate caught up on his beauty rest, Nicki had a chance to check for outstanding warrants and past convictions for Danny's roommate. And what she learned made the ne'er-do-well the primary suspect as far as she was concerned.

She headed for her cousin's suite the moment she finished her list of unsavory details.

~

Nate pulled open his door just as his cousin was about to knock. "Good morning, Nicki. I trust you slept well." He tried to step around her.

"What's your hurry? I thought we could grab something to eat."
She positioned herself in his path.

"Not for me. Thanks to your rich husband-to-be, a huge basket
was delivered to my room filled with fruit, nuts, cheese, crackers,
and sparkling grape juice. What did you tell Hunter? That we're
starving to death in Tennessee?"

"I may have mentioned you were disappointed about no free
breakfast buffet. I received a matching basket in my room." Nicki
covered her mouth with her hand and giggled. "Where ya going
in such a hurry?" She dogged him to the elevator.

"Danny's apartment. I plan to sweet-talk the building super
into letting me inside."

Knocking his hand from the "down" button, Nicki dangled
a key on a plastic ring. "Look what I have for you, cousin. The
easy way in."

Nate's frown was downright ferocious. "Where exactly did
you get that?"

"Let's go back to your room, and I'll explain if you give me a few
minutes. I didn't break my promise. Izzy asked me to come over
this morning because she didn't want to be alone. She insisted it
had nothing to do with the murder."

Nate snatched the key from her fingers. "I'll give you five minutes. This had better be good or you will end up bald."

Nicki clucked her tongue. "Such violent talk from you. Where
does all this latent hostility come from?"

Nate opened the door to his suite and waved her inside. "Some
women bring out the tender side in men. Others instigate duels,
start world wars, and prompt men to sign up for the space pro-
gram. Guess which kind you are?"

Nicki marched to the fruit basket on his desk. "I'm pretty sure
my basket is bigger. Ain't love grand?"

"Thanks for the key." Nate slipped the ring into his pocket.

"But if your visit to Isabelle had nothing to do with the case, why don't we chitchat later? I want to comb through Danny's belonging before some overzealous rental agent hauls his stuff to the curb."

"Because I have *useful* information." Nicki plopped down on the window seat. "Danny had a roommate, a former drug addict who Izzy says was hooked on smack." She wagged her index finger at him. "I really didn't go there about the case. Izzy told me this later."

"Did you get his name? The police didn't say anything about a roommate."

"They probably didn't know because the guy slept on the couch. His name is Titus Sullivan, but he goes by 'Tito.' Danny apparently took in a homeless junkie to rehabilitate. Izzy tried to discourage him, but you know Danny. He had a heart of gold."

Nate pulled out his laptop and opened the lid.

"I already took care of it, boss." Nicki handed him several sheets of paper. "Just printed these out in the business office. Charming Tito has been arrested for drugs six—count 'em—six times, starting when he was fifteen. He's been through court-ordered rehab twice from what I could gather. According to tax records, he's never owned a house or had a tax-withholding job. And here's where it gets interesting. He served eighteen months in prison for assault with a deadly weapon. How 'bout them apples?"

Nate smiled with appreciation. "You managed all of that this morning?"

She shrugged. "Not everyone stays up until two a.m. and then sleeps till ten. Izzy called me at dawn, and since you were still in bed I took the rental car."

"Thanks. You've found a perfect way to be useful, at least until Hunter gets here." He scanned through Sullivan's background information. "No addresses or spots he crashed other than Danny's couch?"

"I haven't found any yet, unless you count his previous addresses at juvenile hall and county lockup, but I'll keep looking."

"I'll check if any of Danny's neighbors know where Tito went and call Detective Marino with an update. Why don't we talk tonight during dinner?"

"Five minutes more," begged Nicki. "There was trouble at Izzy's condo. She doesn't think it's connected to Danny, but who knows for sure? I wanted to tell you so this doesn't come back on me later."

For the second time, Nate pivoted on his heel. "I guess I underestimated you, partner. Why don't you tell me what happened while I eat this juicy red apple? Then I'll either tie you to a chair or give you a raise."

Nicki began a tale of vandalism, prank calls, and obsessive men on first dates. She fidgeted the entire time, as though unnerved by the events.

"In your professional opinion, do you think someone who lurks at open houses may be our murderer?" Nate kept his tone neutral.

"I don't know what to think. But since I promised not to interfere, I wanted to run this by you."

"Even if this Tony Markham turns out to be a stalker, what happened to Danny looked very personal."

The two cousins locked gazes.

"I agree," she said. "Do I have your permission to stick my nose into bad-date extraordinaire?"

He rubbed his chin with the back of his hand. "Sure, from the comfort and convenience of your Carlton suite. Of course, you're free to see Miss Andre for lunch or lattes. After all, we're here on the largesse of Hunter Galen. But if her vandalism turns out to be not a random prank, then I'll handle Markham and any other miscreants that crawl from the gutters of Memphis. Remember, local police have labeled *you* as a wacko." He couldn't keep from smirking.

"Very funny. Just for the record, when Germantown police responded to Izzy's call, I hid in the bathroom."

"What a smart cookie I hired to work for me." Nate headed for the door. "Feel free to stay here and use my computer or return to the comfort of your grander suite and bigger fruit basket. When I get back tonight, dinner will be on me."

Nicki's brown eyes turned huge. "In the French restaurant off the lobby? I've heard nothing but great things about them."

"Nope. I checked their menu. Considering the way you and I eat, a meal would cost an entire week's food per diem." Nate waved his hand to forestall any argument. "If Hunter wants to pull out his platinum card for his bride-to-be, he'll get a chance this weekend. But I will only incur normal expenses. Oh, plus this swanky room, of course."

"You'd better call Marino first. We don't want him putting a leash on you too." Nicki tossed him another plastic ring. "Here are your car keys back. They'll come in handy in the parking garage."

SEVEN

$\mathcal{N}$ate took his cousin's good advice and punched in Marino's number on the drive to Danny's apartment. Because the detective had given him his cell number, he picked up without the hassle of the precinct switchboard.

"Hey, what's up, Price?"

"I received information from Isabelle Andre. Danny had a roommate sleeping on his couch, a heroin junkie. Apparently, Andre felt sorry for the guy and took him in off the street."

"Yeah, that's what I heard from a neighbor. I'm always eternally grateful for little old ladies who refuse to mind their own business. Busybodies come in handy during investigations."

"Miss Andre also gave me a key to Danny's apartment. You don't have a problem with me looking around, do you?"

"Nope. They've already released the crime scene. I don't know what you think you'll find, though. Nothing left behind gave us an idea as to where Sullivan may have gone. No drug paraphernalia. No cash in the cookie jar. No crack hidden among the frozen peas. We have an APB out on Titus 'Tito' Sullivan. I'll let you know when he's in custody."

"Did you get a description of him?"

"Yeah, hang on." Nate heard the rustle of papers. "Short, five three at the most. White, stringy blond hair, eye color hazel, maybe a hundred twenty or hundred thirty pounds. Needless to say the guy doesn't dress for success, if you catch my drift."

"You like him for the murder then?"

"Barring any other suspects, I think so. Lots of bleeding heart do-gooders want to help the disadvantaged and end up getting their hands bit in return. Some lowlifes just don't know how to say 'thank you.'"

"I appreciate being kept in the loop, Chip."

"No problem. Anything for an old Mississippi State Bulldog."

Nate hung up and drove to Danny's. As the detective had warned, he found nothing helpful in the trashed apartment. Anything Danny had owned of value was either destroyed during the fight or already picked over by the superintendent. He probably wanted to get another renter as soon as possible. A few ragged garments in a plastic bag were likely Sullivan's because they were several sizes smaller than those in the closet, but there was nothing in the pockets, and the trash can contained only junk mail and bills addressed to Danny. The only thing Nate found remotely interesting were several wrappers and take-out boxes from a kosher deli on Second Street. According to the menu in one bag, the restaurant probably wouldn't be within Danny's or Tito's price range.

Shoving the menu into his back pocket, Nate scrubbed his hands with the sliver of soap he found in the bathroom and then pulled Isabelle Andre's card from his wallet. She worked at a realty office across town. With plenty of afternoon left, he wanted to hear firsthand about the prank in the middle of the night.

Like Nicki, the blood spatter gave him a bad feeling. In a murder investigation, you couldn't rule anything out too quickly.

～

Just about the time Isabelle's eyes began to cross, a buzz pulled her attention from the listings on her computer screen. Their office intercom was a throwback system, very effective for interrupting agents in the middle of negotiations with clients.

"Miss Andre?" said the receptionist.

"What's up, Janice?" Isabelle pinched the bridge of her nose.

"A Mr. Price needs a few minutes of your time. Should I check to see if his mortgage application is already preapproved?"

"That won't be necessary. Mr. Price isn't here about a house. It's a personal matter."

"Oooh. Can't say I blame you," she whispered. "The guy is totally fabulous looking."

"Let's shelve that train of thought for now," Isabelle said sternly as she shrugged into her suit jacket.

"Sorry, Miss Andre. I keep forgetting you just lost your brother. Perhaps when all of this is behind you…"

"Please show Mr. Price to my office." Isabelle spoke crisply to discourage the receptionist's conjectures. Not that her attempts had ever worked in the past. Some women in their early twenties thought the sun rose and set on romance.

"You got it." A moment later, Janice opened the door and gestured toward a chair in front of Isabelle's desk. "Won't you have a seat, Mr. Price?"

"Thank you, ma'am." Nate took a quick perusal of the room.

"What can I do for you? Nicki told me the coroner issued her findings and my brother's death is officially a homicide." Isabelle tried to utter the words without emotion.

He perched on the edge of the chair as though not planning to stay long. "That's correct. The detective you met on Saturday morning has been assigned to the case. I contacted him earlier today, and they are actively searching for your brother's roommate, Tito Sullivan. An APB was issued to the surrounding counties, including Mississippi and Arkansas. He should be in custody soon."

She nodded. "Did you search my brother's apartment?"

"I did. Unfortunately, Sullivan didn't leave much behind. I found something in the trash that could be a lead."

"Did the police find drugs or syringes?"

"No, nothing like that, but apparently Danny's neighbors didn't like Sullivan much. They heard him ranting and raving in the middle of the night more than once."

She sat mutely, unsure of what would be an appropriate response.

Nate appeared to suffer the same predicament. He shifted and squirmed before continuing. "You and I may have gotten off on the wrong foot, but I will assist with this investigation until Danny's killer is caught."

"Thank you. In return I'll see that your bill is paid." It was a bold statement, considering Isabelle hadn't sold a house all month. If she didn't close on a deal soon, she might end up in a flophouse like the one Danny lived in.

Nate's suntanned complexion paled. "I thought Nicki had discussed the matter of our fee. Nicki's fiancé is paying our expenses, but she and I are working this case pro bono. Nicki won't have it any other way, and neither would I."

"In that case, I appreciate your generosity," she said, tightening her grip on the armrest of her chair.

Except she didn't sound grateful. She sounded angry or haughty or just plain crabby. Maybe it was because Nate was handsome, just as Janice aptly pointed out. Or maybe it was due to the fact she couldn't distinguish decent men from those she should keep far away from.

Tony Markham was proof positive of that.

So was her ex-husband of four years.

"And…the wrong foot we got off on was completely my fault," she added tentatively. "How can I help?"

"Tell me the details of last night's incident. Nicki filled me in on the basics, but I want to hear what happened in your own words."

Isabelle felt her spine stiffen. "I may have panicked Nicki over nothing. The more I think about it, the more I think it was a group of bored kids."

"Humor me, Miss Andre. Please."

Filling her lungs with air, she described meeting Markham on a Sunday afternoon and then agreeing to go out on the most uncomfortable date of her life. "He seemed nice at the open house, very polite and well mannered. He asked so many questions about my job that I thought he planned to take classes to sell real estate." Isabelle rolled her eyes at her naïveté. "When I was locking up the house, he asked if we could meet for dinner. Nothing fancy, just a casual meal. At first I said no because I have never dated a client. But he looked so…disappointed and lonely that I changed my mind."

"So far you've done nothing wrong. Sociopaths are masters at role playing, at least in the beginning. How can a person ever find the right one if they don't show some measure of trust?"

Isabelle wasn't sure if he was talking about her or himself. "I agreed to meet Tony at a restaurant near the mall. When it turned out to be closed for remodeling, his second choice was an Italian bistro out in the country." She met his eyes and then glanced away. "Next, he ordered a bottle of wine after I told him I didn't drink. When the waitress brought a bottle of Cabernet, he insisted on pouring me a glass. For the next twenty minutes it was a battle of wills, for lack of a better word. 'Belle, try a little charcuterie and some of my pasta. Won't you even drink half a glass after I paid so much for the wine?'"

"Markham called you 'Belle?'"

"Yes, and I hate nicknames except with my closest friends." Isabelle felt a blush rise up her neck, remembering the dressing-down she'd given Nate on the riverbank. "I told him to call me Isabelle, but he said the name Belle suited me better."

"So that was it? One interminable meal of fettuccini Alfredo?"

"I'm afraid not. When we finished eating, he insisted we go to the movies. He said it was the last day for something he wanted to see." She crossed and uncrossed her legs. "If only I had stood my ground. In retrospect, everything that came out of his mouth was designed to manipulate me."

"After dinner, why didn't you get in your car and go home? You drove separately, didn't you?"

"Originally we met at the mall restaurant. But when he chose the bistro, he said it was silly to waste gas and opened his car door for me."

Nate growled deep in his throat. "Markham could have been a serial killer. What were you thinking?"

"That I didn't want to hurt his feelings. He seemed so…sad. I know it was stupid, but I didn't want to cause a scene."

A muscle tightened in Nate's neck. "What happened in the theater? Did he try to get fresh?"

"No, but I should've asked about the movie." Isabelle stared at a framed print of windmills in Holland on the wall. "Let's just say it was X-rated with plenty of foul language. After five minutes of total embarrassment, I stood and said I was leaving. Markham pulled me down and told me to give it more time."

Nate's mouth dropped open. "You've got to be kidding."

"I assure you I'm not. I stomped out of the show and called a taxi from across the street. He kept pounding on the phone booth until a crowd started to gather."

"The guy sounds like a psychopath. Thank goodness you didn't accept a ride back to your car."

"There's more, Mr. Price. In the parking lot, Markham called me many colorful names. He said I had ice water in my veins instead of blood like real women." Isabelle felt a flush climb to her face.

"The guy could be dangerous."

As Nate jotted details in a little notebook, Isabelle pushed back from her desk. "Maybe, but we don't know he had anything to do with my balcony. For now let's leave this sleeping dog lie and concentrate on finding Danny's murderer. If Markham didn't toss the blood last night, I don't want to inflame him."

"Why don't I just—"

"No, Mr. Price. Please confine your investigation to my brother's case."

"You're the boss, Miss Andre." Nate's face screwed into a tight mask. "By the way, the medical examiner's office will call when they release Danny's body. As his next of kin, you'll need to make arrangements. If you don't already have a funeral director in mind, they may have suggestions for inexpensive crematoriums." He straightened to his impressive height, his Adam's apple bobbing as he swallowed hard. "Sorry. I didn't mean to imply you can't afford…only that you have options. I'll be in touch." He headed for the door as though a fire alarm had gone off.

"Wait, that reminds me of something." Isabelle braced her hands on the desk.

Nate paused in the doorway.

"Danny didn't like fire. He wouldn't want to be cremated. He wanted to be buried in the ground." When she locked gazes with his unfathomably blue eyes, Isabelle's knees went weak. "I'll arrange a funeral with my pastor. But since I'm new at this church, I was wondering if…" Her voice cracked.

"Say what's on your mind, Miss Andre."

"Would you be one of Danny's pallbearers? I may even need Nicki because I don't know how many mourners will attend. And

I don't know any of Danny's friends." Tears she'd struggled to hold in check slipped from her eyes.

Nate blinked. His expression indicated her request was the last thing he expected. "Sure. As soon as arrangements have been made, you can count on Nicki and me. Give me a call if you need help with anything else." He laid a business card on her desk before moving quickly out of the door and down the hall.

Somehow, they both managed to rub each other the wrong way every chance they got.

EIGHT

When her phone alerted her to an incoming call Tuesday, Nicki picked up on the first ring. Hunter. "Hello, sweet man. What a lovely surprise," she cooed. "You and I have been playing phone tag lately. I hope that means you're doing your civic duty with plenty of competent testimony."

His husky laugh warmed Nicki's heart down to her toes. "When I get done with that father-daughter team, there will be no chance of parole during this millennium. Court has recessed for lunch, so I thought I'd see how Nancy Drew is doing."

Nicki filled Hunter in on the vandalism to Izzy's balcony and her request for help, along with what she found out about Danny's roommate. However, once she described her visit to the ME—a story she'd left out thus far—she raced over the details at breakneck speed.

"What? Slow down, Nicolette. I have a thirty-minute recess and nothing better to do than listen to your sweet voice."

Sighing, she relayed the key details of her encounter with Dr. Blackwood in a decipherable fashion.

"Nate fired you because of one slipup? I will punch that guy in the nose. I don't care if he is my best friend." As usual, her knight in shining armor was willing to ride to the rescue.

"Not fired from the agency, just from this case. He says I can't maintain professional distance because Danny was one of my closest friends."

"And I have to agree with him. What a horribly cruel way to die. How could someone who loved him possibly remain objective? Besides, I didn't want to ruffle your feathers earlier, but if Danny was a musician, he probably hung out on Beale Street. And that is no place for a lady."

"What a sexist thing to say. You're the one getting the sore nose, Galen."

He laughed. "I'll keep an ice pack handy. Come home. You can find plenty of work to do here."

"I think I'll stick to the original plan because I can help Nate on the computer. I want to remain close to the Carlton and still help find Danny's killer."

"Then it sounds like I'm coming to Memphis this weekend. Sooner if the DA wraps up my testimony early."

"By Friday night you'll find me pacing the floors and talking in tongues. A gal can only stare at a computer monitor for so long."

"You should take the Carlton tour. It's delightful."

"You do understand I've spent time in a hotel before, don't you? I think I can find the gift shop, rooftop garden, and work-out room without a uniformed guide."

"Trust me on this, sweet pea. The Carlton is loaded with history. People from all walks of life have stayed there since the Civil War, and some of those lives have been on the wrong side of the law. You'll have enough fascinating tidbits to share at teatime for years."

"Teatime, Hunter? I'm barely twenty-six, not eighty."

"You don't do happy hour, so teatime is your best choice for making new friends."

"Fine. When I finish checking out Danny's roommate, I'll look into it. But remember, if this tour costs money and I don't like it, you're paying me back."

"I have every faith and confidence my five bucks is safe."

~

Truly, Nicki needed a trip to a grocery store because soft drinks from the vending machine or the gift shop were costing her a fortune. But as she stepped off the elevator to hunt down a nearby store, she practically tripped over an ornate stanchion that hadn't been there before. The brass-and-enamel signboard read: "Today at 2:00 p.m., tour the famous Carlton Hotel. Hear tales from its illustrious and colorful past. Admission: general public, $10.00; hotel guests, $5.00; children, free."

"There are no accidents in life." Her mamaw's favorite adage coupled with Hunter's suggestion made Nicki smile.

She checked her watch and went to the front desk. "Excuse me. Where do I sign up for today's tour?"

"Right here, Miss Price." The clerk waved off the crumbled bill Nicki dug up from her purse. "We'll just charge the ticket to your room." She handed Nicki a paper reproduction of the signboard. "The tour starts in half an hour. Meet at the fountain."

Nicki was impressed by two things: One, the whiteness of the clerk's glorious smile. *I'm definitely using the wrong toothpaste.* And two, the fact that the young woman addressed her by name.

For the next thirty minutes, Nicki people-watched at a bistro table in the indoor courtyard. Since mastering the ability to lip-read, she enjoyed other people's conversations, whether young or old, on business or on a family getaway. Usually, those on business were in a hurry, while vacationers maintained far better moods. No surprise there. As the crowd gathered for the tour, their attire suggested everyone fell into the vacationer category.

Also no surprise. Elderly senior citizens, young women with tod-dlers, and lovey-dovey honeymooners closed around their guide as he approached the fountain.

"Good afternoon, and welcome to our hotel." The man spoke with a rich, deep baritone that required no amplification to be heard. "If we haven't had the pleasure yet, I am Robert Prescott, the senior concierge at the Carlton. It's been my honor to have worked here for the past twelve years. This establishment has pro-vided Memphis hospitality throughout several wars, fires, floods, political upheavals, social unrest, and urban renewal. From the day it opened, the Carlton has remained dedicated to excellence in dining, shopping, and superb accommodations."

"Get on with the tour, Bobby. You don't need to toot the hotel's horn." This advice came from an ancient, ebony-skinned man sit-ting in a wheelchair.

Nicki had watched a young woman wheel him to the foun-tain, kiss the top of his head, and then join her friends in the lobby. The girl couldn't be more than twenty, while the gentleman had to be ninety at least.

"Good afternoon, sir, and welcome back." Seemingly unaf-fected, Mr. Prescott bowed to the heckler before resuming his rehearsed narrative. "Why don't I point out some of the details of our grand courtyard, and then we'll head to the mezzanine level?"

Nicki was impressed by the concierge's bearing as well as his polished appearance. He took the definition of dapper to a new level. Not a speck of lint marred his expensively tailored suit. His thick, silvery hair was expertly cut, while crow's feet enhanced rather than detracted from his café au lait complexion.

"Here in the center of the courtyard is our pride and joy—our hand-carved Italian marble fountain and pond, home to our famous fish since 1945." Mr. Prescott explained at length about the yellow marble produced in Siena, Italy, an area of Tuscany famous for violet, blue, or red veins running through the hard stone.

When the concierge began to describe the type of fish that lived in the pond, the elderly guest interrupted a second time. "These folks don't want to hear all that decorator and zoology nonsense. Tell them the story about how the fish got in the fountain in the first place. What about that movie starlet in the fifties who tried to catch one in her champagne glass to take home to Hollywood?" He chuckled at the reminiscence.

Everyone else also laughed, even though only the heckler seemed to know the amusing story.

Mr. Prescott quirked an eyebrow at the man in the wheelchair. "Perhaps later, if time allows. In the meantime, let's move to the gallery upstairs, where portraits of our founders and photographs of some famous guests can be found. You can take either the elevator or the stairs to the mezzanine level." He flourished a hand in the two directions the guests could go.

"One moment, please," interrupted a young woman, one of the lovey-dovey newlyweds. "Was that beautiful starlet Marilyn Monroe?"

"To my knowledge, madam, Miss Monroe never stayed here. However, the Prime Minister of England, the Princess of Monaco, and several presidents have, along with notables from the music and theater worlds as well as the political arena. Guests from the nineteenth century included famous riverboat gamblers and titans of the Industrial Revolution."

"If the folks want to hear history, Bobby, let's tell them about the yellow fever epidemic of seventy-eight. Thousands of people died, and thousands more hightailed it out of Memphis as fast as their legs could carry them. Plenty of hotels went belly-up, but the Carlton kept its doors open as a hospital for the sick. The city of Memphis almost went bankrupt, but the Carlton survived and was bustling with customers a few years later."

Some of the tourists looked skeptical, most flabbergasted, but Nicki wasn't easily fooled. "Are we talking about 1978?" She addressed the older man, but their distinguished tour guide answered instead.

"No, ma'am. The epidemic was in 1878, a year this gentleman remembers fondly. This is Mr. Henry Prescott, my grandfather." Robert shook his head at the heckler-turned-helpmate.

The crowd laughed, the mystery of the pushy guest solved. "Our concierge is your grandson?" Nicki asked Henry, intrigued. "How did you learn so much about the hotel, sir?"

His watery old eyes twinkled with delight. "That's easy, missy. I worked right here for more than fifty years. Everyone knew Henry the bellman because I did a right fine job."

Nicki pulled her camera from her bag. "Fifty years? You should be the one giving the tour. Mind if I take your picture?"

"Don't mind a'tall. I did give tours until my grandson got promoted to top dog. Then Bobby thought I should be put out to pasture just 'cause my legs weren't no good. I was *only* seventy." Henry slapped his palms on his thighs and then smiled for the camera.

The concierge rolled his eyes. "All good things must come to an end. But one day a month we still enjoy your plethora of knowledge during our extended tour. Now, dear guests, let's regroup in the mezzanine, where I'll explain some of the radical changes to the Carlton over the years." He reached for the handles of his grandfather's wheelchair.

"I can roll myself just fine, Bobby. There's nothing wrong with my arms." Henry propelled himself toward the elevator, while half the group headed for the stairs.

Nicki and the concierge exchanged a look. Watching the

family dynamics was well worth the price of admission. Robert's distinguished facade had slipped a notch. A man well into his forties had just been reduced to grandchild status, one in which a person never advanced beyond age fifteen.

When the group reassembled on the upper promenade, Henry allowed the tour to continue uninterrupted for ten minutes. Robert described a former glass-walled tearoom, the grand ballroom, and a mineral-infused indoor pool, all of which had been replaced with modern amenities in recent years.

"It would have been cool to hold our prom here," said the fan of Marilyn Monroe.

"I would love to soak in a warm spa after yesterday's sightseeing," said an older woman, rubbing her elbows.

"Okay, Bobby." The former bellman couldn't remain quiet any longer. "You can't leave out the tale of the Carlton jewels. Everyone would love a story about the good old days." He clapped his hands with anticipation.

Robert drew back a sleeve to check his watch. "They might, but I'm afraid we're out of time. If there's anything I can do to make your stay at the Carlton memorable, do not hesitate to ask." Smiling, he bowed low to a round of applause.

Nicki stayed to ask the concierge how early breakfast was served, and when she turned to talk to Henry, he had already disappeared into the elevator. She raced down the hallway to the staircase, but by the time she reached the lobby, Henry was being helped into a van by a uniformed attendant. The pretty young woman and her pals were nowhere in sight. What a shame! Because if anyone could spin an interesting yarn on a somnolent afternoon, it would be the retired bellman of a four-star hotel.

～

Nate spent his Tuesday morning doing paperwork and thinking about his meeting with the Ice Queen. If Isabelle didn't want him butting his nose into her case of vandalism, he could live with that. But could someone explain why she treated him like a toad while cutting this Tony Markham guy plenty of slack? She had climbed into the car of a total stranger to ride to the country because she *didn't want to hurt his feelings*?

If his memory served him right, bruising egos had been Isabelle's favorite pastime in high school. How many boys had asked her out only to slink away with their tails between their legs? Nate had been one of them. Isabelle hadn't been interested in men from Natchez because she had set her sights on Vanderbilt University and marriage to a premed or prelaw student. Local math teachers, lumberyard supervisors, and bricklayers didn't make the cut. And certainly not someone taking classes in criminal investigation hoping to get into the police academy. But maybe life in Nashville after Vanderbilt wasn't all she'd expected. Something had brought her to Memphis.

The real mystery, though, was how she could still get under his skin. It wasn't as if Nate hadn't dated plenty of attractive women over the years. The fact that he'd never met one to marry seldom bothered him.

He pulled a stick of gum from his pack to chew away his tension. He needed to focus on Danny. The sooner he solved this murder, the sooner he could get back to his orderly life in New Orleans. Nicki wasn't the only fish out of water in this town.

Nate left his car in the hotel's garage and walked to Kurtz's Deli on Second Street. Exercise would be good for both his mind and body. According to the number of take-out boxes in the apartment's trash can, either Danny or his roommate had eaten plenty of meals here.

When the bell above the door signaled his entry, Nate offered the man behind the counter a friendly smile. "How are you doing? I'd like to order pastrami on rye with mayo, sauerkraut, and cheddar cheese."

"Your first time eating pastrami?" The sandwich-maker stopped slicing meats.

"Yeah. How did you know?"

"Just a hunch. Can I suggest mustard instead of mayo and Swiss instead of cheddar? If you don't like it, I'll make it your way no charge."

"Sounds good. Are you Mr. Kurtz?"

"Guilty as charged. You want potato salad with that?"

Nate nodded and pulled out a photo of Danny he'd gotten from Nicki. The snapshot showed them holding up a string of redfish caught one summer morning. "My friend raves about a deli in this neighborhood. I'm curious if I'm at the right one. Do you remember seeing this guy?"

Kurtz leaned over the counter and shook his head. "Nope. He's definitely not a regular."

Nate tucked the snapshot into his pocket. "How about a short white man, around twenty-eight or so with longish blond hair? Most days he's pretty ragged looking."

The deli owner placed a mound of potato salad on the plate and reached for a huge pickle spear. "Are you talking about that homeless guy who hangs around my picnic tables? He watches for people who don't finish their lunch and then digs the leftovers out of the trashcan. Some restaurants pour bleach over their dumpster at night to discourage scavengers, but not me. Everybody's gotta eat, although I wish that guy would spread his patronage around more establishments than mine. People get nervous when he practically stares the food out of their mouth."

Nate handed over his debit card in exchange for the heaping platter. "Does he come around often?"

"Sometimes he's here at lunch, but he usually checks what's on my backyard menu after I close." Kurtz sighed.

After a few bites of bliss, Nate remembered where else he still needed to be. "This sandwich tastes great, but could you wrap it to go? I need to get down to police headquarters."

"No problem. If you're serious about finding this *friend*, I would watch the dumpster out back around nine tonight." Kurtz placed the contents of Nick's plate into a Styrofoam box.

"Thanks, and I'm glad you don't taint your trash. Too much food gets wasted in this country while other people go to bed hungry."

"Yep, that's what my rabbi says." Kurtz handed him the take-out bag. "Make sure you tell your friends how good my sandwiches are."

Nate checked his watch on the walk back to the Carlton to get his car. With any luck he might catch Detective Marino at the precinct because he preferred face-to-face conversations whenever possible. Stretching the truth, evading direct answers, or giving someone the runaround were far easier to accomplish over the phone.

Whether it was luck or help from above, Chip Marino was hunched over his desk when Nate wound his way through the warren of cubicles. "No rest for the weary, eh?" He flashed a grin.

"Price, you're a sight for sore eyes. You ready to go for ribs and a few cold ones tonight?" Leaning back in his chair, Marino laced his fingers over his stomach.

"Soon, but not today. I just had lunch at Kurtz's deli and promised to eat with my partner tonight. That guy makes great pastrami on rye." Nate slouched into the chair in front of his desk.

"I'll keep that in mind. What can I do for you?"

Nate's focus fell on several pictures spread across the surface of the desk. They showed a deceased young woman who hadn't died of natural causes.

Chip tapped the photos into a neat stack and slipped them into a folder. "You here for an update on the Andre case?"

"I wondered if the APB turned up Tito Sullivan yet."

"Nah, those things work a lot faster with folks who drive, use credit cards, or hang out with a predictable group of friends. None of that fits a homeless guy." Chip typed a few words on his keyboard.

"I think I found a lead in the trash in Danny's apartment."

"Rubbish picking. Always a fine idea to put our skills to good use."

Nate resisted the impulse to ask if the detective ever tried it or considered it beneath his dignity. "It's amazing how predictable people are when you check out what they throw away."

Chip typed a few more words before saving his file and then closing the lid on his laptop. "You have my full attention. Did you find the address of a sugar mama who let him crash for a few days? After a long hot shower, of course." He chuckled merrily.

Nate couldn't understand why some people found homelessness a source of amusement. Life's catastrophes could derail the best-laid plans for the future. "I found menus for a deli on Second Street and decided to check it out. The owner didn't remember Danny, but he recognized Tito from your description. He said Sullivan digs through the dumpster almost every night looking for half-eaten sandwiches."

"Yuck. No way I could get that hungry. Can you imagine biting into a sandwich and discovering someone stubbed out a cigarette or parked their used gum?" Marino pulled a sour face.

Nate waited for the homicide investigator to arrive at the obvious conclusion. But instead Marino continued to contemplate what unsavory surprises awaited someone searching for food behind a restaurant. "Be that as it may," Nate said, losing patience, "will you take some officers and watch the alley behind Kurtz's tonight? Sullivan usually drops by around nine."

Marino focused on Nate. "Is that what you think I should do? Just drop whatever I'm working on to chase after a garbage-eating junkie?"

"It's just a suggestion, Chip. There's a good chance you might catch a murderer."

"Got any clue where you are, old buddy? This is the booming metropolis of Memphis. You think Andre is the only homicide I got? Take a look at these." Chip spread a stack of files across his desktop. "We have a home invasion, two car-jackings that didn't end well for the car owner, three drive-by shootings, plus your usual assortment of dead hookers and gang members. And those are just recent cases that came in around the same time as Andre's. We won't even mention the cold cases sitting in file cabinets. You PIs work, what, one or two cases at a time? Our department has dozens to solve." Oddly, Marino's voice contained no anger or resentment, just an unemotional statement of facts.

Nate let a few moments pass before replying. "You're right on all counts. I pick and choose the cases I want and seldom work more than three at once. But you may be able to close this one if you stakeout Kurtz's dumpster tonight."

Slowly, Chip's face bloomed into a grin. "Tell you what. Since tonight ain't our night for spicy ribs at Sonny's, I think I might invite a few brothers in blue to join me for corned beef or smoked turkey piled high on a hoagie roll. Who knows who we might just collar while dining on the taxpayer's dime? I'll keep you posted." Marino lifted the lid of his laptop and returned to his paperwork.

"I appreciate it. And when we do go for barbecue, that meal will be on me."

NINE

On Wednesday Isabelle walked the thirty-something couple out to their car with a friendly smile, despite the fact her throat hurt and her shoes felt two sizes too small.

"Please keep looking, Miss Andre. We want four bedrooms, not three, and two and a half baths. Those homes you showed us today were all too small. Five bedrooms would be ideal with one on the first floor in case we need to move Paul's mother in with us." All this from a young mom of two with a third on the way. "And those backyards didn't offer much for a growing family. We would love a full acre so the children can get some exercise when they play."

"I have two properties in Monroe Heights that may fit the bill. Both homes are large with nice yards. One has an above-ground pool that stays with the house." Isabelle tried to smooth the wrinkles from her skirt.

"Oh, no. Not Monroe Heights," interjected Mr. Smalley. "I read that their school system has dropped a level in the ratings. If we have to pay this much for a house, I can't afford to shell out for private schools too." He wrapped an arm around his wife's waist. "Please confine your search to the better suburbs, Miss Andre."

"And I would like laundry facilities close to the bedrooms, not off the kitchen, and certainly not in the basement." Mrs. Smalley shifted her weight to her other hip.

Isabelle ran her finger down her clipboard at listings in the couple's preferred area. Nothing with their requirements came even close to their price range. "Are you certain one ninety is the most you can manage?"

"Yes, but you assured us this was still a buyer's market." Mr. Smalley frowned. "The minimum down payment will almost wipe out Gretchen's decorating budget the way it is. Who knows what kind of tacky wallpaper the current owners have up on the walls?"

Isabelle resisted the urge to ask if they had heard the term "starter home" or the idea of a wife working while the kids were in school. "Perhaps you could negotiate a thirty-year mortgage instead of a twenty-five with your banker? That might bring monthly payments into a more manageable range."

"Goodness, Miss Andre, I would like my husband to be able to retire before he's sixty." Mrs. Smalley chewed on her lower lip.

The husband opened the car door for his wife. "Let's stick with the preapproved loan amount as it stands and hope something comes on the market soon. We want to move in and get settled before the next school year."

"I'll keep looking and give you a call." Isabelle waved as the couple drove away.

What else could she say to a hopeful couple who only want the best for their growing family? How did she explain they were aiming for the stars? They would need a much larger down payment and better monthly income to purchase such a big house on an acre lot. Perhaps she could show them homes in areas not as posh or convenient but infinitely more affordable.

Isabelle sighed as she climbed into her hot car. She'd been that kind of stars-in-the-eyes bride once, a long time ago. When she'd fallen in love with Craig Mitchell, she planned the rest of her life—three children, maybe four; private schools; good colleges; a cottage by the lake; maybe even a membership at a Nashville country club. Why would the wife of a corporate lawyer, who graduated in the top five percent of his class and passed the bar exam on his first try, expect anything less?

What she didn't expect was Craig having a hard time with the "forsake all others" part of their marriage vows. Isabelle had forgiven his first indiscretion after he begged for forgiveness and promised never to stray again, but when she found receipts in his car for hotels they had never been to, she became suspicious. Then, when someone name Rochelle started texting indecent photos to his cell phone, Isabelle confronted him.

Her husband had offered two options—either turn a blind eye while enjoying a comfortable lifestyle, or pack her bags and move out. Isabelle chose the latter. Because they had no children and had amassed few assets, she received no alimony and a miniscule settlement. Fortunately, she'd studied real estate and pursued her license as a way to pass the time until babies came along. Good thing she was a fast learner because God apparently had other plans for her than motherhood.

Craig decided they should split the credit card debt evenly, which, unbeknownst to her, had turned out to be substantial. And he had amassed huge debts all over town, thanks to his passion for betting on sports. Several bookies came after her, even though she'd been no more aware of his gambling habit than his addiction to pretty women in short skirts. After paying off what she could, Isabelle changed back to her maiden name and moved to Memphis. Danny was the only family she had left, and if her brother needed to live here to find work as a musician, that's where she wanted to be.

But if she wanted to pay the rent this month, she had better find a suitable house for the Smalleys and a few other clients.

When Isabelle stepped through her front door, she found Mr. Chester waiting to be cuddled. Every time she petted her cat, stress from unrealistic clients, worries about money, and aggravation from aggressive drivers or heavy traffic melted away. She had a cool pitcher of lemonade in the fridge, a stockpile of movies, and the entire evening to herself.

Setting down her cat, Isabelle padded to her room for shorts and a T-shirt. A few minutes later, minus her heels and business suit, she popped a frozen dinner into the microwave and filled a bowl with prewashed salad. While she waited, Isabelle intended to clean out her purse of gum wrappers and old receipts, but instead her focus landed on the business card for Price Investigations.

Her breath caught in her throat. Nate Price, bonded, licensed, and insured. *Insured against what, Mr. Price—wreaking havoc in female hearts?* Remembering Janice's reaction when he came to the office made Isabelle laugh. Maybe it wasn't just young women who behaved foolishly in his presence. Shamefully, she remembered her own rude reaction when they met on the riverbank. No matter whether male or female, well-educated or unsophisticated, most people based their initial reaction on physical appearance. And she was no different. She had been intimidated by Nate's good looks, and that negatively affected her treatment of him.

"Who are you really, Mr. Price?" Isabelle spoke to an empty room.

Mr. Chester responded with an impatient meow. His kibble bowl was empty, a transgression not easily excused.

Give me a call if you need help with anything else. The memory of his easy-going style, along with a promise to ride up on a white horse, left her feeling bewildered. "Help from you is the last thing I need, considering my past history with handsome men. If I had half a brain I would give up dating altogether."

Chester frankly didn't care if she remained single for the rest of her life. He let out a howl, restating his simple but urgent demand.

After feeding her cat, Isabelle curled up on the couch with her salad and red-beans-and-rice entrée. She flipped through the movie choices and finally decided on a PBS mystery on the DVR. But the first forkful of romaine hadn't reached her lips when something on the patio caught her eye. Rose petals were scattered across the freshly scrubbed concrete all the way to the sliding glass door. Isabelle bolted from the couch, nearly dumping her dinner on the rug.

Throwing back the draperies, she spotted a floral wreath leaning against the side wall. The rose petals were dried and curled, the flowers of the wreath wilted and brown. The words *Rest in Peace* blazed across the wide white ribbon, while the bottom banner declared, *Dearly Beloved. We'll miss you.*

Someone had stolen the wreath from a grave, probably from a recent burial. And Isabelle had a very good idea who that someone was.

～

The next morning, unable to sleep late, Nicki was up and pacing the length of her suite by six thirty, praying she wouldn't spend another day cooped up in her room. There was only so much a person could learn cloistered inside a hotel. She drank two mini pots of coffee and ate an apple, a pear, and wedge of smoked cheese on Melba toast. She didn't dare call Nate this early. He never rose before eight o'clock no matter what the circumstances.

Their dinners lately had been enlightening, to say the least. From a menu in Danny's trash, her cousin found an establishment frequented by Tito Sullivan. As long as Detective Charles Marino followed through on his pledge to protect and serve the city of

Memphis, Danny's killer may already be in jail. That is, if Marino didn't get called out on a higher profile case and if Tito kept to his normal routine of kosher suppers at Kurtz's Deli. But Nate had spent an uneventful Tuesday night staking out the dumpster alone, without the assistance of Memphis's finest, and Sullivan hadn't shown up. Then he spent an equally nonproductive Wednesday haunting Danny's neighborhood, talking to people who had little to say to someone they didn't know. He'd abandoned his vigil at the dumpster when the skies opened with a deluge.

Would the elusive roommate turn out to be a murderer? The amount of destruction inside the apartment indicated rage, not a simple misunderstanding between friends that had spiraled out of control. Would the smaller-sized Sullivan have been able to overpower Danny in order to inject the drugs? Or did he have someone helping him?

So many questions. Nicki glanced at her watch and sighed. She'd practically worn a path through the carpet, yet it was still only seven a.m. After an invigorating shower, she dressed in a long silk skirt and cotton top. Carrying her laptop down to the lobby, she decided to continue her Internet search in a beautiful spot. If Marino hadn't already slapped the cuffs on the roommate, then maybe something else useful would turn up.

After an hour, Nicki concluded that those living off the grid truly remained off the grid. She tucked her laptop in her tote bag when she spied the concierge reading a newspaper at his desk. He looked almost as bored as she felt.

"Good morning, Mr. Prescott," she greeted. "Things a little slow for a Thursday morning?"

His face brightened with a smile. "Indeed. Where are the guests hoping for theater tickets or dinner reservations or recommendations for sightseeing? I'm even ready for the bus groups eager to see our famous fish." He refolded his newspaper. "How are you this fine day, Miss Price?"

Nicki perched on the edge of a chair. "I'm fine, thanks. That was an awesome tour on Tuesday. I truly enjoyed it."

The concierge studied her curiously. "Which part? The part where my grandfather tried to needle me into repeating unsubstantiated rumors and idle gossip?"

"Absolutely. I adored your grandpa because he reminded me so much of my own. Did Mr. Henry really work here for fifty years?"

"He did. The hotel hired him when he was only twenty years old. Over the years, he made himself downright indispensable. At least, that's how Granddad describes his tenure here. No one's still alive to either verify or refute him."

"Goodness, the changes he must have witnessed, not just at the Carlton, but in the city of Memphis and the country as a whole."

"You're exactly right. That's why it's hard for my grandfather to accept a quiet life in Oakbrook Center."

"He's stuck in a nursing home?" Nicki hoped that didn't sound judgmental.

"Not at all. He's in an assisted-living apartment. He cooks his own breakfast and lunch, and he eats dinner with people his age in a gracious room with white tablecloths and fine china. The only trouble is his peers only talk about their grandchildren or the latest episode of *Survivor.* A steady diet of that bores him to tears after living through the aftermath of World War II, Korea, Vietnam, and two Gulf Wars. My grandfather saw the fall of the Berlin Wall, the Civil Rights era, the decline of Memphis, and the city's eventual rebirth. When Granddad came to work here as a bellman, his father was still farming with a mule. I wouldn't have believed it, but he showed me an old photograph."

Nicki nodded. "My grandparents are retired farmers living in Red Haw, Mississippi, and Papaw still owns a mule to this day."

They both shared a chuckle. "Was that pretty girl who brought him here his granddaughter?"

"She's his *great*-granddaughter. Antoinette is my daughter, but she dotes on him endlessly. Me? I get a new tie and card on Father's Day and that's it." His expression revealed amusement instead of hard feelings over the favoritism. "Antoinette brings him here for brunch once a month. Afterward, she shops with her girlfriends while my grandfather follows me around as I give the tour. This week he called for the Oakbrook van driver to take him back early. The spicy Creole he ate for lunch upset his stomach."

Nicki thought of her grandfather with a pang of homesickness. Papaw had to give up his favorite Cajun dishes too. "I understand why Mr. Henry can't stay away. This hotel has been part of his life for so long."

"Granddad was as much a fixture at the Carlton as our famous fish are now. The regular guests knew and remembered his name from year to year. His responsibilities went far beyond opening doors. The bellman performed many of the same duties I have today, but often on the sly. Henry arranged meetings with famous musicians for blues aficionados, obtained front row seats for unadvertised appearances, and always made sure guests knew where to find a church in their denomination. Back then, everyone went to church. People didn't consult their day planners first." Robert shook his head. "Forgive me, Miss Price. I seem to have inherited Granddad's penchant for waxing poetic without provocation."

"Frankly, I'm grateful for someone to talk to. I don't have much to do until my fiancé arrives this weekend to show me around."

"Then may I recommend the trolley—"

Nicki held up a hand. "Not until Hunter arrives. I've been ordered to stay put and not spoil his plans. But I would love it if you told me about the Carlton jewels. Sounds like my kind of story." She absently fingered her engagement ring, the only real piece of jewelry she owned except for a small gold cross, a gift from her mother for her confirmation.

"The Carlton *jewels*." Robert shook his head. "Sounds like something out of an Agatha Christie novel. Granddad developed a flare for the dramatic over the years."

Nicki folded her hands in her lap and waited, looking as hopeful as a child in a toy store.

"I see he worked his magic on you." Robert sighed. "Take a stroll with me, Miss Price, if you have time to kill. I need to stretch my legs."

On their way through the inner courtyard, he greeted guests sipping tea, reading the paper, or simply enjoying the elegance of a bygone era. They paused at the marble staircase leading to the second-floor mezzanine, which was seldom used because most employees and guests chose the elevator.

"Unlike my grandfather, I don't know all the details of the story. I only know that in the fifties several well-to-do Memphis couples arrived for a long weekend each year to escape from demanding careers, family obligations, and everyday routines. Life can become tedious even for the very rich." He winked, a charming gesture that didn't diminish his dignity in the least.

"I'm quite sure foundation board meetings and charitable fund-raisers can be exhausting," Nicki said in a haughty tone.

"Exactly. The story goes that when they decided their trip to the Carlton would be a yearly event, one of the couples conceived the idea of a scavenger hunt. They went out and purchased gifts—one prize for the husband and one for the wife. I can't remember what any of them were, but they hid the 'jewels' somewhere in the hotel. Then once a day the couple provided hints to the other couples. These clues eventually led to the hidden treasure."

Nicki's mouth dropped open. "Wasn't the hotel filled with guests?"

"Absolutely. That was part of the fun. There was always a chance Mr. and Mrs. So-and-So from Little Rock celebrating an anniversary would spot the baubles first. The hotel *did not* sanction this scavenger hunt. In fact, at first they weren't even aware of its existence. But one year the society pages published a photo of the winners wearing the booty. After that, hotel management turned a blind eye because these couples were the movers and shakers of Memphis. The scavenger hunt was kept secret so their employees didn't spend their time searching instead of working."

"But your grandfather knew?"

Robert paused during their leisurely stroll around the balcony overlooking the lobby courtyard. "Yes. That's how fond people were of him. They not only trusted him, but Granddad often provided a distraction so the jewelry could be hidden."

"Good thing crooks didn't read the Memphis society pages in the fifties." Nicki leaned against the polished brass railing.

"Indeed. Some people did find out about the hunt and wanted in it. The hotel staff was ordered never to divulge the identities of the five couples or reveal the dates of the next scheduled hunt. Of course, the couples weren't too hard to figure out." When the concierge's phone buzzed, he glanced discretely at the screen. "I brought you up here for a reason, Miss Price. Take a look at this picture."

Nicki leaned close to the framed photograph he indicated. Two middle-age women in expensive ball gowns, along with husbands in dinner jackets, flanked a bright eyed, ebony-skinned young man. "Is this your grandfather with a pair of winners? Who are the other folks?"

"Yes, but he's the only person I recognize. You can't even make out what they won."

"I'll bet Mr. Henry would know."

"He may, but unfortunately I'm needed at the front desk. I

look forward to making the acquaintance of Mr. Galen this weekend. Good morning, Miss Price."

"I'll ride the elevator down with you," she said, keeping pace at his side. "With your permission, I'd love to visit Mr. Henry. Do you think he would be willing to see me?"

Mr. Prescott pressed the down button. "Granddad loves company, so I'm sure he would. But if you get him talking about the scavenger hunts, you'd better clear your schedule for the rest of the day." He jotted an address and phone number on a business card during the ride to the first floor. "If there's any other way I can be of service, do not hesitate to ask." He handed her the card with a smile.

An idea flashed through Nicki's mind. "One more thing, sir. Could I borrow the picture from upstairs to refresh your grandfather's memory?"

The concierge narrowed his eyes. "Because that photograph is property of the Carlton Hotel, I'm not at liberty to grant such permission. But if it were to mysteriously go missing for a few hours, I doubt anyone would even notice. And if someone did, I would imagine it would be back in place before anyone summoned the Pinkertons."

Nicki thanked him before going back up to her room and googling car rentals in the neighborhood. She needed her own car while in Memphis. Robert easily could have arranged that for her, but she felt she had reached her question-quota for the day.

Besides, she was an investigator, wasn't she?

TEN

*N*ate smiled at the note slipped under his door while he'd been sleeping: *Gone to visit a sweet old man I met during the hotel tour. He lives in Oakbrook Assisted-Living Center. Don't wait up. Nicki*

That was his cousin—always the person with the biggest heart in the room. He was glad she wasn't fighting him tooth and nail to stay on Danny's case. To catch this killer he needed to prowl some of the city's worst neighborhoods, and until Sullivan was in custody, it would be safer to talk to potential witnesses alone. And not busybodies with too much time on their hands. In his experience, people often put a spin on what they saw, and interpretations could be very different than reality.

Once Nate reached Danny's block, he parked along the curb and strolled leisurely toward the apartment building. Along the way, he attracted plenty of attention. Maybe next time he should rethink Dockers and a golf shirt in the inner city. He probably looked like a parole officer or social worker out to catch parents indulging in destructive habits. He didn't know which would be worse for his image.

Two storefronts from Danny's entrance, Nate spotted a young woman hunched over a large tablet. Behind her was a ratty backpack and a couple of soft-sided coolers, giving the impression she spent long hours in this spot. Nate assessed her sidewalk artistry. The caricatures weren't bad, but if she made her living selling them, she could use a few lessons. "How ya doing, miss? Those are pretty good."

She peered up at him through heavy eye makeup. "Keep moving, loser. I ain't that kind of girl."

Nate was taken aback. She couldn't be more than eighteen. The possibility she might sleep on the streets broke his heart. The idea of her being *that kind of girl* made his stomach queasy.

"Of course you're not, and you've got me all wrong. I'm just interested in your sketch of the Road Runner. Will you take ten bucks for it? I've always loved that bird."

She stared at him until he pulled a crumpled ten from his pocket and dropped it by her feet. Then she started sketching furiously, her focus not leaving the paper. "You a cop or something? If you're undercover, you really need a better disguise."

"Nah. I flunked covert operations. That's why I'm a private investigator out of New Orleans. I'm looking into Danny Andre's murder for personal reasons. He was a friend of mine."

Her thick pencil hovered above the sheet for a few seconds. "You don't look like one of his pals." She went back to work.

"People change. I knew Danny in high school, and then we kind of drifted apart. But I don't like that somebody killed him and dumped his body in the river."

Her industry came to an abrupt halt. "That's what happened? I heard he was dead but didn't really believe it. I thought he owed somebody money and was layin' low."

Nate sat next to her on the stoop. "I wish that were the case. Someone beat him up real bad."

The girl focused on the building across the street, her eyes shiny and moist. "Danny was a sweet guy. He'd give you the shirt off his back and half his lunch if you asked. If I knew who wasted him, I'd tell you, Mr. Private Investigator, but I don't."

"What about Tito Sullivan? You think he could have done this?"

She snorted. "Why would he? Danny was the reason Tito ain't on smack anymore."

"Maybe he…relapsed?" Nate couldn't remember all the street terminology.

But the girl didn't seem to notice. "Not that I'm aware of. Tito's been straight since Danny hooked up with him up at that outreach center."

"Did Danny ever use, to your knowledge?"

"Oh, please." Her young face scrunched into a scowl. "You *have* been out of touch. Danny would never do drugs. He saw too many messed up lives working in the bars on Beale. He didn't even drink."

Nate took a moment to reflect. "That's what I thought, but I wanted to hear it from somebody else. Could you point me in the direction of this outreach center? Maybe they know who had a grudge against Danny."

"It's in the basement of that big Baptist church on Fifteenth. You can't miss it. Fresh Start or New Hope or something like that." She tore the top sheet with the Road Runner off her pad. "You owe me ten more bucks for the conversation."

Nate pulled a couple twenties from his wallet to add to the ten along with his business card. "Call me if you think of anything else. And thanks for the sketch. I'll hang it on my office wall."

The girl looked at the money and then shoved it into the pocket of her jeans. "Here's some free advice: Save your cash for somebody with useful information."

"You've been more helpful than you know."

With that the neighborhood's artist-in-residence grabbed her backpack and coolers and disappeared into the alley.

Nate headed toward Fifteenth Street and easily located the Baptist church, but the outreach center was another matter. No sign indicated "Fresh Start" or "New Hope" or anything similar. After driving around the block twice, he finally parked and tried the doors of the sanctuary and entrance to the church office. Both were locked. But off the back alley, a leaf-strewn set of concrete steps led to a heavy, reinforced door. Nate went down the stairs and knocked twice. When patience produced no results, his intuition prodded him to turn the knob.

The door opened into a low-ceilinged room that smelled of bleach, dryer softener, and chicken soup. Despite the fact no one had answered his knock, the room was filled with occupants either napping or staring at a television. Cast-off sofas and upholstered chairs were arranged for cozy conversations. Along the wall, long cafeteria tables with metal folding chairs waited for the next meal.

A brusque command curtailed Nate's perusal of the decor.

"Don't just stand there, man. Close the door," said an under-fed teenager. "If you're looking for a meal or a place to crash, sign in on the sheet." He pointed at a clipboard with pen attached with a string. "If you're selling something or taking a survey, or you're here for any other reason, get lost. Nobody wants to talk to you." With those instructions the boy disappeared through a door marked "Men."

Nate couldn't help but notice the teen's blackened teeth, a dead giveaway of his drug of choice—methamphetamine. *Well, perhaps his former drug of choice.* Nate signed his name in the column indicating he needed a meal. Not that he was hungry, but he was at a loss as to how to proceed. One of the room's occupants, a hollowed-eyed man sitting on the couch, had kept his gaze on Nate since he arrived. The man was around forty in clean but faded clothes, his black hair buzzed close to the scalp, his skin a rich shade of ebony. The newspaper on his lap was open to the front page.

"Mind if I join you?" asked Nate.

"Free country," the man said with a shrug. "You don't look like you need a meal or a place to crash. You some reporter trying to grab a Pulitzer with a new angle on junkies?" His laughter held little humor.

"I can barely write a grocery list, let alone a prize-winning article." Nate sat at the end of the couch and stretched out his legs. "I want to talk to whoever runs this place about a friend of mine."

The man's smile revealed straight white teeth. Meth was apparently not his demon of choice. "The director's name is Carl Fuentes. When he ain't here, I'm in charge to make sure nobody gets out of hand and busts up the place. I'll throw 'em out on the street if they forget how to behave." He crossed his arms over his chest, further accentuating his biceps.

"Nate Price," he said, offering his hand. "Any idea when Mr. Fuentes will return, Mr...?"

"My name is Wallace, not Mr. Anybody." He shook with little enthusiasm. "Ain't seen Carl for a couple days, but he don't punch a time clock around here. You can sit and wait, or come back tomorrow, or come back next week. Don't make no difference to me. But I don't recommend staying for supper. None of these guys know the first thing about cooking, and I ain't nobody's maid."

"Does Carl do the cooking?"

"Most of the time. Him or one of the volunteers."

"Carl helps men get clean here?" Nate dropped his voice very low.

"If this looks like rehab to you, Nate Price, you must live under a rock." Wallace sneered with contempt. "We provide a meal, a place to sleep, and somebody to talk to *after* you're discharged from rehab. If an addict goes back to his old crowd on the street, sobriety ain't gonna last long."

A lightbulb illuminated in Nate's head. "Was Danny Andre a counselor here?"

Wallace watched Nate from the corner of his eye, apparently gaining his own insight. "Danny the friend you're so curious about?"

"Yeah, and now he's dead. I want to talk to someone who knew him. Is that how Danny helped out?"

"Danny was a great mentor, the best one I ever met who hadn't walked the road himself." Wallace rolled up one sleeve to reveal well-healed needle marks. He waited until Nate nodded with comprehension before pulling down his sleeve. "When Danny took someone under his wing, he stayed with them until they were clean. Night and day, for better or for worse, if you catch my drift, no matter how long it took."

"Danny was a stand-up guy." Emotion welled up Nate's throat upon hearing the former addict's respect for his old friend. "Did Danny meet Tito Sullivan here?"

Wallace nodded. "Yep. Just one of his many success stories."

"Does Sullivan volunteer now that he's clean?"

"Man, you are clueless. Sullivan may be clean, but if he starts hanging around those still on smack, he'll fall off the wagon for sure. If he ain't already using now that Danny's dead." Wallace made a point of looking at this watch. "Either you start cooking us a pot of chow or move along. I gotta get one of these boys busy or there'll be a revolt."

Nate jumped to his feet. "I appreciate your time, Wallace. One more question. What's the name of this place? I couldn't find your sign."

"The name is New Horizons. Those who need us find the way. Advertising usually brings nothing but trouble."

Halfway to the door, Nate broke his promise of only one more question. "Do you think Mr. Fuentes will be back tomorrow?"

"No idea. This is the first time he's been gone more than a day in the five years I've been here." With that, Wallace disappeared through the swinging doors.

Nate glanced at the recovering addicts, whose focus hadn't budged from the game show they were watching, and then walked out the door to the stairs to the street. He was halfway back to his car when his phone rang. Caller ID indicated Detective Marino.

"You'll be happy to know we collared Sullivan last night." The detective said in lieu of a greeting. "He's in a holding cell waiting for a public defender before we question him. He lawyered up. Here I'd been counting on a full confession." Chip laughed with animation.

"*Last night?*" asked Nate. "I was expecting you Tuesday night. I sat there in the shadows all alone and came back last night until it started to pour. "

"You gave up too soon. Sullivan showed around three o'clock in the morning. And you ain't the only name on my dance card, old buddy. I thought you would be thrilled."

"Yeah, I am, Chip. Thanks for letting me know."

"You're welcome. I gotta take another call, but stay in touch, okay?"

Marino clicked off, leaving Nate with plenty of questions, surprisingly little satisfaction, and no thrill whatsoever.

ELEVEN

*F*ollowing a sleepless night, hours of time wasted on paperwork, two fruitless sales appointments, and a depressing stop at the funeral home for final arrangements, Isabelle was desperate to go somewhere after work. With Danny gone and her remaining family still in Natchez, she regretted never taking the time to make friends in Memphis or Germantown. Maybe it was her dearth of girlfriends that led Isabelle to the Carlton late that afternoon. It was a long shot, but she hoped Nicki was back from wherever Danny's case had sent her. If not, she would sit in the lobby and wait, all night if necessary. Just so she didn't have to go home yet.

Isabelle pulled up to the curb just as a minivan drove away, vacating a spot with nearly an hour left on the meter. Even more fortuitous, Nicki was pacing the sidewalk in front of the hotel, punching numbers on her cell phone.

"Nicki," Isabelle called, climbing out of her car during a break in traffic. "You are a sight for sore eyes."

"Isabelle? What on earth are you doing at the Carlton? Did something happen?" Nicki slipped her phone in her pocket, her face clouding with concern.

Isabelle mustered a brave smile. "You go first. Tell me why you're patrolling the street at rush hour on a Thursday afternoon."

Nicki released a screech of exasperation. "That stupid rental agency has kept me dancing on a string for hours, ruining my plans to visit my new friend Henry at his assisted-living center. At first the manager refused to rent me a car without a personal credit card. So I told him I had a company card for Price Investigations. But when the guy came to drop off the car, he wouldn't give me the keys without Nate's signature. Then he drove away with my Buick."

"Why would Nate have to cosign your rental agreement? You're over twenty-five." Isabelle jumped back as a bus splashed water onto the sidewalk.

"Because Nate's name is on the card. I just made partner recently, but I haven't had trouble using it until today." She rolled her huge brown eyes. "That's what I get for letting either Nate or Hunter make arrangements for me."

Isabelle hooked her arm through Nicki's elbow. "Let's go have a cup of coffee and formulate a plan. You look ready to punch someone's nose, and that's never a good thing."

Once they were seated with steaming mugs before them, Nicki's tense posture relaxed. "Thanks, Izzy. You were right. I was overreacting to a situation easily remedied. Either Nate will sign for the car in the morning or Hunter can when he flies up tomorrow afternoon." She took a long swallow of her coffee.

Isabelle's anxiety ebbed as well as she focused on someone else's life. "Tell me about this mysterious fiancé of yours. Have you been dating a long time?"

"A little over six months, but it was pretty much love at first sight for us. Hunter was my client, so I fought romantic notions for as long as possible. He was a murder suspect. By the time I *knew* he didn't do it, I was head-over-heels." Nicki ducked her head to hide her embarrassment. "It will make more sense after you meet him."

"You're engaged to a former murder suspect? I can't wait to hear the details." Isabelle refilled their cups from the silver carafe on the table.

Nicki happily complied, her irritation with the rental company forgotten. She launched into a complex saga of a dead business partner, a broken engagement, a conniving ex-fiancée, and a father who would do anything for his daughter. When Nicki finished her story, Isabelle still had many questions, but she was certain of one thing. Nicki was engaged to a nice man who loved her very much. And that conclusion filled Isabelle with envy.

She swallowed down her shameful feelings. "Have you set a wedding date?"

"Not yet. We'll sit down to work out the details once Hunter finishes his court testimony and I'm back in New Orleans. But watch your mailbox for an invitation."

"I'll start looking for a dress right away."

Nicki reached for Isabelle's hand, her exuberance fading. "You didn't drive here after work to hear about my wedding plans. Tell me what happened, Izzy. I'm sorry I ran away with the ball."

"Honestly, I'm glad you did." She glanced everywhere but at her friend. "I just didn't want to go home until I told someone about last night."

"Here I am, ready to shut up and let you talk."

Now that the floor was hers, Isabelle's words stuck in her throat like a chicken bone. If the adage "misery loves company" was true, maybe people with disastrous lives didn't like to share with those with hopeful futures. Disaster was the only way to describe her recent sales record, her failed marriage, and her every attempt at dating. Underneath it all lay the niggling conviction she might be responsible for her brother's death.

"First on the agenda, the medical examiner released Danny's body to the funeral home. The…" Her voice cracked just saying the word. "The…undertaker thought a closed casket would be best, but I insisted on one hour of viewing before the service. I thought you'd like to see Danny in better circumstances than on the banks of the Mississippi." Tears streamed down her face. "The funeral will be at ten o'clock at Germantown's United Methodist on Saturday. Will that be all right?"

Nicki chewed on her lower lip, gripping her coffee mug tightly. "Thanks. I would like to see him. And Saturday is perfect since Hunter will be here. If there's anything I can do, say the word."

"Perhaps Hunter could be a pallbearer? I'm not sure who will come to the funeral." She wiped her face with a napkin.

"Done. He will be honored." Nicki sat quietly for a while and then squeezed her hand. "Go on, Izzy. I know something else has you spooked other than funeral arrangements. What happened last night?"

Isabelle stared at her hands. "Those neighborhood kids were up to mischief again."

"What kids?" Nicki set down her mug. "Do you mean someone threw more blood on your balcony?"

"We still don't know if that was actual blood. I don't have the results from Germantown Police yet. At any rate, no blood. This time someone left a cemetery wreath on my balcony. Two dozen red roses along with ribbons that said 'Dearly Beloved' and 'We'll miss you.' They trailed dead flower petals to my sliding door like bread crumbs in Hansel and Gretel."

Nicki's eyes were round as an owl's. "Was someone *inside* your apartment?"

"Not that I could tell. I think someone climbed to the balcony, which would be no easy feat." Isabelle tore her napkin into shreds. "Would you come to my apartment and take a look? Maybe it's not teenage vandalism. If this is retaliation from a bad date, then it could be related to my brother's murder. I...I may be the reason why Danny's dead."

Nicki grabbed her arm and shook it hard. "That's ridiculous. The only one responsible is the thug who injected Danny with heroin. Nobody else." She pulled out her cell phone. "I'll call Nate and ask him to meet us there."

Isabelle grabbed the phone from Nicki's hand. "No. Can't you just look into this?"

"No, I can't. I'm sorry, but Nate's the PI on this case. I've been demoted to background checks and behind-the-scenes work. Maybe you should tell me why you don't like my cousin."

Her fingers curled around the wad of shredded paper. "It's not that I don't like him, but every time we're in the same room I manage to insult him without provocation. If he described me as rude and arrogant, I couldn't disagree."

"I get that you rub each other the wrong way, but Nate's a good investigator—the best in Louisiana or Mississippi. He needs to see this wreath and check your building's security system. He'll get the results of the blood DNA quicker too. In the meantime, you should move to the Carlton until Danny's killer is caught. Also until we can prove Tony Markham is behind those terrible things on your balcony. For all we know, the killer and Tony are one and the same."

Isabelle shook her head. She'd checked the rates after Nicki mentioned where she was staying. With taxes and parking, even a few nights would equal a month's rent on her condo. "This is definitely out of my price range."

"I mean stay in *my* suite. Goodness, there's enough room for both of us. I could be your bodyguard and still be out of Nate's way."

Isabelle smiled at a friend she didn't deserve. "I see why my brother adored you. You really are a nice person."

"Danny also liked salamanders and snapping turtles, so his judgment can't be trusted. Will you come stay with me?"

"No thanks, Nicki. Tomorrow your fiancée will arrive. Won't he be sleeping on your sofa?"

"Absolutely not. He'll sleep in Nate's room."

"Well, I have a fat calico who needs me, so I'll stay in Germantown. I appreciate the offer, though."

"All right, but you need to swallow your pride and work with Nate. If you give him a chance, I know he can get to the bottom of this. Trust *my* judgment. He's a nice person too."

Isabelle drained her mug and pulled the business card from her blazer pocket. Without another word, she punched in Nate's number. When he picked up on the third ring, she cleared her throat. "Hello, Mr. Price? Isabelle Andre. At the moment, I'm having coffee with Nicki at the Carlton, but there's something I would like you to see. Do you have time this evening to meet me at my condo?" She held her breath and waited.

"I'm two blocks away at a red light, so I can follow you back to Germantown. Please tell my cousin she's to find out everything she can about the New Horizons Outreach Center. It's in the basement of First Baptist on Fifteenth Street. And ask her to do a background check on Carl Fuentes, same address as the center. That's where Danny met Tito Sullivan. Danny mentored addicts recovering from both drugs and alcohol."

Isabelle jotted names on her napkin while exchanging glances with Nicki. "Danny was a sobriety mentor?"

"You weren't aware of this?"

"Unfortunately, I assumed my brother slept all day when he wasn't playing music in bars. I didn't know the extent of his humanitarian nature."

"Families are complicated. I'm not here to judge, Miss Andre. Tell Nicki to watch for the name Wallace in connection to the shelter too. Not sure if it's a first or last name."

"I'll give her your message. How soon will you be here?" Isabelle passed the napkin filled with notes to Nicki.

"I'm double-parked next to your green Prius as we speak. When you're finished with my cousin, I'm at your disposal."

Isabelle flushed for no apparent reason as she said goodbye and ended the call. She looked at Nicki. "Nate's already outside, and I don't want to keep him waiting. This is the name of the outreach center he wants you to check out, along with Carl Fuentes and someone named Wallace. Could you use this for our coffee?" Isabelle pulled a ten from her wallet and then impulsively kissed Nicki's cheek. "Thanks for being here for me."

～

Nate waited until the dressed-for-success Realtor buckled her seat belt and pulled into traffic before falling in behind her. Isabelle drove like a little old lady. Or maybe she didn't think he could keep up with her in traffic. She seemed to have zero confidence in any of his abilities. At the next red light, he punched in Nicki's number.

"I'm not even back to my room, boss. Stop bugging me. I'll check out the names you gave me, but I need a little time." Nicki sounded like her normal, sassy self.

"That's not why I called. I want to know why Miss Andre came to the Carlton and why she called me. I don't like walking into situations blind."

"She was afraid to go home alone. More trouble at her condo last night. These aren't out-of-season Halloween pranks, Nate. Somebody is stalking her."

"And she wanted you to investigate." He didn't hide his pique.

"Well, I am a PI and licensed to carry a gun, but don't get your underwear in a twist. I told her to call you since this might be related to Danny's murder."

"Marino arrested Tito Sullivan last night, so he'll be in custody for at least the next forty-eight hours. I just found out this afternoon."

"That's good news, no?" Nicki didn't sound convinced.

"We'll see. Sullivan may have a rock solid alibi for all we know. Right now, tell me about Isabelle."

"Somebody left dead flowers from a grave on her balcony. Pretty icky, don't you think? One ribbon said 'We'll miss you.'"

Rage surged up Nate's spine. He closed the distance between his car and Isabelle's. "That sounds like a threat to me. I'll call the Germantown PD and have them meet us there. We'll need police reports to substantiate future restraining orders or to get an arrest warrant on stalking charges. Why don't you dig up everything you can about this Tony Markham too?"

"You got it, but this could take all night. Better bring back a deluxe pizza, double cheese."

"When does Hunter arrive? Does he need me to pick him up at the airport?"

"Tomorrow after six, but he insists on a taxi. I'm so glad he'll be here for Danny's funeral. It's set for Saturday at ten at Germantown United Methodist."

"Good to know. Miss Andre already asked me to be a pallbearer. I'm glad Hunter can serve instead of a skinny girl like you." Nate expected Nicki to rail against the description, but she didn't. Discussing her best friend's funeral didn't bring out her sparring nature.

"Hunter won't mind at all. Good thing I brought a dress along. Do you think navy will be okay? I don't own any black."

"I'm sure navy will be fine. Gotta go, Nic. Miss Andre is getting on the expressway and traffic is heavy." He disconnected the call to make sure Isabelle never left his sight.

When they arrived at her condo, Nate parked in a guest slot

and followed her to a three-story building. In the elevator she seemed nervous, but considering his own clammy palms he wasn't surprised. It took more than one attempt before her key turned in the lock.

"Sorry. I'm more flustered than I thought," she said when the door finally swung open.

"Who wouldn't be?" Nate stepped into her meticulous living room. There wasn't a stack of old magazines, unread junk mail, or empty pizza boxes in sight. Every time he visited someone else's home, he always walked around with a trash bag the moment he returned to his. An overweight cat bumped against his leg, startling him. "Who are you, little missy?" Nate said as he reached down to scratch the feline's head.

"That's Chester. You're the first male he's ever approached." Isabelle rubbed her forearms as though cold.

"I have that effect on children and small animals. It's big people who run in the opposite direction from me." Nate had no idea what triggered the confession, but when he looked at Isabelle, she held his gaze for several seconds.

"Why don't I show you to the latest addition to my balcony?" She crossed the room to the slider and opened the drapes.

The sight of the morbid decoration turned Nate's blood cold. "Did you handle the wreath or touch the railing? The police will want to dust for fingerprints."

"You called the cops?"

"Yes. I don't think this is child's play, Miss Andre. If Tony Markham is a threat, we'll need documentation. Do you have a problem with that?"

Several seconds spun out before she replied. "Not if he's the one behind this. I just don't want to make trouble if he's not." Her gaze darted around the room nervously.

"Neither do I, so maybe you should tell me about anybody else with a grudge against you if you're uncertain this is Markham's handiwork." Nate hooked a thumb toward the balcony.

Isabelle shifted from foot to foot, like a child getting scolded, but she remained silent.

"Look, if you want my help, I need to know about people you've alienated since moving to Memphis—clients unhappy with houses you've sold, mail carriers disappointed with their Christmas tip, other former suitors spurned after some unforgivable faux pas."

"*Suitors*? This isn't the Victorian era." She set her purse on the counter between the kitchen and living area with a thud.

"Dates, beaus, potential mates—pick a noun, Miss Andre, and start talking or I'm out of here." Nate stuck his hands in his pockets. "The Germantown police will soon be here to take your statement."

Isabelle's eyes darted between the door, the balcony, and his face. "I'm surprised they're not here already."

"This isn't an emergency. They have to respond to 9-1-1 calls first."

"Of course. I should have thought of that myself. Please have a seat, Mr. Price. My list of unhappy acquaintances won't take long."

When he settled on the couch, she lowered herself to a chair. "I moved to Memphis four years ago after my divorce to be close to Danny. He's all the family I have left except for a couple of aunts and cousins in Natchez. We shared an apartment until I found a position in the Germantown office. My brother had no desire to move to suburbia." She attempted a smile that didn't quite work.

"What about your ex-husband? Maybe he's tired of paying alimony payments or still mad about the divorce settlement."

Isabelle laughter sounded hollow. "I never received a penny of alimony. My share of the property settlement amounted to half the debts he accrued during our marriage, even though I worked two jobs to put him through law school."

"A lawyer should make a decent living, even if he's a court-appointed defense attorney."

"I'm sure he does, but Craig has a new girlfriend to spend his money on. Around the time a major Nashville corporation hired him for their legal team, Craig decided the vow of fidelity was far too restrictive." Isabelle tucked a lock of shiny hair behind her ears, revealing a bit more of her flawless complexion. "I hope I don't sound bitter, because I'm not. After some counseling, I was able to let go of my anger and resentment. The only reason I bring up my ex-husband is because at the time of our divorce, Craig owed a lot of people money. And I'm not talking about student loans. He acquired a gambling habit during college, betting on sports. I helped him pay off as much of it as I could, but I had half the credit card debt to deal with and a car constantly breaking down. So one day I pulled up stakes and moved away, absolving myself of any further responsibility for his debts." Her green eyes turned luminous as they caught the lamplight. "You don't think some bookie found me here and took his revenge out on Danny, do you?" Her lower lip trembled either from fear or sorrow.

"That's not very likely." Nate stood. "Put that out of your head. Most likely it was Tito Sullivan, who's already in custody. If not him, then Tony Markham would be my next guess. Nashville bookies wouldn't come after a penniless ex-wife in Memphis four years later." He felt his face redden and grimaced. "Sorry about the penniless comment. I meant no offense."

This time her smile looked genuine. "None taken. I am barely surviving here in the land of upwardly mobile, two-earner families. I leased this condo to be close to my office, but I should have stayed in the city with Danny. Then he wouldn't have taken in a dangerous roommate and maybe he would still be alive." Her eyes filled with tears.

"Hold on a minute. None of this was your fault. Danny chose

to volunteer with former addicts at the outreach center. That kind of work comes with a measure of risk. Maybe he wasn't given a long life, but it's what we do with our number of days that counts."

"Thank you for saying that. Does your philosophical attitude come from a strong spiritual base?"

Nate knew this was one question he needed to be absolutely truthful about. "Yes, I guess it does. That's how I was raised, and that's what I believe, although I don't talk about it much. "

Isabelle nodded with understanding. "Death makes us consider our own mortality and what comes next. I'm glad you and Nicki will be with me during the funeral."

The way she stared at him turned his legs to jelly. "Ten o'clock on Saturday? Nicki and I will meet you at the United Methodist Church at nine. You'll get through this, Miss Andre. We'll make sure of it."

A knock on the door signaled the arrival of Germantown's finest. Nate was never happier to see the police in his life. Every time he was alone with Isabelle Andre his confidence and composure plummeted to zilch. Why this tiny, hundred-and-fifteen-pound woman would have such an effect on him, he had no idea.

TWELVE

*N*icki jumped out of bed Friday morning with the energy of three women. She would be spending the day with not one but two handsome men. Now that Hunter had arranged for a rental car to be delivered to the hotel at nine o'clock, she planned to visit Henry Prescott, the Carlton's former bellman. Later Hunter would arrive by taxi in time for dinner. Her heart had definitely grown fonder during their week apart.

She dressed in a pair of chino slacks and a cotton twinset. After coffee and an in-suite breakfast of crackers, cheese, grapes, and a pear from her bottomless fruit basket, Nicki went to the lobby to await her rental car. The concierge was already at his desk, concentrating on his computer screen.

"Good morning, Mr. Prescott. Isn't this a lovely morning?"

He glanced up at her over his wire-rimmed glasses. "It is indeed, Miss Price. I just got off the phone with your fiancé. Mr. Galen requested the best table in the house at Chez Francois this evening. I was more than happy to oblige."

Nicki checked the drop-off zone for the Buick she'd requested from the window. "I can't wait to try that place. My tightwad cousin refuses to eat there." Noticing Mr. Prescott's reaction she added, "Sorry. I have a bad habit of saying whatever comes to mind. I just meant five-star dining isn't in our budget this week."

"I consider frankness an asset, not a detriment. Won't you have a seat? The rental car courier knows to bring me the keys."

Nicki perched on the edge of a chair in front of his desk. "I'm visiting your grandfather today unless you think that wouldn't be a good idea."

Mr. Prescott grinned. "Unfortunately, Granddad's days are far too routine and predictable. He'll welcome your company. I'll call ahead to make sure he wears his favorite shirt."

Spotting a young woman with a car logo on her shirt, Nicki jumped up. "One more thing before I go. You may want to skip the second floor mezzanine as you stroll around the hotel today."

"Duly noted. And if you're not back by the time Mr. Galen arrives, I'll send out the cavalry. My grandfather has been known to hold an audience captive for hours."

⤳

When Nicki walked through the doors of the assisted-living center, she was pleasantly surprised. Her only experience with elder care facilities had been a visit to a great-aunt in a sad place reeking of disinfectant. Patients had lined the hallways in their wheelchairs or sat in their rooms looking forlorn. But at Oakbrook's front desk, Nicki was greeted with a friendly smile.

"I'm here to see Henry Prescott, ma'am."

"You must be Miss Price. I'll show you to the sunroom. Mr. Prescott's grandson requested some refreshment for your visit. You must be very special." The woman led her down two hallways and through double doors into a high-ceilinged conservatory that brought to mind the elegance of British mansions.

Henry Prescott sat in his wheelchair wearing an argyle cardigan and bright smile. Two glasses of lemonade and a plate of cookies waited on a side table.

"Hello, Mr. Prescott. Do you remember me? I'm Nicki Price."

He blinked several times, his face a craggy topography. "Have we met, young lady?"

So much for her being a special guest. "Yes, sir. On Tuesday's hotel tour you started telling us about the famous Carlton jewels."

"Oh, that's right. You were pushing that tyke in a stroller. Little girl, right?"

The desk clerk disappeared as Nicki pulled a chair close to him. "No, sir. I was alone during the tour." She handed him a gift-wrapped box as her expectation for details about the scavenger hunts dimmed. "I brought you some chocolates. I hope that's okay."

"I love candy. Thanks. If you live as long as me, people stop telling you what you can or can't eat. Yesterday, I ate two pieces of sweet potato pie, and today I had bacon for breakfast. My arteries still feel fine." He tucked the box into a cloth pouch attached to his wheelchair. "Yes, now I remember you. Funny thing about getting old. I can remember forty years ago clear as a bell, but sometimes I can't recall what I wore yesterday to save my life." He laughed heartily while holding his stomach with one hand.

"Who cares about clothes anyway? I'd love to hear more about those scavenger hunts. How did they get started?"

Henry offered her a cookie and took one himself. "Brainchild of Mrs. Smithfield, to be sure. She bought the first set of jewels and planned the whole shebang. She and the mister arrived two days early to figure out where to hide the prizes and decide what clues to give out."

"Do you remember what year that was?"

"Sure do. It was 1955." Henry leaned forward in his chair. "The Smithfields had the deepest pockets, if you know what I mean.

They were the richest of the five rich couples. They bought some kind of diamond trinkets. Gimme a minute to recall exactly what."

"Diamonds," Nicki murmured. "Pretty nice prizes for a scavenger hunt."

Henry's dark eyes twinkled. "Don't know what kind of people you come from, Miss Nicki, but these folks didn't live like most. They dressed fancier every night for dinner than most folks do on their weddin' day. They had maids and valets and chauffeurs, and they brought more luggage for three days than my wife took to Texas for a month."

"No, that's not like my people. Mine can pretty much fit everything into two brown grocery store bags," Nicki said, smiling at him as she finished her cookie.

Laughing, Henry slapped his knees. "You're a funny gal. Have more cookies." He pushed the plate across the table.

"What were the rules to this game? Surely the Smithfields set down specific guidelines."

Henry scratched his head as he thought. "Let's see…prizes had to be hidden in plain sight. No rippin' up carpeting or punching holes in walls, for obvious reasons. For a while the Carlton management knew nothing about them. None of the staff either, 'cept for me. Mrs. Smithfield took a liking to me 'cause I chased a thief seven blocks to get her purse back. She set it on the luggage cart for a minute and a scoundrel grabbed it and ran off." He clucked his tongue with dismay. "After that, the Smithfields had me run their errands after my shift was done."

"If your work was finished for the day, didn't you resent their demands?"

"Nope. Back then, one of Mr. Smithfield's tips was more than a day's pay. 'Sides, I was single at the time and didn't have much else to do." Henry leaned back against the chair, his expression sly. "I thought up the first hiding place."

"Where was it?" Nicki sputtered around a mouthful of cookie crumbs.

His smile bloomed with the memory. "After all the guests went to bed, I met Mr. and Mrs. Smithfield in the lobby. Hotel didn't have no night staff in those days. Folks knew better than to check in after nine o'clock. Can't understand why places stay open for twenty-four hours—even Walmart. Who needs to buy gardening gloves or paper towels in the middle of the night?"

Nicki placed a hand on his arm. "Tell me more about the first year's jewels," she prodded.

"Oh, yeah. Miz Smithfield showed me a diamond band for a lady to wear in her hair, like half a crown for a queen. I looked up at the lobby ceiling and saw the crystal chandelier, all sparkly, just like those diamonds. 'There's our hiding spot,' I said."

Nicki swallowed a mouthful of lemonade. "How on earth did you get up to the chandelier? Surely you didn't drag in an extension ladder inside the building."

"Didn't have to. Back then, the chandeliers could be lowered on a chain for dusting. All we had to do was stay out of sight till the last maid went off duty. Then I lowered the chandelier and the missus attached the…the…"

"Tiara?"

"That's it, tiara, and a cigarette case studded with diamonds for the mister." Henry beamed with the recollection. "That first year's clues were easy. At dinner on the second night, one of the couples figured it out from the clue 'Always ready to shed some light on a dark corner.' Once folks went to bed that night, down the chandelier came again so the winner could claim the prize. Nobody else was the wiser."

Henry's head started to bob, the room's warmth apparently making him drowsy.

"May I ask one more question, Mr. Prescott?" Nicki pulled the framed photograph from her tote bag. "Do you know who these people are?"

His eyes snapped open. "Let me see that." He held the picture two inches from his nose. "Sure I do. That's Mr. and Mrs. Smithfield." A crooked finger tapped the left-hand couple. "And that's who won the prize in '55, Mr. and Mrs. Whitley." He tilted the frame to catch more light. "She got that tiara already in her hair."

Nicki took the photo from him just as it slipped through his fingers. With his eyes shut, she thought Henry had fallen asleep. But before she reached the door to the main hall, his scratchy voice called to her. "You keep diggin', missy. Maybe you'll be the one to find the lost jewels."

That stopped her dead in her tracks. Returning to the elderly man, she shook him awake. "What do you mean by that, sir?"

"Just what it sounds like. Not all them prizes were found. Not that there's much either of us can do about it."

Nicki stared at the photo, growing more excited by the moment. "But I'm a trained private investigator."

"Then I'd say you now got something to 'vestigate." Henry closed his eyes with a smile.

～

Nate finished the last of his taco from a street vendor just as his phone rang. *Nicki*, according to the face on the screen. "It's about time you returned my call. You're still on the job until five o'clock." After spending the morning on the phone with his New Orlean's secretary tying up loose ends in old cases, he wasn't in the best of moods.

"Didn't you get my message, boss? I had a date with a sweet old man."

"Who you see behind Hunter's back isn't my concern. Tell me

what you found out about Carl Fuentes, the director of New Horizons."

"I found out plenty. Carl Fuentes, Americanized from Carlos, did prison time for drug possession on three different occasions. His rap sheet goes back to his juvenile days, all drug related. Cultivation of marijuana, possession with intent to distribute, and sale of controlled substances. He never moved significant quantities, so his sentences weren't too long in minimum security at Turney Prison. Then he got clean ten years ago during his last incarceration. Most likely some judge threatened to throw away the key."

Nate wiped salsa off his chin and pitched his empty wrappers into a trash barrel. "Anything violent on his rap sheet? Assault, domestic violence?"

"Nothing like that. And here's the best part. Fuentes studied theology while behind bars and is now some kind of preacher. He's one of the pastors at First Baptist, which might have helped him open the outreach center in the basement."

"Any recent complaints against Fuentes from parishioners or disgruntled rehabbers?" Nate was having trouble picturing a former junkie as a preacher.

"*Nada.* Mr. Fuentes has been straight as an arrow. Not even a parking ticket in recent years." Nicki slurped something in the background.

"Any complaints from neighbors or police reports for unruliness at the center?"

"Nothing. I'm telling you, Nate, New Horizons appears to be a model organization in the community. Several Baptist churches hold yearly fund-raisers for them, and Fuentes accounts for every dime he spends. If you were hoping to tie him to Tito Sullivan in a bad way, sorry I couldn't help."

Nate climbed into his car and started the engine. "I don't have a personal agenda, Nic. Where are you heading now?"

"Back to the hotel for a bubble bath and to have my hair fixed into something sophisticated. I'm dining at Chez Francois with a handsome man tonight. Care to join us as a third wheel?"

"Thanks, but I just ate Mexican. Enjoy yourself but get plenty of sleep. We need to be at Miss Andre's church by eight thirty tomorrow morning."

Nicki was a silent a moment. "Hunter and I will meet you in the lobby by eight. Bye, Nate."

He felt like a heel. It was the probably the first time all week Nicki wasn't thinking about Danny, and he'd just cast a shadow on her fun evening. What was wrong with him? Was he jealous because his cousin had found someone to spend her life with? Being single had never bothered him in New Orleans, but on the road, out of his element, he felt more than just alone. He was lonely.

Shifting the car into gear, Nate drove to county lockup. It was time to meet Titus Sullivan. You could tell a lot about a person face-to-face, and Danny's former roommate turned out to be no exception.

Nate identified himself as a private investigator from Louisiana working with Memphis homicide, checked his weapon at the desk, and waited for Tito to be brought in. He was expecting a multi-tattooed, hard-as-nails thug with an attitude. But Tito looked like an emaciated, frightened kid who had never pumped iron or talked trash in his life. It would be miraculous if he stayed alive long enough to stand trial.

"Who are you?" asked Tito, slumping into the chair on the opposite side of the table.

"Name's Nate Price. I'm a friend of Danny Andre's. I came to town to investigate his murder." He kept his expression neutral.

"Oh, man! It's good to finally see a friendly face. I'm going crazy in this place. You gotta get me out of here. I ain't even been charged yet." Sullivan's eyes darted left and right, as though danger was closing in.

"Why would you think I'd be friendly with you? You're about to be charged with Danny's murder."

"No! That ain't right." Tito sliced the air with his hand. "I would never hurt Danny. He was my *friend*. I weren't nowhere around the night he got killed. I got no idea who done it, but it weren't me."

Nate was taken aback by the verbiage. An English teacher would jail Sullivan based on bad grammar alone. "I take it you have an airtight alibi for last Thursday night?"

The small amount of color in Tito's complexion faded. "That's just it. I was someplace I shouldn't have been." His voice dropped to a whisper.

With little knowledge of the world Sullivan inhabited, a visual montage of opium dens and crack houses ran through Nate's mind, courtesy of TV crime dramas. "Did you fall off the wagon but don't want to get your dealer in trouble?" Scorn turned Nate's words brittle.

Tito stared at him. "No, man, nothing like that. I swear I'm clean." He placed a bony hand across his heart. "I ain't got no supplier."

Nate was no expert on substance abuse withdrawal, but wouldn't Sullivan be sweating or trembling or have dilated pupils if he'd been using? The pathetic soul sitting across from him looked like he needed a good meal, not a fix. "If you had nothing to do with Danny's death, you should start talking, at least to me. I'm not interested in bringing other criminal charges against you, only murder."

Tito glanced at the camera mounted on the wall. "I guess I got nothing to lose. I spent the night locked in the sound room at the Blues City Club. Danny introduced me to the sound guy who works all the big shows. When there's gonna be a standin'-room-only crowd, he lets Danny and me sneak in to hear the band. Danny had the night off, so I thought he'd show up, but he never did."

Nate leaned back in his chair. This had to be the last thing he expected. "Go on. How did you get locked in?"

"They rented the balcony for a bachelor party and set out a spread of food. Wings, hoagies, ribs…even fried okra. I never had it fixed that way." Tito's eyes glazed over with the memory. "Never saw so much grub. I waited till those boys wouldn't care who wandered into line, but I didn't touch no booze. You gotta believe me. I filled my plate a second time for Danny and hid in the closet of the sound room. Then I fell asleep. When I woke up, the door was locked and I had to wait till Gus came to work the next night to get out. Gus told me if he ever laid eyes on me again, he'd break my arm." Tito rubbed the sleeve of his jumpsuit.

The guard unlocked the door and cleared his throat, signaling that Nate's time was up.

"I didn't lay a hand on Danny. I was still a block away from the apartment when I heard that he was dead."

"So why would you run if you had nothing to hide?" Nate rose to his feet.

"I ain't got good history with cops." Something raw flashed in Tito's eyes and then was gone. "They'll look at my rap sheet and not believe a word I'm sayin'."

"Thanks for talking to me, Mr. Sullivan. I suggest you do whatever your attorney says."

"What you gonna do for me, Price? I told you I was stuck in Blues City all night!" Tito's pleas followed Nate out the door.

∼

The only thing he could do, whether or not it was for Tito, was call Detective Marino. "Hey, Chip. How's it going?" Nate trotted out his friendliest tone. "I wanted to make sure you knew Danny Andre's funeral was tomorrow morning."

"Is that right? Give me the details and I'll make a point to be there."

Nate provided the time and place and then asked, "You eager to see who shows up? Maybe the killer will be lurking behind the headstones?"

"Nah. I already got the killer lurking in a cell. I'm hoping Andre's sister is so grateful she'll go out with me. Get this. Tito Sullivan was wearing Danny's clothes and watch when we arrested him. I sent a picture of the nice wool sweater to Isabelle, and she confirmed she bought it for Danny last Christmas, along with the watch. Sounds to me like Sullivan wanted them in a bad way and things got out of hand. Plenty of neighbors will testify that Tito had a temper."

Nate didn't know what bothered him more, Marino trying to get a date with Isabelle or his foregone conclusion he'd arrested the right man. "I just talked to Tito. He said he spent last Friday locked in the Blues City Club overnight. Crashed some kind of bachelor party and overstayed his welcome."

"Wow, you're like a dog with a bone, ain't you? Yeah, I ran that alibi by the soundman at the club. The guy said he didn't know what Sullivan was talking about."

"The soundman may have motivation to lie." Nate crossed the parking lot to his car as sirens whined in the distance.

"And Sullivan doesn't? Man, why won't you let this go? Sullivan was wearing expensive property that didn't belong to him, his alibi doesn't hold water, and the guy has a rap sheet a mile long, including both theft and assault. You wanted me to catch Andre's killer and I have. Now, pick a night we can go for ribs and forget about that loser."

Marino disconnected the call without as much as a goodbye.

But the detective's rudeness didn't matter to Nate. It was the inkling that he'd helped railroad the wrong man.

THIRTEEN

efitting the occasion, the morning of Danny's funeral dawned cool and rainy. Nate put on the fanciest clothes he'd brought to Memphis—tan chinos, white cotton shirt, and dark sport coat. The Carlton concierge had everything starched and pressed last night. Mr. Prescott was only too happy to help Nate because Nicki had brightened his grandfather's day. Nate smiled. If she wanted to sniff out something that happened sixty years ago, he couldn't be happier. Just as long as she stayed out of harm's way.

Nicki and Hunter were waiting in the lobby at the appointed hour. Nicki looked demure in a navy dress with white collar and cuffs, while Hunter's Armani suit underscored his distinguished appearance. Maybe it was the haircut or his French accent, but Hunter would probably look dignified dressed in a clown costume. Even if Nate tripled his yearly income, he couldn't come close to Hunter's élan.

As the three of them walked outside, the valet had a Lincoln Town Car waiting at the curb. "I thought you were renting a Buick," Nate whispered in Nicki's ear while Hunter walked to the driver's side.

"Hunter made the arrangements. He thought something bigger would be more comfortable."

The somber occasion affected everyone's mood during the drive to Germantown. Hunter made polite conversation about his court testimony, carefully avoiding anything that might upset Nicki. He was not only rich and well dressed, but diplomatic as well. Nate tried to inventory his personal assets and came up with only "never licks his fingers in public" and "never wears socks with sandals." Not exactly a compelling list of reasons for women to dream about him. But once they arrived at Isabelle's church, Nate forgot his self-absorption.

Isabelle Andre stood on the steps with the minister and a man who had to be the funeral director. Dressed from head to toe in black, she looked paler and smaller than normal. Her almost waist-length black hair was wound in a knot at the back of her head.

Hunter parked just behind the hearse and limo and walked around to open Nicki's door. As soon as she was out of the car, Nicki ran straight up the steps into Isabelle's arms. For several long moments the two women hugged and cried while Nate and Hunter watched helplessly. Both men wanted to offer comfort but were afraid to intrude.

"I'm so glad you came." Isabelle's plaintive words floated on the breeze. "It didn't hit me until today that he isn't coming back."

Nicki choked out something undecipherable, wiped her eyes, and then blew her nose. "We'll stay as long as you need us. Izzy, I'd like you meet my fiancé, Hunter Galen." Nicki reached for Hunter's hand to draw him close.

Feeling like an interloper, Nate hung back with the minister and funeral director on the sidelines. He watched one white-haired woman enter the church.

Suddenly Isabelle extended her hand toward him. "Mr. Price, I am so grateful you're here too." She pulled him into the inner circle. "It's just as I thought," she whispered next to his ear. "Most of the mourners are from the women's club or members of the church choir. Danny didn't attend this church, and I didn't socialize with couples. I feared there wouldn't be enough pallbearers."

Nate liked the feel of Isabelle's hand so much he would have agreed to carry the casket on his back. "We'll have enough now. Should we go inside?"

"Yes, before they close the casket," said Nicki. "Hunter never got to meet Danny. This will be his last chance." Her face crumpled with misery as Hunter walked with her into the sanctuary.

Nate extended his elbow to Isabelle as a vehicle screeched to a stop in the parking lot. The painted lettering indicated the van came from Memphis First Baptist. Judging by their rough attire, it didn't take a PI to deduce the mourners were Danny's former clients. One by one the reformed addicts entered the church, somber and respectful. One man, better attired than the others, approached the funeral director and spoke quietly.

Nate was halfway up the center aisle before realization dawned. *Carl Fuentes…no longer missing in action.* But with Isabelle leaning on his arm, now wasn't the time for crime solving. As Nicki wept in front of Danny's casket, Nate cleared his mind of everything but the moment at hand. For ten minutes mourners filed past Danny, paying their last respects as a pianist played hauntingly beautiful music. Nate had to bite the inside of his mouth to keep from crying for a man he barely knew.

When the funeral director closed the casket, the minister opened the service with Scripture. Then some of those who knew the deceased stepped forward to offer tributes. Although Nicki, Danny's best friend, and Isabelle, his only close relative, both spoke, the most stirring words came from those Danny had mentored. Half a dozen men walked to the pulpit one at a time, and each one described how Danny saved his life. Each insisted he would be dead if not for Danny's intervention, how he refused to give up even after several failed attempts at rehab. According to their testimonies, Danny had exemplified the Christian code of kindness, selflessness, and generosity. Many of the men broke down and wept at the pulpit. By the time Carl Fuentes delivered his tribute, there wasn't a dry eye in the house.

Nate gazed around the sanctuary as the soloist delivered a mournful "Amazing Grace." Several older women had slipped into the last row after the service had begun, along with Chip Marino. The detective nodded when Nate's gaze met his. At the song's conclusion, the minister delivered his final prayer, directions to the cemetery, and instructions as to where lunch would be served. Nate had no chance to talk with Marino, Fuentes, or any of the New Horizons clients. Isabelle clung tightly to his arm as they followed the casket down the center aisle. When the wheeled contraption arrived at the church steps and could go no farther, Nate and Hunter stepped forward to carry the casket to the hearse. But Fuentes and five of Danny's clients reached for the brass handles first.

"Please, let us do this for Danny," said the center's director. "It's nothing compared to what he did for us."

Nate returned to where Isabelle leaned against a pillar. "I didn't know how cherished my brother was," she said softly. "I guess I didn't know him at all." A single tear ran down her cheek.

"Most people have many sides, Miss Andre. You saw the side reserved for sisters, the one he wanted you to see." Nate squeezed her hand as they walked toward the Lincoln.

As the cortege drove through the streets of Germantown, no one spoke. Nate expected Isabelle's silence, but he couldn't remember his cousin ever being that quiet. Even the charismatic Hunter Galen stared out the window as the drizzle increased to a downpour. Although the Carlton concierge had provided two large umbrellas for the graveside prayers, the residents of New Horizon stood in the rain without complaint. Finally, the funeral director instructed mourners to place a long-stemmed rose on the casket and say their final words.

"I'd like a moment with you before you leave, Mr. Price." Carl Fuentes appeared at his side.

"Sure. Just give me a few minutes." Nate accompanied Isabelle across the uneven ground to deliver her flower. Once she and Nicki were safely inside the Lincoln with Hunter, he sought out the former addict-turned-pastor. "What can I do for you, Mr. Fuentes?"

"I'm sorry I missed you the other day when you stopped by the center. I was in Biloxi a few days for a family matter. Is there something I can help you with?"

"I wanted to know about Danny's role at New Horizons, but that was cleared up at the funeral today. Thanks for coming, by the way. Hearing how instrumental Danny was in the men's lives was a powerful tonic for Miss Andre."

"I didn't bring them. They would have come without my van. Once they heard what happened, they were very upset."

"Even Tito Sullivan?"

"Especially Tito. He was crushed by Danny's death."

"Doesn't look good that he disappeared when the police wanted to question him."

Fuentes stared at the endless rows of graves. "When you've had as many run-ins with the law as Tito, you become reluctant to step forward. And when you made a lifetime habit of lying, everyone assumes you're incapable of the truth. But that doesn't make him a murderer. I assure you, Mr. Price, that Tito loved Danny. He wouldn't kill him over a watch or a sweater or anything else."

Nate's surprise that the director knew the details doubtlessly showed on his face. "So you heard he was caught wearing Danny's clothes?"

"I spoke with his public defender last night after the DA

charged him with second-degree murder. I'll tell you the same thing I told the lawyer. Tito was wearing the sweater and wrist-watch to help him blend in at Blues City. He borrowed Danny's clothes often, and Danny didn't mind. They were roommates."

"The soundman at the blues club didn't corroborate Tito's story."

"No surprise there. If management found out he let people sneak in, he would be fired. Why would he risk his job for some-one from the streets?"

"If you're certain it wasn't Tito, who *would* want to harm a nice guy like Danny?"

Fuentes shrugged. "Don't know, but if I were you, I'd stop looking at former users and start looking where Danny made his living…on Beale Street. From what I've heard, Danny was in demand when clubs needed a stand-in sax player. For musi-cians not in a band, good-paying gigs are hard to find. Every time Danny got picked, some other musician went hungry that night." Carl pulled up his collar with a shiver. "If you have any more ques-tions, Mr. Price, you know where to find me."

Nate watched him shuffle back to the van, hunched over in the rain, and then returned to Hunter's rental car, more confused than ever by the enigma of Danny Andre.

~

Isabelle cringed when she saw Detective Marino approach-ing the car. Nicki and Hunter had stepped out to confer with the funeral director about the luncheon. Poor Nicki was worried the ladies' auxiliary wouldn't provide enough food for hungry men, so Hunter was trying to arrange for some deli trays and buckets of fried chicken. When the homicide cop tapped on her window, Isabelle had no choice but to open the door.

"Come in out of the rain, Detective." She scooted over on the spacious backseat.

Marino shook the rain from his trench coat like a spaniel and ducked into the car. "Don't mind if I do. Man, I don't think the forecasters called for this kind of monsoon." He smiled without parting his lips.

With zero knowledge of the day's weather report, Isabelle changed the subject. "I wanted to thank you for coming to my brother's funeral. And also for arresting the man responsible for Danny's death." She offered him her hand to shake.

Marino squeezed her fingers. "No need to thank me. I felt bad about your seeing your brother on the riverbank that way. And tracking down that lowlife moocher was just doin' my job. Some guys not only don't know how to say 'thank you,' but they bite the hand that feeds them. Throwing Sullivan in jail was my pleasure."

"Just the same, I am grateful for your diligence on Danny's case. Others may have drawn the wrong conclusion about my brother based on where he lived and his choice of friends." Isabelle glanced out the window, hoping Nicki and Hunter would hurry. "Will you stop for a sandwich back at First Methodist? Even a busy detective has to take time to eat."

"Since you asked so nicely, Miss Andre, I'm sure I can spare another hour." Marino glanced at his watch and then let his gaze drift over her dressy suit. "I need to talk to my old buddy Nate, anyway. I'll meet y'all over there. And if you ever need a shoulder to cry on, give me a call." He set his card on the leather upholstery.

Suddenly a knock on the glass jarred their attention. Isabelle lowered the window to see a woman in a full-length black raincoat, her face obscured by its deep hood.

"Miss Andre, I'm sorry to interrupt you, but I wanted to express my sympathy for the loss of your brother." She pushed back the hood to reveal classically pretty features with high cheek-bones and full lips. But the woman's eyes were bloodshot, and her complexion was so pale as to be almost ghostlike.

"Thank you for coming today. Did you know my brother well?" Isabelle reached for the woman's hand.

She clasped Isabelle's fingers briefly. "I considered Danny…one of my closest friends. His death came as a shock to me."

"Would you like to get out of the rain? Join us, and we'll drive you to the luncheon."

"I'm sorry, but I must get home. I just wanted to tell you he was the sweetest man I've ever met." Then, as quickly as she appeared, the woman vanished into the downpour.

"With that I'll take my leave too. See ya at the church." Detective Marino climbed out on the opposite side.

Isabelle released a whoosh of breath when he exited the vehicle. Despite her appreciation for his work, the detective made her skin crawl. Although plenty of people used weddings and funerals as occasions to catch up with friends and relatives, it seemed tacky to say so to the bereaved. She shook away her criticism. Maybe that's why her likelihood of ever marrying again was zero—she over-analyzed and judged every thought, word, and deed from every-one. Except for Craig. During their marriage she had kept her head buried in the sand until he walked out on her.

Isabelle leaned her head back and closed her eyes. Part of her couldn't wait for this day to be over. Yet when it was, her brother would no longer be part of her life. She would shut the door on her family forever. She and Danny had been close when they were young. When she moved to Memphis, he'd been so excited to look for an apartment together. *"Since I sleep late and I'm gone most evenings, we won't get in each other's way. Plus, splitting the bills and chores will lighten the burden on both of us."* Danny's hopeful declarations returned to haunt her.

Yet he had started to annoy her within days. Why couldn't men put something away when they were finished with it? Then housecleaning wouldn't be an all-day affair. And did the TV volume have to be so loud when she was trying to sleep? Even though she nagged endlessly about the toothpaste cap, shoes in the middle of the room, and taking out the trash, Danny had never complained. He stoically put up with her idiosyncrasies until the day she declared the experiment a failure and asked him to move out.

Isabelle's eyes flew open as the car door squeaked.

"Sorry if I startled you." Nate dropped into the spot recently occupied by Detective Marino. "Hunter and Nicki arranged for sandwiches and buckets of Kentucky Fried to be delivered to the church social hall. They'll be here in a minute."

"I'm sure the food would have been sufficient," she murmured, although she wasn't at all certain.

"My guess is Nicki feels sorry for those men."

"I do too, so let's have any leftovers delivered to New Horizons afterward." Isabelle tried to speak normally, but suddenly she couldn't control her tears.

"Consider it done, but I shouldn't be bothering you with inconsequential details."

She shook her head. "I was just thinking about the tributes those men paid my brother. I had no idea how valued Danny was at the center, how revered. They knew him better than I did."

"Danny wasn't one to toot his own horn. That's probably why he never talked about his work there. That and because he didn't want you to worry." Nate turned toward her on the seat. "Mind if I ask what Chip wanted? If it's not my business, just say so," he said, his face earnest.

"I'm not really sure. He said he enjoyed arresting Danny's roommate. And that if I ever need someone to talk to when this was over with, I should call him. Then he gave me his business card…again."

"At the risk of upsetting you, I'm no longer sure Sullivan's our man. He could be, but I'm not as certain as Marino."

"What changed your mind?" Isabelle tamped down her surprise.

"Everybody at New Horizons swears Tito would never hurt Danny. And when I talked to him in county lockup, I pretty much got the same feeling. If it's okay with you, I'll stay on this longer and keep digging."

"Why would you need my permission?"

"This is Memphis Homicide's murder investigation, so Detective Marino has the final word. If he's ready to close the case, then I don't want to make things harder for you." Nate splayed his fingers on his knees.

Instead of Nate's bombshell upsetting her, Isabelle felt the knot between her shoulders begin to dissipate. "I don't want the wrong man to go to jail, Mr. Price, so please continue until you're certain one way or the other."

"Thanks for your vote of confidence. For now, let's not tell Nicki until I check out the director's alibi. Carl Fuentes could be every bit as standup as he appears. And if that's the case, he offered a possible alternative to Tito Sullivan."

"We'll say nothing to Nicki. Let her take comfort from Hunter this weekend." As Isabelle watched Nicki and Hunter approach the car, huddled together under an umbrella, the green-eyed monster reared its ugly head once more.

Nicki ducked into the front seat while Hunter held the umbrella for her, and then he walked around the car to get in behind the wheel. "Weren't you touched by what those men said about Danny?" she asked, pivoting around to face them.

"I was," Isabelle murmured. "My brother's mentoring gave them a real chance to stay clean."

"When Hunter gets back to New Orleans, he's going to instruct the Galen Charitable Foundation to cut New Horizons a check in memory of Danny." She smiled warmly at her fiancé.

"In both of our names, dear heart." Hunter kissed the back of Nicki's fingers before pulling onto the main road from the cemetery.

"That's very kind of you both," Isabelle said. "Thank you."

With Nicki's attention no longer on the backseat, Isabelle glanced at Nate. Worry lines across his forehead had deepened since their first meeting. Her brother's death had affected him even though they hadn't known each other well in high school. Nate Price was a good man...a decent man. Maybe it would be nice having a friend for a change. Like Nicki had in Danny. And Danny had with her.

Maybe Isabelle wasn't destined to find one great love. Considering her romantic past history, one good friend sounded infinitely more appealing.

FOURTEEN

*T*he next morning Nicki awoke to the sound of impatient knocking on her door. Glancing at the clock, she scowled. Only one person would have the salt to bother her at this hour. And that would be the man she planned to spend her life with. Slipping on her robe and knotting the belt, Nicki swept open the door. "What do you want, Galen?"

Fully dressed, Hunter stepped around her into the suite. "I merely seek asylum from your cousin's snoring. He would keep Rip Van Winkle awake."

Nicki's sigh was deep and full of resignation. "I'll call down for a pot of coffee. Let's sit at the table and talk." Nicki pointed at a bistro chair as she dialed room service.

"Coffee with a Mississippi belle with a view of the Mississippi River. What could be finer?"

After making the call and then hanging up the phone, Nicki sat in the other chair. "That was a lovely dinner last night. Thank you."

"You and Isabelle barely ate a bite at the funeral luncheon. Were you saving your portions for the men at New Horizons?" He patted her hand affectionately.

"I suppose, subconsciously. Nate mentioned mealtime is a challenge since only Carl knows how to cook."

"They will be okay, my love. Those men are survivors."

"Maybe not all of them. Danny sure wasn't one." Nicki stared out the bay window, trying to forget how he looked that horrible morning.

Hunter tactfully changed the subject. "I've picked out a church if we can both be ready in an hour. Calvary Episcopal. According to the website, it's Memphis's oldest public building in continuous use and one of the city's most beautiful churches."

"Because you attended St. Louis Cathedral since your First Communion, you should feel right at home in a fancy church. You sure you're okay with our wedding at Grace Baptist? It's very small and plain."

"I would marry you in a broom closet. The bride picks the church, remember?"

"What about your mother's guest list? What if they all show up in Red Haw for the ceremony?"

"We'll rent a circus tent with loud speakers. Then we can throw a luncheon for all the locals who refuse to drive to New Orleans for the reception."

"You are the world's smartest person," she teased before taking a bite of an apple.

"I believe love has clouded your judgment. What would you like to do this afternoon—sightseeing? The art museum? How about the zoo?"

"There is a place in the country I'd like to visit if you don't mind. Do you remember when you recommended the tour of the hotel? On it I learned something curious about the Carlton's illustrious past. Then last night when I couldn't sleep after the funeral, I searched the Internet and discovered a clue."

"Hold that thought," said Hunter. He jumped up to retrieve their coffee at the door.

While he poured, Nicki talked about meeting Henry, finding the photo with Robert, and her subsequent visit to Oakbrook.

Hunter took a long swallow and smacked his lips. "Now I'm ready for anything. Tell me more about these scavenger hunts. Are you thinking about organizing one for our friends some day? The French Quarter has several historic hotels that would be perfect. One or two are even reputed to be haunted."

"Maybe, but with less extravagant prizes. More on the order of restaurant gift cards. In the meantime, I want to learn everything I can about the Carlton jewels."

Hunter set down his cup. "But Nate said Danny's killer has been arrested. Aren't you coming home with me? The Quarter isn't the same without you." He winked as he refilled their cups.

"I miss you too, but I would like to stay a little longer. I have a gut feeling Nate isn't convinced Tito Sullivan did it. And the detective in charge of Danny's case didn't strike me as the most thorough of investigators."

"Surely the DA wouldn't indict without sufficient evidence."

"I know, but if you can afford it, I would like to be here in case Nate needs background help."

"My desire for you to come home has nothing to do with my bank account." Hunter leaned across the table for a kiss.

"Give us a few more days. Danny deserves no stone unturned. And I also want to look more into the scavenger hunts."

Stretching, Hunter rose to his feet. "It's settled then, but right now you should jump in the shower. The clock is ticking. I'll wait for you downstairs."

～

After church, Nicki and Hunter ate waffles with strawberries and whipped cream at a restaurant instead of brunch at the hotel. Decent PIs worth their paycheck couldn't intuit on an overly full belly. Halfway through his second waffle, Hunter asked, "I believe it's time to tell me about the clue you discovered last night when you couldn't sleep."

Nicki set down her fork and dabbed her lips with the napkin. "Henry the bellman told me the winners of the 1955 Carlton jewels were a Mr. and Mrs. Whitley. He didn't mention their given names, but he distinctly recalled the prizes—a diamond-studded cigarette case for the husband, and a diamond tiara for the Mrs. Did women really wear such affectations back then?"

"What is amazing is so many people smoked that a cigarette case was a common accessory."

"Good point. At any rate, I looked online for Memphis businesses during the era, those owned by a sole proprietor or a family. There weren't that many prominent Whitleys, but one stood out with potential. Marcus Whitley owned several car dealerships. He and his wife, Diana, lived on an estate north of Memphis. And get this, Mr. Galen. The house still stands. According to county records, Tabitha and Jon Grant now own the property. Tabitha *Whitley* Grant." Nicki grinned so broadly her face started to hurt.

"Well done, Agatha! Did you call them and set up an interview?"

"No, it was too late last night. Then I didn't wish to interrupt their Sunday morning. So I thought we could crash the gate or scale the walls and then sneak through the bushes."

Hunter laid money down on the check. "Great plan! Since my lawyer works on retainer, count me in."

One hour later, the Lincoln's GPS navigated them up a long, tree-lined driveway well off the beaten path. The home of Tabitha and Jon Grant had neither a twelve-foot wall to scale nor a gate to crash. There was only a discreet sign in the bushes identifying their security system. Hunter parked under an ancient live oak, but before they could climb the stone steps to the columned front entrance, Nicki spotted someone in the garden pruning rose-bushes. The middle-aged woman did not look like a gardener.

"This might be easier than I thought," she murmured.

"Should we put on the fake mustaches I bought?" he whispered.

On their way up the driveway, Nicki delivered a sharp elbow to his gut. "Mrs. Grant?" she called. "May we have word with you, please?"

The woman peered up at them from under her hat brim. "If you're collecting for a charity, leave the literature on the steps for me to look at later." She resumed deadheading the flowers.

"No, ma'am. That's not why we're here. I'm Nicolette Price, and this is my fiancé, Hunter Galen. We're from New Orleans. Could we have just a minute of your time?"

Mrs. Grant tossed a handful of spent blooms into her basket. "Oh, no. Not another pushy bride-to-be! This is a private resi-dence, and we never rent it out for weddings, young lady."

"No, ma'am. Our wedding will be in my hometown outside of Natchez." While Hunter hid his laughter behind a cough, Nicki produced the expression that usually got her an extra cookie from Mamaw.

Mrs. Grant studied her curiously, and then she peeled off her gardening gloves. "All right. Suppose you tell me what this is about."

"I'm a private investigator who came to Memphis on a personal matter. While I've been staying at the Carlton Hotel, I found out about the scavenger hunts that took place in the 1950s." Nicki took a few steps forward.

"That has to be the last thing I expected. How old do you think I am? I wasn't even born until 1960." Her chuckle was a good sign as she closed the distance between them.

"Of course, but I believe your grandparents were the Whitleys who participated years ago. Did your grandmother ever mention this?"

"Wait a minute. Are you writing a story? My husband and I don't like publicity. It will only bring more donation seekers, salespeople, and brides-to-be." Her friendliness slipped a notch.

"Absolutely not. I'm merely looking into the mystery to help an elderly gentleman who was there but whose memory is faulty."

She shrugged. "Yes, you have the correct Whitleys, but there's no mystery, Miss Price. It was just some fun between friends. The scavenger hunt lasted five years, until the deaths of the Smithfields. My understanding is that after that the remaining couples lost interest in the game." Mrs. Grant lifted her basket to her hip. "Both my grandparents are dead, as I suspect most of the participants are."

Nicki pulled the framed photograph from her tote. "Have you seen this?"

Mrs. Grant gazed down at the image. "Not for a long while. Goodness, Granny was beautiful. That's my grandfather next to her, and that's Paul and Agnes Smithfield. The tiara and cigarette case were sold long ago to help settle estate taxes after their deaths. I don't know what else I can tell you."

"As winners of the '55 game, they would have planned the '56 hunt. Do you remember what your grandmother bought for the prizes?" Nicki took the framed photo back.

Mrs. Grant's eyes grew round. "I do, come to think of it. Emeralds. According to my mother, Granny got in trouble for going overboard when she bought the jewelry. It was an emerald bracelet and cuff links that set my grandfather back quite a bit. But I'm afraid that's all I can tell you. I don't know who won those emeralds, but they must have been gorgeous. Grandfather curtailed Granny's spending for months after that."

"Thank you, Mrs. Grant. You've been very helpful." Nicki followed her down the garden path toward their car. "We'll be off now."

"Best wishes to you, Miss Price, Mr. Galen. Thank *you* for not asking to turn my front yard into the set for *Gone with the Wind*."

～

Nate glanced at his watch for the third time as Nicki walked into the coffee shop Monday morning. "It's not like you to be late for breakfast. Still have provisions left in your larger-than-mine fruit basket?"

Nicki sat on the opposite side of the booth. "Nope, it's finally empty. But I had to drop off Hunter at the airport first. No way would I let him take a taxi when I have a Lincoln at my disposal." She grinned as she picked up a menu to scan.

"Hunter left town? Then why are you still here, Nic? I told you after the funeral you could go back with him."

"Key word *could*, but I don't want to. Something is fishy with Danny's case, Nate, and I want to know what it is." Nicki leaned back as the waitress filled her coffee cup. "I'm not leaving until we can leave together."

"Eggs, over easy, rye toast, hash browns, sausage links. Thank you," he said to the waitress. To his cousin he released a sigh. "You should sit on Jackson Square with a crystal ball, the way you read minds."

"Mamaw would take a broom to me," she said after telling the server she would have the same. "How did you spend your Sunday? We called you last night to join us for dinner, but you didn't pick up."

"I found a church with an 11:00 service and then drove out to Starkville, home of my alma mater. Walked every block of the campus and then stopped in Oxford to see how our old rival has changed, Ole Miss."

"Sounds lovely. Now tell me what you found out."

"While you were having dinner with Hunter, I did my own Internet search and made a few phone calls. Carl Fuentes was telling the truth about being in Biloxi the day Danny was killed."

"So what? We never figured Tito had an accomplice."

"True, but because Carl was telling the truth about that, I started to wonder what else he might be right about. I did some checking into private parties at Blues City. I had to charm the socks off their event planner, but sure enough, there was a bachelor party the night Danny died. The caterer delivered wings, ribs, hoagies, and fried okra to the reserved balcony. The planner remembered because it was the first time okra was ever requested for a bachelor party."

Nicki rolled her eyes. "The culinary tastes of unmarried men are utterly fascinating, but what does this have to do with anything?"

"Only that Tito Sullivan may have been telling the truth. He told me he sneaked into the party, gobbled down a plate of food, and then filled a second plate to take back to the sound room for Danny in case he showed up later. How would Tito know they served fried okra if he wasn't there?"

"So the sound engineer lied."

"That's my theory, but proving it will be hard. I'm not going to Marino until I have hard evidence. He already thinks this case is closed."

"Not the most diligent of public servants. How do you want us to proceed?"

"In the direction Carl Fuentes pointed me. I've been focusing on former drug addicts and the underbelly they inhabit, but I'm no longer convinced that's our best lead. How much do you know about Danny's work? Everybody has bills to pay, even in low-rent buildings like his."

"He played the saxophone in a band. Playing music professionally had been his dream since we were kids. He knew the songs of the old masters—that's what he called B.B. and Muddy, John Lee Hooker and Robert Johnson. He said they were like Rembrandt and da Vinci in the art world."

"Except that Danny wasn't in a band with a regular gig in Memphis. He was picking up work as a stand-in on Beale Street. Apparently, it's harder to get steady work there than for a starving artist to find a rich patron. If a sax player was sick, or in jail, or any one of countless reasons they can't show up, the band leader would hire someone for the night. Fuentes seemed to think Danny's expertise was in demand."

"I'm not surprised. I've heard him play. He was great, but why would that get him killed?"

"Pageant contestants sabotage the competition's face cream. Olympic skaters bash kneecaps with metal pipes. Why wouldn't musicians be prone to fits of jealous rage?"

"That is a stretch, boss."

"I know, but it bears looking into. We've both chased down thinner leads than this."

"Okay. Let's head to Beale Street as soon as we're finished here. I am raring to go."

Nate smiled at her. Even after graduating from a school for criminal investigation and clearing Hunter of a murder charge, Nicki was still a babe in the woods. "Think about it, Nicki. It's not even ten. Musicians working the club scene are fast asleep. The blues world is definitely after-hours. You, on the other hand, are in bed by ten with a novel."

Her hackles rose like fur on a startled cat. "I once pulled an all-nighter playing Crazy Eights in my treehouse. I can stay up when the occasion demands. Why are you so critical of me?"

"I think you're an incredible investigator or I wouldn't have made you my partner, but Beale Street isn't much different than the neighborhood that Danny lived in. Plenty of dangerous characters mingle with upstanding aficionados of blues music. Hunter wants you to come home safe and sound." Nate realized the error of his ways the moment the words left his mouth.

Nicki set her coffee cup with a clatter. "I should have known he put you up to this. I will skin him alive when I get back to New Orleans."

Nate clucked his tongue. "Such violent talk from a Sunday school teacher. All right, Hunter *may* have asked about my plans, but he didn't put me up to this. I'm your boss, and I call the shots."

Nicki huffed like a dragon. "Perhaps I can investigate ladies suspected of passing coupons after their expiration date."

He tried not to laugh. "I still need your help, but just not prowling the clubs on Beale. Besides, Hunter mentioned you're making progress on the Henry Prescott mystery."

"You're the one I'm going to skin. I intend to needle Hunter to death with endless *girlie* requests. *'Oh, darling. Can you loosen this pickle jar lid? I've just had my nails done.'*"

"Don't be mad, Nicki. Part of the reason I don't need you is that this might be a dead end. I have my male ego to protect."

She stood, her bearing regal. "I find I'm not hungry after all. Text me with any background checks or research requests. In the meantime, I shall retire to my suite to plan my trousseau." Miffed, she stomped off.

Nate remained in the booth even after his breakfast was finished. There was no fooling his partner. Hunter had asked him to keep Nicki out of harm's way. After-hours clubs were no more savory than drug rehab centers. He wasn't sure how this partnership would work out once they returned to the Big Easy. But for now, Nate knew Hunter loved Nicki more than anything in this world. And she loved him. Sometimes a career wasn't all that important. Not when you considered the sum total of a person's life. Danny's career might have been what got him killed.

FIFTEEN

By the time Nicki left the coffee shop and reached the grand lobby, she was no longer peeved with Nate. Or with Hunter. Or with anybody else. Hunter loved her, and his only motivation was to protect her. And this was still Nate's case. If there was any chance Tito hadn't killed Danny, she wanted Nate to find out who did. Her unfortunate tangle with Memphis Homicide and the medical examiner wasn't that long ago, and those involved hadn't forgotten her. Because she would be more of a hindrance than a help, she needed to stay behind the scenes.

She couldn't stop thinking about Izzy. Danny's sister was another reason Nicki didn't want to go back to New Orleans yet. Had Izzy's composure during the funeral been an act? Until Nicki felt confident Izzy would be okay without her brother, she wasn't going anywhere. Especially since someone kept reminding Izzy just how alone she was.

Nicki glanced at her watch. If Nate didn't need her at the moment and Izzy was working, she had time to track down scavenger hunt participants. Tabitha Grant had confirmed her grandparents won the diamonds and purchased emeralds the following year—jewelry that got Mrs. Whitley in hot water with her husband. Funny how poor people thought about money all the time, but the rich usually didn't worry about such matters. Those baubles must have been extraordinary. But she couldn't very well search for buyers of emeralds sixty years ago. No Internet back then.

On the elevator ride up to her room, an idea popped into her head. Nicki pushed the button for the ground floor and headed to her rental car as fast as her legs could carry her. It took less than a minute to Google the address of a Memphis newspaper, the *Commercial Appeal*, and less than fifteen minutes to drive to their corporate headquarters on Union Street. But it took quite a bit longer of pleading and cajoling to gain access to the newspaper's archives. A helpful tech stayed by her side the entire time to make sure no journalistic espionage happened on his watch. But with patience and plenty of smiles, Nicki was allowed to skim the society pages of November and December 1956 on an old-fashioned monitor in the basement.

Goodness, it was hard to imagine that trivial details, such as the names of bandleaders and menu selections for a Christmas cotillion, were newsworthy. But the world was different back then—a genteel, fairy-tale world, at least for rich, white society. After an inordinate number of soirees, fund-raisers, and engagement announcements, Nicki found what she was looking for—a grainy black-and-white photograph. Two couples wearing broad smiles and formal evening attire posed in front of the fireplace in the Carlton Hotel. Nicki practically levitated off the metal chair when she read the caption:

> *Mr. and Mrs. Marcus Whitley (left) presenting this year's lucky recipients, Mr. and Mrs. Blake Koehler, with their prizes. The Koehlers are the latest winners of a secret scavenger hunt among Memphis's inner circle. Details regarding the next scavenger hunt are guarded better than*

*the gold in Fort Knox. From the expression on Bunny
Koehler's face, Santa arrived at the Carlton Hotel a few
weeks early this year.*

At the moment Nicki wasn't concerned with the gold in Fort
Knox, but with the wealth encircling Mrs. Koehler's delicate
wrist. She knew from Tabitha Grant that the jewels were emeralds. From the way Blake Koehler held up both wrists, she sur-
mised his prize were cuff links. Even in a grainy, black-and-white
photo, the size of the stones was impressive.

Nicki leaned back in the chair and closed her eyes, transport-
ing herself decades into the past. She smelled the crackling fire in
the hearth, heard instruments tuning up for dancing in the ballroom, and tasted vintage champagne bubbles on her tongue—
even though champagne wasn't something she drank, vintage or
not. And there was Henry Prescott as a young man, smiling as he
greeted new arrivals or bid departing guests a fond farewell.

She liked Hunter's idea. After she was back in New Orleans
and the wedding of the century (according to Hunter's sister) was
behind her, she would plan an annual getaway for her friends.
Except right now her friends were scattered all over the country, and most weren't part of a couple. Times change. Who says
friends had to be married to participate? But first she needed to
deal with the task at hand.

Nicki swiveled around to the young man. "Could you print
me a few copies of this?" she asked.

Leaning against a metal filing cabinet with his arms crossed, he
couldn't look more bored. "Sure, for a buck each."

When the kid made no move, Nicki realized he was waiting
to see her money. "Here's a five." She pulled a bill from her wallet. "Please print three copies of this page and keep the change."

"Gee, thanks," he said, pushing off from the cabinet. After he made a few taps on the keyboard, the printer on the far wall rumbled to life.

While he retrieved her copies, Nicki studied the monitor again. The emerald bracelet and cuff links won by the Koehlers in 1956 provided another piece of the puzzle. She had no idea where this would lead, but she knew what she would do with the copies. Besides keeping one for her investigation, she thought Tabitha Grant might be curious about the recipients of her grandmother's largess. And Nicki was certain Henry Prescott would love a picture of the Whitleys and Koehlers. As people aged, the years fell away. Often the distinction between long ago and the present began to blur. The photo would bring back fond memories for Henry of an exciting period in his life.

Nicki thanked the tech, tucked the copies in her purse, and left the newspaper's headquarters. She called Hunter as soon as she climbed into her Lincoln.

"Hey, how was your trip back? How are you? Where are you? Have you unpacked yet?" She hurled questions at him in rapid succession.

Her fiancé responded in the manner she'd come to love. He laughed. "Slow down, *O'lette*. My trip was uneventful. I am fine. I came straight to the courthouse, so I'll unpack tonight. I have only a minute, so tell me what you discovered. I can tell by your voice it's something good."

"I found a newspaper clipping of Tabitha Grant's grandparents. They are awarding the Carlton jewels to Blake and Bunny Koehler. No joke—the wife's name was Bunny. Who would name a kid that? Because both husband and wife are holding up their wrists, the prize appears to be a bracelet and cuff links."

"The super sleuth has worked her magic again. Are those the emeralds which landed Mrs. Whitley in hot water?"

"One and the same. I wonder where Bunny found them. Maybe hidden under the carrots in the cornucopia centerpiece?"

"What an imagination you have. Now you know which couple planned the 1957 hunt. Good luck tracking down Bugs and Bunny. Call me tonight after you climb from the rabbit hole. I love you, *O'lette*. Be safe."

"The feeling is mutual, sweet man." She spoke even though the line had gone dead. Hunter had said those three words dozens of times, yet they never failed to kindle a flame inside her. A flame that kept her warm no matter how damp or dreary the day.

On her way back to the Carlton, Nicki punched in Izzy's number. "Hey there, girlfriend, it's Nicki. My ball-and-chain has returned to New Orleans. How about joining me for supper? I'm thinking greasy pizza with double cheese."

Izzy laughed. "Sounds delightful, but I have two houses to show tonight. Between now and then I'm tied up at the office. Can I have a rain check?"

"Of course. Call me whenever you're free." Nicki hesitated and then added, "I want to spend time with you." She wasn't sure how her true confession would be received. The two of them weren't very close in the past.

But Izzy quickly responded. "I would like that too, Nicki. I'll be in touch."

Nicki slipped her phone into her pocket. She had rest of the day before Nate got back with an update. And nothing better to do than find out what she could on Tony Markham. The guy had probably already moved on in life and forgotten about Isabelle. Maybe he regretted his childish bullying outside the restaurant. But she owed it to Danny's memory to make sure Isabelle was safe from potential stalkers, disgruntled clients, or balcony defacers.

～

Isabelle was filled with regret the moment she got off the phone with Nicki. Her boss, her pastor, and the neighbor who occasionally fed her cat told her that being with people would be therapeutic after Danny's funeral.

"Don't allow much downtime to wallow in grief."

"Don't spend too much time alone thinking about Danny."

"Stay busy; stay distracted; and when you come up for air, the pain will have lessened."

Who came up with these helpful tips? Not everyone dealt with loss the same way.

Unfortunately, neither couple scheduled to view homes tonight were willing to reschedule. Otherwise she would have loved grabbing a pizza with Nicki. In the brief time they spent together, Isabelle saw what her brother had loved about his friend. Nicki was forthright— almost to a fault. She said exactly what was on her mind without a duplicitous bone in her body. What you saw was what you got with Nicolette Price. After a long tedious day trying to make buyers and sellers happy, Isabelle yearned for a few hours of honesty.

Having a friend, a real friend, would be wonderful. Perhaps she would lose her own pretentiousness. A man like Craig wouldn't have been attracted to her unless they shared some of the same qualities. That realization had struck like a lightning bolt as she left Danny's graveside. Nice people didn't worry much about the impression they were making. They were more concerned with others than themselves. While she and Nate waited in Nicki's backseat, Isabelle realized he was a nice guy. She doubted he would use that term to describe her, but perhaps it wasn't too late to change.

Hours later, Isabelle waved goodbye to the last couple and climbed into her Prius, exhausted but relieved. Although the first family hated the small bathrooms, the treeless backyard, and just about everything else about the house, the second couple expecting their first child had loved it. Perhaps they were tired of throwing money away on rent or the limited space in their apartment, but they offered an amount close to the asking price. The current owners accepted their bid without further negotiation and within an hour a formal contract had been drawn up, signed, and notarized. The young couple was on their way to becoming homeowners, and Isabelle would be able to make her own rent payment this month.

Glancing at her watch, she decided she was too tired to cook pasta or even chop vegetables for a salad. After seven hours in the office and then four hours in the field, she was famished. Jack's Deli, right on her way home, made the best Greek salads in the world. Or at least in Germantown.

Isabelle parked on the street, placed her order at the counter, and breathed in the fragrance of garlic bread sticks. Soon she was carrying out a romaine feast, complete with fava beans, blue cheese-stuffed olives, a marinated chicken breast, and homemade croutons. Jack was famous for personalizing each salad to his customers' specifications rather than adhere to a standardized recipe.

"Hey, there, Isabelle. Got your regular takeout order?" A man's voice drifted soft and melodic from the shadows. A moment later, Tony Markham stepped into a yellow pool of streetlamp light. "I thought Wednesday was your Greek salad night. Tonight is only Monday." Markham acted as though he'd made some kind of joke.

Isabelle tightened her grip on both the paper bag and her car keys. "What are you doing here?" Unfortunately, her voice cracked on the final word of her question.

"Do you mean in Germantown? I love this place. I told you when we were together that I'm watching every new listing for something in my price range." He smiled with the assurance of a confident man.

"No, I mean *here*." Isabelle hooked her thumb over her shoulder. At least the deli's facade and front window were well lit. A few customers still lingered at the round café tables.

"You mean at Jack's?" Tony sounded confused by the question. "I love this deli." He lifted a brown paper sack to match hers. "Turns out the Greek salad is my favorite too. Like you, I always get the full size. After all, how many calories are in lettuce, a chicken breast, and those *divine* stuffed olives?"

"How do you know what I usually order?" she demanded, imagining a tiny transmitter hidden under her jacket lapel. "Have you been following me?"

"Relax. Just because you and I broke up doesn't mean I can't patronize my favorite take-out place. Besides it's easy enough to figure out Jack's specialties, especially among the ladies."

Isabelle didn't know what upset her more—his knowing her culinary preferences or that she was such a creature of habit. "You and I didn't 'break up,' Tony. We had one date and things didn't exactly click for us." She rotated the ring of keys inside her palm so the longest key could be ready as a weapon. If she had the stomach to use it.

He shrugged. "If it makes you feel better, use whatever terminology you prefer." He stepped closer so he could stare down at her. "Look, it's a lovely night for a walk. What do you say we take our salads to Municipal Park to eat?"

Her mouth dropped open. "Don't you remember telling me I had ice water in my veins instead of blood like a real woman? After you called me foul names? I don't want to walk to the park or anywhere else with you."

"Can't you cut me some slack?" His voice rose in volume. "I was in a bad place then, but I've started going to church. I know that's important to you. Don't you believe people can change?"

Suddenly the deli's front door opened and a pack of noisy

young women spilled onto the sidewalk. Bolstered by their prox-
imity, Isabelle lifted her chin and looked him in the eye. "I'm
happy for you, but I'm not interested in chatting in the park or
sharing a meal. I'm tired and I'm going home."

She tried to walk around him, but he blocked her path,
undaunted by the group of women. "I'm trying to be nice here,
Belle, considering everything that's happened."

Her heart hammered against her ribcage. "What are you talking about?"

"Your brother's death, of course." Tony feigned an expression
of concern. "And I must say, your boss at Realty World is pretty
heartless to make you wear that gaudy-colored blazer. Women
should be allowed a period of mourning, don't you think?"

Isabelle almost snapped a retort about her clothes being none
of his business until a more insidious thought came to mind.
"How do you know about my brother?"

Tony stretched his neck from side to side. "I must have seen
the death notice in the paper."

"Few people check the obits, and it only appeared one day in
the Memphis newspaper, not Germantown's."

"My mother started me in the habit. If you don't watch the
death notices, you'll never know when an old friend might need
you. But you didn't need much comforting, did you, Belle?"
Markham's muttered words held ill-concealed hostility.

But Isabelle heard him loud and clear. "You were at Danny's
funeral? You didn't even know my brother."

"But I know you, and I had such high hopes for us." His lower
lip protruded like a child having a tantrum.

"Then you're living in a dream world. Stay away from me, Tony.
Don't be concerned with the food I eat, or what I wear, or the
places I go. I'm warning you."

"Or what?" he growled. "You'll sic your new boyfriend on me?

I thought you were a decent person. Your poor brother is barely cold in the grave, and you're already hanging all over some rent-a-cop from Louisiana. Your parents would be ashamed. It's a good thing they're not here to see the spectacle you made of yourself at the funeral."

Isabelle stumbled back into a bike rack. Markham's hand shot out to steady her, but she slapped it away as if it were a hornet ready to sting. "Leave me alone! If I see you near my condo or my office, I'm calling the cops."

"Oh, really? It's not a crime to look at condos in your development, and Realty World is the largest agency in Germantown. I would love to live in the Glades. Besides, the police aren't usually quick to believe floozies with bad reputations."

She wavered on her high heels. Then she sucked in a steadying breath and marched toward her car. Along the way she tossed her supper into a trash can. Her appetite had vanished the moment he'd mentioned his duplicate order. Engaging him in conversation had been a mistake. Discussions were only effective between reasonable and sane people. Tony was neither. Issuing threats had merely provoked him like a bully on the playground.

What had she done to attract the attention of a madman? Trembling uncontrollably inside her vehicle, Isabelle watched him saunter to his SUV with his head held high. Tony cast a final glare in her direction, started the engine, and peeled down the street.

Isabelle hated confrontations. Maybe that's why she'd allowed Craig to manipulate her for so long. Briefly, she considered stopping by the Germantown Police Department, but much of what Markham said was true. It wasn't against the law to frequent her favorite deli, or look for apartments in her neighborhood, or even attend a graveside service. His assertion that he hoped they would get back together was too close to the truth not to be believed.

Remembering something Nicki had said, Isabelle jotted down the date, time, and description of Markham's car in case she needed it. Then she punched in Nicki's number, but disconnected before the other end rang. It was late. Nicki might already be in bed.

She'd much rather call Nate, yet she couldn't bring herself to take on the role of helpless female—a woman who remained aloof except when the situation warranted. She needed Nate. Not because he carried a licensed, registered weapon. Not because he had a working knowledge of the law, along with connections at the police department. And not because he was a big man who could put Tony Markham in his place. She needed a friend. A real friend, like Nicki had had in Danny. Something she had never had in her life.

Once she was safely inside her condo, Isabelle closed the blinds, checked the doors and windows, placed a metal rod inside the patio door runner, and punched in Nate's number. Just before the call went to voice mail she heard a deep, husky voice.

"Hello? That you, Miss Andre? What's wrong?"

"Nothing, Mr. Price. I-I hope I'm not calling too late, but I wanted to ask you something."

"Of course. What is it?" In the background she heard the unmistakable pop of an aluminum can.

"Would you be my guest for dinner? I have questions and a few things I'm concerned about. How about tomorrow?"

"How about tonight? I'm starving and could be there in less than thirty minutes."

"Do you mean right now?" she asked after a short hesitation.

"Sorry. You've probably already eaten. Why don't we make it tomorrow after—"

"No, I haven't eaten. Should I meet you, or would you mind picking me up?"

"I don't mind at all. I'll be there as soon as I can."

After he hung up, Isabelle stared at the moonlight dancing on the wall from clerestory windows. Then she tucked the phone in her purse and pulled a chair next to the door. *Why not eat with Nate tonight?* After her confrontation with Markham, she wouldn't get much sleep anyway.

Thinking of a restaurant that stayed open twenty-four hours was easy. Figuring out how to dissolve her awkwardness with Nate Price would take every available moment she had until he arrived.

SIXTEEN

*N*ate wasn't sure what got into him, but he had approximately twenty-five minutes to figure it out. Then he would have to face Isabelle, the chief character of his adolescent fantasies and the snooty sister of their dead client. Except maybe she wasn't as arrogant as he'd originally assumed. Maybe a chilly exterior covered a lack of self-esteem and confidence. Isn't that what the pseudo-psychology books claimed? Maybe Isabelle was just as clueless about how to make a good impression as he was.

Maybe. Or maybe not.

She'd surprised him when she'd agreed to have dinner tonight. Most women didn't want a man to know their calendar was free and clear, but he didn't have a limitless amount of time in town. Anything she wanted to discuss, whether related to Danny's case or on a personal level, needed to happen quickly. Because as soon as he felt sure Marino had the right killer behind bars, he planned to put Memphis, birthplace of the blues and rock and roll, in his rearview mirror.

Nate never could understand the cat-and-mouse shenanigans in dating. Or in anything else in life for that matter. He just learned a few years ago that a man wasn't supposed to divulge his income, even if directly asked. And when a woman asked, "How do you like my haircut or new dress," honesty was seldom the best policy. He also had trouble with the advice "never act like you care for someone until certain of her feelings." It all seemed like a colossal waste of time.

Maybe that's why he was pushing thirty and still single.

But Isabelle hadn't called him to have dinner because she regretted snubbing him in high school. He'd heard fear in her voice. Something had happened, and Nate suspected it had something to do with Markham.

Isabelle's condo was on the second floor of the last building in her complex. Beyond the parking lot was a pond and then dense woods. Her shady street was the most private and the least secure in the development. Nate parked at the curb, flicked on his emergency flashers, and jogged up the walkway. But before he had a chance to ring the bell, Isabelle hurried out the door.

"Looks like you're as hungry as I am," he said, pivoting on his heel.

She smiled thinly. "A little, but I'm more eager to leave before someone spots us."

Her response caught him by surprise. "Is there a secret husband I should know about? You invited me out, remember?"

Isabelle looked up and down the street before climbing into his car. "Of course I remember, and no, there's no secret husband." She hit the lock button before fastening her seat belt. "I found out tonight that Tony Markham has been following me."

"Tell me what happened." Nate turned the key in the ignition.

"I will, but let's get out of here first." She slouched down in the seat. "When you reach the main highway, turn left and head toward the mall. It will be around four miles on your left."

Nate complied, while Isabelle sat silent and motionless until away from her complex. Once they were surrounded by traffic, she explained running into Markham outside of Jack's Deli.

"It was no accident, Nate. Tony knew what I usually order. He said it's easy to guess what women like best, but that's ridiculous. The deli has a dozen options for salad on the menu, and no two female agents in my office ever order the same one."

"He's stalking you, Miss Andre, and that's against the law."

"Isabelle, please. I hope you're not holding my initial rudeness against me."

"I hold nothing against you. After finding your brother on the riverbank, you were in shock." Once again, he'd said exactly what was on his mind, a trait he must have picked up from Nicki.

"It's still no excuse for bad behavior, so I appreciate your understanding."

Nate squared and relaxed his shoulders. A knot of tension had formed where his neck met his spine. "Go on with your story, Isabelle."

"I think Tony has been following me because I don't go to Jack's any particular day of the week. He'd ordered the exact same food and then suggested we go to the park to eat."

Nate lifted an eyebrow. "And you said no?"

"Yes, and he didn't like it very much. He also said he's looking for a condo in my neighborhood. And there's not a single thing I can do about where he chooses to live." Isabelle gripped the arm rest tightly.

"True, but we can make sure he doesn't come within twenty feet of you."

She peered out the window as though in a daze. "Oh, my. We're at the mall already."

Nate turned into the landscaped entrance. "Which restaurant did you decide upon?"

"Let's eat at the Apple House. People go there at all hours."

"Don't worry about Tony coming near you tonight. Not with me around." Impulsively, Nate patted her forearm.

Isabelle's eyes shimmered with tears. "You don't know what he's like. He's crazy, Nate. He talked about 'when we were together' and that 'he's hoping to get back with me.' He and I were *never* together. He's imagining a relationship that didn't take place."

"That's common among sociopaths." Nate parked the car and turned to look at her. Common among sociopaths? Who had he become in the last fifteen minutes—Sigmund Freud?

"His delusions make me very uncomfortable." She exhaled her breath in a whoosh. "Tony said he'd changed and that he'd started going to church because it's important to me. How does he know I attend church regularly?" The sophisticated real estate agent suddenly sounded like a little girl.

"Because he's been following you, just like you suspected, but that doesn't mean we're helpless to stop him. Let's go have dinner before they start passing out breakfast menus. We'll talk more inside."

Nate hopped out and walked around to her side of the car, feeling nothing but pure rage. He wanted to track down Markham and rearrange his face. Not very professional and not very Christian. He'd better control his emotions for his sake and hers. So instead he offered Isabelle his arm, and they walked in like characters from a Jane Austen novel.

Inside the well-lit restaurant, surrounded by people of all ages, Isabelle seemed to relax. She ordered chicken fried steak with mashed potatoes and iced tea. Comfort food. Nate glanced at the menu and decided on his usual cheeseburger, fries, and a Coke. After the waitress left with their order, Isabelle resumed her painful narrative.

"He called me 'Belle' more than once, even though he knows I don't like pet names and no one has ever called me that."

Nate resisted the impulse to revisit calling her 'Izzy' as he had done on the riverbank. "That's simply another way he tries to feel connected to you. Don't dwell on his antics. We must take steps to rid you of him before his behavior escalates."

Isabelle leaned back as the waitress delivered their beverages, her expression unchanged. "Tony knew that Danny was dead. He came to my brother's funeral, but I never saw him. He said he read about it in the obits, but I don't believe that. The death notice didn't appear until that morning, more of a formality than anything. Everyone who needed to know already did." She tried to sip her drink, but the glass slipped through her trembling fingers.

Nate moved the glass away and wiped up the spill. "That psychopath watched you during the funeral? Tomorrow we'll go to the Germantown police station, and you'll tell them everything you told me. It should be enough for a restraining order."

A flicker of relief crossed her delicate features. "Thanks, Nate, for helping me through this, but you need to hear the rest."

Unfortunately, the waitress chose that moment to deliver their meals. *How could the food be ready so fast? Did they have burgers and chicken fried steak waiting under heat lamps?*

Nate pushed his plate to the side. "I have all night. Tell me everything."

"Tony knows about you too. Or at least in his sick mind who he thinks you are in my life." Isabelle didn't meet his eyes. "He said he saw me...hanging...all over you at the funeral. He called you my boyfriend. And he said that my behavior would have made my parents ashamed. It sounded as though he knew my parents are gone and that I'm alone in the world."

"First of all, this is just more manipulation. You can't let him get under your skin. Secondly, you're not alone. You have Nicki and me. And we're not leaving Memphis until you're safe from this man." Nate popped a French fry into his mouth.

She pulled her plate of food closer, the aroma of grilled

mushrooms and onions whetting her appetite. "You and Nicki can't protect me forever. You have your own lives in New Orleans."

Nate added a liberal amount of catsup to his burger. "True, but you can always pack up and move to the Crescent City. New Orleans could use a little class."

Isabelle laughed, maybe for the first time that evening. "That sounds more appealing than you know, but my job is here." She cut up her chicken patty and ate a piece.

"Then we won't get ahead of ourselves. For now, let's eat. Tomorrow I'll take you to get that restraining order. Someday this will be behind you. I won't say you'll laugh, because there's nothing funny about this, but it *will* be over."

She reached for his hand a second time. "You have no idea how good it feels to have a friend."

He nodded and bit into his sandwich. After the comment about being her boyfriend, coming up with an appropriate reply was beyond his ability.

After Nate walked her to her door and said goodnight, he couldn't bring himself to actually leave her neighborhood. For a while he cruised the streets and then parked down the block in the shadows under a tree. He didn't like the idea of Markham stalking her, even though someone might accuse him of the same thing. Finally, he called Germantown police and asked that her home be put on their regular patrol as a professional courtesy. Once he spotted a squad car drive by her building, Nate returned to the Carlton, exhausted.

Nicki would describe him as smitten, but what he really had was a bad feeling in his gut.

❧

The next morning, Nicki called for room service. The pizza she'd had delivered for supper last night was long gone. Today she would treat herself to a pot of coffee, croissants, and a fruit cup. Later on she would pick up English muffins, Swiss cheese, and a bag of oranges from the grocery store. She refused to pamper herself on Hunter's tab. She was here for work, whether or not her cousin needed her help.

Nate hadn't returned to the hotel last night before she fell asleep, and he still wasn't responding to her texts. Instead of stomping her foot like a woman—Nate's favorite expression—or wasting energy feeling sorry for herself, Nicki got busy with her own case. By the time they brought up her continental breakfast, she had narrowed her search for the correct Koehler among the era's rich and famous.

A Blake Koehler had owned a chain of furniture stores in Fayette, Tipton, and Shelby Counties, and in northern Mississippi during the fifties, sixties, and seventies. He sounded like an excellent possibility for the winner for the 1956 scavenger hunt. But after Mrs. Grant's less than warm reception in her garden, Nicki decided to be sure. A quick phone call to the hotel's favorite bellman might just do the trick.

"Hello, Mr. Prescott? This is Nicki Price. We met on the tour of the Carlton Hotel and then I came to see you last week."

Two or three seconds passed before he said, "Who?"

So much for leaving a memorable impression. Then Nicki recalled that almost every time she phoned her grandparents, their initial response duplicated Mr. Prescott's. Remembering to slow down, speak loudly, and enunciate clearly, she repeated her introduction and waited for the tumblers to fall into place.

"Oh, yes. I remember you, Miss Price. How ya doing with that rabbit trail I sent you on?" Henry released a good-natured chuckle.

"Very well, I think, but I need to ask a question. Do you think the Mr. and Mrs. Blake Koehler who won the jewels in 1956 were the Koehlers who owned a bunch of furniture stores?"

"One and the same, missy. That's him, for sure. He sold them stores to a big corporation out of Atlanta sometime in the eighties. I bet they offered him a pretty penny, if you know what I mean. Mr. Koehler wanted to retire and take it easy. They didn't have no children to carry on the business, nary a one. I used to joke with the mister that they could have one of mine. Just say the word and I'd pack their bags." He laughed with gusto.

Nicki smiled to herself. She wondered what the distinguished Robert Prescott would think of his grandfather offering one of his brood to a white couple in the suburbs, even in jest. "He didn't accept your offer?"

"Nope. Said right about the time his missus got attached to the youngin', we would miss him and ask for him back."

"Sounds about right. Did you ever hear anything about the Koehlers after that?"

"That's all I know, but you keep me posted, okay? Folks have come to make sure my heart's ticking. Can't they see me still breathing?" Henry huffed into the phone.

"I'll come visit you again real soon. I have a picture for you too."

"Sounds real nice. Good luck, Miss Price."

The phone line went dead, but Nicki had a lead. Selling a chain of stores to a major corporation would have made headlines in the business pages. Rich people had a more difficult time remaining anonymous than poor people. Within the hour she'd located the name, address, and phone number of the legal firm that had handled the transfer on behalf of Mr. Blake Koehler. At least the phone number of a firm in business thirty years ago. But according to the string of names recited by the receptionist, a descendent was still working at the law firm today.

"Good morning. It's of upmost urgency that I speak with Mr. Bennett. This is Miss Nicolette Price of New Orleans calling." Nicki duplicated the hoity-toity accent of her future mother-in-law, Mrs. Clotilde Galen of the Garden District.

The young woman was flummoxed. The Galen name meant nothing in Memphis, yet she was reluctant to dismiss someone with the authority implied in Nicki's delivery. *Practicing in front of a mirror while applying makeup worked!*

"I'm sorry, Miss Price, but Mr. Bennett is with a client. Is there another partner in the firm who can help you?"

"No, thank you. Please give him my name and number, along with my request for expediency in this matter."

"Of course. I'll give your message to him as soon as I can. May I tell him what this is regarding, ma'am?"

Nicki sighed. "No. I can't discuss it. I'm afraid it's of a...sensitive nature."

"Yes, ma'am. I'll have him contact you as soon as he's free."

Nicki felt guilty about her subterfuge, yet she knew her drama wouldn't hurt anyone and might just make an elderly man happy.

Plopping down on the thick, plush carpet of her suite, Nicki launched into exercises aimed to mitigate her love of chocolate and raspberry cheesecake. But before she finished the dreaded situps, Mr. Bennett returned her call.

"Miss Price, Nicholas Bennett. What can I help you with?" His accent was smooth as a pond in winter, her Mamaw's pet expression.

"Thank you for responding so promptly, Mr. Bennett." Nicki said, using Clotilde's accent. "I represent an elderly gentleman who is desperate to reconnect with old friends before he passes. I'm afraid he's lost touch with these people and has something...valuable to share with them before it's too late."

"I don't know how I can help, Miss Price. Perhaps a PI firm can track down these friends..."

"Yes, of course, and I already have a very good PI. But I noticed the name Horace Bennett appears on a real estate transfer executed by your office. We are attempting to track down the heirs of Blake and Bunny Koehler." Nicki allowed her voice to trail off. Mrs. Galen once told her only a silly person or one with something to hide prattled on endlessly.

The pause proved effective. "Horace Bennett was my grandfather. He practiced law here until his death."

"Oh, dear me. Do forgive my insensitivity, and please accept my sympathy for your loss. I shouldn't take up another minute of your time."

"Thank you, ma'am, but Grandfather passed on quite a while ago. Let me check our system for information on the Koehlers that I can share with you."

Nicki was placed on hold. A few minutes later, Mr. Bennett returned to report that after Mrs. Bunny Koehler passed, his firm had handled probate of her estate. But Mr. Blake Koehler was living at Sunnybrook Care Center in Millington. No further details could be conveyed due to privacy laws.

Nicki thanked the lawyer profusely and was soon inside her Lincoln, heading north into the Tennessee countryside. *A living participant of the Carlton scavenger hunts.* Henry Prescott would be pleased. She was pleased. She felt like a real live PI for a change, an experience that had eluded her since arriving in Memphis.

Unfortunately, Mr. Blake Koehler wouldn't be the key to unlock her puzzle. He was indeed alive but well into his nineties and residing in the Alzheimer's wing of Sunnybrook. Nicki felt profound sorrow for a man she'd never met before. What a cruel twist of fate to live not knowing who you were and what was important to you. She hoped Mr. Koehler had had a personal relationship with God, who never forgot His children.

At the nurse's station of the Alzheimer's wing, Nicki encountered a second obstacle. Her name wasn't on the list of approved visitors. No one had ever seen her before, and employees were reluctant to expose impaired residents to strangers. Unlike her inflated charade on the phone, Nicki opted for the complete truth with the nurse on duty.

"I'm a friend of Henry Prescott, a retired bellman of the Carlton Hotel. Henry is trying to connect with old friends. Blake Koehler and his late wife, Bunny, were two of those friends from the 1950s. May I please speak with Mr. Koehler? I promise not to upset him in any way."

"You are aware of Mr. Koehler's impairment?"

"Yes, ma'am. I have two photos I'm hoping may trigger fond memories for him."

Nancy Lansky, RN, according to her name tag, frowned at the pile of papers spread across her desk. Nicki fully expected to be sent on her way. "I couldn't allow an unsupervised visit, but it's almost my break. I could sit and eat lunch with Mr. Koehler. That should give you half an hour."

"That'll be more than enough." Nicki resisted the impulse to hug the woman.

When they entered his tidy room, Mr. Koehler was sitting in a wheelchair and staring out of the window. He turned and smiled, and Nicki's heart filled with sadness for the second time.

"How are you feeling today, Blake?" asked Mrs. Lansky.

"How do you do, Mr. Koehler?" Nicki said simultaneously. "Mr. Henry Prescott sends his regards from the Carlton Hotel."

The elderly man peered from one to the other with little interest. Undaunted, Nicki pulled the framed photo from her tote bag. "Do you remember Henry? That's him right there." Nicki tapped the middle smiling face. "And that's Mr. and Mrs. Smithfield, and those are the Whitleys. Everyone says hello to you."

Blake looked at the photo without one iota of recognition.

"I told you not to get your hopes up," murmured Mrs. Lansky. She perched on a chair and unwrapped her sandwich.

"How about this picture, sir?" Nicki produced one of three copies made from the newspaper clipping. "That's you and your lovely wife, Bunny."

The gentleman held up the picture and traced her outline with one finger. A grin bloomed on his craggy face.

Nicki hadn't indicated which woman was Bunny. "He recognized his wife," she whispered to the nurse.

"That's wonderful. I hope you'll let him keep that picture. Although he has a bunch of old photos, including plenty of Mrs. Koehler." The nurse walked to the closet and pulled a box from the shelf. "Blake, why don't you show Miss Price your mementoes?"

For the remainder of the nurse's lunch break, Nicki took item after item from the crate—furniture store flyers, golden anniversary invitations, and pictures of people no one in the room recognized. Nicki tried her best to illicit responses without success. Blake merely watched as she drew out the next treasure, a silly poem about coins in a fountain and Dorothy McGuire.

When Mrs. Lansky finished her bag of chips and apple, she began to shift restlessly. Nicki was about to repack his keepsakes in the box when her fingers landed on a black-and-white of two couples in formal attire. Her breath caught in her throat, and her heart beat faster.

"That's you, Mr. Koehler. You and Bunny." She handed him the snapshot, eliciting a faint smile. "Who are these people, sir?" Nicki pointed to the other couple. "Please look again, because it's very important." She switched on the light over his shoulder.

"I'm afraid you're wasting your time. It's been sixty years, for goodness' sake." Mrs. Lansky gently pulled the photo from his fingers and turned it over. "There's your answer. Horace and Betsy Bennett, 1957."

Nicki carefully repacked his box, hugged Blake goodbye, and thanked the helpful caregiver profusely. So much for her own extraordinary PI skills. Nevertheless, she had her answer. Horace Bennett wasn't just the Koehlers's attorney. He and his wife were their friends too. Although from the picture she couldn't tell what their prize had been, she still had another piece of the puzzle.

SEVENTEEN

*N*ate finished two cans of Coke in the hotel lobby before his partner strolled in whistling a tune.

"Where have you been?" he demanded.

Nicki stopped dead in her tracks. "At a care center in Millington. If you would have answered your phone last night or this morning, you would have known that. What's up?"

"What were you doing there?" Nate tossed his soda can into a nearby recycle bin.

"Tracking down a participant in the Carlton scavenger hunts. Wait until you hear—"

Nate held up both hands. "Save your wild-goose chase story until later. I want you to call Isabelle to see if she'll go to a blues club tonight."

"*Go out?* She just buried her brother, Nate. Besides, I thought you saw her this morning for the restraining order. At least Izzy takes my phone calls. Why didn't you ask her then?" Nicki walked around him toward the elevator and pressed the button.

"I don't want it to sound like a date. This is related to Danny's case."

Nicki cocked her head to the side. "Sounds like a date to me, cousin. What's going on?"

"I want it to *look* like a date so we can blend in better on Beale Street. I think Danny's murder has more to do with his music than his work with recovering addicts. If you can manage to stay up past ten, I want you to come too."

"You're lifting my house arrest?"

"You're hardly in solitary confinement if you spent the morning gallivanting to Millington."

Nicki let the doors open and close without stepping in. "If being on a date is your idea of clever camouflage, why would you want me as a third wheel?"

Nate clenched his back teeth. "To take the pressure off. Isabelle makes me nervous."

"Oh, you still don't like her." Nicki pushed the button again.

"No," he said, deciding to go out on a limb. "I do like her. A lot. That's the problem."

Nicki's eyes almost bugged from her head. "You're kidding me! You, Nate Price, smitten by the Ice Queen? Isn't that what you used to call her?"

"Taking the pressure off does *not* include trotting out ancient history. Forget I asked. I'll go alone." This time when the elevators doors opened he stomped inside.

Nicki followed at his heels. "Relax, Romeo. I was joking. I'll call Izzy and insist she come with us. What time should I be ready and where should I sit? In the backseat or between you two up front like a chaperone?"

"I don't want Isabelle to think this is a date. Tell her we'll pick her up at eight. Please, Nicki. I need your best behavior tonight."

"Hmm. I'll try not to remember the times you chased me with snakes, or put bugs in my sleeping bag, or stranded me in a gator habitat." When they reached their floor, Nicki skipped down the hall.

Nate was left with several hours to figure out how to pump

distrustful musicians for information, and how to impress a woman he couldn't stop thinking about.

ᵔᵕ

When the cousins arrived at her condo, Isabelle made the decision about seating arrangements for them. When Nicki jumped out to greet her, Isabelle hopped into the backseat without much consideration. She was far more concerned about clubbing on a weeknight.

"Why did you pick a Tuesday to meet some of Danny's fellow musicians?" she asked, leaning over the front seat. "Wouldn't the weekend be better?"

"Yeah, that was my thought too at first, but then I realized Tuesday and Wednesday are when many stand-ins take the stage if a regular needs a night off. Sunday and Monday most clubs are dark. Thursday through Saturday the clubs are filled to capacity, so regulars wouldn't dare not show up. Plus, some small clubs have an open mic tonight. New musicians can show off their talent in case established bands are looking to replace someone. This actually should be our best shot at finding those who may have known your brother."

"I'm impressed, Nate," said Nicki. "You were busy while I was in Millington."

"Sounds good, as long as we're not out too late," said Isabelle. "I have a long day tomorrow."

"Music starts early on Tuesday, and I brought you this if you need it." He handed her a bottle of energy drink.

"Thanks. I'll save it for the office tomorrow." Isabelle settled back on the seat. "Tell me what you're hoping to find out."

"Because I'm not convinced Tito is our man, I want to know how Danny got along with the other musicians. If he had any enemies on Beale Street."

Isabelle sighed. "I doubt it. Everyone who met Danny liked him. It was that way his whole life. He had the magnetic personality in our family."

Nicki pivoted on the seat. "Your personality is just fine, Izzy. Not everyone can be as outgoing as Danny."

"I agree," said Nate, glad Nicki was there to voice his thoughts. He hated to hear Isabelle criticize herself, yet anything he said would sound like transparent flattery. "Besides, tonight we're simply three friends out to relax and listen to good music. I found out that Blues Nation is playing at Jimmy's Downunder. Two guitars plus a bass player, drums, keyboard, and a saxophone. Danny played the sax, right? Maybe members of the band knew him."

Nate glanced at Isabelle in the rearview mirror. She looked on the verge of tears. Bringing her along so soon after the funeral had been a mistake. But there was little he could do now but scan the radio stations for distraction until they got to Beale Street.

Jimmy's Downunder turned out to be a dark, cavernous club with a jukebox so loud that conversation, witty or otherwise, was virtually impossible. Nate wouldn't have to worry about putting his foot in his mouth. Because they arrived earlier than the average club-goer, twenty bucks secured a table in front of the stage.

"Out with *two* lovely ladies tonight," purred the hostess. "Aren't you the lucky one?" She winked at Nate before tottering away on ridiculously high heels.

"That I am." Nate pulled out Isabelle's chair and then reached for Nicki's. But she was already snapping photos of musicians as they tuned their instruments. "Exercise a little subtlety, if you don't mind," he cautioned.

"Why? I'm just an enamored fan of the blues."

"Not everyone likes their picture taken," Nate hissed in her ear. Sure enough, a wiry, dreadlocked guitarist was trying to stare holes through his cousin.

Nicki put away her phone and ordered an assortment of

appetizers, two Cokes, and one Budweiser from the waitress. "I know you don't drink, but I ordered you a beer. You know, as part of our cover," she whispered in her cousin's ear. "It can just sit there."

On second thought, why hadn't I just brought Isabelle and left Nicki back at the hotel?

But by the time they ate their overpriced tourist food, concerns about proper club etiquette were forgotten. The Blues Nation warmed up with a few instrumental versions of popular tunes and then launched into music that took Nate's breath away. Driving beats that reverberated in his chest, perfect pitch harmonies, guitar chords that would make the masters weep, and sorrowful lyrics that had given the genre its name. The guitar player with laser vision turned out to be the lead singer. His R&B style reminded Nate of a rawer, earthier Al Green or Barry White, but with none of the romance. The range of his vocals kept the three of them mesmerized for an hour, all thoughts of food, beverages, or their purpose forgotten.

When the band took a much-deserved break, Nate walked up to the tip jar and threw in a hundred-dollar bill—currency he kept tucked in his wallet for a special occasion. The singer's voice, along with guitar work that rivaled the late Stevie Ray Vaughn and sax playing that brought to mind E Street Band's big man, warranted no less.

Nate's largesse didn't go unnoticed. The guitar player's eyes rounded when he spotted the hundred atop the ones and fives. He mopped his forehead, took a swig of water, and sauntered toward their table as though he had all the time in the world. "Either you've had too much to drink, or you really liked our first set. Considering you've barely touched your beer, I'd say it was the latter." The man looked long and hard at each of them in succession, his gaze lingering longest on Nate. "Unless you folks have another reason for being here."

Nate shrugged. "I haven't heard live music in a long time. I forgot how much I liked it. And that was better than any I can remember."

The musician stretched out his hand. "Tyrone Biggs. Thanks for coming to Jimmy's Downunder. Me and the boys have been playing together a while now." He angled his head toward the stage.

Nate got the feeling that Tyrone Biggs had seen and heard more than the average man. The moment they locked gazes, Nate knew he couldn't fool him about anything. "We're in town for a funeral. Our friend and her brother." Nate nodded at Isabelle. "He recently died. Since he played the blues, we're here to honor him before going back home."

"Danny played the saxophone, just like him," said Isabelle, pointing at a shaved-headed musician talking to a group of women.

"You're Danny Andre's sister?" asked Tyrone.

"I am. Did you know my brother?" Two large tears ran down Isabelle's face.

"Yeah, and I'm real sorry 'bout what happened. He sat in with us once or twice. Nothing too regular, though." Tyrone pulled up an empty chair.

Unfortunately, Nicki took this opportunity to make her presence known. "We're hoping to talk to other stand-in sax players. Maybe some of them were friends of Danny's."

Tyrone thought for a bit and then rattled off three names. "I can't think of anybody else not hooked up with a regular gig." He waved over the waitress, ordered a beer, and told her to put it on Nate's tab.

Nicki jotted the names on a napkin and tucked the list in her purse. "Did any of them need work even more than Danny?"

Tyrone glared at Nicki as though he suffered a case of indigestion. "Anybody here look independently wealthy to you, lady? This ain't no hobby for us."

"No, but I want to know if someone had a grudge against my best friend," Nicki shot back at him fearlessly.

"You tryin' to hang this on a sax player? You're barking up the wrong tree. I heard they arrested some junkie uptown." The tension between Nicki and Tyrone could be sliced with a knife.

Isabelle touched the musician's sleeve. "We just want to speak to them, Mr. Biggs. Please," she added softy.

Tyrone focused his bloodshot eyes on her. "Then you should talk to Leon Perkins. He weren't as good as your brother, so every time Danny got work, Leon went home with empty pockets. Far as I know, he still lives in the projects on the east side." He rose to his feet just as the waitress delivered his beer. "My sympathies, Miss Andre." He bobbed his head. "And thanks for the brew," he said to Nate. Nicki he ignored.

That hadn't been the most subtle approach at interrogation, but it had gotten the job done. Nate had a suspect.

～

Wednesday morning, Nicki munched on a cold bagel and broke an orange into sections. The neighborhood grocery didn't have fluffy croissants, and the packaged cheese had looked far too brightly colored to be natural. However, her financial outlay was far less than a twenty-eight-dollar room service bill added to Hunter's tab.

Apparently, their night out on Beale Street had been a complete success. All Nate did was talk about everything that happened and repeat every word said, especially those uttered by Isabelle. If Nicki didn't know better, she would think her cousin had a crush on Danny's sister. Izzy had certainly loosened up quite a bit since their initial meeting. From her clandestine surveillance, Nicki spotted Izzy glancing at Nate when she thought he wasn't looking—and vice versa. Yet Nicki knew nothing would come out of this. She and Nate would soon be heading south while Izzy remained here in the land of the Delta blues. Long distance relationships seldom worked.

Nate was also thrilled to get the names of other sax players. He planned to track down Leon Perkins today. Unfortunately, he had refused to let her tag along. Nate said the public housing described by the Blues Nation bandleader was no place for ladies to go. He apparently forgot why she was here, along with the fact her mother lived in subsidized housing in Natchez.

Not everyone in this world was rich…or even remotely middle class.

Nicki had seen poverty her entire life, from the soles of her shoes up to the tarpaper patches on Mamaw's roof. She wouldn't have been shocked or afraid.

Instead, she was trapped in her luxury suite waiting for Nicholas Bennett to return her call. The lawyer hadn't been quite so polite when she called the first thing this morning. Perhaps it was because she forgot to use Clotilde's accent. More likely it was because she started rambling about expensive gems.

"Tell me again who you represent, Miss Price."

"Mr. Henry Prescott, a retired bellman of the Carlton Hotel. Mr. Prescott knew your grandparents, Horace and Betsy, during the fifties and considered them friends."

Nicholas made a dismissive click of his tongue. "Even so, both of them have passed on. Any sort of reunion would be impossible."

"I understand that, sir. But I'm piecing together the scavenger hunts for Henry in case other participants are still living. Because Horace and Betsy won in 1957, they would have planned the next year's event. Do you know who won the 1958 hunt?"

"I haven't the least idea," Mr. Bennett said, sighing wearily.

"What about the prizes your grandparents won? Any idea what kind of matching jewelry they found hidden inside the hotel?"

"What exactly is this bellman after? Some kind of claim on my grandparents' estate over a scavenger hunt prize?" His tone of boredom morphed into distrust.

"Absolutely not. He and I only wish to locate any surviving participants. I'm curious about the prizes only so I can piece together the past for Mr. Prescott. You have my word."

Of course, the word of a stranger might not be worth much.

Mr. Bennett seemed to be pondering the matter. "If I have time this morning, I'll call my mother to see if she remembers anything about this. She assisted with their estate."

"Thank you, sir." Nicki supplied her cell number again but had little hope of hearing from him.

Sometimes, however, people surprised you in delightful ways. Two hours later, after watching several reruns of *Petticoat Junction* and finishing one hundred sit-ups, Nicki's phone rang.

"Miss Price? Nicholas Bennett. I have only a minute, but my mother remembered the scavenger hunts you referred to. My grandmother won a sapphire pendant, while Granddad won a sapphire tiepin. Rather lovely stones, she recalls. Grandma was so fond of her prize she insisted she be buried wearing it. No clue what happened to his. Maybe Granddad lost it."

"Did she mention anything about who might have won the following year? Your grandparents would have planned the next hunt and purchased the prizes."

"I asked, but the only other thing she knows was that the sapphires were found in a decorative vase on the fireplace mantle. Apparently, this porcelain vase was in the library, a gentleman's meeting place to enjoy a cigar. The room was off-limits for women in those days. But Grandma got an inkling based on a clue given at dinner and sneaked into the room during the middle of the night. That's all I can tell you, Miss Price. Please don't call me again."

"I won't, sir, and thank you very much."

Nicki's gratitude went unheard because the busy man had already hung up. Undaunted, she jotted down the pertinent information on a chart she was constructing for Henry. She'd begun this quest due to boredom and a desire to make a sweet old man happy. But now that she was convinced the last set of jewels was still somewhere in the hotel, she couldn't wait for the next sleuthing opportunity. Finding them and returning them to the rightful owner could make someone very happy.

However, right now she should call Izzy. Maybe Nate didn't need her, but her friend did. Venturing into Danny's world had been a rude awakening for both of them. Nate seemed unmoved by the dark, smoky, cavernous club, but she had been shocked. Nicki didn't think smoking was allowed in any public places, but clubs that didn't admit those under twenty-one were exempt from the law as long as they didn't have full restaurant menus. Nicki had to send her favorite blazer to the dry cleaners and shampoo her hair twice to get the smell of smoke out of it.

But it wasn't just drinking and smoking that made Beale Street an odd place for a former choirboy to work. Although the music had been the best blues she'd ever heard, she'd sensed desperation among the musicians. Apparently, the take-home pay and retirement benefits left much to be desired. Danny had been one of them. He loved the blues. So for his sake, Nicki hoped Nate was wrong about one of his peers being a killer.

EIGHTEEN

Musicians stayed up until the early hours of morning and then slept late the next day. Nate tried to spend his morning hours productively with emails and expense reports, yet like a lemming he found himself in the car on his way to Isabelle's. After seeing nothing out of the ordinary at her condo, he drove to her realty office in the center of town to check on her. Even though the Germantown police had put her building on their nightly patrol, he still worried about her. Men like Markham were unpredictable. And that made him nervous.

Spotting her car in the employee lot behind the building, Nate relaxed and headed back toward Memphis. When he reached the outskirts of downtown, he punched the last known address of Leon Perkins into the car's GPS. According to the helpful bandleader, Tyrone Biggs, Perkins lived on the east side, close to the zoo. Nate had checked public records for the correct street and unit number.

City streets in need of repair, barricaded doorways and boarded up windows of foreclosures, and weedy yards neglected by absent landlords indicated he'd reached the less fortunate residents of Shelby County. Nate parked on a narrow street clogged with vehicles in various states of disrepair. It wasn't until he had stepped out of the car that he began to doubt the wisdom of visiting the musician alone. If Perkins was the killer, he was walking into his house without anyone knowing his whereabouts. He could wash up on the riverbank in the same spot as Danny. Nate released the safety on his weapon and cautiously approached the concrete block building. Fortunately, no one on the street paid him much mind.

A young woman of about twenty-five answered his knock on the door. "Can I help you?" she asked.

"I'm looking for Leon Perkins. Is he home?"

"What you want?" The woman seemed more curious than suspicious. "He owe you money? We ain't got it if that's the case."

"No, nothing like that. I want to talk to him about a friend of mine—"

"Charlene, you go on in the kitchen. I got this." A young man, muscular and multi-tattooed, moseyed into the room. Nate had never before seen anyone slouch while they walked.

"I'm Leon Perkins. Who are you and what do you want?" He lifted his chin with an air of authority.

"I'm Nate Price, a friend of Danny Andre's. Could I come in for a minute and talk?"

"You got a warrant?"

"I'm not a cop, so that would be no."

Perkins studied him with deeply hooded eyes and then shrugged. "Come on in. I ain't got nothing to hide. Just don't go wandering around. A man's home is his castle." He strolled toward the recliner facing the TV.

"Thanks," Nate said, stepping into the tidy room. Although none of the furniture was new and the decor wouldn't make *Southern Living* magazine, it looked like a family who respected what they owned lived here. A laundry basket filled with stuffed animals and an infant swing next to the couch indicated Leon and

Charlene were parents. "I understand you play the sax, just like Danny." Nate perched on the sofa but didn't settle in.

"Who told you that?" Leon crossed his arms and glared.

"Tyrone Biggs." Nate watched the kitchen door from the corner of his eye.

Leon uttered a foul word and rolled his eyes. "Biggs. That guy just won't give it a rest. You want to know who whacked your friend and threw him in the river, and Biggs sends you *here*?"

He started to repeat the foul verbiage until a child about four years old bolted into the room. The boy wore Hercules pajama bottoms, but he had apparently escaped before his mother could put his shirt on him. With a baby on her hip, Charlene entered hot on her son's tail.

"Come here, you." Leon swept up the giggling child and set him on his knee. "Who you runnin' from?"

"He's slippery as an eel." Charlene tossed Leon the pajama top and then tucked the baby into the swing.

"What's your son's name?" asked Nate. "You have a pair of real cute kids."

"Isaiah, straight from the Bible." Leon pulled the shirt over the boy's head. "And we got three. One's in school." He cranked the handle on the swing to start the rocking motion and turned back to Nate. "Is that it, Price? You think I killed Danny Andre? Why would I do that?"

Nate tried to think of a safe answer but came up empty. "Tyrone thinks Danny took good paying gigs that could have been yours."

"That's…" Leon glanced at Charlene and reconsidered. "That's baloney."

"Tyrone said Danny may have been a better sax player." Nate expected Perkins to balk or argue the assertion. With the man's wife and children in the room, he went out on a limb.

Leon's nostrils flared, but he kept his composure. "Danny was better than me. I ain't gonna lie about it. But Danny ain't why I don't get my fair share of work on Beale."

Nate's surprise must have shown on his face. "So Danny really was good?"

Leon snorted. "Funny how Andre was supposed to be your friend, but it sounds like you never heard him play."

Nate felt a flush climb his neck. "I lost touch with him a while ago. I'm trying to make up for that now."

"It's a little late, don't you think? He was every bit as good as the sax player in Blues Nation, but that guy has worked for Biggs a long time. You don't fix something that ain't broke." Leon set the boy on the floor, who took off down the hallway at lightning speed. "I didn't have no beef with Danny. Fact is, I liked the guy. Just about everybody did. He gave work to me a couple times when I had rent due or a sick kid. Besides, I got an alibi for when Danny was killed. I was in Mobile for a few days with my family."

Charlene huffed. "You'd better give him the address where we stayed so you don't get locked up for no good reason." She hurried down the hall after Isaiah.

Leon rolled his eyes after she left the room. "Looks like you're wasting your time talkin' to me."

"Starting to sound that way. Got any idea why Biggs sent me here?"

Leon's face filled with hatred. "Biggs is the reason I don't get my share of gigs. He badmouths me every chance he gets. Says I steal from the tip jar when nobody's looking. He's the one who goes from table to table, pocketing whatever he can shake down folks for."

Nate remembered seeing Biggs slip the hundred into his pocket real fast. Maybe he didn't plan to share with the band at the end of the night.

"I ain't no thief!" Leon pounded his fist on the sofa.

"I believe you, Mr. Perkins. Not that it does much good." Nate rose to his feet. "Thanks for talking to me. And I appreciate what you said about Danny's music. For the rest of my life I'll regret not hearing him play." He was halfway to the door before he stopped in his tracks. "You said *almost* everybody loved Danny. You know somebody who didn't?"

Leon frowned. "Why would I jam up somebody based on nothing? That's what Biggs tried to do to me."

"You said Danny was a nice guy. Anyway, I'm not a cop. You're not jamming up anybody."

"Tell him about Jimmy Watts." Charlene said from the kitchen doorway.

"Ain't you got something to do, woman?" he snapped at her. "This is *my* business." With another roll of his eyes he looked at Nate. "Jimmy hated Danny. He thought Danny was some rich boy hanging out in the slums like it was spring break at the beach."

"Because Danny was white?"

"Nah, because Danny passed up work and loaned money to just about anybody. I told Jimmy that Danny worked with junkies out of some church basement, and that made him even madder. He said he hated do-gooders even more than rich kids playing poor."

"Danny didn't have two dimes to rub together from the day he was born."

"I know that. But you just can't tell some folks nothin'."

"Know where I can find this Jimmy Watts?" Nate asked, inadvertently holding his breath.

"I ain't got an address for the guy, but if I wanted to talk to him—which I don't—I'd hang around the Blues City Club. If a band needs a stand-in at the last minute, they can usually find one there." Perkins's expression turned hard as nails. "And that's the last thing I'm gonna say to you, Price."

At least Nate now had somewhere to go.

~

Isabelle spent the entire day in a daze. It was a good thing that she had no houses to show or she might have tried to sell a one-bedroom loft to a family of six. She kept replaying the previous evening with Nicki and Nate in her head.

Nate turned out to be nothing like what she had originally assumed—an arrogant, sexist jock concerned solely with sports or what others thought of him. Although he still loved the Mississippi State Bulldogs and the New Orleans Saints, he didn't seem to have an egotistical bone in his body. He wasn't afraid to show his softer, gentler side either. Nate had been as touched by the unforgettable music as she had been. Why else would he tip the band so generously? He'd tried to hide the bill's denomination, but details seldom escaped Isabelle's eagle eye.

How could she not like a man who loved the blues like Danny?

But Nate wasn't the only thing distracting her. Seeing Danny's fellow musicians in a venue where he had worked was a rude awakening. Whenever he had talked about playing his saxophone, she pictured a small auditorium or a cozy coffeehouse with a raised center stage. Seeing Jimmy's Downunder up close and personal erased all images of chamber orchestras from her mind. Although tourists made up the majority of the club's patrons, Isabelle hadn't been prepared for the amount of alcohol being consumed or the rowdy behavior from some guests. It was hard to picture her sweet brother hanging out there. Whether or not Nate learned anything helpful from the names supplied by the guitar player, Isabelle was glad he'd called her. Beale Street, like the New Horizons Outreach Center, had been Danny's world. How heartbreaking she hadn't known her brother better when she had the chance.

The raucous buzz of the intercom jarred her attention. "Miss Andre?" asked the receptionist.

"Yes, Janice. Do we have a walk-in client?"

"No, but there's a Craig on line two. He won't say what this is about, but he insists on speaking to you."

"It's fine. Please put the call through." Isabelle cringed. Her ex-husband. What did he want?

"Hi, Craig, what's up?" She struggled to keep her tone neutral.

"Hey there, Izzy. How are things going?"

An innocent enough question, but it set her teeth on edge. Should she tell him about her brother? As far as she knew, Craig still lived in Nashville. Most likely he hadn't heard about Danny's passing. But he had paid little attention to her brother the few times they met. He called him flakey and ill-equipped to deal with the real world. As fate would have it, Craig had been the ill-equipped one, considering his expensive habits. So after a moment's hesitation, Isabelle chose to let the opportunity pass.

"I'm fine but very busy this afternoon. I trust you have something on your mind?"

"Yes, I called you for a reason." He breathed heavily into the mouthpiece. "I'm getting my license to practice law reinstated. Part of the process is to prove I've made restitution to everyone I owed money to—back income taxes, overdue rent, and every credit card that still had a balance at the time of our divorce."

Isabelle knew she shouldn't ask, but couldn't seem to stop herself. "If you've been unable to practice law, how on earth could you pay back all that money?"

"I put in sixteen-hour days as a law clerk at two different firms. I've slept less than four hours a night for the last two years and worked Saturdays too. Cassie has been paying all the bills from her paycheck so I can comply with the bar association's requirements."

Oh, yeah, Cassie. Isabelle had almost forgotten about the

red-haired paralegal Craig hooked up with before the ink had dried on their divorce decree. Not that she had a grudge against the woman. Cassie had nothing to do with their breakup. Perhaps someday Cassie would realize she was enabling a dishonest manipulator with a weakness for horseracing and the blackjack tables.

"That's very nice of her." Isabelle spoke before the silence grew uncomfortable.

"She's a wonderful girl. You would like her if you got to know her."

Refusing to state the obvious, she said, "Sounds like you're getting your life together. I'm happy for you, but why call me today?"

"Because I have a favor to ask. One of the bar association referees may contact you at some point."

"What on earth for? We've been divorced for four years." His gall left a bitter taste in her mouth.

"To see if I made financial restitution to you."

"And you expect me to lie?" Isabelle didn't hide her annoyance.

"You were able to manage the debt you walked away with."

"You didn't give me much choice. You implied your life was at stake from some bookie."

"Look, Izzy. Can you cut me some slack here? I've been struggling to get my life together. If I had extra money, I would send it your way. But Cassie wants us to buy a house as soon as we're married."

"You're engaged?" Isabelle had no clue why that news irritated her. She certainly didn't want the man back.

"Yes. We'll marry as soon as my license is restored. I don't want her to be saddled for life with a man who can't provide…a loser."

It was a good thing he couldn't see her face. "That's probably a wise choice, but I won't lie for you, Craig."

"I understand, but you don't have to stab me in the back either.

Can't you tell the referee we both left the marriage with an agreed-upon amount of debt? That's pretty much the truth."

Isabelle pinched the bridge of her nose. She didn't want to talk to him another minute longer, but her Christian upbringing mitigated any need for revenge. "Fine. If they call I'll tell them that."

"I'm grateful, Izzy. And I really hope you find a special person someday too."

How does he know I already haven't? "Thanks. I wish you and Cassie lots of luck. But, Craig? If you ever have reason to call again, don't call me Izzy anymore. I prefer Isabelle." She hung up the phone with satisfaction.

For a long while Isabelle stared at her computer monitor, scrolling through properties on the market. Yet she couldn't remember what any of her clients were looking for even though she reviewed her notes less than an hour ago. On a lark she punched Nicki's number. She needed a female shoulder to cry on after her depressing conversation with Craig.

"Hey, girl, you got plans for tonight? I'm going stir-crazy in the office and hoped we could catch an early dinner."

"You must have read my mind. I planned to call *you* after I got off the phone with Hunter. I've been pacing the floors of paradise with no place to go all day."

"Nate wouldn't take you with him to talk to the musicians?"

"Nope. He thought the neighborhood was too rough. So I've been confined to my ivory tower. Maybe he's forgotten where we both grew up."

Isabelle felt her shoulders relax just hearing Nicki's voice. "I, too, heard from an endless source of irritation this afternoon. Why don't I come rescue you, Rapunzel? I can finish up and be there in an hour."

"I'll be tapping my toe in the lobby since nobody's climbing up my golden tresses. Too many split ends."

Isabelle couldn't wait to get to the Carlton. Nicki had really grown on her. And if Nicki had any news to share about her handsome cousin, she wouldn't change the subject.

～

True to her word, Nicki bounded through the doors as soon as Isabelle arrived at the front entrance. "I thought you *never* would get here," she said, jumping into the passenger seat. "Drive around the block to the parking garage. The place I picked out is within walking distance." Nicki unfolded a brochure from the information rack. "Shrimp, oysters, snapper, catfish... Just reading the menu makes me homesick."

"Sounds delightful, especially because I like seafood. And since you just got off the phone with Hunter, you can give me an update on your wedding plans."

Isabelle looked for the ramp into the garage while Nicki launched into a delightful tale of bridesmaids, honeymoon destinations, her mother insisting on the church in Red Haw, Mississippi, and her future mother-in-law pressuring for a reception on a yacht in Lake Ponchartrain. Nicki talked while they were seated inside the restaurant and only took a breath to place her order. She didn't seem the least bit discouraged. If anything, she was enjoying the challenge.

"Are you pretty sure this Hunter Galen is the one?" Isabelle teased when she able to get a word in edgewise.

Nicki blushed to her hairline. "Sorry, Izzy. I've monopolized the entire conversation with Mr. Perfect. I'll probably discover *something* mediocre about him once we're married. He's sure in for a shock the first time he sees my hair in the morning. But I'm so happy at this point that I'll do everything I can to make this marriage work."

"You strike me as Miss Independence, yet Hunter manages to keep you practically confined to your hotel room and you don't seem to mind. Now that I think about it, he should seem super controlling, but oddly he doesn't."

Nicki reflected before answering. "I guess a man's motivation makes the difference. I know Hunter loves me. He gives me space and shows me love on a daily basis, so I know he fears for my safety in Memphis. I do have a bad habit of blundering into danger. But that's enough about us."

"I enjoy hearing about happy couples. Gives me hope I'll find my own happy-ever-after someday." Isabelle looked down as she fluffed a huge napkin across her lap.

"No doubt in my mind that you will. What was the irritating news you heard?" Nicki moved her iced tea to the side as a spread arrived that would be enough for four people. Salads, sweet corn, fried okra, and mashed potatoes with gravy accompanied their entrees of smoked salmon and fried catfish.

Isabelle sighed and repeated the conversation with Craig almost verbatim. "I don't hear from him for years and now this?"

Nicki pondered for a moment. "What bothers you more, his asking you to cover for him with the referee or his getting married again?"

"Am I that transparent?" Isabelle set down her fork. "Good thing I don't play cards."

"We're all transparent when someone hurts us."

"The truth is that any hard feelings toward Craig are long gone. I hope he's kicked his addictions and will make Cassie a good husband." Isabelle looked everywhere but at Nicki.

"Go on," Nicki prodded. "Get it all out."

"It's just that…well, because I was the wronged party in our divorce, I really thought I'd be the one to marry first. But here I am, still self-righteous and not even dating." She covered her face with her hands. "I know how awful that sounds, Nicki, but you told me to get it off my chest."

Nicki pulled her hands away. "That sounds perfectly normal to me. There's no reason you can't meet a nice guy, but you may have to let down your guard." She dug into another piece of fried catfish.

"Can you blame me, considering what's going on with Tony Markham?"

"Of course not, but you'll scare away any potential diamonds in the rough along with the psychopaths."

"Like your cousin? I sure scared him away with everything that came out of my mouth."

"Stress doesn't bring out the best in people, but Nate deserves another chance. I wouldn't call him a diamond in the rough, but you never know what common ground you two may have."

Isabelle opened her mouth but lost her nerve before she could ask about Nate's romantic status. With her brother not even gone two weeks, this wasn't the time to dive into a romance. Yet if her intuition was correct, the number of possible opportunities was dwindling fast.

NINETEEN

*N*icki was anything but tired when she returned to the Carlton from the seafood restaurant. Over refills of sweet tea, she had filled Izzy in on the scavenger hunt mystery and received a surprising amount of encouragement from her. Nicki feared Izzy might prefer her to stay focused on Danny's case, but apparently she had full faith and confidence in Nate.

Nate. He had been very much the elephant in the room during dinner. Nicki could tell Izzy liked him and knew for a fact he liked her, yet she didn't know how to get those two together. Tonight she would say a prayer that two lost lambs could bridge the gap created by hurt feelings in high school and too many years gone by. As eager as Nicki was to return to New Orleans and the adorable Hunter Galen, she didn't want to leave until Nate and Izzy were at least good friends. Both of them could use one.

Unfortunately, when Nicki wandered through the lobby, Robert Prescott had abandoned the concierge desk. Even the most dedicated employee had their own life to go home to. Anxious to share the latest developments with someone and wired by too much caffeine, Nicki tossed and turned for hours in bed. She had tried calling Nate, but the call went straight to voice mail, indicating her boss was probably on a stakeout. No point in leaving a message. When she finally dozed off, bizarre dreams of bejeweled phantoms chasing her down dim hallways peppered her sleep.

When she awoke the next morning tangled up in the sheets, Nicki couldn't wait to jump in the shower to wash away the last of her nightmares. By the time she bought a bagel and coffee at the lobby deli, the hotel concierge had arrived at his desk.

"Good morning, Mr. Prescott. How about a coffee?"

"Good morning, Miss Price. Thank you, but I'll pass. I've had my limit." He tugged down his cuffs and opened his laptop computer. "What can I do for you? Dinner reservations? Tickets to the theatre? How about a sightseeing excursion down the Mississippi?"

"No, thank you. I wanted to bring you up to speed on the Carlton jewels mystery because I may need your help."

Robert looked as though he'd bit into a lemon. "There is no mystery, Miss Price, only my grandfather's unreliable memories of his youth. I appreciate the attention you're paying to a lonely old man, but I think Memphis offers more interesting diversions while you're in town. Have you seen our Cotton Museum or the National Civil Rights Museum? How about—"

"Thank you, sir, but I want to track down everyone who participated in the hunts and find out what happened to them. For Henry's sake and because I'm interested too." Nicki produced her most glorious smile.

"Have you tried the new equipment in our workout room?"

"I hate getting sweaty."

"I could arrange a trip to Graceland. Are you a fan of Elvis?" Robert tugged on his tie.

"I'm not too familiar with his music, but I know my grandmother loves him. Perhaps I can take *her* there someday."

He studied her over his reading glasses. Then he sighed. "Very well, Miss Price. Have a seat and fill me in on your progress. You're a very persuasive young lady."

"I have been described that way a time or two." Smiling, Nicki pulled up a chair and told him about her conversation with Nicholas Bennett and his grandparents, Horace and Betsy. "They won the sapphires in 1957, but unfortunately they have both passed away. Their grandson doesn't remember what kind of jewels his grandparents purchased the following year or who the lucky winners were."

"Congratulations on tracking down another piece of the puzzle, but this sounds like a dead end to me." He plucked a brochure of culinary delights in the Memphis area from his drawer and handed it to her.

"Thanks. This looks fabulous." Nicki accepted the brochure graciously. "It's not really a dead end because I have an idea how to proceed."

"And this is where you need my help?"

"Yes, sir. I thought I was at the end of the road until I had a flash of brilliance in the middle of the night. Because the Bennetts won in fifty-seven, they would have planned the fifty-eight hunt. Then whoever won in fifty-eight would have planned the fifty-nine hunt. All we have to do is find out who arrived a day or two early for the fifty-nine hunt, and we'll know our fifty-eight winners."

Mr. Prescott sighed again with disappointment, feigned or otherwise. "A brilliant deduction, but I'm afraid our computer archives don't go that far back."

"Yes, but hotels kept register books in those days. Leather bound, no? I've seen guests sign them in old movies." Nicki tried not to look smug. "I would bet the Carlton has them stored somewhere."

He blinked several times. "You really are clever besides persuasive. We do have those old registers in a basement storage area, but that area of the hotel is off-limits to guests."

"Oh, I completely understand. But perhaps you could

accompany me to the basement? Most likely no one will notice us peeking inside some dusty old books."

Mr. Prescott checked his watch. "Why don't we go now while I'm not busy? You're the only guest who gets up this early."

Nicki clapped her hands. "Thanks so much."

He turned his nameplate around to read, "The concierge will return shortly." Then he smiled at her, extended a hand, and said, "Let's be off, Miss Price, before I come to my senses."

They took a staircase labeled "Employees Only" to the basement. Mr. Prescott unlocked a metal door labeled "Private" and gestured for her to enter ahead of him. Nicki felt a surge of adrenaline seeing old furniture, shrouded paintings, and decorative pieces past their prime. "Now this is what I call sightseeing."

"The register books would be stored in here." Mr. Prescott unlocked a wire cage of a room containing rows of filing cabinets.

"I thought security like this would only be found in the Pentagon," said Nicki, awestruck. She read aloud the tags marking each cabinet until she came to the right one. Opening the drawer, she said, "Goodness. Shouldn't these be in the Smithsonian? They're so old!"

"Not really. They contain little historic significance." He pulled out two leather-bound tomes labeled 1958 and 1959 and handed them to her. "You may use that table while I wander around the basement. I still haven't seen everything down here."

"Thank you, sir." Nicki carried the heavy registers to the spot he had indicated, giddy with excitement.

Because the five couples usually selected a weekend between Thanksgiving and Christmas for their annual getaway, she pored over the registered guests in late November through December 25, 1959. It didn't take her long to locate the weekend when Mr. and Mrs. Bennett, Mr. and Mrs. Koehler, Mr. and Mrs. Whitley, and Mr. and Mrs. Smithfield all stayed at the hotel. All she had to do was cross reference the names of guests who arrived one day early with the names of guests who stayed at the hotel during the 1958 scavenger hunt to discover one common name: Mr. and Mrs. Reginald Fitzhugh.

Nicki stared at the name as though apparitions might suddenly float from the page.

"Mr. Prescott, I found the winners in 1958!" Nicki shouted so loud, anyone in the basement would have heard.

The concierge returned to her side within seconds. "Well done, Miss Price. Now I can get back to my post." He replaced the volumes in the correct filing cabinet and switched off the overhead light.

Once they reached his desk, at Nicki's urging Mr. Prescott typed "Reginald Fitzhugh" on his laptop's keyboard. Within moments his mouth dropped open. "I don't believe it."

"What is it? Did the name Fitzhugh pop up as belonging to influential scions of Memphis society?" Nicki circled his desk to read over his shoulder.

"No, this is even better." He stared at the screen as though fearful the information might change. "I searched the hotel's database instead of googling the name. Mrs. Reginald Fitzhugh is still an occasional guest at the Carlton. She checked in a couple of years ago and stayed for two nights."

"Do you think it's the same person who knew your grandpa?" Nicki's shock equaled his.

"Does that sound like a common name to you?"

"Wow, she's still alive. She must be in her nineties. Let me jot down her address and phone number. I can't wait to—"

He quickly closed his laptop. "Absolutely not, Miss Price. I will not break privacy laws even for you."

"Don't you think she might enjoy chatting with Henry after all these years?"

"Maybe. Or maybe she has no recollection of a bellman from sixty years ago."

Ridiculously, Nicki almost burst into tears. "You won't help me?"

Mr. Prescott looked stern, but he seemed to be fighting back a smile. "Because Mrs. Fitzhugh left a number on file with us, I'll call and tell her about you and your project with my grandfather. With your permission I will pass your phone number along to her. Then it will be *her* choice whether or not to pursue this."

"Good idea. Tell her I'm a *real* nice person and completely harmless."

His dimples deepened. "Nice, absolutely, but harmless? That remains to be seen, young lady."

～

After catching up with paperwork and mail, Nate had a little time to kill before returning to the Blues City Club at suppertime, so he put on sweats and sneakers for a run. A park stretched along Riverside Drive with some fine views of the Mississippi and Wolf Rivers. Running usually cleared the cobwebs from his head, burned away extra calories of rich Southern cooking, and gave him perspective on where he was going in life. Too bad it wasn't working so well for him today. Two hours later, breathless and sweaty, he hiked up the hill to Third Avenue with no better sense of who he was than when he left.

He wasn't stupid and didn't imagine things. Isabelle had enjoyed his company two days ago at Jimmy's Downunder as much as he had enjoyed hers. Once or twice he'd felt her gaze on him. As mesmerizing as the music had been, it was hard not to stare back. He had a bad case of the Isabelle Andre. And if he learned anything at all during high school, there was no cure.

Yet when he dropped her at her front door, all she had said was: "Thank you for an enjoyable evening. I hope we can get together again before you return to Louisiana."

That sounded like something you said to your boss after an obligatory event.

He was a desperate man out of options. As much as he hated to admit it, he might have to ask his cousin to intervene.

Nate showered, dressed casually, and tucked his gun into an ankle holster. Wearing a sport coat would only brand him as an undercover cop or a city inspector out to slap stiff fines on the club for safety infractions. Either way nobody hanging around waiting to pick up work would want to talk to him.

At five thirty in the afternoon, more employees were scurrying around the Blues City Club than paying customers. Waitstaff rearranged and refreshed tables, restocked coolers, and unloaded dishwashers. Bartenders took inventory of stock. Nate took a seat at the horseshoe-shaped bar and ordered a Coke. Along with his soft drink he was brought a menu and a separate list of appetizers served during the show. He chose a half slab of ribs with fries and coleslaw.

While waiting for his supper, he surreptitiously observed the musicians arriving singly and in pairs. Many went straight to the stage to check equipment, while others milled in small clusters, talking and joking in low voices. Nate sipped his drink and stared into space as unobtrusively as possible. Once his food arrived, he needed no further distraction. The ribs were the best he'd eaten in years, and the fries were exactly how he liked them—crisp, but soft on the inside. He savored the food and ambiance of the night world coming to life. Instruments were tuned and guitar riffs floated through the air. Customers soon began to drift through the double doors, filling the round tables around the stage first.

As the crowd thickened, Nate was able to observe more freely.

It didn't take long to find a bear of a man carrying a saxophone case. Judging by his unhappy expression, Nate was fairly certain he found the right musician. He left a twenty atop his bill and slid off the stool.

"Are you Jimmy Watts?" Nate asked in a soft voice.

"Maybe. Who are you?" The man's frown deepened the lines around his mouth.

"Nate Price. I'm a friend of Danny Andre's. Can I buy you something to drink and maybe dinner? I'd like to ask you a few questions."

"Do I look like I can't buy my own food if I'm hungry? And I don't drink when I'm working." Watts's eyes hardened. "Yeah, you sound like Andre's friend…another do-gooder who can't keep his nose out of people's business. So ask your questions. Then I'll decide if I've got anything to say."

"Look, I just want to know how Danny ended up dead. If that happened to your friend, you'd be curious too."

Watts laughed. "It's happened to lots of friends of mine, but I'm smart enough to stay out of it. People live longer that way."

There was no mistaking the threat behind Watts's words, but Nate refused to react. "Well, maybe I'm not that bright. I heard you hated Danny and I'm curious as to why. You were both sax players. I would think there would be camaraderie among musicians."

"This look like a high school marching band to you? We're down here picking the strings or blowing a horn to make a living. Danny was just a bleeding heart, always spouting 'love thy fellow man' and 'turn the other cheek' like a Sunday school teacher. The last thing I need when I'm trying to make money is somebody sounding like my old granny." Watts moved a step closer, his size downright intimidating.

Nate was unsure what to do. He didn't want to fight with

Watts as much for the man's sake as his own. If the guy needed a gig tonight to pay the bills, no one would hire a musician in a combatant mood. So he waited patiently for Watts to break the silence.

"I'm so sick of white boys who think they can change the world. Like it's all up to them 'cause they're so much better than everyone else."

"Danny didn't think he was better than anyone." Nate had had enough of the bitter man's venom. "He really liked people, even someone as unlikeable as you, Jimmy."

Watts released a dismissive snort. "And see what that got him—floating facedown in the river. Maybe he should've just played his horn and minded his own business." Watts slid off the stool with catlike grace and placed a hand on Nate's shoulder. "I suggest you not make the same mistake, *friend*." Then he picked up his case and strolled out the fire exit without a backward glance.

Nate shook off a sudden chill. Then he went to find Gus Crane, the club's soundman according to the bouncer at the back door. That tidbit of information had only cost him twenty bucks, a paltry amount if Crane admitted he'd lied to the cops about the night Danny died.

TWENTY

*I*sabelle had plenty of reasons to look forward to leaving work: A movie she'd been waiting to see was free on cable. She'd just signed contracts for two new homes and uploaded the particulars into the database. Because neither seller demanded an unrealistic price and the homes contained the amenities most young couples wanted, she would probably be able to find qualified buyers within a week or two. And after her encouraging conversation with Nicki, she had decided to become proactive with Nate.

What was she waiting for? The moment he confirmed Danny's killer was already behind bars, he would be on his way back to New Orleans. Tito Sullivan had been an argumentative roommate caught wearing Danny's sweater and watch—gifts from her—with an alibi that didn't pan out. Sometimes the person who looked guilty really was.

But when Isabelle reached the parking lot, her hopes for a quiet evening at home vanished. Covering the back windshield of her Prius was the same copper-smelling, rust-colored liquid that had been splashed across her balcony, a substance finally identified as pig's blood in the lab report. An icy chill ran up her spine. Agents and customers had been in and out of this lot all day, yet no one had noticed? On wobbly legs she moved closer to inspect. The blood had barely begun to dry.

Pivoting in place, Isabelle scanned the lot in every direction as though expecting to see Tony Markham across the street with an empty bucket in hand. But whoever the culprit had been, they were gone. She punched in the number for the police and reported the incident, and then she questioned the receptionist and other agents. The police arrived within a reasonable amount of time and initiated a familiar course of action with unfortunately the same end result.

Had anyone in the office seen someone suspicious lurking around her car? No one had.

Had any of her clients recently been dissatisfied with her performance? None that she was aware of.

Can you think of anyone other than this Tony Markham with a grudge against you?

"No, there isn't anyone else," she said, struggling to hold her temper. "Aren't you going to arrest Markham? What good is the restraining order if he can still torment me whenever he pleases?"

The taller of the two officers stopped writing and met her eye. "I know how frustrating this must be, Miss Andre, but unless someone saw Markham in the vicinity of your car, we can't drag him in for questioning."

"We take the temporary protection order very seriously," said the other officer, "but if we don't follow the letter of the law, Markham can file a harassment complaint against the department or obtain a TPO against you, as ridiculous as that sounds."

Isabelle retreated to her office and watched from the window while police photographed her car, took samples of the blood, and finished their report. Three hours and one splitting headache later, she drove straight to the best car wash in town and then arrived home to a dark condo and a huffy cat.

"Are you hungry, Mr. Chester?" She lifted the tabby into her arms. Something about hugging a furry animal settled her nerves. She filled his bowl with salmon pate and petted his silky fur while he ate. By the time Chester was licking his paws, she felt almost human again. Reaching for her favorite afghan, Isabelle curled up on the couch with the remote control.

Twenty minutes into the movie, a pebble thudded against the patio door, an odd occurrence considering the overhanging balcony above hers. Isabelle jumped to her feet, the little hairs on her neck standing on end. She parted the drapes an inch in time to spot a dark SUV driving away. The same SUV that had taken her to the Italian bistro out in the country. Markham's car.

With shaky fingers, she punched in 9-1-1. This was no after-the-fact complaint without witnesses. She had seen her tormentor's car within the radius protected by the restraining order. Within minutes, the police arrived, the same officers who had responded to her earlier call.

With her description of his vehicle, they intercepted Markham leaving the development. However, upon questioning, he produced a page of condo listings, both rentals and those for sale from another agency. He explained that the restraining order was nothing but a mistake, but he was complying nevertheless. He claimed he'd been interested in the Glades long before he'd met Isabelle but would only consider units beyond the TPO's specifications. Without sufficient cause to arrest him, Markham was sent on his way.

Isabelle pulled up Nate's number in her list of contacts the moment the police left. Tonight she just needed to talk. Maybe swap work stories or reminisce about former teachers at Forrest High School or share news about old friends. She didn't want to discuss Markham or her frustration with the legal system. Or appear like a needy, hysterical woman once again. When he picked up on the second ring, her heart almost burst in her chest.

"Hi, Isabelle. I planned to call you last night about my visit to Leon Perkins, but according to the text I got from Nicki you were having dinner with her. Then I tried calling you all day. What's up?"

"I muted my phone earlier and then forgot I had done that. Sorry about missing your calls. Right now I'm just hanging out with my cat, watching a movie. If you have no plans, why not join me? I'll send out for pizza."

Nate hesitated less than a second. "I ate ribs and fries at the Blues City Club while waiting for the musicians to show up, but I've never turned down a slice of pizza in my life. I'm on my way."

"The Blues City Club? You went clubbing without me and Nicki?" She felt herself start to relax.

"Only this once. What should I bring for movie night?"

"I have plenty of Coke in the fridge, so just bring yourself. And the sooner the better." Isabelle hung up relieved she hadn't disintegrated into an emotional train wreck. After a quick check of the street, she called the pizza shop and filled a bucket with ice.

Nate arrived at the same time as their supper. She tipped the delivery man generously and set the pizza on the counter. But as soon as the man left she burst into tears.

"What's happened?" Nate locked the door behind him. "I thought I heard something in your voice that made me uneasy."

"I didn't want to act like this when you got here," she said, fighting for control. "I want us to have a n-normal evening."

"Okay. I'm not sure what normal looks like, but I'm willing to give it a try."

She sniffed and then reached for a tissue to blow her nose. "Then let's sit down and eat some pizza before it gets cold. Why don't you get our soft drinks from the fridge?" Isabelle had only a short while to pull herself together. When he returned with two Cokes and the ice bucket, she was sitting on the couch with the pizza, plates, cups, and napkins on the coffee table.

"I gotta admit it smells good." Nate settled at the other end and filled their glasses with ice and Coke.

"I didn't realize how hungry I was." Isabelle separated slices with a spatula and placed two on each plate. Handing one to him, she began to devour her piece of pizza.

Nate watched for a moment and then duplicated her actions down to wiping his mouth after the second slice. "Okay, we've eaten. Now suppose you tell me what happened today that has you spooked?"

Isabelle swallowed her last mouthful. "I'm not much of an actress, am I?" She gazed into his worried but sympathetic face.

"You already have a career, so start talking."

She recounted the incident with her car at work, the police response, and then seeing Tony's vehicle on her street. "The same officers responded, and we had talked about the TPO earlier at my office. They caught him at the other end of the complex, but he produced a page of condo listings from a different real estate agent. He said nothing in my restraining order prevents him from moving to the Glades."

Nate leaned his head back. "Markham has this whole thing figured out. My guess is you aren't the first person he's stalked."

"That doesn't give me much comfort. What can we do, Nate?" She threw her balled napkin down on her plate. "The police said they are powerless to act without proof he's in violation of the judge's order."

"Proof may be hard to get." The corners of Nate's mouth pulled down. "I'll look into Markham's history to see if Nicki missed something. Maybe I can find something to show a pattern of stalking. In the meantime don't let him get you down. Most stalkers want to intimidate, not harm their victims. They derive pleasure from seeing you squirm, so don't let him win."

"How exactly do I accomplish this?" Isabelle tightened the afghan around her shoulders.

"You start by eating another piece of pizza. Then we'll open two more Cokes, and I'll tell you what I learned from a couple of sax players. One of them wasn't a big fan of your brother's." Nate waited a few seconds before he added, "Then we can watch a movie and maybe get to know each other."

She felt her face turn warm. "I'd like to get better acquainted. As for the rest, I'll give it a shot."

He offered a lopsided grin. "That's good enough for me."

"I have a DVD of last year's best movie, but it's more than three hours long. How much time do you have?"

"You have plenty of food, a comfortable couch, and that afghan looks warm. I'll call Nicki and tell her where I am. My time is my own, Isabelle, and tonight there's nowhere else I would rather be."

Isabelle glanced away as her emotions bubbled to the surface. "Thanks, Nate. I'm grateful. What will we do if Tony comes back?"

"Let's see…we could call the police. But they've already done their duty twice today. So why don't I drag him from his car and beat the stuffing out of him?"

"That doesn't sound very professional…or very Christian."

"No, it doesn't, but it does sound infinitely satisfying."

They both laughed. Then while Nate served up two more slices of pizza, she went in search of a movie for later. There was no more talk of Markham, or beatings, or the Germantown police. Isabelle settled back as Nate described his visit to a famous blues club. It hurt knowing that Jimmy Watts had hated Danny for no other reason than he was generous and tried to help people.

But it was lovely listening to Nate—a man trying so hard to

find her brother's killer. Simply being in the company of someone willing to take on Tony Markham made her feel that anything was possible.

~

Nate awoke with a crick in his neck and a stiff back. But the scent of bacon wafting from the kitchen, along with the realization of where he was, relieved plenty of discomfort.

"Good morning," he called. "And what a fine day it is. Bathroom down the hall?"

Isabelle peeked around the corner, her dark hair loose and flowing down her back. "Last door on the left. I set out towels, a new toothbrush, and a shaving kit Danny left here. Breakfast will be ready in ten minutes." Her head disappeared back into the kitchen.

Nate lumbered to his feet and worked out the kinks in his spine. On his way down the hall, he couldn't help but glance into the other rooms. Most men probably weren't curious about a woman's tastes in furniture, yet he wanted to know everything about Isabelle. Last night he found out she cried during Hallmark commercials, loved buttered popcorn, and still looked gorgeous at eleven o'clock.

The first room on the left had to be a guest room. Half a dozen pillows were arranged on the bed, a comfortable chair sat by the window, and there wasn't an ounce of clutter. When he looked into Isabelle's room on the right, he felt a frisson of shame, as though he was no different than Tony Markham. But his mind had already registered the details: wall-mounted flat screen TV, bright area rugs, and dark wooden shutters instead of drapes. She had a stuffed bear on her blanket chest and enough jars and bottles on her vanity table for a movie diva.

Inside her sunny bathroom, Nate washed his face and hands,

shaved, and brushed his teeth, but he avoided inventorying her medicine cabinet and linen closet. He had never snooped like this in his life except while on a case, but suddenly he wanted to know everything about her.

"You're a perfect hostess," he said after joining her in the kitchen. "Thanks for the hospitality."

She turned to face him. "You can't be serious. I'm in your debt, not the other way around. I haven't slept so soundly since this ordeal started. Something about a man with a gun gives a person a sense of security." With a deft hand, Isabelle flipped pancakes on the griddle and pushed bread down in the toaster. "Not that I would want you to shoot Markham. I prefer that he just go away and forget about me."

Nate settled into a kitchen chair. "The offer of stuffing removal is still on the table."

She smiled on her way over to him. "Coffee? It's regular, but I can make instant decaf."

He held up his mug. "Fully caffeinated, please, and keep it coming. What time do you have to be at work?"

"Not until ten, so we have plenty of time. I'm manning the office today." She flipped pancakes onto a platter next to the toast and a pile of bacon and carried it to the table.

"That is a lot of food, but I doubt we'll need two hours to eat." He speared two pancakes along with several strips of bacon.

"True, but I want you to tell me everything that's happened since high school. And which do you prefer—dogs or cats, the Saints or the Titans, paper or plastic? How did you like Mississippi State?" Her voice softened. "Any ex-wives in your past? What about kids?"

"I will be happy to reveal my secrets as long as you're willing to do the same." Nate stirred sugar into his coffee far longer than necessary.

Isabelle studied him over her mug. "Absolutely. I'll even go first. I went to college at Vanderbilt and got married right after graduation. We stayed in Nashville for four years while my husband went to law school and I worked. Nashville is a great town with plenty to do. Unfortunately, I haven't done much with my business management major because you don't need a degree to sell houses." When she paused to refill her mug, she seemed reluctant to continue.

"We don't have to stir up bad memories if you don't want to. You have enough annoyances to contend with."

"I want you to know everything, Nate. Besides, any bitterness I once had is long gone. Craig called a couple days ago to say he was getting married. After the initial shock, I was happy for him."

"How long did your marriage last?" Nate took another strip of bacon.

"We were married for four years and have been divorced for four. No kids. We decided to wait on them until he passed the bar." She nibbled a piece of toast. "I hate the idea of divorce, but sometimes it's unavoidable. I know it was in our case."

"What brought you to Memphis if you were fond of Nashville?" At the risk of being nosy, Nate loved hearing the details of her past.

"Danny. Right around the time my marriage disintegrated, my brother decided to leave Natchez and move to the blues capital of the world. He loved playing his sax. He was never a fan of the bar scene, but he would put up with almost any environment to play the blues. Sometimes he got hired to play at country clubs or weddings, or one of the festivals such as the International Blues Challenge or the Delta Jubilee in Clarksdale. That was a thrill for him." Her voice faltered, betraying her grief.

But Nate didn't interrupt. She needed to talk to heal.

"Our parents were both gone by then. Other than a few aunts, uncles, and cousins in Mississippi, Danny and I had only each other. So I decided to move to the area and found a broker in Germantown who happened to be hiring." She met his gaze with a wry grin. "Danny and I shared an apartment for a while, but as much as I loved my brother I couldn't live with him. He played his sax while I tried to sleep, and he slept at odd hours. He was allergic to Mr. Chester, and he wasn't the tidiest man on earth."

Nate glanced left and right. "You do run a tight ship, Miss Andre."

"What did our grannies used to say? 'A place for everything and everything in its place.'" As they both laughed, her grief seemed to recede.

"So that's when Danny moved to the city?" Nate noticed his self-consciousness had receded as well.

"Yes. He had a steady stream of roommates who couldn't pay their half of the bills. But from what I learned from you and Nicki, I really didn't know my brother during the last few years. I judged him to be immature or irresponsible, or that he had gone over to the dark side. I couldn't have been more wrong." Tears filled her eyes. "Now I find out he'd volunteered at a halfway house to help give ex-addicts a fresh start."

Nate considered how much to tell her and opted for full disclosure. "One of Danny's fellow musicians told me he passed work on to guys with children to feed or rent past due."

Isabelle wiped her eyes with a paper napkin. "That doesn't surprise me. Danny had a heart of gold when we were growing up. If all he had was a dollar, he would still give you fifty cents. All someone had to do was ask. Apparently, his heart glowed even brighter after moving to Memphis." Her face turned wistful. "Someday I hope to tell him how proud I was."

"He knew you loved him, Isabelle."

"Yes, he did. And that helps me deal with a bagful of regrets."

She poured syrup over her cold pancakes and began to eat. "Now it's your turn. Should I repeat my list of questions?"

"Nope. My mind is like a steel trap. I prefer paper over plastic, but the best are cloth shopping bags. I root for the Saints, but I prefer college football to the pros. And because Chester is watching me from the doorway, I pick cats over dogs."

"Smart choice. Chester can turn vicious if given proper incentive."

"I loved attending Mississippi State, but unfortunately I took football more seriously than my studies. My degree was in sports management, but I also took classes in criminal justice and law enforcement. I planned to start as a cop and work my way up to commissioner of police."

She ate another piece of pancake. "And your personal status?"

"Never married, therefore no children. Never even got close to the altar. My mom thinks I should hurry because I'm past my prime."

"From what I've seen, Mr. Price, I beg to differ with your mother. I feel very safe with you, and I'm glad we've become friends."

He pushed away his plate but didn't take his focus off the cow-shaped cream pitcher. "Since we're laying our cards on the table, I want to make sure I'm clear about something. If friendship is all you want, I can live with that. But I don't feel toward you what I feel with my other friends." Nate forced himself to look her in the eye. "Would you like to go out with me, Isabelle? I know you just lost your brother, and this Markham business has you—"

"Yes, I would," she interrupted. "Except right now I should pop into the shower and get ready for work."

"Work sounds good, because I'll need at least eight hours to get my composure back." Nate ran a finger along the inside his collar. "I seem to have broken out in a sweat."

TWENTY-ONE

When her phone rang for the third time that morning, Nicki was tempted to let it go to voice mail. She'd already spoken with Hunter, who was eager to fly up that evening and spend the weekend with her. And she was just as excited to see him. A week was too long for an engaged couple to be separated.

The second phone call from Nate arrived on the heels of the first. Her cousin apologized for letting her spend another afternoon and evening alone watching TV in her suite. Then he summarized Izzy's latest terror at the hands of Tony Markham and his night spent on her couch waiting for the lunatic to return. So far that morning there had been no lunatic sightings, but Izzy had apparently cooked him one fine breakfast.

Nicki was good at reading between the lines or, in this case, gaps between Nate's sentences. Izzy and Nate seemed to be getting along better, and for that she was grateful. Nate planned to follow Izzy to the office and watch surreptitiously to see if he could catch Markham in the act. Apparently, that's what it would take to put him behind bars. His one request for her was to find out what she could about Jimmy Watts.

So when the phone rang as she was about to step into the multi-jet shower, Nicki hesitated. Fortunately, her intuition kicked in and she picked up. "Nicki Price."

"Miss Price?" A scratchy voice sounded a thousand miles away. "I was informed yesterday that you wished to speak to me."

Mamaw? Mrs. Galen? Her old high school teacher who still kept in touch? Several names of elderly women came to mind, yet none sounded quite right. "Um…yes, ma'am. Who is this?"

"Mrs. Violet Fitzhugh. I received a call from the Carlton Hotel that a young woman wished to speak with me."

The phone nearly slipped from Nicki's fingers. Scrambling, she jammed the phone to her ear and shrugged into her bathrobe. "Yes, ma'am. I do. I just didn't think you'd call back…so fast." She clenched her teeth to stop rambling.

"Why wouldn't I? Mr. Prescott assured me you were a lovely young lady."

"That was kind of him. What I'm trying to do is locate folks who participated in the annual scavenger hunts at the Carlton."

"Who on earth would be interested in them after all these years?"

"Mr. Henry Prescott, a retired bellman. He's the grandfather of the current concierge. Henry and I are working on this project together."

Several seconds passed before she asked, "Henry is still alive?"

"He sure is, and he'll be happy to hear you are too." Nicki uttered the words before she could stop herself. "Sorry. That didn't come out right."

But the woman only chuckled. "I'm amazed every morning when the good Lord allows me another day. I'll be ninety-seven soon. Whoever thought I would live this long?"

"Is your husband still…with you?"

"Oh, no. Reginald passed years ago, and I've outlived two of my three children. That's very difficult for a mother."

"I can't even imagine." Nicki's mind raced to devise a reason to visit instead of chatting on the phone."

Mrs. Fitzhugh solved the conundrum for her. "Would you like to come to my home, Miss Price? I don't get many visitors, but I would prefer to meet the person I'm sharing my secrets with." Her laughter sounded like tinkling wind chimes.

Nicki did a little jig. "I would love to."

"Why don't you come for tea? I live in Tipton County near the town of Gilt Edge. Do you have pen and paper for my address?"

"Yes, ma'am." Nicki flew into the bedroom to jot down the street name and number along with the town. "But isn't teatime in the late afternoon? I might hyperventilate by then. Could I possibly come sooner?"

"Mr. Prescott warned that you were persistent. Delightful but persistent. Very well, come have lunch on the terrace. The weather is supposed to be lovely."

"Oh, no. I couldn't trouble you to cook for me and then fuss with dishes afterward. Why don't I pick up sub sandwiches or a bucket of chicken?"

"I don't eat either sub sandwiches or fried chicken, my dear, but have no fear. My cook will prepare our luncheon and my maid will clean up. I'll expect you at eleven, Miss Price." Mrs. Fitzhugh hung up, preventing further discussion.

Glancing at her watch, Nicki knew she should spend some time doing what Nate needed her for. The scavenger hunt shouldn't distract her from their case. Twenty minutes later Nicki stepped under the shower stream barely able to breathe. Another living scavenger hunt participant, and this one seemed to be in complete possession of her faculties.

After changing outfits three times, Nicki left the hotel in a Sunday dress with sheer stockings and sensible pumps, her hair in a long, single braid down her back. The drive north into the Tennessee countryside was stunning. At times industry encroached on the mighty Mississippi, destroying the expectation of scenery created by nineteenth-century novels. In other areas stately, columned mansions rose high on bluffs above the delta farmland—jewels unto themselves that had withstood floods and the War Between the States.

Violet Fitzhugh resided in one of those mansions overlooking the river. After she had mentioned her cook and a maid, Nicki wasn't surprised. What did surprise her was an armed guard at the gate. The guard requested her ID, which he ran through a database. After passing security clearance, Nicki drove up a half-mile driveway that was flanked on both sides by ancient live oaks.

A butler opened the front door before Nicki was able to knock. "Miss Price?" he asked. "Mrs. Fitzhugh is waiting for you on the terrace."

Nicki fell in step behind him. Despite having dined several times in Hunter's ancestral home in New Orleans' Garden District, the trappings of the ultrarich still astonished her.

The stroll through the house seemed almost as long as the driveway. Then the butler opened French doors onto a flagstone terrace straight from the movies. Potted plants. Tiny lights strung through the trees, which had been landscaped around instead of cut down. Comfortable chaises, several wrought iron dining tables, and, of course, a lily pond with a gushing fountain.

A tiny woman wearing a peach-colored dress and a string of pearls sat in a wheelchair next to the pond. "Miss Price," she murmured and extended a hand no bigger than a child's.

At five feet eight, Nicki seemed twice the woman's size. She often wondered if people truly shrank as they aged or if those born before a certain generation were genetically smaller. *Will I end up to be a petite five four before I die?*

Nicki crossed the terrace and gently clasped the woman's delicate fingers. "Mrs. Fitzhugh, I can't thank you enough for inviting me to your magnificent home."

The woman cocked her head to one side. "It *is* a pretty house. I often take my grandfather's legacy for granted. Please have a seat. Tea, lemonade, coffee?" She gestured toward a cart being wheeled in by a maid.

"Tea, please."

After frosty glasses of sweetened iced tea were set before them, Mrs. Fitzhugh leaned in her direction. "Why don't you get started with your questions while they serve? I hope you like chicken salad."

"I love it." Nicki took a sip of tea before pulling out her notebook. "I understand you won the scavenger hunt in fifty-eight and therefore would have planned the following year's event."

"Ah, we certainly did! What fun we had during those getaways." Years seemed to slip away as she spoke. "Rubies were the prize that year—earrings for me and a ruby-studded money clip for Reginald. Money clips…who even uses those things anymore?"

"Maybe in Las Vegas," offered Nicki, amazed how animated the woman had become.

"Perhaps." She tucked her silver hair behind her ears, revealing stunning ruby earrings on her lobes. "I usually keep these locked in the safe because I have little use for them anymore. But I wore them for you, Miss Price. I hope you won't tell the etiquette mavens about my faux pas. You're never supposed to wear jewels before six."

"You have my word." Nicki was mesmerized by their sparkle. "I never appreciated rubies before today."

Mrs. Fitzhugh paused as a plate of chicken salad on a croissant with fresh fruit was placed before her. "Yes, these are no ordinary rubies. The couple who purchased them—the Bennetts—must have searched high and low for such quality." She leaned toward Nicki and winked. "The Bennetts were always competing with the Smithfields."

"I'm sorry to tell you that Mr. and Mrs. Bennett have passed on." Nicki fluffed out her napkin.

"I know, dear. I attended their funerals." She patted Nicki's hand. "When you've lived as long as I have, you outlast practically everyone."

"Well, you haven't outlived Henry, and he would love to see you. Unfortunately, he's in an assistant living center."

She produced a sad smile. "I would like to visit Henry because I remember the bellman fondly, but alas." She tapped the arms of her wheelchair. "I rarely leave the house anymore."

Nicki took a bite of her sandwich, her mind whirring a mile a minute. Then she noticed Mrs. Fitzhugh cutting her food with a knife and fork. "Excuse me, ma'am. I'm lacking in social graces." She set down the sandwich.

"Nonsense. Picking up a croissant is perfectly acceptable. I would do it too if not for my dentures."

Nicki resumed her interview. "Because you won the rubies in fifty-eight, you would have planned the fifty-nine scavenger hunt. Do you remember the prizes you purchased?"

"Of course. They were gold watches—Rolexes, to be exact. The Bennetts weren't the only ones in competition with the Smithfields."

Rolexes—for a getaway weekend game with your friends? Nicki reached for her iced tea.

"I can anticipate your next question, Miss Price. It was the Smithfields who found the watches on the very first night, but I can't say we hid them very well. They were on the newel posts of the grand staircase. After Reginald read the clue, it turned into a footrace in tuxedoes and high heels." She chuckled at the memory. "The Smithfields, who came up with the scavenger hunt idea, were first to get to the stairs. Once they had their prizes in hand, they announced we would be looking for diamonds again next year. Unfortunately, they were killed during the scavenger hunt in 1960. After that we abandoned the silly game."

"I know it's been many years, but I'm sorry for your loss."

"You *are* a very sweet girl, just like Robert said."

"May I ask where you found the rubies?" Nicki still couldn't take her eyes off the woman's earlobes.

"Ah, that was no walk in the park. On the final night of clues, Reginald and I discovered them hidden in the music salon. Unfortunately, that room was later turned into the first floor deli." Her nose twitched with distaste.

"I'll never buy snacks there again."

"I don't know what else I can tell you other than I've enjoyed your visit. Please give my regards to the best bellman the Carlton has ever had."

"Thank you. I can't tell you how helpful you have been. Would you mind if I took a couple of photos of you to show Henry? And maybe your maid can take one of us together?"

"I wouldn't mind at all." She smiled graciously.

While the two women finished lunch, one starting a new life and one in her waning years, Mrs. Fitzhugh told Nicki what she remembered about the final hunt. And Nicki told her about Hunter, their upcoming wedding in a small country church, and the extravagant reception aboard her mother-in-law's yacht. "I can assure you," she said, "I'll be glad when the entire hullaballoo is over and I'm fixing mac-and-cheese for my new husband."

Mrs. Fitzhugh laughed. "That's pretty much how I felt about my wedding day. But try to enjoy yourself. If you're a fortunate woman, this marriage will last your entire lifetime."

Nicki kissed Violet Fitzhugh's powdered cheek when she left, a stranger no longer. On the way home, she pondered not only her new clues, but the lesson learned from a woman who defined class and charm…qualities that had nothing to do with wealth.

～2

"Hi, Nate. What's up?"

Nate blew exasperation out through his teeth. "I'll tell you what's up. If you hadn't picked up this time, I was calling the cops to report a missing person. Where are you?"

"Simmer down. As usual, you're overreacting. I talked to you this morning while you were at Izzy's. Hey, should I head there now to relieve you as her bodyguard?"

"You should not. She'll be at the office all day and then has an open house scheduled. I have it covered. And stop trying to change the subject. Why didn't you answer your phone?"

"Because it would have been rude to answer during my lovely luncheon." She put special emphasis on the final word.

"A Quarter Pounder and fries doesn't qualify as a *luncheon*." Nate turned onto the expressway leading back to Memphis.

"True, but I've been dining alfresco on the terrace of Mrs. Reginald Fitzhugh of Tipton County near Gilt Edge." Nicki deepened her accent for the sake of drama. "Isn't that the perfect town for a rich lady to live in?"

Nate bit back an impolite word. "Either tell me what's going on or I'll reach through the phone and strangle you. I told Hunter I would keep an eye on you, and you drive up to Tipton County without telling me?"

"You tell Mr. Hunter Galen that leg irons have been outlawed in the civilized world. I'm still free to move about the state." Nicki sounded more annoyed than usual.

"I'll tell him. In the meantime, are you on your way back to the Carlton?"

"I am. Aren't you curious as to how I got an invitation to lunch with the charming Mrs. Fitzhugh?"

"Yes, I would love to hear the explanation." He used such a sweet tone that Nicki launched into a fifteen-minute summation involving hotel registers, rubies, Rolex watches, music rooms, a society matriarch who had patronized the Carlton for more than sixty years, and a terrace overlooking the Mississippi. Nate's mind was swimming with more details than catfish on the river bottom. "Can't you ever tell a story in less than a thousand words? I'm already back downtown."

"Nope. It can't be done, and I'm still thirty minutes away. Should I meet you somewhere? Where are you going?"

"I'm headed to the Blues City Club to talk to Gus the soundman. He had last night off, but he should be on duty tonight. If I can get him to corroborate the roommate's story, then I can get Detective Marino to release Tito. The more I talk to musicians, the more convinced I am that he was telling the truth. Then I'll point Marino in the direction of Jimmy Watts. That sax player hated Danny, and for no other reason than Danny had a big heart."

"Hold on a minute, Nate. While you were eating breakfast in Germantown, I checked up on Jimmy Watts. He may be creepy, but he has an alibi for the night Danny was killed."

Nate pulled to the curb to hear what his cousin had to say. "I thought you were busy with the mystery of the missing jewels all morning." He imbued the words with unnecessary sarcasm.

But Nicki took no notice. "How long does it take to dig into public records if you know where to look? Jimmy Watts was in county lockup for forty-eight hours. Apparently, no one bailed Mr. Personality out after police arrested him for disorderly conduct and resisting arrest. My, my. That young man has a bad temper. However, that barroom fistfight gets him off the hook for murder."

"Wow. Thanks for checking this out before I sent Marino down the wrong path. Our favorite detective won't tolerate too many missteps from a PI, even from a fellow Bulldog."

"You're welcome. I'm headed to the hotel to call Hunter. I can't wait to tell him what I discovered. Keep me in the loop about Gus Crane. Oh, I almost forgot. In case Gus doesn't choose to cooperate, I dug up a tasty tidbit on him too. A warrant has been issued for his arrest in Texas. The man has eight hundred fifty dollars' worth of unpaid parking tickets in Houston. Doesn't exactly qualify him for the FBI's most wanted list, but he probably doesn't want local law enforcement to know."

"Thanks, Nicki. And you're doing a great job tracking down Henry's old pals. He'll be thrilled one of the participants is still alive."

"Two of them," she corrected. "Maybe Henry and Mrs. Fitzhugh can trigger Mr. Koehler's memory. See ya later."

Nate ended the call and then pulled back out onto the street. Not long later, he was turning into the parking lot of the club. After bribing both a bouncer and a cocktail waitress, he was pointed toward the sound room behind and above the stage. A huge picture window with sliding panels overlooked the floor below. As expected, Gus had just arrived for work, thermos and lunch cooler in hand.

"Mr. Crane?" Nate asked as he stepped into the cluttered room.

"I'm Gus Crane. What can I do for you?"

"Name's Nate Price. I recently moved here from New Orleans." He offered a tourist-friendly smile. "They told me downstairs you might be able to help me."

Gus's suspicion meter lowered one notch. "I will if I can. What do you need?" He pointed at a folding chair.

Nate sat and crossed his legs. "Thanks. I'm marrying a Memphis gal in a few months. We have a reception planned on one of those river barges, but the band is short a sax player. I don't know if you heard, but Danny Andre died. He was supposed to play at our wedding. How can a band play the blues without a proper set of horns?"

"A sax isn't a horn. It's actually a woodwind. What's the name of the band you hired? I might be able to recommend someone."

"I stand corrected." Nate placed a hand over his heart. "But you've never heard of these guys. They're friends of mine from college who still get together occasionally. They're not bad, really. Danny said he would round out the sound. I can't believe he's gone."

Gus's interest in the upcoming wedding flagged. "Look, I gotta check equipment for tonight's show."

"The gig pays four hundred per man for five hours of music, including breaks. The bride's family is pulling out the stops for our wedding. You sure you don't know someone who could use the work?"

Gus returned to the conversation. "I might know a musician or two."

"I want somebody good, not just someone twiddling their thumbs. Tell me honestly, Gus, who was as good as Danny? I loved hearing him play his sax." The words internally made him sad. He would regret never hearing Danny to his dying day.

The soundman stroked his scraggly goatee. "I can think of a couple guys, but they don't always get along with amateurs, if you catch my drift. I guess your best shot would be Sam Jessup. He lives in an apartment above the Laundromat on Cooper near Central. Don't know if he's available. Maybe he found a permanent gig by now." Crane copied down a phone number off a bulletin board.

"Did you like Danny Andre?" Nate asked, tucking the slip of paper into his pocket.

The question caught Gus by surprise. "I got along with him well enough, not that we had much interaction."

"I'm sure you respected him enough to want his killer locked up behind bars."

Gus's gaze narrowed. "Why wouldn't I want a killer locked up? What's this about?"

Nate rose to his full six feet three inches. "This is about you lying about Tito Sullivan. He got locked in your sound room overnight, but you wouldn't corroborate his alibi. I don't think he killed Danny, but thanks to you the wrong man is in jail."

"What do I care? You'd better get out of here before I call security. You don't need to hire a sax player. You've just been playing me." His face took on a sheen of perspiration.

"Actually, I just don't like the wrong man going to jail."

"What do you care about Sullivan? He's a worthless bum."

"He's a human being who cleaned up his act. And you're going to call the detective on the case and tell him the truth about where Sullivan was that night."

"And if I don't?"

"I would hate to spread gossip about Texas arrest warrants, but I want the real killer behind bars."

"Parking tickets," he snarled. "You'd get me fired over that?"

"That's not my desire, Mr. Crane. Call Detective Marino. He'll just think you're doing your civic duty after your memory kicked in. Then nobody will have to hear about the money you owe the city of Houston."

"Yeah, and if management finds out I let Tito in without paying a cover, I'll get fired over that."

"Nobody will hear it from me or the detective. We just want Danny's killer caught."

Gus plucked the card from Nate's fingers. "I'll call tomorrow. Now get out of here before I change my mind."

Nate left the Blues City Club and sauntered down Beale Street whistling.

Two birds…one stone. Let's just hope both Gus Crane and Sam Jessup live up to expectations.

TWENTY-TWO

As Nicki neared the city limits of Memphis, she saw no reason to return to the hotel if Nate was busy tracking down leads. She was glad she straightened him out about Jimmy Watts, but now she had her own new lead to contend with.

Besides serving a great lunch, Mrs. Fitzhugh brought her full circle regarding the scavenger hunt participants. The whole game began and ended with Mr. and Mrs. Smithfield. They had planned the first hunt and the final one...on the weekend which turned out to be their last on earth. Mrs. Fitzhugh told her they had been killed on Saturday. The guests were given the first clue during dinner on Friday and then took off in different directions to search. No one had found the diamonds by the time everyone went to bed. Paul and Agnes Smithfield, however, had left the hotel earlier in the evening to attend a concert. On their way back, a drunk driver ran a red light and killed all three of the taxi's occupants. None of the guests knew what had happened until the next day.

Nicki's heartrate quickened as a mental picture took shape. Mr. and Mrs. Smithfield hid the jewels on Thursday night. On Friday the first clue was presented to contestants, but it didn't lead to an early discovery. Then the couple was killed. According to Mrs. Fitzhugh, most of the participants hung around the hotel until lunchtime, uncertain what to do. Once the Smithfields' children arrived to collect their belongings, one by one the friends went home, never to congregate for the same reason again.

When Mrs. Fitzhugh accompanied Nicki to the front door in her wheelchair, Nicki had asked if she thought the diamonds might still be where the Smithfields had hidden them.

"Don't be ridiculous, dear girl. I'm sure they were discovered by a clever handyman or a lucky maid long ago."

Maybe. Maybe not.

Nicki drove straight to the offices of the *Commercial Appeal.* This time when the young man accompanied her to the basement archives, he allowed her to scan the old news stories alone. Although he remained in the general vicinity, he no longer hovered over her shoulder.

She easily found the first story about the deaths of Paul and Agnes Smithfield in December 1960. The accident took place shortly after one a.m. at the corner of Beale Street and Riverside Drive. Unfortunately, thieves reportedly stole some of their jewelry before the ambulance and police arrived. Witnessess at the Carlton reported the couple had been wearing watches and rings that evening that weren't found at the scene.

Most likely the gold Rolexes they'd won the previous year, Nicki thought. Their friends would remember those watches, especially the Fitzhughs. Nicki shuddered. What kind of people stole jewelry off dead bodies? Although it had been emptied of cash, Mr. Smithfield's wallet still contained identification and a valet parking ticket for the hotel. According to the news article, the taxi driver had also been killed, but the other driver walked away with only minor injuries.

Nicki hoped the police had checked his pockets before they arrested him for vehicular homicide. The remaining report contained a lengthy description of who the Smithfields were and their enormous contributions to Memphis charities. They seemed to have been patrons of many creative endeavors and sat on the board of multiple foundations. Nicki learned this not from the initial news story, but from the many that followed during the aftermath and subsequent funeral. The Smithfields' entourage rivaled that of a foreign head of state. Nicki studied photos taken at the funeral with her magnifying glass, recognizing not only Henry, Violet Fitzhugh, and Blake and Bunny Koehler, but the likenesses of the Whitleys and Bennetts as well. Nicki experienced a sense of loss for a couple she had never met. The Smithfields had touched many lives with their generosity, and they been loved and respected by their peers.

After paying for some photocopies, she climbed back into her car just as her phone rang. She looked at the screen. "Hello, Mrs. Fitzhugh. I didn't think I would hear from you so soon."

"I've thought of little else other than that last scavenger hunt since you left. See what you started? You asked me about the clue we received at dinner that night."

"Yes, ma'am. You said you couldn't remember."

"You know how memories go. Not thirty minutes after you left it popped into my head. Then it took some more time to find that piece of paper with your phone number. Well, I won't drag out the suspense. The clue was this, more or less: 'Some places soar to great heights, some command a view of the world, some soothe the soul with tranquil waters, while others warm both body and soul. This location does all this and more.'"

"What do you think that meant?"

"Most people, including my Reginald, insisted it meant the rooftop patio and garden. It was the highest part of the hotel, and it had a great view of the city. The 'tranquil waters' could be the river, and certainly the sun heats the rooftop year round. But my friends and I scoured every inch of that rooftop to no avail, even with flashlights after dark."

"What do *you* think the clue meant, Mrs. Fitzhugh?"

"I thought it meant the grand lobby. It's two and half stories high, it has great views from the balcony mezzanine and warmth from the huge fireplace. And some guests say the sound of the fountain calms them. But there're just too many nooks and crannies to search the entire lobby. I tried but came up empty. Good luck, Miss Price, and keep me posted."

Nicki couldn't get back to the Carlton fast enough. She parked the Lincoln in the garage and bolted through the back door. Because it was late on a Friday afternoon, tons of people were arriving to start their own getaway weekend. Both levels of the grand lobby were beehives of activity, but that wouldn't deter a trained investigator from Mississippi. As surreptitiously as possible, she checked under huge potted ferns, looked behind framed prints of the famous fish, and ran her fingers under the edge of the balustrade around the entire balcony. Just as she lifted a heavy oil painting off the wall, two security guards appeared over her shoulder.

"What on earth are you doing, Miss Price?" To her good fortune, Robert Prescott accompanied the armed guards.

"Hi, Mr. Prescott. You won't believe who I met today out in Tipton County. She was so helpful and encouraging." Nicki replaced the painting on its hooks and clasped her hands behind her back.

"I know exactly whom you talked to." The concierge's brows knit together. To the security guards he said, "This woman is a guest here. I will vouch for her."

The guards gave Nicki another once-over, shook their heads, and left.

"Follow me, young lady, and don't touch *anything* along the way."

"I'm convinced the jewels hidden by the Smithfields are still here someplace, but I probably should have waited for a less busy time to look," Nicki murmured as they stepped into an empty meeting room.

"Oh, you noticed we're at full capacity this weekend? Your fiancé booked the last suite. And everyone seems to have arrived at the same time."

"I'm sorry, Mr. Prescott. I won't keep you from your duties. Hunter and I will make this up to you before we leave."

His expression softened with her apology. "I'm charmed by your enthusiasm for the Carlton, but I cannot have you ransacking the place—"

"Understood. I'll be a model of decorum while I'm here."

"At least try to contain yourself until your fiancé arrives. Then you're someone else's responsibility." Robert opened the door for her but blocked her path. "Truly, Miss Price. It's been sixty years, and the hotel has undergone extensive renovations, not to mention normal cleaning, polishing, and maintenance. It's inconceivable that something valuable wouldn't have been found by now."

"Of course you're right. As you say, I'm just overly enthusiastic." She smiled sweetly at him.

He wasn't fooled. "Remember, guards patrol the premises twenty-four hours a day. Public areas are also monitored with security cameras. It isn't like when my grandfather worked here and everyone went to bed at a decent hour."

"I understand, sir. Again, I'm sorry I caused you trouble."

After he let her go, Nicki practically skipped to the elevator. The mention of Hunter's name reminded her she needed a quick shower and fresh outfit. She couldn't wait to see him and tell him all about her plans for the hotel's oldest unsolved mystery.

⁓

When Nate left Gus at the club, he didn't waste time appreciating the sights and sounds of Beale Street as the area came to life. He hiked up Second Street back to the garage for his car and drove to the corner of Cooper and Central as fast as traffic and jaywalkers would allow. Only one apartment building sat on the corner, a ten-story edifice with a Laundromat on the first floor. Squeezing his car into the only spot at the curb, Nate entered the lobby and perused the eighty or ninety names printed next to the apartment numbers.

Today was his day for catching a break. Only one "Jessup" lived at the Winston Arms. Nate pressed the button for 432 and waited.

"Yeah, who's there?" A voice crackled through the archaic system.

"Nate Price. I'm here to speak with you about a job. Gus Crane supplied the recommendation." He used his most dignified tone.

After a few seconds, Jessup replied. "You're too late. I already lined up a gig."

"Why not hear me out, Mr. Jessup? You might want to change your mind when you hear what I'm offering."

A buzzer sounded, unlocking the door. Nate stepped through the doorway and scanned his surroundings. A long hallway led to back units, while a staircase led to the upper floors. The sole elevator displayed an out-of-order sign, the tape yellow with age.

Thank goodness the Jessups don't live on the tenth floor.

Nate climbed the steps to the fourth floor and knocked on 432 harder than necessary.

"Hold your horses! I'm coming." The door swung wide, and a man loomed large in front of him.

"Are you Sam Jessup?" asked Nate, breathlessly. "Nate Price. May I come in?"

The man opened the door wide. "Don't make no difference to me. I tried saving you the steps. Like I said, I already accepted a job, but you can talk while I pack." Sam headed down a dimly lit hallway.

Nate followed him through an austere apartment. "How long has the elevator been broken?"

When Sam entered a small bedroom, Nate stopped at the doorway. "That elevator's been busted the entire time I've lived here. Two years, at least.

"And people climb nine or ten stories every day?" Nate's sense of justice couldn't comprehend the legality of such an inconvenience.

"Nah. If you live on the fifth floor or above, you can use the freight elevator through the back alley." Sam resumed what had apparently been interrupted by the buzzer. Clothes were stacked in neat piles on the bed, along with shoes and toiletries. A battered instrument case, doubtlessly containing his saxophone, sat close to the door.

Nate slipped a hand under his jacket to his weapon. "I see you're packing. You in a big hurry to leave?"

Sam pulled a duffel bag and a suitcase from the closet and began stuffing the duffel with clothes. "Like I said, I got offered work out of town. Tell me about the gig you have in mind."

Nate leaned his shoulder against the jamb. "I'm getting married soon. Some of my musician friends will play for the reception, but I've come up short a sax player."

"*A wedding*? You're offering a one-night gig? Don't waste my time." He placed the rest of his belongings into the suitcase.

"That one night pays four hundred a man for five hours of blues. I'll even throw in a catered meal." Because he was making up the story, Nate embellished as he went along.

Sam glanced over at him. "That's good pay. If I didn't have to leave soon, I'd take you up on it. But I landed a permanent position at the Hyatt Regency in St. Louis. They need me there tomorrow. Tell Gus to line up choice number two for you." He zipped shut the duffel and hefted it to his shoulder. "I finally won't have to scramble around week after week to pay the bills."

"Actually, Mr. Jessup, *you* were choice number two. Danny Andre was number one." Nate opened his jacket to reveal his shoulder holster and nine millimeter. "I'm real upset that someone killed a friend of mine."

Jessup's gaze rotated between Nate's face and the gun. "You think *I* had something to do with Andre's murder?"

"You seem to be leaving town in a hurry."

"Like I told you, I got hired by the Hyatt. Their fancy restaurant wants a blues band—lead and bass guitars, drums, keyboard, sax, and trumpet. We gotta wear tuxedos five nights a week. Fortunately for me, they're providing those. You can check if you don't believe me."

"I plan to." Nate let his jacket fall back in place, covering his weapon. "Maybe you got the job because Danny was no longer around. Maybe *he* was the one they wanted."

Jessup dropped the bag on the floor. "You got this backwards, Price. Danny ran into an entertainment director from St. Louis. The guy said he already hired the other musicians, but he still needed a sax player. 'The old-time sound,' he called it. Danny set me up with the audition because he didn't want to leave Memphis. He said he needed to stay because of his sister. The guy liked me and offered me the job."

Nate studied Jessup's face. If he was lying, he was very good at it.

"Danny said he would bring his sister to St. Louis sometime to hear us play, but he would give us six months to figure out what we were doing first."

"That sounds like something he would say," Nate murmured.

"I'm sorry about your friend. Danny was an okay guy and not bad on the sax. Just not as good as me." Jessup picked up his suitcase, duffel bag, and instrument case. "The hotel guy who hired me was named Cramer. Give him a call, but please don't mess things up for me. This is the best work I've ever been offered."

Jessup stepped around Nate on his way to the front door. "Hey, if you see anything you can use, grab it. Since I'm taking the bus to St. Louis, this is all I can carry. The stuff might be other folks' discards, but most of it is still good. Once I'm gone, the other tenants will pick through it before the landlord rents out the place."

Nate gazed around at a hodgepodge of secondhand furnishings Sam had probably acquired in the same fashion. Not wishing to insult his generosity, Nate walked over to a large clay pot on an end table. "Is this some type of cactus?"

A grin filled Jessup's face. "It's a Christmas cactus. My ma brought me that when I moved in. She said a cactus is a good plant for a man since he'll usually forget to water it."

Nate clutched it in the crook of his arm. "Then it will be perfect for me. Thanks."

"Man, I hated to leave that behind, but how do you deal with a cactus on a bus?"

"I'll take good care of it."

"It never bloomed 'cause I forgot what my mom told me to do."

"I'll look it up online. Good luck in St. Louis, Sam."

"Good luck with the weddin', and I'm sorry about your friend." He disappeared into the hallway, leaving the door open behind him.

Nate walked down four flights of steps encumbered with a prickly plant. He hoped Isabelle would agree to plant-sit for a while, because carrying it aboard an airplane would be even trickier than onto a bus.

TWENTY-THREE

*I*sabelle left the office feeling more relaxed than she had in a long while. Nate couldn't prevent bad things from happening, and he certainly couldn't stay with her twenty-four hours a day, seven days a week, but just his friendship relieved much of her anxiety. He cared about her. And not just for her safety, like a bodyguard.

She had plenty to be happy about at work too. Considering the hours she had logged in at the office and her open house tonight, she could take tomorrow off. Real estate agents almost never had a free Saturday. Many potential buyers worked long hours during the week, and their only time to house hunt was on the weekends.

If Nate could spare some time from the investigation, maybe they could spend the day together. Unfortunately, cowardice had kept her from extending an invitation when she had the opportunity. She was rusty at dating, but with any luck she would get another chance tonight.

Isabelle arrived at the four-bedroom, three-bathroom colonial an hour early. This allowed time to make sure toys were put away and no damp towels littered the bathroom floor. The tidiest homes could get out of hand with people's busy lifestyles. Even kids had active calendars between sports, clubs, hobbies, and part-time jobs. She placed a bouquet of flowers in a vase on the kitchen counter, spread utility bills across the dining room table for monthly estimates, and opened the drapes to the waning sunshine. Then she turned on some lights so the house would appear warm and cheery. And the crowning touch to guarantee a sale? Isabelle rolled refrigerated cookie dough onto baking sheets she'd brought from home and cut out three dozen gingerbread men. Not only would visitors receive a sweet treat, but the cinnamon and sugar would scent the air.

With everything ready, Isabelle glanced at her watch. Ten minutes to spare. Ten minutes to daydream about Nate, something she'd been doing a lot of lately. What would her life have been like if she hadn't focused on marrying a lawyer? Had she only been concerned with potential earning power? Or with the prestige that accompanied certain vocations? Honestly, she couldn't remember why she'd set her sights on Craig, but she hadn't done either of them a favor.

Before she fell into hopeless melancholia that accomplished nothing, the first carload of customers pulled into the driveway. Out of the van tumbled three energetic youngsters. This would be the perfect home for a big family—spacious kitchen, fenced yard, expansion potential above the attached garage for a playroom…or another bedroom. The woman lumbering up the walkway was obviously expecting her fourth child soon.

"Welcome," greeted Isabelle as she opened the door. "Come in and have a look at what could be your new home."

So began one of the most productive open houses of her career. Potential buyers maintained a steady stream through the front door. Women opened closets, peeked in cupboards, and measured bedrooms with retractable measuring tapes. One diligent man even stuck his head inside the fireplace to assess the chimney.

Buyers who arrived with other brokers appeared eager to return to the office to draw up purchase offers.

Isabelle felt confident about selling the house even before the last gingerbread man was consumed.

Suddenly her cell phone rang, cutting short her praises of the local school system. "Isabelle Andre, Realty World."

"Miss Andre? This is Justine Thoreson from Jackson. Bob and I seem to be lost, and unfortunately we don't own a GPS. Can you help us find you?"

She glanced at her watch. "The open house has only another thirty minutes left. Perhaps we can reschedule a viewing for another time?"

"Please don't give up on us." The woman's voice sounded near tears. "We drove more than an hour to get here, and we have been driving around Germantown for another hour. We won't have another chance until next weekend."

The house will surely be sold by then, Isabelle thought. "All right. I'll wait for you. Tell me exactly where you are." Isabelle pulled up MapQuest on her laptop and supplied the grateful Thoresons with directions. Once she returned to the other attendees, it was another forty minutes before she shooed the last family out the door. Yet the Thoresons still hadn't shown up.

Isabelle packed her baking supplies into her tote bag, closed the bedroom closets, and locked all the doors. As she dimmed the living room lights, she noticed a sedan creeping down the street. With Tony Markham never far from her thoughts she froze, paralyzed in a strange house on a deserted street. A frisson of fear spiked up her spine as she watched the taillights turn the corner. A minute later the car returned from the opposite direction. It stopped at the curb directly in front of where she peeked through the curtains.

Pull yourself together and do your job. Isabelle flashed the porch light off and on to flag down the confused couple. However, it wasn't a lost pair of house hunters who responded to her signal.

The sedan turned into the driveway and screeched to a halt behind her Prius. Two uniformed policemen jumped from the vehicle with their weapons drawn. One ran up the front walk in a low crouch, while the other disappeared around the side of the garage. Isabelle flattened against the wall and dropped to the floor. Like an insect, she scuttled behind the hall tree, uncertain what to do.

"Germantown Police!" The cop shouted as he pounded on the door. "Open up."

Isabelle reached the front entrance on shaky legs, turned the lock, and shrank back. "Come in," she called. She lifted her hands into the air.

"Are you Isabelle Andre?" Stepping across the threshold, the officer glanced around the room, his weapon pointed at the floor. "I'm Jeff Anderson of the Germantown Police Department."

"Yes, and I have permission to be here. I'm a licensed real estate agent with identification in my bag." She gestured toward the hall table.

"Who else is in the house, Miss Andre?"

"No one. Everyone has left. Tonight was an open house, but I was just locking up now. The owners should be home soon."

"You can lower your hands, ma'am. We're here to protect you, not arrest you. We saw the porch light flash and thought it was a distress signal."

Isabelle dropped her hands to her side. "Did the owners of the house ask you to stop by?"

"No, we got a call from Nate Price. He requested we check on you as a professional courtesy. In light of the restraining order and your recent troubles, we were happy to comply."

"Everything's locked up tight out back," a voice barked through Anderson's radio.

"We're good here too. Call it in." To Isabelle, he said, "Would you like me to do a walk-through?" He crossed the foyer and craned his neck to look up the stairs.

"It's not necessary, Officer. I was ready to leave when I saw your car slow down. I thought you were expected late arrivals. One couple got lost on the way here."

Davis pulled back the drapes to check the street. "Any sign of Tony Markham tonight?"

"None whatsoever." She slung her purse over her shoulder and picked up her tote bag.

"Why don't I walk you to your car, ma'am?" Just as Anderson opened the front door, they saw the other cop, along with a frightened-looking man and woman.

"These folks say they are the Thoresons from Jackson," said the officer. "They said you were expecting them. Is that true, Miss Andre?"

Isabelle peered from one face to the other and nodded.

"I take it we're too late," said the wife in a tiny voice.

"Yes. Mrs. Thoreson, I'm afraid so." But Isabelle relented when she saw the disappointment in Mrs. Thoreson's face. "However, since you came all the way out here, I can give you a few minutes to take a quick look."

The grateful couple hastily went through the house, and then once Isabelle felt confident they were safely on their way back to Jackson, she headed home, exhausted but happy. Her joy stemmed from several potential buyers clamoring over her listing and from knowing Nate Price had been thinking about her. That made her even happier than a fat commission check.

She pulled into the lot behind her building and punched in

his number before her courage flagged. When he answered, she said, "Thanks for sending out the cavalry, Nate."

"You're welcome. Realtors at open houses could be sitting ducks if no one shows up."

"True, but tonight I was overrun with moms, dads, and rambunctious children. Markham would have been trampled by the throng."

"Good to hear, but I'll wait until you're inside and flash your balcony light. Give me the same signal you used for the Thoresons." He chuckled good-naturedly.

Isabelle froze halfway to her building. "Where are you?"

On the street one of the parked cars blinked its headlights.

"Goodness, Nate. You seem to be everywhere at once." She lifted her hand in a wave.

"I'm hoping your next restraining order won't be against me." His laugh didn't sound quite so self-assured.

"Not this month it won't be. Would you like to come in for a cup of tea?"

"You're probably worn out. We'll talk tomorrow. Good night, Isabelle."

"Wait, tomorrow…that reminds me. I don't have to work, so I thought we could spend the day together—see the sights, have a picnic, maybe float down the river on a raft like Huck Finn. And if you're short on time, at least let me buy you coffee and a donut."

"I'll clear my calendar. When should I pick you up?"

"Let's say ten o'clock. Wear sensible shoes and come hungry. And just so we're clear, tomorrow everything is my treat. I'm hanging up now so you can't put up any argument." Isabelle disconnected just as she entered her condo. After sliding the deadbolt in place, she ran to her balcony doors and flashed the light, hoping the gesture wouldn't draw another batch of Germantown's finest.

Nate signaled back and drove away. Isabelle waited until his car disappeared around the corner before she fed her cat and chose a frozen dinner to microwave. However, even if a million dollars was at stake, she couldn't have described what she ate or the shows she watched on TV. Her mind was already planning her date with Nate down to the smallest detail.

ᔫ

Nicki met Hunter the next morning for breakfast a mere ten minutes late. She had to make sure her outfit and hair looked perfect. With Nate practically working alone, Hunter had been begged her to come back to New Orleans. She missed him too, but she wasn't ready to leave, not when she was so close to solving the case of the missing Carlton diamonds. She chuckled at how ridiculous that sounded, even to her. Yet, until she ran out of leads, she planned to stick with it.

"Good morning, handsome man," she greeted, kissing him on the cheek before sitting across from him in the booth. "I hope you haven't been waiting long."

"It was worth it. You look beautiful. Why don't you wear your hair like that more often?"

"Too much trouble when I'm working. This coiffure took me twenty minutes with the blow dryer and curling iron. How did women manage in the previous century with rollers and bobby pins and hairnets?"

"Still dabbling in the fifties, I gather." Hunter peered over his menu. "I'm here to drag you kicking and screaming back into the current millennium."

Nicki picked up her menu as well, more to hide her expression than peruse the selections.

"What looks good to you, *O'lette*? I heard from a reliable source that the bananas Foster is worth every fat gram."

"You already talked to Mr. Prescott?"

"I did, and he supplied us with these." Hunter spread a bevy of brochures in the space between them. "We are seeing the sights today, missy. Prepare to wear your shoe leather paper thin."

A cheery waitress arrived at their table. "Coffee, Miss Price? And are we ready to order?" She turned her dazzling smile on Hunter.

"I believe we are." He laid down his menu. "I'll have the bananas Foster, an order of country ham, and wheat toast. How does that sound, dear heart?"

Nicki shook her head. "Nope. Coffee, tomato juice, oatmeal, and fruit. Thank you," she said to the waitress.

Once the woman left, she leaned across the table. "After what we ate for dinner last night? Do you really want me to weigh four hundred pounds by the wedding?"

Hunter laced his fingers over his flat stomach. "That was some fine barbecue, wasn't it? Anyway, a few more pounds just means more of you to love." He reached for her hand.

She slapped at his fingers. "That dress is already costing a fortune for tulle and silk. I intend to avoid expensive alterations by controlling myself."

"Suit yourself, but don't even think about stealing my whipped cream." He winked as he glanced through the pamphlets. "Why don't we hit the Civil Rights Museum today and Graceland tomorrow? I know you love history, and who doesn't love Elvis?"

Nicki sipped some coffee. "Both worthy attractions, I'm sure, but not today."

"How about the zoo? They have giant pandas." Hunter wiggled his eyebrows.

"Maybe tomorrow, but today let's pay a social call."

"Oh, no. Does this involve showing up on someone's doorstep

unannounced and asking nosy questions?" Hunter leaned back as the waitress delivered his toast and her bowl of fruit.

"Goodness, no, but as long as you're willing, I'd love to visit a delightful gentlemen who gets so lonely in his senior center." She opted for a pitiful expression.

"Would this be the senior Mr. Prescott, who has *dozens* of children and grandchildren doting on him?"

"Well…yes, but they're usually busy with their own lives. Please, Hunter? I'm dying to tell Henry what I learned out in Tipton County and show him the pictures I took. He'll be so happy to hear Mrs. Fitzhugh is still alive."

His face turned tender. "Have I ever denied you a single wish? Of course we can visit Mr. Prescott. As long as you assure me you're not falling in love with an older man."

"Thank you! And although Henry is cute as a bug, your patience with me keeps your boat floating even at low tide."

Hunter fluffed his napkin across his lap as the chef arrived to flambé his breakfast. "All right. Your high praise merits one taste of my bananas, Nicki, but not a bite more."

Nicki picked up her fork. "How did you know what I planned to ask next?"

⟶

Two hours later, Nicki and Hunter arrived at Oakbrook Assisted-Living Center laden with magazines, DVDs of remastered old movies, and a huge box of candy. Henry was in the barber shop getting a haircut, so Nicki and Hunter waited for him in the courtyard in the shade.

"The residents turned this into a bird sanctuary." Hunter pointed at several different styles of feeders and a variety of seed types scattered across the flagstones. "There must be a dozen nesting boxes for wrens and even a purple martin house." He pointed at the apartment-style birdhouse on a tall pole.

"Look at all those." Nicki pointed at several hummingbird feeders mounted on brackets next to windows. "Folks can refill the feeders from inside their apartments, sit back, and enjoy the show."

Hunter tilted his head back, the glare deepening the creases around his eyes. "I could see myself living in a place like this in old age. Three squares a day, big-screen TV, bingo on Saturdays. Do you think we'll finally be married by then?"

Nicki grabbed him by his jacket lapels. "We haven't even been engaged a year. You must learn patience, Galen. You'll be on my short leash before you know it." She stretched up to kiss his cheek as an aide opened the door to the courtyard.

"Mr. Prescott is back in his room, Mr. and Mrs. Galen."

Nicki smirked but didn't bother to correct her. She loved hearing the sound of that despite Hunter's insistence she was dragging her feet.

When they entered his room, Henry was in his usual spot by the window. She made a mental note to bring a hummingbird feeder and bottle of nectar during her next visit. "Hi, Mr. Prescott. It's Nicki Price. I have an update for you on the Carlton scavenger hunt, and I brought someone for you to meet. This fortunate man is my fiancé, Hunter Galen."

"Hello, Miss Price." Henry offered a toothy smile. "But I believe you're supposed to let the gentleman decide how lucky he is." Henry extended his hand to Hunter.

Hunter shook heartily. "Nicki is not one to stand on convention, as you've probably noticed. How do you do, sir?"

"Fine and dandy, young man. Now sit down and tell me your news."

"Guess who I had lunch with?" Nicki pulled her chair closer to him. "Violet Fitzhugh! She's alive and well, and she's living about an hour from here. Your grandson helped me track her down, and I went to see her." Scanning through the photos on her phone, she found the one taken on the terrace at lunch.

He studied the picture for a long moment. "Would you look at that? Barely changed a'tal. That woman is still a beauty."

"She is, and she sends her best regards to you." Nicki explained the details about the fifty-eight and fifty-nine scavenger hunts to bring Henry and Hunter up to date.

"I'm surprised Bobby is helping you. He can be straight-laced when it comes to his job. He has rules about this and rules about that."

Nicki laughed. "I had to coerce some of his help, but I really do like your grandson. Thanks to him, the newspaper archives, and Mrs. Fitzhugh, I pieced together the details for every year except the last. According to Mrs. Fitzhugh, Mr. and Mrs. Smithfield won in 1959. So they would have arrived a day early in 1960 to plan the game and hide the prizes—diamonds."

Henry's eyes focused on something no one else could see. "Diamonds," he said. "It's only fitting the game would come full circle. That's what the first prizes were. So the Smithfields went out and bought another set of diamonds."

"The Smithfields were very generous to their friends," said Hunter. He perched on the arm of Nicki's chair. "Do you remember what business Mr. Smithfield was in?"

"Let me think a moment." Henry tugged on his earlobe. "Yep, I do. He owned one of them fancy designer companies."

"Like a group of interior decorators?" asked Nicki.

"Oh, no. I mean he had architects, engineers, and construction folks working for him. If somebody got a notion how they wanted a building to look, they went to Mr. Smithfield and he could make it happen. 'Course, that all came with a big price tag. That's how he got so rich."

Nicki and Hunter exchanged a look. "Did the Carlton ever hire Mr. Smithfield for work on the hotel?"

Henry's eyes widened. "Sure did. Smithfield handled a big renovation 'bout the time all this was going on."

"Do you think it was in 1960, the last year for the scavenger hunts?"

"I couldn't say for sure. What you got in mind, missy? I see those little wheels turning in your head."

Hunter grinned and slapped Henry on the back. "You're a very observant man. I should take lessons from you."

While they guffawed, Nicki wrinkled her nose at Hunter. "I think I may know why no one ever found the last prizes—at least, no one we know of. What was changed during the renovation?"

Henry shook his head. "You give my memory too much credit. Maybe Bobby can look that up for you."

"That's a good idea, but in the meantime let me read you something. This is what Mrs. Fitzhugh remembers about the first clue given them at dinner on Friday evening." Nicki pulled the notes from her purse and said, "'Some places soar to great heights, some command a view of the world, some soothe the soul with tranquil waters, while others warm both body and soul. This location does all this and more.'"

Nicki sat back to watch Henry's and Hunter's wheels spin as they tried to knit the clues together.

After a few moments of dumbfounded silence, she said, "Most of the guests thought it meant the rooftop—highest level, best views, the serene waters of the Mississippi River, and warmth from the sun."

Henry slapped his knees. "It gets real hot up there. That's why they put up a shade pavilion."

"But the participants combed every inch of that rooftop and found nothing. What do *you* think the clue meant?"

"Don't know. That's why I put you in charge, missy. Those Smithfields were too clever for their own good." Henry yawned, an involuntary reflex, but also a signal they were intruding on his afternoon nap. "Good to see you, Miss Price. Thanks for bringing me that sack of goodies." His eyes closed and his chin bobbed.

Nicki and Hunter rose to their feet to leave, assuming Henry had already fallen asleep. She laid the photocopy of the well-attended Smithfield funeral on his dresser, along with a print she had made of Mrs. Fitzhugh. But before they reached the door, he called to them.

"Nice meeting you, Hunter. You come back anytime, and we'll get started on those lessons. Best to understand women *before* walking down the aisle."

TWENTY-FOUR

*I*sabelle inventoried her backpack for the third time. Sandwiches—check. Chips, fruit, bottled water—check. Sunblock and insect repellent—check. She'd better stop or she would resemble a pack mule instead of a fun-loving, energetic woman out to woo a former jock. She was so out of practice, both in having fun and impressing a member of the opposite sex.

All work and no play had made Isabelle a dull girl. Long hours, coupled with bitterness after her divorce, had sapped her carefree spirit, even without the Tony Markham factor. But all that was behind her. Even with the madman still roaming free, just knowing she was no longer alone changed her perspective.

Isabelle braided her hair and let it hang down her back. Then she dusted her cheeks with blush, applied dark eyeliner, and dabbed on taupe eye shadow. But somehow the makeup looked silly with shorts and a T-shirt. After wiping most of it off, she used only pink lip gloss and tinted sunblock. Unfortunately, her sneakers looked exactly what they were—brand new. Thanks to late hours and open houses almost every weekend, her plan to take up power walking had never been realized.

The raucous sound of the buzzer curtailed further consideration of her outfit. Isabelle spoke into the intercom. "Good morning, Nate. I'll just lock up and be right down." She met him in the doorway to her building.

"Are these duds okay? I didn't know what we were doing."

The first words out of his mouth made her smile. Apparently men worried about their appearance too. "You're perfect for what I have in mind."

Nate reached for her backpack. "Let's see…you don't have that giant tote bag, so that rules out the mall. You're wearing long shorts and a T-shirt, so that eliminates a matinee at the Orpheum Theatre. And you're not wearing a helmet, so no motorcycle racing, steeplechase, or dirt bikes." He crossed his arms over his chest. "I give up. Where are we going?"

"Sounds like you've been studying tourist brochures." Isabelle walked around to the passenger side of his car. "We're riding bicycles in the park. No motors, no electric starters. Just the power of feet on pedals, but don't worry. They'll have helmets as well."

Nate opened her door for her. "Fresh air, sunshine, and blue skies. I'm happy as a clam. Is this park far away?"

"No. Shelby Farms is one of the biggest urban parks in America, and it's right here in Memphis. Forty-five-hundred acres of fishing, paddleboats, hiking, and horseback riding."

"Sounds great." Nate smiled down at her as she settled herself in, and then he went around the car to get in on his side. He started the engine and pulled away from the curb, pausing at the first stop sign. "By the way, how long do you plan to keep me? These are the only clothes I brought."

"Only one day, but it will be a long one." She gave him directions to the park before saying, "We can rent bikes at the trailhead. And step up the pace. We have miles to cover before lunch." Isabelle tried to tamp down her excitement, to no avail. "Oh, did I mention the buffalos?"

"Buffalos? You're sure we're not riding to Yellowstone? What do you have planned for the afternoon—sailing around Cape Horn?"

"Wait and see. I want today to unfold spontaneously."

"Translation—you're waiting to see if someone falls off his bike and breaks an arm."

She laughed but otherwise ignored that. "According to my map, there are four lakes. We're bound to find one of them eventually."

For the next ten minutes Nate talked about riding around Red Haw with his younger brother and Nicki. "Once we rode all the way to Natchez, but our bikes didn't have headlights, so my dad had to come pick us up. All three of us were grounded for the rest of summer."

"For that reason, let's make our selections very carefully. Turn right, and we're here." Isabelle jumped out the moment he parked and ran to the bike racks. Nate picked out a twelve-speed with knobby tires and a battery-powered headlight. Isabelle's had five speeds, a bell, and a basket. "We'll rent for four hours please," she said, stepping up to the counter.

"Let me get this." Nate pulled out his credit card. "You packed the lunch."

Isabelle elbowed him to the side. "Oh, no you don't. You agreed to my terms on the phone." Isabelle held out her own credit card. "Besides, having a private bodyguard would cost me a fortune."

The middle-aged clerk looked from one to the other and took Isabelle's card. "This lady apparently means business, sir, so I suggest *you* mind your *p*'s and *q*'s."

"Yes, ma'am." Nate said with a tip of his ball cap.

With the map in her pocket and their lunch strapped to the basket, Isabelle was soon flying down the trail. She forgot how much she enjoyed bike riding, especially with no traffic to contend with. They rode for miles through wooded glens and across grassy fields, passing joggers, hikers, and parents pushing baby strollers along the way.

Nate matched his pace with hers, slowing down on ascents and letting her decide the speed on the downhill runs. With the warm sun on her arms and shoulders, Isabelle allowed herself to relax completely. So much so that she recklessly failed to brake on a curve. Her front tire ran off the hard-packed surface into the soft grass. Before she realized what was happening, she flew from the bike, landing in an inglorious heap on the ground.

"Isabelle! Are you all right?" Nate was off his bike and at her side in an instant. He hauled her to her feet as if she were a small child.

His hands on her arms unhinged her worse than the embarrassment of falling off the bike. "Let go of me! I'm fine." She shrugged away from him.

Nate stepped back, holding up his hands in surrender. "Hey, I wasn't trying to get fresh. I just overreacted to your fall."

Brushing off the back of her shorts, she saw disappointment in his face before he turned away. "Sorry. I'm the one who overreacted. I'm not used to a lot of physical contact. That must sound silly coming from someone who has been married, but my parents weren't the touchy-feely type, and neither was Craig."

"Duly noted. I won't make that mistake again." Nate inspected the spokes and wheel rims on her bike. "I don't think anything's bent, so we're good to go." He rolled her bike to the trail and then picked up his from the grass without looking at her.

"Nate, please don't be offended." Isabelle followed close behind. "I told you how things were, not how I want them to be. Truth is, I've always been jealous of women like Nicki who can show affection easily…and accept it in return. I don't want to be like this."

Nate studied her for a moment. "All right. We'll start slow by hooking our little fingers. Then we'll graduate to holding hands for fifteen-minute intervals." He wiggled his pinkie at her.

"You're making fun of me."

He shrugged. "Only because I don't know what else to say or do. You threw me for a loop."

"I have a talent for that. Can we forget about this? Trust me, I'm getting better. You should have seen me a year ago. I wouldn't even shake hands with clients." She lifted the kickstand and grabbed the handlebars. But instead of climbing on, she walked her bike down the hill toward the water. "That's Beaver Lake, a good spot to eat lunch. Have you worked up an appetite yet?"

"I was born hungry, so I hope you have something in that backpack other than granola bars."

"I know *exactly* whom I'm feeding today." Isabelle found a flat grassy spot and shook out a large checkered towel. "How about sandwiches, sliced peaches, pretzels, and peach-flavored tea?" She plopped down in the grass and spread out the food. For several minutes, Nate praised her turkey and Swiss, and she accepted his compliments graciously. Then their conversation took an unexpected turn.

"You're not the only one whose parents left a mark on her life," he said. "Without intending to, my father created a difficult situation between Nicki and me and the rest of my family." Nate focused on canoes in the distance. "Dad covered up the truth about how Nicki's father died to protect my brother, Sean. Recently, Nicki dug up the past to solve her father's homicide, a seventeen-year cold case. She didn't want his killers to get away with murder."

"How does Nicki get along with her uncle now?"

"My dad died of cancer a few years ago, taking his secrets to the grave."

"Did you know, Nate?" Isabelle broke a pretzel into pieces.

He met her eye before answering. "No, and Sean was only eight at the time. But every time Nicki mentions her father, I remember that mine let Uncle Kermit's killer go free for a long time. See what I mean about parents scarring us forever?"

"I would say we're both lucky to have Nicki in our lives."

Nate finished the rest of his sandwich. "As cousins go, she's not bad, but that's enough sad stories for one day. I say we mount up and ride."

Isabelle repacked the leftovers and ran toward her bike. "It's time for me to show you where the buffalo roam. Then we'll take a scenic shortcut back to the Germantown trailhead. I have plans for later, so conserve your energy."

After they returned their bikes, Nate pestered her with questions as to where they were going next. Finally, on the way back she relented. "We're headed to the Beale Street Landing. We'll stop at my condo so I can wash up and grab a sweater. Then we'll stop at the Carlton for your jacket. It might get chilly on the river tonight."

Nate's head snapped around. "Are we really floating down the Mississippi? I think we'll need more sandwiches."

"How does pulled pork, grilled chicken, sweet corn, and apple pie sound? We're taking the Memphis Queen III instead of a raft. They'll even have a live band for dancing under the stars. Are you up for that much fun?"

"I'm not sure. It sounds awfully romantic. How will we manage slow dancing with only hooked pinkies?"

She laughed in spite of herself. "You're incorrigible. Do you know that?"

"So I've been told."

When they got back to her condo, Nate slouched down in the seat, pretending to nap. "I'll wait for you here. I'm saving my energy for tonight."

Isabelle ran upstairs to wash and change clothes, but she couldn't stop grinning the entire time she was gone. What was the matter with her? Either she'd hit her head when she fell or the unthinkable was happening. She was really starting to like Nate Price.

Nate's stop at the Carlton was equally brief. Fifteen minutes later, he emerged wearing a fresh shirt and carrying a Saints jacket. "I left a note for Nicki and Hunter to join us if they get back in time. According to her message, they went to see the former bellman of the hotel. Nicki won't rest until she discovers what happened to those people sixty years ago."

"I love her perseverance."

"She may solve her case before I solve your brother's." Nate sighed wearily. "My latest lead with yet another sax player didn't pan out. Detective Marino left a message too. He just released Tito Sullivan after the soundman confirmed his alibi."

Mustering her courage, Isabelle placed her hand over his on the console. "Let's not talk about the case. I want us to relax tonight."

Nate's smiled. "Then that's what we shall do."

At the landing they sipped cool drinks and watched boats on the river until it was time to board the ship. They talked about work and play, friends and family, Nashville and Natchez and Memphis. But they didn't discuss Tony Markham or Tito Sullivan or even her brother. Just for one night, Isabelle forgot she was alone in the world, barely keeping her financial head above water, and being stalked by a madman. She and Nate strolled the deck, ate deliciously fattening food, danced under the stars, and enjoyed each other's company. And when he walked her to her door at the end of the evening, Isabelle reached for his hand.

Nate paused on the sidewalk. "Are you sure about this, Miss Andre?" he asked, tightening his grip. "You're making quite a leap."

"Sometimes a girl has to throw caution to the wind, or she'll risk missing the good things in life. And I think it's time you called me Izzy. If you want to, that is."

"I seem to have leaped a tall building and crossed a sea full of crocodiles, all within two weeks."

She didn't need a mirror to know she was blushing. "You must think I'm hopelessly neurotic."

"Not anymore. I think you're downright sociable, along with being very pretty. But we better say good night before I do something stupid and try to kiss you."

Isabelle felt her blush deepen as she closed her eyes and waited to be kissed. But when she opened her eyes, Nate was getting into his car.

"Goodnight, Izzy," he called. "Thanks for the best day I've had since the Bulldogs won the division championship for Mississippi State."

ᘒ

Nate drove back to the hotel barely aware of traffic, songs on the radio, or parking next to Nicki's Lincoln in the garage. His mind was on Isabelle Andre...*Izzy.* He didn't know how they would manage long-distance dating, but a relationship was exactly what he wanted. He was so distracted he didn't notice someone close to the elevator until he was a few yards away.

"Man, you are lucky I'm not a mugger, Price. I could've whacked you on the head and lifted your wallet before you knew what happened."

Nate's attention jerked back to the here and now. "Hey, Marino, how's it going?"

The detective pushed the button and squinted his eyes. "I don't have to ask where you've been all day. The stupid grin on your face, the la-la-land attitude—I'd say you were with Isabelle Andre."

"Guilty as charged. We spent the day seeing the sights of Memphis. Your city has a lot more to offer than I imagined."

Marino tossed his cigarette down on the concrete when the elevator door opened. "Yeah, I figured you two were getting cozy. I called her a couple times, but she gave me the cold shoulder. When I asked her to spell it out, she said she had recently met someone. I figured it was you."

"You win some and you lose some, old buddy." Nate made every effort to sound pleasant, even though he didn't want to discuss Isabelle.

"Yeah, well, I didn't come to talk about chicks." Marino's tone underscored his change in mood. "Why don't you buy me a beer inside your swanky hotel while I spell out a few things for you, *old buddy*."

As they strolled into the lobby from the back entrance, Nate nodded at the employees who had grown familiar to him. They headed to the ornate mahogany bar in the center of the courtyard where guests could sip libations or enjoy a snack near the fountain and fishpond.

"This place looks like something straight from the Roaring Twenties," said Marino, sliding onto an upholstered barstool. "I almost expect to see Al Capone walk in with his machine gun."

"I hope there will be no gunplay tonight." Nate signaled to the bartender. "Pick your poison."

"I'll have a draught Budweiser." Marino said, with his attention locked on a pair of attractive women at a bistro table.

"Same for me." Nate waited until the bartender delivered their drinks before he turned to his college pal. "So you have a bone to pick with me?"

Marino swiveled around to face him. "I'll make it short and sweet. Stop sticking your nose in my case. You ain't a cop, Nate, let alone a homicide detective, and this sure ain't New Orleans." He tipped up the mug and drank several swallows.

Nate considered his next words carefully. He wasn't worried about their future friendship, but Marino had the power to hobble him while he was in Memphis. "Sorry, Chip. I'm just trying to help. I know you have a heavy caseload, and Danny was my friend. That's all. Any update you can give me I would appreciate."

"Like I said in my message, Crane came to see me. His memory about the day Danny died seems to have miraculously returned. He confirmed that Tito Sullivan spent the night in the sound room. Then he said you assured him I wouldn't jam him up with management at the Blues City Club." Marino wrapped his fingers around the frosty stein. "Where do you get off making promises like that?"

Nate sipped his beer, grateful it wasn't one of those dark, heavy microbrews that tasted like medicine. "I knew he was lying. I made the promise so he would come clean. I also knew you wouldn't want the wrong man rotting in jail while the killer goes free."

Marino pulled over a bowl of mixed nuts and poured some into his palm. "You're lucky I'm a nice guy, Price. Some cops would run you out of town."

Nate laughed, yet he had no idea if Marino was joking or not. "What about Tito Sullivan?"

"Since you have a big heart for ex-addicts, you'll be happy to hear the DA dropped all charges. I personally drove Tito home after I bought him lunch at Kurtz's Deli. I'll bet that was the first time he ate inside the joint instead of in the alley." Marino snickered in adolescent fashion. "I no longer thought Sullivan was our man, but I liked having him locked up for a while. Tito had a place to sleep and three meals a day. In the meantime, the real bad guy might lower his guard and say or do something stupid."

Nate studied the detective. "Should I tell you what I learned? Or will it give you a reason to run me out of town?"

"Oh, I know what you've been up to." Marino finished the mug and gestured for a refill. "I have been one step behind you for days now. You sure got a bug about the killer being another musician, don't you? You've gotten under quite a few collars on Beale Street."

"Innocent people have nothing to worry about."

"Nobody is all that innocent." Marino stared at his reflection in the ornate mirror behind the rows of bottles. "So we know it wasn't Leon Perkins, because he has a solid alibi. And Jimmy Watts may have hated Danny's guts, but he was in jail at the time. Although I should have arrested him for a total lack of personality. Let's see. The last I heard you were headed to the Winston Arms to see Sam Jessup."

"You have been following me."

"Like a bloodhound on the trail, not that it was my choice. So what did you find out? Did Jessup throw himself at your feet and confess?"

"No." Nate poured himself a handful of nuts. "Danny helped Sam get a job in St. Louis. So that takes away any kind of motive. Jessup liked Danny, and he seemed like a nice guy too."

"Three sax players later and you're out of suspects, right?"

Nate hated to admit the truth, but the detective was right. "I was sure it was some kind of rivalry among musicians."

"Yeah, I thought the same thing. That's why I didn't clip your wings sooner. But now you're starting to annoy people. And annoyed musicians clam up worse than run-of-the-mill folks. I'm not done with the jealousy angle, but let me do my job. Don't muddy the waters any more than they already are." Marino swallowed another mouthful and pushed away his mug. "Thanks for the brew, but I gotta run. I am worn out, and tomorrow I have a date with a supermodel, so you can keep your black-haired, green-eyed real estate agent." He jumped to his feet.

"Good luck with that, and thanks for keeping me in the loop about the case. But do me a favor and keep life copacetic for Gus Crane."

"No problem. A soundman sees plenty up in his booth. You never know when that might come in handy. And, hey," he pointed at the bowl of mixed nuts, "don't think this gets you off the hook for ribs down the road. That night is going to cost you *plenty*." Marino laughed much too loudly for a bar in a five-star hotel as he strode toward the door.

Nate sat for several minutes contemplating a man he hadn't really known in years, if at all. Had Marino been following the same leads? Was he really planning to drop charges against Tito Sullivan even before Gus's confession? As cases went, Nate felt he wasn't any further forward on this one than he was the first day he landed in Memphis.

TWENTY-FIVE

*I*sabelle contemplated burying her head beneath the pillow and skipping church. What an exhausting day yesterday had been, considering how far they had pedaled in the park and how long they had danced on the riverboat. Neither of them had wanted to sit down for a single number that the band played. It had been after midnight when Nate dropped her off at her front door and after one before she'd calmed down enough to sleep.

Never before had she enjoyed herself so much.

Never before had she felt this way about a man. She never sang along with the band or danced cheek-to-cheek while married to Craig. Her ex-husband had been buttoned-up in public while living in some high-rolling fast lane behind her back. At long last, maybe she'd found someone to love and someone who could love her, which provided plenty of incentive to go to church and give thanks.

Throwing back the covers, Isabelle turned on the coffeemaker and headed to the shower. Forty minutes and three cups of coffee later, she ran up the steps of Germantown United Methodist. Inside, the congregation was already singing the opening hymn as the choir entered the sanctuary from a side door. Isabelle crept along a side wall, but she couldn't find an empty seat until she was three-quarters up the aisle. Her mother always joked that sinners sat in the back to keep a low profile. Whenever she asked her mom, "Aren't all Christians sinners?" her mother would laugh heartily. "Yep. That's why if you're late, the only empty seats are up front."

Squeezing in next to a family of four, Isabelle reached for a hymnal to join in. After announcements, an update on missions, and the Scripture reading, the pastor launched into his sermon. His message about stepping out in faith contained special meaning for her. How many times had she shrunk in fear? How often had she been reluctant to attend parties by herself or volunteer for projects or committees? She had been afraid others would see her as inexperienced, ineffective, or simply alone. Why had she given the opinions of others so much power over her?

When the service concluded, Isabelle joined the throng in the center aisle, wishing she had invited Nate to join her. Not only would he have liked the message, but they could have gone to breakfast and then back to Shelby Farms for a leisurely stroll through the woods. Maybe if they spent more time together, Nate would forget about going back to New Orleans. After all, he wasn't a Louisiana native. He hailed from the river delta of Mississippi, the same as her.

"Good morning, Belle," a voice called out, interrupting her woolgathering.

Stumbling on the church's stone steps, Isabelle caught the metal handrail in the nick of time. She scanned the crowd and spotted Tony thirty feet away. He stood beneath the shade of an ancient live oak, his eyes hidden behind dark sunglasses.

"What are you doing here?" She closed the distance between them, not eager to share her shame with her fellow parishioners. "My restraining order requires you to stay away from me."

He shrugged as though a helpless victim of circumstances.

"Hey, you're the one who approached me. I told you long ago I was moving to Germantown, and this is the only UMC in town. Since I was raised Methodist, why wouldn't I attend this lovely church?" His gaze lifted toward the steeple and cross high overhead.

"I don't believe you were brought up *anything*, Tony. You probably crawled from beneath a rock or the sludge from the river bottom." Isabelle hissed rather than spoke the words.

His features registered surprise along with something more insidious. "There's no need to get nasty. The preacher's words of love and forgiveness seemed to have gone over your head. Maybe you had something else on your mind."

"There's another Methodist Church in Collierville. I suggest you start going there. Because if I see you here again, I'll file a police report and have you arrested." Isabelle lifted her chin defiantly, refusing to succumb to fear. Showing weakness to this man would only fuel his obsession.

But instead of slinking away, he inched closer. "Are you *threatening* me, Belle? Because if you are, I suggest you think long and hard about this before you report any alleged infractions to the police." He brushed a piece of lint from his sport coat. "Let's suppose some of these holier-than-thou folks are willing to sign statements that I ventured into your sacred zone." He flourished his hand in a circular motion. "I might be arrested and thrown in jail, but do you think that worries me?"

"It should. A man like you wouldn't like being surrounded by other bullies." Isabelle mustered every bit of gumption she had.

A smile pulled his lips into a thin line. "My attorney will post bail, and I will be released within a few hours, a day at the most. In the meantime, you will have pissed me off royally." He leaned closer. "That stupid TRO covers you, Miss High-and-Mighty, not your friends."

"What do you mean?" She asked the question while already knowing the answer.

"Consider your old pal Nicki Price. I've seen her walking down the street texting on her phone or reading a brochure and not watching where she's going. She could step off a curb and never know what hit her. *Splat*," he enunciated, slapping his hands together. "Half the time that bubblehead leaves her car unlocked, yet she never checks the backseat before getting in." His voice dropped to a low murmur. "Sometimes she drives to the country on lonely back roads, getting lost more often than not. What if she got a flat? Who knows what could happen before Triple-A comes to change her tire?"

"You stay away from Nicki! She has nothing to do with this." Isabelle's hands balled into fists, even though she'd never punched anyone in her life.

Tony shrugged. "Okay, what about Nate Price? I'd say he has *plenty* to do with this." His eyes narrowed. "You think I don't know who you were bike riding with in the park? That was a real *nice* picnic on the banks of Beaver Lake. Your restraining order doesn't include private detectives who come to town butting their noses into police business or honing in on another man's girl."

There was no rational response to his words. There could be no reasoning with Tony, because when Isabelle looked into his eyes she saw a madman. "What exactly do you want from me?"

His face softened. "A little kindness, that's all. Answer the phone when I call. Listen to me talk about *my* hard day once in a while. It's not all about you, Belle. Maybe we could have lunch or see a movie. I know I rushed things and frightened you off. But this time I'm willing to be patient. I won't expect anything romantic until you're ready."

For a moment Isabelle was afraid her legs wouldn't hold her up. "Let me think about this, Tony. I'm not agreeing, but I'm also not calling the police today." She forced out the words as she shakily stepped back from him.

But he wouldn't let her escape so easily. He closed the distance and grabbed hold of her chin. "That's all I'm asking for—another chance. In time, you and me and Nicki can all be friends. Wouldn't that be better than something horrible happening? I would hate for Nate to end up like your pathetic little brother." Tony turned and walked away, whistling a tune as if it were any other lovely spring day.

Isabelle stared at his back until he turned the corner. *Something horrible happening to Nate?* Yes, Tony would certainly be caught and convicted. But Nate, the man she was falling in love with, would still be dead. And that frightened her more than anything Tony could do to her.

‑‑‑

After attending church with Nicki and Hunter, Nate spent most of his Sunday afternoon thinking about Isabelle. Correction—Izzy. But now that she'd given him permission to use her inner circle name, he preferred the one her parents had given her. Isabelle. How his perception of her had changed since that misty morning on the riverbank. How different she was from their high school days. Of course, he wasn't the same sports-oriented jock with no interest in anything else. In his case, change had been a good thing. He only wished Isabelle hadn't experienced a disastrous first marriage and now a bad date turned into a stalker.

Yesterday, Nicki pestered him for details about their outing to Shelby Farms and the river cruise, but Nate had refused to say more than, "Things are proceeding along as best as can be expected."

His answer hadn't satisfied his cousin, but Hunter finally

intervened to stop Nicki's interrogation. How could he say more with so little confidence in their relationship? Nate vacillated between wanting to beat the tar out of Markham or follow Isabelle around to keep her safe.

Nate decided to give her some space to rest up after an exhausting day and time to think seriously about him. If they had a future, she had to make the next move. So he boarded the downtown trolley, which provided locals with transportation and showed tourists the landmarks. He'd been on most of the streets before, but you saw so much more when you weren't driving. During the late afternoon he called Isabelle but reached only her voice mail.

When his phone rang twenty minutes later, he answered without bothering to look at caller ID. "Hi, Izzy. Did you have an open house scheduled for today?"

After a pause, a voice indicated it definitely wasn't the woman of his dreams. "I ain't no Izzy, man. That you, Price, the PI from New Orleans?"

Nate recognized the gravelly tone of the bandleader from Jimmy's Downunder. "Is this Tyrone Biggs of Blues Nation?"

"It is. I remember that you and two pretty gals came to the club one night, more to nose around than drink beer and listen to music."

"That's not true, Mr. Biggs. I would say my motivation was equally split between the two. Your guitar riffs were the best I've heard in a long time."

"Well, I suppose I can't argue with that conclusion." He released a soft laugh.

"How did you get my number?"

"You've been leaving your card with musicians all over town. All your poking around is starting to get on folks's nerves. So I decided it was time you and me had another chat, but not when

I'm surrounded by paying customers and musicians looking to pick a beef with me."

"Will this chat involve the Danny Andre murder case?"

"Well, I sure ain't hiring you as a backup singer, but that pretty black-haired gal could hum along and shake a tambourine any time she wants to down here."

Nate swallowed his initial response to Tyrone's suggestion and waited.

"Yeah, it has something to do with Danny. My band doesn't play tonight, so the Downunder will be dark. Come by in an hour."

"I'd like to bring along the homicide detective who's in charge of the investiga—"

"I don't care what you'd *like*, Mr. PI. Come alone or you ain't gonna find me." Biggs hung up, putting an end to the possibility of further negotiation.

Nate thought long and hard about how to proceed. During their first encounter, he'd had a feeling Biggs knew more than he'd let on, but his tip about Leon Perkins had been a dead end, borne out of a private beef between two musicians. On the other hand, Marino's warning had been clear. He didn't appreciate Nate's involvement with the case. The next time he went behind his back, Nate was sure Marino wouldn't be quite so nice about it.

In the end, Nate entered the back entrance of the Jimmy's Downunder alone, without Marino watching from the shadows across the street. If Biggs had evil intentions, he could carry them out long before the cops busted through the door with guns blazing. Nate didn't have a death wish, but he also saw no alternative to getting the information Biggs seemed to want to share.

Biggs sat at the bar alone, drinking from a crystal tumbler with his back to the door. Nate passed two security guards and three cleaning personnel, who paid him zero attention as he wound his way to the main showroom. Biggs apparently held plenty of clout inside the vintage blues club.

"Mind if I join you, Mr. Biggs?"

Tyrone patted the vinyl barstool beside him without turning around. "Got this seat saved for you, Price."

By the time Nate sat down, a bartender materialized from the shadows, opened a Budweiser, and placed it in front of him. Then he refilled Tyrone's glass from a bottle of bourbon and vanished as quickly as he had appeared.

"You remembered what I drank. Thanks."

"I don't miss much that goes on." Biggs swiveled around on his stool. With all the houselights turned up for cleaning and restocking, the master guitar player looked older than Nate had pegged him to be. Deep creases underscored his eyes and framed his mouth, while his hair was more gray than black. "Thanks for coming alone. I was pleasantly surprised." Smiling, he sipped his drink. "Since you showed me respect, I'm going to return the favor."

Nate took a swallow and wiped his mouth. "Would that favor be helpful information about Danny? Or another wild goose chase out to Leon Perkins's house, who turned out to be a nice guy, by the way."

"You're funny, Mr. PI, so I'll overlook your opinion of Perkins." Tyrone laughed from his belly. "Yeah, I have some helpful information for you." His demeanor quickly soured. "Stop looking on Beale Street for your friend's killer. You're focusing on us because we're easy targets. Plenty of musicians got rap sheets because not knowing the next payday can lead a man down the wrong path, but you're wasting your time looking for the killer down here." Scowling, he set his glass down with a thud. "Let me tell you about the time I met Danny."

Nate's stomach tightened. He was afraid he was going to hear something about Danny he didn't want to know…or tell Isabelle. "I'm listening."

"I wasn't happy when Danny started hanging around the Down-under, trying to pick up gigs. He was always real friendly, like he was one of us. Most of the guys didn't mind, but he got on my nerves. I said to him one night, 'What does a white boy like you know about playing the blues?' Danny didn't bat an eyelash. He asked me if I ever heard of Eric Clapton or Stevie Ray Vaughn or maybe the Fabulous Thunderbirds. I said to him, 'You trying to aggravate me? Those are all guitar-pickers like me. And you ain't got no guitar in that case of yours.'"

The bartender placed a second beer in front of Nate even though his first was only half finished. Tyrone waited until he left to continue.

"Danny unlatched his case and said, 'No, Mr. Biggs, I play the sax just like Kenny G. Have you heard of him?' Then he pulled out his sax and starting playing 'Songbird,' right on money."

The musician laughed at the memory. "Then I said, 'Anybody can practice one song till they get it right. That don't mean nothing.'"

"'Name your tune, Mr. Biggs.' Danny wasn't the least bit nervous. So I started picking songs from our usual playlist that have heavy sax, and he played every one of them note perfect. Even my regular sax player was impressed."

Nate cracked his knuckles. "Danny and I go way back, but I never heard him play. You have no idea how bad that makes me feel."

"Is that so?" Tyrone sounded surprised. "Then you missed a real treat. Danny was a natural. He could hear a song once and pick it up. You give him half an hour, and he would play it perfectly. Sure, musicians gotta eat, but nobody killed him because they were jealous of his talent. Bluesmen love the music, first and foremost. Everybody liked Danny, even me after a while. And the few who didn't…well, they pretty much don't like anybody."

Nate watched a waitress wrap napkins around silverware. "If not on Beale Street, then where should I look? Point me in the right direction."

Tyrone finished his drink but waved away the bartender when he reappeared. "Since you never heard Danny play, you probably didn't know about his love life either. When Danny started filling in on Tuesdays and Wednesdays, this woman started showing up to listen. Tall, blonde, short skirts. She would sit right there, bat her eyelashes, and clap her hands like a woman in love, l-u-v."

"And you think Danny's girlfriend beat him up and threw him in the river?"

"What I'm telling you is that high-maintenance girlfriend has a nasty ex-husband, bigger than an ox. He came around one night and started making trouble. He was some rich guy who didn't like his ex's new downtown friends, if you catch my drift. The bouncers weren't too nice when they threw him out 'cause of all the trash that guy was talkin'. But it was no easy task to remove him." The band leader rose to his feet. "That's all I can tell you. Time for me to go home. I'm here too much the way it is."

Nate extended his hand, and after a moment's hesitation, Tyrone shook. "Thanks. I appreciate the information, along with what you said about Danny."

But when Nate started to take out his wallet, he clamped a hand on Nate's wrist. "Keep your money in your pocket, Mr. PI. That round and the advice were on me." Tyrone gestured with his chin toward the door. "I think you can find your way out."

TWENTY-SIX

*W*hen Nicki met Hunter in the hallway Monday morning, both of them were smiling. "Good morning, handsome man," she greeted. "What has you in such a good mood?"

"Certainly not the idea of returning to New Orleans without you. But all in all, I would say we had a bang-up weekend. Don't you agree?" Hunter pressed the elevator button and leaned over for a quick kiss.

"I do, indeed." Nicki returned the kiss with all the ardor public spaces permitted. "I'm glad you got to meet Henry. And I'm overjoyed we ironed out a few wedding details with your mom."

Hunter rolled his eyes as they entered the elevator car. "In this case, FaceTime worked out infinitely better than being in person. We are not allowing her to turn our reception into an opportunity to pay back her social obligations."

"Do you think limiting her to three hundred guests was cruel and unusual punishment?" Nicki tried to maintain a straight face.

"I do not. Because your mother wants an open house in Natchez after our honeymoon, some of her guests probably won't drive to the Big Easy. Once the RSVPs roll in, my mother may be able to increase her number."

"My mom will come, but Mamaw isn't comfortable out on

water of any kind—river, pond, or lake—and Pawpaw has never been on anything bigger than a fishing boat. Unfortunately, some of my aunts feel the same about a yacht reception. Are you sorry you proposed to a country gal?" She fluttered her eyelashes.

"You must be joking. I'm just glad Mother hasn't scared you away with her pushiness."

"Actually, her arranging the reception is a load off my mind. Once I found out what Tournedos Rossini and langostinos were, I even like her menu."

"Feel free to change anything you want. This is our day, Nicki, yours and mine, not my mother's." His arm around her waist tightened into a hug.

Once the elevator doors had opened and they made their way through the lobby, Nicki spotted Robert at his desk. "Hunter, while you have the valet bring the car around, I would like to ask the concierge something."

He lifted an eyebrow. "Does this have anything to do with my chief competition? Henry needs to remember I saw you first." He buzzed her cheek before exiting through the double doors.

Nicki approached the concierge on a mission. "Good morning, Mr. Prescott. Do you have time to research something while I drive Hunter to the airport?"

"Let me guess." Robert cocked his head to one side. "You're interested in any hotel renovations orchestrated by Smithfield Interior and Design around the year 1960."

"My motives seem to be rather transparent today."

"Granddad called me Saturday night after your visit. He was quite excited. I appreciate your interest in him, but did you visit any of the places I recommended to your fiancé?"

"Yes, sir. Saturday night we drove to the Ground Zero Blues Club in Clarksdale. Yesterday we went to the zoo after church and finished our day at Riverfront Park."

"It's a start, I suppose." He turned on his computer. "Go, Miss Price. Your car is here. I'll have whatever information is available on Smithfield's work when you return."

Two hours later, Nicki sat in the coffee shop staring at schematics for a renovation to the grand lobby. Clever as she was with a computer, an architect or engineer she was not. Most of the cosmetic changes involved lighting, wall coverings, and the relocation of the reception desk. The only major addition was the ornate fountain in the middle of the courtyard's pond. Constructed of Italian marble, the fountain was the lobby's artistic centerpiece besides being a functional water supply for the fish. Nicki rubbed her tired eyes and sighed. No matter how long she stared at the blueprints, she didn't discern any potential hiding spots for diamonds that would have hidden them for decades.

With the blueprints in hand, Nicki marched back to the concierge and waited patiently her turn. After a group of senior citizens secured a trolley schedule, dinner reservations, and directions to Graceland, Nicki spread the schematics across Robert's desk.

"The more I study these, the more I'm convinced the jewels are in the fountain. Even Mrs. Fitzhugh thought the original clue meant the main lobby. After all, it's two-and-half-stories high, has great views from the balcony mezzanine, and the fireplace can provide the warmth mentioned in the poem. Besides, everyone knows the sound of water is calming. Plus, the fountain was the only new piece added that year."

"I noticed the same thing, but that fountain has undergone regular maintenance since its installation. I can't tell you how many times the motor has been replaced. The fishpond has been regularly drained and inspected for sixty years. Any diamonds hidden would have been found by now." He gathered the blueprints into a pile and rolled them into a tube.

"But don't you think—"

"No, I don't. And if I see you sloshing around in that pond, Miss Price, I'll drag you out by your ear and lock you in your suite until Mr. Galen comes back." His expression didn't encourage debate.

"I understand. But if you don't mind, I would like to hang on to these a little longer." Nicki grabbed the roll and ran away before he could stop her.

Back inside her room, she set aside the blueprints and pulled out her copy of the newspaper's article on the Smithfields' death. Rereading it carefully, her brain latched onto an error in semantics. Reaching for her phone, she called the only living participant of the scavenger hunts with a memory. "Hello, Mrs. Fitzhugh. It's Nicki Price. Do you have time for a few more questions?"

"All I have left is time, my dear. Any progress with solving the final hunt?"

"Maybe. I'm looking at blueprints for renovations to the lobby, which include the addition of a marble fountain. Because Mr. Smithfield's company oversaw changes to the pond, those jewels have to be hidden in that vicinity just like you thought."

"All well and good, but remember, according to the rules prizes had to be accessible without damage to the Carlton and without creating a ruckus. So climbing a fountain or draining the pond of water wouldn't have been permitted."

"Yes, ma'am, but there's something else I'm confused about. You received a poem on Friday that sent folks scurrying to the rooftop, where they found nothing. But according to the newspaper stories, Mr. and Mrs. Smithfield died *late Saturday* night, approximately at one a.m., which actually would have been Sunday morning. Wouldn't they have given out another clue at dinner that evening?"

Mrs. Fitzhugh was silent for so long Nicki grew uneasy. "Forgive me, ma'am, if I sound disrespectful to their memory. I know they were good friends."

"Thank you, dear. It is horrible to lose those you love unexpect-edly. After we heard about their accident, we abandoned the game and forgot all about the clues. But you're correct. We had been given another silly poem at dinner. The Smithfields always had to be so clever—too clever for my amusement. The only detail I can remember was something about Dorothy McGuire, but I'm sure that name means nothing to you."

Remembering Mr. Koehler and his box of keepsakes, Nicki felt the hairs on the back of her neck stand on end. "I wouldn't be so sure of that, ma'am."

"You are a nice young woman, Miss Price, for listening patiently to an old woman's stories. Most people your age are too busy. And the people in my life have heard my stories many times before. But may I give you a little advice?"

"Yes, of course." Nicki forced her mind back to the present conversation.

"Stop wasting your time on old memories—mine and Henry Prescott's. Instead, make some wonderful new ones of your own. Where did you say you're from?"

"Mississippi, but my fiancé and I plan to make our home in New Orleans."

"Perfect! New Orleans has plenty of lovely hotels. Get your friends together for a yearly scavenger hunt."

Nicki giggled, thinking about her old college buddies. "None of my friends or even my fiancé can afford diamonds or Rolexes for prizes."

Mrs. Fitzhugh clucked her tongue. "Who says they need to be jewels? Why not a pair of tickets to a Saints game, or maybe a fishing charter on Lake Pontchartrain? Select things your friends would enjoy and everyone can afford. Forget about what the Smithfields hid that year. Somebody has undoubtedly found those diamonds long ago but was afraid they would have to give them back if they said anything."

"That's what the concierge said, along with my fiancé and everyone else—except for Henry."

She laughed softly at that. "They could be right, but don't think I'm trying to get rid of you. Please stay in touch, Miss Price. Let me know how you like married life. I might have a pointer or two for you and a great recipe for mac-and-cheese."

～

Isabelle had spent all of Sunday figuring out what to do about Tony. Several times she almost picked up the phone to call the Germantown Police Department. After all, she had a court order forcing him to keep his distance and not contact her via phone, email, or through the post office. He would be arrested and charged with aggravated stalking, a class C felony punishable by three to fifteen years in jail. But Tony was right. It wasn't as though he would be thrown in a cell, denied bond until his trial, and given a life sentence without chance of parole.

He would be released, probably much sooner than she could sell her condo, change her name, and relocate to a new city. Isn't that what stalking victims were often forced to do? Disappear into new lives and never stop looking over their shoulder? Or, as Tony suggested, into the backseat of their car? Remembering his thinly veiled threat against Nicki kept her from reporting the violation of the TPO.

He was right about Nicki too. After growing up in Red Haw, Mississippi, she was woefully naive. Spray-painted graffiti on billboards, mailbox bashing, and shoplifting at Rite Aid weren't the same as urban crime. Of course evildoers could live anywhere, but Nicki was too trusting and too eager to believe the lies that people told. Nate, although far more worldly than his cousin, might lower his guard long enough to fall victim. Could she take that chance? Most people obeyed the law to avoid the consequences of crime, but someone as deranged as Tony had no barometer to keep their behavior in check. Isabelle couldn't let her friends suffer because of her own poor judgment in picking dates.

That Monday morning, the office phones rang constantly with buyers seeking specific amenities and sellers checking to see if any offers had come in over the weekend. Along with several walk-ins demanding to see homes listed on the website, Isabelle barely had time to drink her cold coffee before lunch. She appreciated the distraction of work, but when Janice appeared in her doorway, she welcomed the interruption.

"What a morning, huh?" Janice opened her blinds, filling the room with sunlight.

"You're not kidding. Every buyer who checked the multiple listings or newspaper classifieds over the weekend wants to see the properties today." Leaning back in her chair, Isabelle rubbed the back of her neck.

"Mr. Price asked me to deliver a message. Apparently, he's called your direct line and also left messages on your cell." Janice gave a sly grin. "He says if he doesn't hear from you soon, he'll throw himself into the river and forget he knows how to swim. He can't stand being ignored."

Nate's ridiculous threat may have made her laugh if not for her heartbreaking decision. Now his persistence only made what she had to do harder. "Thank you for delivering his message. I'll call him right now."

The receptionist stood by the window, as though hoping to listen in. When Isabelle remained motionless, phone in hand, Janice pushed off from the windowsill. "I'll leave you to it," she said as she closed the door behind her.

Once she had some privacy, Isabelle listened to Nate's sweet messages on her voice mail. Then she dialed his number and held her breath.

Nate picked up on the first ring. "Must I buy a house for you to take my calls, Miss Andre? What kind of girl dances with a fellow under the moonlight Saturday night, holds his hand, and then ignores him all day on Sunday? If you would have answered yesterday, we could've gone to the zoo with Hunter and Nicki. Did you know they have giant pandas?" He didn't allow her time to get a single word in edgewise. "No, forget I mentioned that. I know you're a nice girl who spent Sunday doing good deeds until the sun went down. And since you're probably Realty World's top producer, you're up to your eyelashes with work today." Nate paused to catch his breath.

"I'm not the office's top producer. I came in third last month." Of all the things Isabelle could have said, she chose the most inane.

"Even the *third* top saleswoman still needs to eat. Why don't I come to Germantown and take you to lunch? Didn't you tell me your favorite deli was nearby?"

Jack's Deli near Municipal Park—a place that Tony knows well. A shiver ran through Isabelle's body. "No, Nate. I brought a sandwich to eat at my desk. Mondays are always crazy around here."

"Understood. How about dinner? Hunter went back to New Orleans, so why don't we take Nicki out? She's been dying to try Bleu, and that's not a place where you dine alone."

"Then you should take her…without me." Isabelle left her final words hanging in the air.

A moment or two passed before he spoke. "Are you tied up with clients tonight? Nicki and I can wait until tomorrow since we'll still be here. Hunter paid for another week for our rooms. He and I exchanged a few words about him footing the bill, but he insists he's getting a great weekly rate, as though that has anything to do with it. If he wants to pay for Nicki's suite, fine, but not mine."

Nate was not going to make this easy for her. "I'm sure you'll work out the bill with Hunter. In the meantime, I think you and I should take a couple steps back."

"*What?*" Nate's single word spoke volumes.

Isabelle fought to keep her voice level. "In my opinion, our date got a little out-of-hand. Give me time to think this whole you-and-me idea through."

"What's wrong, Isabelle? Did something happen with Markham? You didn't think we were moving too fast on Saturday. You told me to call you Izzy, remember?"

"Nothing's wrong," she lied. "And I certainly remember everything I said and did."

"Did I offend you in some way? I'm pretty rusty with dating etiquette, so don't be afraid to point out my shortcomings."

"No, it's nothing like that," she snapped impatiently. "I just want us to take a break for a couple of weeks and then reevaluate our feelings."

"*A couple of weeks?* I have a lead that may crack Danny's case wide open. So if it pans out, *in a couple of weeks* I'll be back in New Orleans while you'll still be here in Memphis." His tone betrayed his incredulity.

"We both have email and cell phones, Nate. Louisiana isn't Outer Mongolia if we're meant to have a future together. So why don't you tell me about your lead in Danny's case?"

An uncomfortable ten seconds spun out while Nate processed her bombshell. "I need a little time here. Why don't I see if this tip pans out first? I'll give you a call in a few days with an update."

"All right. That's how we'll leave it for now." She couldn't have sounded colder.

"Goodbye, Isabelle."

The click of his disconnect sent a sharp pain between her ribs, but she saw no alternative. If she told him about Tony visiting her church, Nate would have made the decision for her. Wheels would be set into motion that could have disastrous consequences for people she loved. Tony was her problem, and she needed to take care of him once and for all.

As a plan came together, Isabelle felt more empowered than she had in years, maybe in her life. She would stall Tony until her friends were back in New Orleans, out of harm's way. Then she would set a trap and have him arrested for stalking and menacing. She could only hope that the DA would make a strong enough case to put him in jail for a long time. With Tony behind bars, she would tell Nate the truth. Maybe he wouldn't want a relationship with a flighty nutcase like her, but it was the chance she had to take to keep him safe.

TWENTY-SEVEN

*N*ate pushed himself back from his laptop when the pounding on the door threatened the wood frame. "I'm coming!" he shouted.

After he had swept open the door, Nicki strolled into his suite in a mint green sundress, canvas shoes, and a sunhat meant strictly for the beach. "Are you deaf or are both of your legs broken?" She headed straight for his mini refrigerator. "Got any soda?"

"No," Nate said briefly as he shut the door with his heel.

Nicki grabbed a bottle of water and sat down on his sofa. "Wow, what an afternoon. I'm convinced the missing prizes are hidden near the fountain, but Mr. Prescott won't let me drain the pond for proper examination. So I'm stuck going over these with a magnifying glass."

While she unrolled and spread out a stack of blueprints, Nate tried to recollect what Nicki had told him about the bellman's theories. "So one of the scavenger hunts went unsolved?"

"Yes. Well, Henry and I believe—are hoping, anyway—that the prizes remain where they were hidden in 1960." Nicki lifted her focus from the blueprints. "What's wrong with you?" she demanded. "Have you been crying? Your eyes are bloodshot."

Nate shook his head. "Of course not. Must be pollen in the air. Maybe ragweed."

She didn't appear convinced. "I don't remember your having allergies when we played hide-and-seek in the woods."

"I'm fine." He picked up one of the drawings to hide behind. "Tell me what you discovered."

"Nothing from these blueprints. That's why I'm seeing Mr. Koehler tomorrow at his nursing home."

"Who's Mr. Koehler?" Nate dropped the blueprint atop the others.

"Don't you listen to a word I say? He was the winner of emerald cuff links in 1956. Hey, what time are we picking up Isabelle for dinner? I'm so anxious to try that place I've already put on my outfit." Nicki stood and then held out the full skirt as she twirled in place. "Does this dress call for heels, or will my flats be okay?"

"You look just fine, but it'll be just you and me tonight, cousin. I hope you're not disappointed." Nate stared out the window, where rush hour traffic was picking up steam.

"Is that why you're down in the dumps? Because you didn't see Izzy yesterday and you won't see her tonight?" Nicki dropped her voice to a mournful whisper.

"Who said I'm down in the dumps? I've been working all afternoon. I'm not here in Memphis for an appearance on *The Bachelor*."

Nicki marched over to where he stood and crossed her arms. "Spill your guts, Price. Did you two have a fight? Should I talk some sense into that woman? She can be so much like Danny."

Nate gently took hold of her arms. "Izzy wants us to take a break from each other. You and I will respect that decision and give her space. Please, Nicki, don't interfere."

Her face finally registered the seriousness of the situation.

"Okay. Whatever you say, but this doesn't sound right to me. I know for a fact that—"

"Stop. Whatever you *knew* is no longer the case. Let's leave it at that." Nate dropped her arms and walked back to the desk. "Pull up a chair. I need your natural PI instincts because I've run into a brick wall."

Nicki dragged over an upholstered chair. "You want my help with Danny's murder?"

"I do. I no longer think Danny's killer is one of the Beale Street musicians. Leon Perkins was in Mobile with his family for a few days. Jimmy Watts was in county lockup when Danny died. And my last lead, Sam Jessup? He was hired for a permanent gig at the Hyatt Regency in St. Louis and is on his way there."

"Maybe the Hyatt originally wanted Danny for the spot."

"They did, but Danny didn't want to leave Isabelle behind in Memphis, so he recommended Jessup and set up the interview. No motive there."

Nicki scratched her head while sorting out the details, much the way she did with the scavenger hunts. "What happened when you saw Tryone Biggs yesterday? Did he send you on another wild goose chase?"

Nate recounted everything he learned from the guitar player about Danny's girlfriend.

Nicki's eyes grew rounder the more he talked. "Danny was in love and he didn't tell me?"

"Apparently, it was a fairly new relationship. Men aren't like women, Nicki. They wait until something concrete develops instead of posting on social media the moment something looks promising."

"Are we talking about you and Izzy again?"

Nate cringed at his transparency. "No, I'm just telling you why Danny hadn't shared his relationship yet. Since talking to Biggs,

I called everyone I could think of who might have seen Danny and this woman at the Downunder. Everyone confirmed Biggs's opinion—the mystery woman was in love with him. But Danny never introduced her, so nobody knows her name."

Nicki slapped her forehead. "She came to Danny's funeral."

Nate jaw dropped open. "Are you certain?"

"Who else could she have been? I saw her when I was talking to the funeral director, and, more importantly, Izzy spoke to her. Not for long, though. Just call Izzy. She might remember, or maybe the woman signed the guest book."

Nate couldn't look at his cousin. "Do you think you could ask Izzy?"

"Wow. You can't even bring yourself to talk to her about Danny?"

Nate hoped he didn't appear as embarrassed as he felt. "She doesn't want me to call her. She said she needs time to…think. I'm to get back to her after I track down this lead. If I can't figure out any other way, I want you to ask her."

"Men sure have strange ways of dealing with romance problems."

"Izzy never allowed our relationship to advance to the romance stage," said Nate, no longer caring about transparency or his embarrassment. He left her and moved back across the room to the window.

Nicki followed him and slipped an arm around his shoulder. "Not to worry. Your old pal Detective Marino was there when that woman walked up to the car. Maybe he remembers her name."

Nate kissed the top of her head. "Thanks. As cousins go, you're as good as they get. Why don't you go put on high heels for that fancy restaurant? I'll knock on your door right after I call Chip."

"Don't take too long. I'm starving." Nicki skipped to the door.

After she left, Nate paced the room like a caged animal. As

much as he wanted to call Isabelle, even if only to hear her voice, he couldn't. He had no choice but to give her space. Funny, in high school when she rebuffed him, he had been angry. Now he felt nothing but sadness. It was time for him to solve Danny's murder like he promised and go home…and the sooner the better.

When he called Marino, Nate forced a carefree tone to his voice. "Hey, Chip, it's Nate. I'm on my way out the door, but I needed to check with you about something."

"Like what I'm doing for dinner tonight? Smoked ribs and curly fries sure would slide down smooth." The detective made a smacking sound with his lips.

"That sounds good to me too, but I promised to take Nicki to Bleu tonight. And with their prices, I can't afford both of you."

Marino whistled through his teeth. "Your cousin has expensive tastes, so I'll catch you another time. What's on your mind?"

"Think back to Danny Andre's funeral. Do you remember a woman who walked up to Isabelle? She might have been Danny's girlfriend."

"You talking about the blonde with long legs? She wore a long raincoat, but underneath that skirt was a little short for a funeral, if you ask my opinion." He emitted a rude noise.

"That would be the one. Did you happen to catch her name?"

"I did. After she paid her respects to Isabelle, I followed her back to her car. Later, I ran her plates. I make it my business to get the names of everybody who comes to a funeral in a murder investigation. You never know when something will turn out helpful. But I hope you're not sticking your nose into my case. You know how I feel about that."

"No way. I learned my lesson. Now that some time has passed, Isabelle wants to reach out to her. Express her sympathy, but she doesn't remember the woman's name." Nate regretted his lies but saw no alternative.

"Hang on while I look it up."

Nate stared out the window while he listened to Chip flip pages.

"Okay, found it. That lovely young lady was named Carlene Bradington. Are you sure you're not the one who wants to express his condolences?"

Nate snorted. "Not this time. Thanks, and I'll be in touch about those ribs."

On his way down the hall to Nicki's suite, he uttered a simple, "Thank You, God." If he was going to solve this case and move on with his life, he needed plenty of divine intervention.

TWENTY-EIGHT

When the concierge arrived at his desk Tuesday morning, Nicki was waiting. "Hello, Mr. Prescott. I trust traffic wasn't too onerous on your drive to work."

"Good morning, Miss Price. Traffic was no worse than usual. What is all this?" He gestured at the containers lined up neatly on his blotter.

"Coffee, juice, and croissants from Starbucks on South Third Street. I thought we could have breakfast together before the crowds arrive." Nicki scooted her chair closer. "Oh, dear. I hope you haven't already eaten. Your grandfather said you usually have only coffee at home."

"Why am I not surprised you talked to Granddad already?" He shot his impeccable white cuffs and sat down. "This looks delicious. Tell me, did you enjoy dinner at Bleu last night? I trust the table I arranged was satisfactory for you and your partner, Mr. Price?"

"It was the best in the house. And the food was wonderful. I had the grilled grouper, and Nate had the salmon roulade. But I'm really not his partner while we're in Memphis. More like a thorn in his foot."

"I can't fathom that." Mr. Prescott chuckled softly behind his cup of coffee. "May I make reservations for you for this evening?"

"No, thank you. I'm not sure when I'll be back, which brings up my next topic of conversation." She stirred two sugars and a cream into her cup. "Isn't Tuesday the day you give the history of the hotel tour, and Henry sometimes has lunch with your daughter, Antoinette?"

He smiled warmly at her. "Since you even remembered Toni's name, I doubt you need much confirmation. But yes, unless she made other plans for her day off, Toni and Henry should be here around eleven."

Nicki finished her pastry and dabbed her mouth. "That's what I thought. How do you feel about my taking Henry out to visit Mr. Koehler at his nursing home instead?" She decided not to mention Mr. Koehler's memory impairment. "I can call ahead and arrange lunch trays for us so we can eat with him. People living in nursing homes don't get anywhere near enough visitors."

The concierge cleaned crumbs from his blotter with a few quick swipes. "I'm well aware of that, but you can't manage Granddad and his wheelchair in your car. My daughter meets him here because she knows that Oakbrook drivers will help load and unload, along with our staff and myself."

Nicki leaned forward. "I thought of that. So after I talked to Henry, I spoke with Oakbrook's director. She said their van can go to Millington at no charge. And because Sunnybrook is a nursing facility, there will be plenty of help while we're there."

"It sounds like you've thought of everything, Miss Price. Granddad doesn't need my permission if he wants to visit an old friend. Are you simply seeking my blessing?" He folded his hands on his desk.

"I suppose I am. As much as I want Henry to see Blake Koehler, I'm a little nervous. Does your grandfather have food allergies I should be aware of or medications that must be taken on schedule? What if there's a medical emergency while we're in Millington? Of course, I would call paramedics, but do you have any advice for me?"

"The van driver will provide written instructions if he needs meds while you're gone, and he's not allergic to anything other than mangoes. Those seldom appear on institutional food trays. Did you ask Toni if she wished to accompany you?"

Nicki nodded. "I did, but she passed. She said she comes to the Carlton every few weeks because senior care centers are too depressing."

Mr. Prescott mulled this over. "Firm up your plans with Oakbrook and Sunnybrook while I make some calls. Have the van driver bring Henry here since it's on their way. Then you won't have to drive. Don't worry about anything today, Miss Price." Robert stood and extended his hand. "And thank you for bringing me breakfast."

Nicki shook with an enormous sense of relief. "I don't want *you* remembering me as a thorn in your foot when I leave this lovely hotel."

"Never. I will recall a sweet young woman who paid special attention to my grandfather."

Nicki threw away their trash and started making calls, but when she walked through the hotel's front doors at eleven, she was in for a surprise. Dressed in a casual shirt, chinos, and loafers, Robert was waiting for her. "Are you coming with us to Millington?"

A smile brightened his face. "Yes, indeed. I found someone to fill in at the desk, so I'm taking a personal day. I can't think of a better way to spend it."

"Your grandfather will be delighted," she said as the Oakbrook van pulled up to the curb.

However, as they climbed into the van's second row, Henry's

exact words were, "What are *you* doing here, Bobby, on the one day I finally get to spend the day with somebody pretty?"

Bobby didn't seem the least bit offended. "I'm here to make sure Miss Price minds her manners. She's been quite a handful around the Carlton lately. Who knows what mischief she has planned for Sunnybrook?"

Henry rubbed his hands together. "That's what I like to hear! Tell me your news, Miss Price. I can't wait to hear the latest developments in our case."

During the first half of the forty-minute drive, Nicki repeated her conversation with Mrs. Fitzhugh practically verbatim. Then Henry described the ongoing debate at his assisted-living center. Some residents wished to implement a Friday cocktail hour in the courtyard, while the teetotalers insisted that alcohol be confined to residents' rooms.

"Goodness, I'm surprised that people are still squabbling when—" Nicki abruptly came to her senses before finishing the sentence.

"When they're old and gray?" Henry cackled with delight. "People will disagree, young lady, whether they are twenty or one hundred and five. Don't you agree, Bobby?"

"Yep. It's human nature." Robert kept a steadying hand on Henry's chair despite the locks on the wheels.

Nicki noticed Robert's change in demeanor. She was pretty sure he wouldn't use the word "yep" at the concierge desk if his life depended on it.

Once the three of them trooped into Sunnybrook, Nurse Lansky greeted them cordially. "Right on time," she said. "Blake is waiting in the private solarium. We'll bring your lunch trays there. You'll have more space than in his room. I'll show you the way."

Inside the sun-filled solarium room sat Blake Koehler, wearing a navy-checked shirt, dark trousers, and, unfortunately, a blank expression.

"Hi, Mr. Koehler. It's Nicolette Price. We met recently. And look who I've brought to visit you. Henry Prescott, a former bellman at the Carlton Hotel. He couldn't wait to see you after all these years!"

Blake looked from the nurse to Nicki but with the same benign disinterest. But when Robert rolled his grandfather front and center, something flickered in his eyes. Blake blinked several times and stared at Henry.

"Hello, Mr. Koehler." Henry scooted his chair to get as close as possible. "It's Henry, your bellman from the good old days. Take a good look at my wrinkly face and see if you don't recognize a friend."

Blake did exactly as instructed. He leaned forward and studied the craggy, ebony features and…laughed.

"Either he remembers what a jokester I used to be, or he just saw the funniest-looking person on earth," said Henry, settling back in his wheelchair.

"Either way, you're off to a good start," said Nurse Lansky. "I'll leave you four alone. This ought to keep conversation lively until your lunches arrive." She set Blake's keepsake box in Henry's lap and wheeled a low table beside the two elderly men. "I won't be able to stay with you today, but if you need anything, just push that intercom button." She pointed at the wall monitor and left the room.

Nicki and Robert dragged over chairs, one on each side of them. Henry opened the box and held up the first treasure—a yellowed newspaper insert. "What's this, Blake? The furniture you had on sale in your stores that week?"

Koehler peered at the flyer, his features registering curiosity rather than recognition.

"Wow. Check out those prices." Henry tapped the bottom of

the page. "An entire suite of bedroom furniture for two hundred dollars. Mahogany, no less. Can't buy that hardwood anymore. No, sirree. We gotta protect the rainforests before they're all gone."

Nodding as though in agreement, Blake laid the paper on the table as Henry pulled the next item from the box.

"Good golly, will you look at this? You and the missus in your younger days." Henry held the Polaroid snapshot close to his face before passing it to Blake. "You two sure had a handsome pair of sons. Children are such a blessing...most of the time."

As Blake examined the photo, a smile bloomed across his weathered face. Nicki and Robert exchanged a silent glance. Neither wanted to break the tenuous connection being established between the two older men.

"Looks like one of your boys played college football." Henry handed him a picture of a young man wearing a helmet and shoulder pads. "That's the logo for the Clemson Tigers." Henry slapped his knees. "Hmmm, they always had a good team."

Blake tucked the gridiron photo into his shirt pocket and waited to see what was coming next. For the twenty minutes Henry presented Blake with a montage of his life, including civic honors, professional awards, anniversary celebrations, and the milestones of family life over dozens of years. Henry had no idea who these grandchildren and perhaps great-children were, but it didn't matter. Birthday parties, graduations, weddings, and vacations at the beach provided universal common ground.

When lunch arrived, Nicki was reluctant to interrupt. Even though he never said a word, Blake seemed to enjoy the trip down memory lane. "Let's let our sandwiches sit for now," she whispered to Robert.

"I couldn't agree with you more." He tipped a water bottle to his lips. "There will always be another lunch, but days like today are few and far between for these two. "

As much as Nicki was enjoying herself, she and Henry had a second agenda, one whose likelihood of success dimmed as Henry neared the bottom of Blake's keepsake box.

"Would you look at this? Here's what Miss Price remembered from her first visit to you, Blake." Henry held up a vellum card embossed with a poem, a poem which had made no sense at the time.

"Read it aloud, Granddad." Robert unwrapped Blake's sandwich and set his tray across the arms of his chair.

"Don't mind if I do." Henry cleared his throat and began to read,

> Remember to take your spare change
> When you look for Dorothy McGuire
> The king of the sea sees all
> So one promenade left
> A reach for the stars
> And one sashay right,
> And a girl's best friend shall be yours.

"I believe you found what you're looking for, Miss Price," said Henry, handing her the card.

The cryptic message meant nothing to Blake as he took a bite of his chicken salad on rye, but Nicki leaped to her feet. "That's it. I'm not sure how, but this is our key, Henry." She began to skip around with her excitement.

"Settle down, Miss Price," said Robert. "Let's not frighten Mr. Koehler."

"May I make a photocopy of this, sir?" Nicki showed Blake the paper and then pointed at the door.

He continued to eat with no interest in the poem.

Nicki raced to the nurse's station to find Mrs. Lansky. As soon as a photocopy was safely in her purse, she was back in the solarium eating lunch with her friends.

Henry loved seeing his old friend despite Blake's limitations. Blake seemed to appreciate new faces or perhaps the change of scenery. Robert enjoyed spending time with his grandfather away from the Carlton.

And Nicki? She suspected that a decades-old nut was about to crack wide open.

TWENTY-NINE

While Nicki and her favorite bellman took off to Millington, Nate was left to track down the elusive Carlene Bradington on his own. Fortunately, his skills proved up to the challenge thanks to her uncommon name in the Memphis area and the magic of Google. Search engines furnished several pictures that matched the description supplied by Marino and Tyrone Biggs. Danny's former girlfriend and the mysterious mourner turned out to be Mrs. Raymond Bradington of Bartlett, an upscale suburb east of Memphis. He had to pull out every PI trick in the book to obtain their address.

Was the fact his paramour was still married the reason why Danny had been murdered? Nate didn't know, but he doubted Danny knew that rather consequential detail, or he never would have asked her out.

On his drive out to Bartlett, Nate couldn't stop thinking about Izzy. He'd been tempted to ask her to accompany him to Carlene's. After all, the girlfriend had approached Isabelle after the graveside service and expressed sympathy. Because she hadn't been hiding her identity that day, she might answer questions from Danny's sister.

Yet Nate knew Izzy would recognize this for what it was—an

obvious ploy to spend time with her and find out why she needed to take a break from him. Regarding annoying euphemisms, that one had to be in the top five on everyone's list. Part of him didn't care how obvious his motives appeared. He wanted Izzy to spell out exactly what unforgivable blunder had slammed the door on their future. But if she needed time, she would have it.

Thanks to GPS, Nate easily found the private community where Carlene and Raymond Bradington lived. Unfortunately, a guard was posted at the electronic gate, and Nate's name wasn't on the Bradingtons' list of usual visitors. "What did you say your name was again, sir?" asked the security guard.

"My name is Nate Price. I'm a friend of Isabelle Andre, who's a friend of Mrs. Bradington. Miss Andre asked me to come today on her behalf. She was called away at the last minute." His explanation, although delivered with perfect sincerity, sounded lame even to him.

"Sorry, sir. I don't see the name Isabelle Andre on the list either." He peered up impatiently from his clipboard.

"Please check to see if Mrs. Bradington is home. I'm here on an urgent matter for Miss Andre. Couldn't you just call her?"

After another skeptical perusal of him and his vehicle, the guard punched a number into his phone. Then he turned his back on Nate.

Returning a minute later, the guard's surprise rivaled Nate's own. "Mrs. Bradington said you should drive up to the house. Stay on the main avenue until the third stop sign, Mr. Price. Then turn left and go about a mile and a half. The Bradingtons' home will be on your left, adjacent to the golf course, 458 Pine Hollow." The man actually tipped his cap.

Mr. Price? Suddenly he was no longer a dubious interloper trying to access an exclusive world? "Thanks." Nate drove through the gate the moment it lifted much faster than necessary.

After passing a variety of opulent homes that failed to generate even a spark of jealousy, Nate found the Bradingtons' driveway and parked in the turnaround. *Just the landscaper's bills must cost these people a fortune.* When Nate rapped on the double front entrance, the elusive Carlene answered the door. "Mrs. Bradington?"

"Mr. Price? Please come in." She opened the door wide with a friendly smile.

The foyer soared upward two stories and was larger than his living room and dining area combined. "This is rather impressive." Nate let his gaze travel up to the crystal chandelier high overhead.

"Thank you, but I can't take any credit for the decor. My husband didn't trust my taste when we moved in, so he hired a decorator. If you're a sports buff, you may have heard of him—Ray Bradington. He played for the Titans a few years back." She looked at him with a certain expectation on her face.

Nate wracked his brain but came up empty. "Sorry. I follow college ball more than the pros."

"No matter. Why don't we have a seat in here?" Smiling graciously, Carlene led the way into a comfortable living room. She pointed at the sofa and then chose a chair by the window.

Nate admired the high-gloss floors, glass étagères, and paintings on the walls. He quickly concluded that football players made substantially more money than private investigators. "Thanks for seeing me without an appointment. I should have called first." He sat, even though he didn't expect to be there long.

"That would have been difficult since I didn't give Isabelle my number when I paid my respects."

The fact Carlene hadn't left her address either hung uncomfortably in the air. Nate scanned the room again before meeting her eye.

"Isabelle appreciated that you came to the funeral, but you

were a bit of a shock to her. She didn't know Danny had been dating someone. A few days later, she wanted to reach out to you and asked me to help. She was planning to visit today, but something urgent came up at work."

Carlene's cheery demeanor diminished. "I suppose you're wondering, and rightly so, why a married woman was dating Danny."

"Yes, I am a little curious."

"Have you ever been married, Mr. Price? Sometimes marriages run off track. Even couples who are deeply in love occasionally have problems. Ray and I had been separated for eight or nine months. He moved out and I filed for divorce." Carlene twirled a long lock of hair into a ringlet. "It was during this difficult period that I met Danny."

Unless Nate was imagining things, just mentioning Danny's name brought a pained expression to her face. "Where did you two meet?"

"I went with a few girlfriends down to Beale Street to listen to music." Carlene rubbed the backs of her fingers. "Don't think late on a weekend night—that's too crazy for my taste. We shared a bucket of barbecue ribs and heard some great blues at seven o'clock on a Wednesday. Danny was filling in for another musician, but he played a few solos. I've always loved the sax. And I fell in love with Danny almost as easily."

The fact that she admitted she loved him astounded Nate. "In that case, I'm sorry for your loss, Mrs. Bradington."

She frowned at the use of her formal address. "Thank you, and please call me Carlene. I was devastated when I heard about his death. That's why I came to the funeral. I wanted closure for a brief but enjoyable period of my life."

"I take it you and your husband have reconciled." Nate decided it was time for the obvious question.

Carlene reached for a pillow and hugged it to her chest. "Yes. He promised to go to counseling. We both went to a marriage counselor, and now our relationship is better than ever." She produced a glorious smile—the smile that probably won the hearts of Raymond Bradington and Danny Andre alike. "Marriage is a sacrament, and we both took vows till death do us part. I'm happy to report we're getting along much better."

"I wish you two the best of luck." Nate forced himself to say the words, but they sounded phony in his ears. "Mind telling me if you went back to your husband before or after Danny died?"

Just for a millisecond Nate saw panic in Carlene's blue eyes.

"Before, of course," she snapped. "As soon as Ray agreed to counseling, I agreed to give him another chance. I went to the club where Danny played and told him of my decision to reconcile. Danny understood perfectly. He wished me luck, just as you did, Mr. Price." Carlene rose regally to her feet. "Please thank Isabelle for her concern and reiterate my condolences. I will always remember her brother as a kind man whose friendship I treasured during a difficult period." Then she strode from the room toward the front door.

Nate had no choice but to thank the glamourous housewife and slink back to his car. His interview with Danny's last love was over, and he was just as nowhere as the last time Tyrone Biggs had fed him a false lead.

THIRTY

When her phone rang, Isabelle looked at the caller ID and groaned. Nicki, again. As much as she adored her new friend, she couldn't talk to her today or any day until she came up with a good excuse as to why she was avoiding her. But when the phone rang again five minutes later, Isabelle knew she couldn't avoid a showdown any longer.

"Hi, Nicki. Sorry I haven't been able to get back to you."

"Izzy Andre, is that really you? I was starting to think I had bad breath or you had developed an aversion to frizzy-haired blondes."

"Your breath is fine, and your hair isn't the least bit frizzy." Guilt over her rude behavior made Isabelle's palms sweat.

"Then why the cold shoulder? I'd hoped you would join Nate and me Monday night for dinner at Bleu. Golly, we ate some awesome food."

"I heard they were good, but I got tied up with a showing on Monday."

"Understood, but it's already Wednesday. How about tonight? Nate, you, and I can stay on budget with pizza on the levee or maybe on the hotel's rooftop. It's a real nice place to watch the sunset if you have another late showing."

"I don't think that's a good idea." Isabelle rubbed the spot between her eyebrows.

"Okay, I get that something isn't right between you and Nate. And maybe, just maybe, it's none of my business. So how 'bout just you and me—a girls-only night out?"

Isabelle felt the lump in her throat expand big enough to choke her. "I'm swamped at work, Nicki, and that's the truth." She wasn't lying, but the hitch in her voice betrayed it wasn't the sole reason.

"Are you crying? You *have* to tell me what's wrong, Izzy. Have I done something to make you mad?"

In that instant, Isabelle knew there was no way around this. She had to hurt Nicki's feelings or chance a far worse fate at the hands of Tony Markham. Inhaling a deep breath, she chose the only logical excuse. "No, Nicki, you haven't done anything. But spending time with you reminds me that Danny is dead. It's not your fault, but as long you and Nate stay in Memphis, I'll *never* get past my grief."

Nicki was speechless for what seemed like forever. Then she said softly, "I was under the impression you wanted us here on Danny's case."

"Yes, at first I did. But it's been almost three weeks, and neither of you are any closer to finding his killer."

"That's because the police focused on Tito Sullivan as their suspect. We can only assist homicide, or they will run us out of town—"

Isabelle feigned indignation. "It doesn't matter the reason! His killer will never be caught. It's been too long. Do you know how many murders go unsolved each year?"

"Too many, granted, but this is Danny we're talking about!" Nicki mustered her own indignation.

"I know that, but I just want to put this behind me—"

"Along with me and Nate? You want to put us behind you too?"

Isabelle felt her gut twist into a knot, but she couldn't postpone the inevitable any longer. "Yes, I think that would be best. I can't look at either of you and not see Danny lying on the riverbank."

"Maybe in a few months…or…or for my wedding—"

"No, Nicki. I know you love your cousin and wanted us to get together, but that's not going to happen. It's time for the two of you to pack up and head back to New Orleans. I'm grateful for what you've done, but I think it's best to let Memphis Homicide finish the investigation."

"Whatever you say, Izzy. Hunter already bought his plane ticket for Friday, so we'll stay through the weekend. I have something planned with my *friend* Henry anyway, but come Monday morning, I'm leaving Memphis in my dust. Nice knowing ya." Nicki was sobbing when she hung up.

Isabelle also burst into tears and laid her forehead on her arm. She cried so hard she attracted attention. The receptionist and another agent ran into her office.

"What's wrong, Miss Andre?" asked Janice, slipping an arm around her shoulder.

"I'm sorry I bothered you," Isabelle whimpered, lifting her head. "I had a horrible quarrel with a friend. Now I'm just over-reacting to something she said." She dabbed her eyes with a tissue.

Her two coworkers looked at each other and then at her. "If you say so," said Janice, but she made no effort to leave.

"I'm fine now. Honest. Let's all get back to work."

"I was on my way to see you anyway." Janice slowly withdrew her arm. "A Mr. Markham is waiting on line two. He will only talk to you about a property you showed him. But isn't he the creep who—"

"No, Janice. Markham is a common name. I'll take his call. Thanks." Isabelle waited until they left her office before picking up the phone. "Mr. Markham, what can I do for you?"

"Ahhh, Belle. So nice to hear your voice. Seems like ages since Sunday."

She ignored his familiarity. *Could this afternoon get any worse?* "What property were you interested in? I can look up when the next scheduled open house is."

He laughed with a horrible brittleness. "We both know I'm not buying anything. There's really no need."

Her stomach twisted into a knot. "I thought you wanted to relocate to Germantown, but at the moment I have another client in my office. Perhaps you could make an appointment."

"Let's cut to the chase, shall we? I'm thinking dinner tonight. How about Italian? Let's replay our first date but with a far happier ending." His voice dropped to a soft, melodic cadence that turned her blood to ice water.

"Tonight is impossible, Mr. Markham. I'm showing a house to the couple sitting in front of me."

"Okay, Belle. I'll give you the benefit of the doubt that there really are people with you. But we came to an understanding last Sunday. I want another chance to prove we can be happy together. So go sell your fancy houses and act like Miss High-and-Mighty, but I don't plan to be patient forever."

"I understand. Why don't we get together next week?"

As Nicki had just done, Tony hung up on her. But unlike Nicki, he disconnected with a rage that was almost palpable.

Nicki and Nate would be gone by Monday. Isabelle bowed her head and prayed. *Please, God, keep my friends safe until I am rid of this madman once and for all.*

She was still trying to get herself together when, a few minutes later, Janice ushered back a couple eager to speak with an agent. They had driven up from Hattiesburg, Mississippi, after learning the husband would soon be transferred to the Memphis area. The enthusiastic pair tied her up for two hours as they discussed every listing remotely within their price range. After Isabelle arranged for several showings and provided addresses for three open houses, the couple left.

Checking her voice mail one last time, she found no more calls from Tony. How in the world could she get him arrested without entrapment or coercion on her part? She hoped she had bought herself enough time to get Nate and Nicki safely back in Louisiana.

When she finally left the office, Isabelle was even too tired for her favorite Greek salad. After all, she would have to park the car, stand in line at the counter, and wait while they chopped up a chicken breast. Instead, a cheeseburger and fries from a drive-through window would have to suffice.

Entering her dark condo, a mournful whine lifted her spirits. She dropped her purse, take-out bag, and the mail on the table and swept her cat into her arms. "Mr. Chester, are you hungry? Won't *anybody* give a starving cat something to eat?"

Chester's reply was a loud *meow*. Nuzzling his head with her chin, Isabelle opened the cupboard where cans of salmon pate and turkey giblets were stored. Then something odd caught the corner of her eye, freezing her midstride. Someone was sitting on the couch in her living room.

In that instant, Isabelle knew she had two or three seconds to act—a span of time that could change her life forever. Remembering her cell phone in her pocket, she lowered the cat to the floor and hit her speed dial. It wasn't for the Germantown detective who had taken her complaint and helped secure the TPO or even 9-1-1. The only number she'd set was for Nate Price, a man she'd broken up with two days ago. She pressed the button, along with the mute feature, and switched on the light, illuminating the features of Tony Markham.

"How on earth did you get in here?" she gasped, swallowing the taste of bile in her mouth.

Tony rose to his full six feet three. "You didn't think this building had good security, did you?"

"Not anymore I don't." She planted her feet and divided her weight evenly.

"Those overhangs allow anyone reasonably in shape to climb up to your unit. You'll soon discover I'm in much better than *reasonably* good shape." His neutral expression morphed into something feral. "And the locks installed on sliding glass doors are a joke."

"Good to know. So my next question is *why* are you here? I thought we came to an agreement on the phone that we would get together next week." She tried to ignore her cat's meows, but Mr. Chester let out an impatient howl.

"Either shut up that stupid cat or I will." Tony took a step toward the cat.

"He's just hungry. If I feed him, he'll quiet down." Isabelle picked him up and walked into the kitchen. As much as she hated confined spaces, she couldn't chance Tony lashing out against Chester.

"He's not the only one." He followed her into the kitchen and dropped a Jack's Deli sack on the counter. "I thought Wednesday was your day for Greek chicken salad. I picked up two and a lovely bottle of Pinot Grigio. I couldn't think of any Greek white wines, so I went with Italian."

Isabelle concentrated on opening a can of Nine Lives and scraping it into Chester's bowl. When she turned around, Tony was inches away.

"Why on earth would you pick up burgers?" He sprayed spittle as he roared. Like a split personality, his angry side had reared its ugly head. "Wednesday is Greek salad night!" He extended his arm and opened his fist. Her takeout bag, compressed to half its former size, dropped to the floor. With a vicious kick, Tony sent it skittering across the floor.

Isabelle hiccupped from holding her breath too long. "I was so exhausted after work I couldn't bear standing in line." With trembling fingers, she placed Chester's bowl in the corner of the pantry.

"Oh, Belle, you mean you really did have clients in your office when I called?" He swung from the evil Mr. Hyde to the benign Dr. Jekyll. "I'm sorry I doubted you. Sit and make yourself comfortable. I'm going to pour us a glass of wine."

As he crossed the room, she picked up the bag from Jack's and stepped around him. "This kitchen smells like salmon. Let's eat in the dining area, where we'll be more comfortable."

Tony frowned but didn't protest. "If that's what will make you happy." He followed at her heels with the bottle of wine and two glasses.

"I'm just opening the sliding door a few inches for some air," she said, and then she lowered herself primly onto a chair.

He watched her every move before sitting across from her at the table. "I just realized I never answered your earlier question."

"Which question was that?" Isabelle tried to act normal in the midst of the most terrifying situation of her life.

He filled their glasses and set one in front of her. "You *thought* we had an agreement to get together sometime next week." He sipped his wine but never broke eye contact. "Let's be clear. I never agreed to that. Once again, you're making the decisions and acting like they are the law of the land. A relationship is a partnership, Belle. We will *share* in the decision making." With each statement his voice rose with intensity until he was shouting. "I don't care if you pick a stupid movie to watch or which nights we go out to eat, but when I want to spend quality time with you, I will *not* be put off!"

Isabelle's hands turned clammy, and a bead of sweat ran down her temple. "That wasn't my intention."

"No? Then drink up. That bottle of vino cost me twenty bucks."

"You know that I don't care for—"

Tony slapped her across the face, an action which startled more than injured her. "I *said* have a drink."

Isabelle lifted the glass to her lips, spilling several drops on her blouse. Swallowing a sip, she forced a smile. "It's delicious, but may I have some of my salad first? I'm afraid the wine will go right to my head."

"Of course. Let's eat. We have a full night ahead of us." Tony pulled both salads from the bag. "I truly don't want a queasy stomach to ruin what I have planned." He spread out napkins and plasticware and added salad dressing as though they were any other American couple enjoying an easy supper.

Isabelle speared a tomato with her fork, but when she brought it to her lips she began to gag.

"What is wrong with you?" he snarled. "You had no trouble chowing down the food on that touristy riverboat. You didn't choke on your dinner with Nate Price." Without warning, he grabbed her wrists and hauled her to her feet as though she were a ragdoll. Dragging her away from the table, he slapped her hard across the face a second time and threw her on the couch.

"Please, Tony. I want to eat my salad. It was the wine I'm not used to. I know you paid good money—"

"Stop lying, Belle. In fact, stop talking altogether! I tried to play nice and it got me nowhere. You're about to find out what happens when a woman forgets her place in the world. I'm going to make you very sorry." Digging his knee into the center of her chest, Markham pinned her to the couch like a moth.

Isabelle opened her mouth to scream.

"I could have sworn I told you to shut up." Markham encircled her neck with his hands and began to squeeze.

In the distance she thought she heard sirens, but it was probably wishful thinking. Closing her eyes, Isabelle hoped she would die quickly so she wouldn't have to be with him another minute longer.

"Get off her, Markham! Or I'll put a bullet in your head long before the cops can save you."

A familiar voice penetrated her muddled senses. Isabelle hovered above a deep black chasm.

In the next instant the suffocating weight was off her chest. Isabelle struggled to sit up and focus her bleary eyes. Nate had an arm around Tony's throat and a gun pressed to his temple. Tony was gasping for breath, his face bleached of color. Outside sirens blared, car doors slammed, and men shouted orders.

"Nate," she gasped. "Please don't shoot him." She coughed and sputtered. "The police are here. They can arrest him."

Nate looked her in the eye for a long moment. Then he pulled out a cable tie, threw Tony to the floor, and secured his wrists behind his back. The big man who'd been so brave bullying her was now whimpering like a child.

"Germantown Police! Open up!" The shout was accompanied by a pounding fist.

Holstering his gun, Nate unlocked the front door. In the next instant, he wrapped Isabelle in the protective shelter of his arms.

"I worried you wouldn't figure out what was happening," she said into his shirt. "Then I worried you might ignore me. I certainly gave you plenty of incentive."

Nate hugged her tightly. "You know us MSU boys never walk away from a challenge. I was about to call and ask if you had enough thinking time yet. Sometimes too much thinking can be worse than not enough. It makes you afraid to take a leap of faith."

Isabelle lifted her face to his. "If not for you, he would have killed me. Thank you." Her two words sounded pathetically inadequate.

"Miss Andre, do you need medical attention?" A police officer intruded on their moment.

She rubbed a tender spot on her throat. "No, I don't think so." Nevertheless EMTs soon surrounded her to shine lights into her eyes and attach a blood pressure cuff.

One officer read Markham his rights while another hauled him out the door. With a gun barrel no longer against his temple, he shouted an assortment of foul names and detailed his plans for her once he was released from jail.

Nate pulled a microcassette from his pocket and followed the assemblage into the hallway. When he returned, he was grinning. "From the time I reached your balcony I recorded every word Markham said and every one of his threats. This will help the DA win more than just a stalking conviction. He tried to kill you. We got him on felonious assault and attempted murder." Nate squeezed in between the medical technicians.

Even though she was being poked, prodded, blinded, and monitored, Isabelle had never felt so happy in her life.

And so protected.

And so much in love.

For the next hour, police officers took photos, bagged evidence, and asked an inordinate number of questions about the progression of events. Finally, she and Nate were left blissfully alone, although she would have to meet with the DA tomorrow and sign a formal statement.

No words could express her gratitude, so Isabelle just wrapped her arms around Nate's waist and hugged him. For a long while they simply enjoyed the quiet after a long and ugly storm. "It was him all along, wasn't it? Tony killed my poor brother to get back at me."

"I don't know, but we're leaving that question up to Detective Marino of Memphis Homicide. After all, what good are friends in high places if I still have to work so hard?" Nate brushed a kiss across her forehead. "In the meantime, you and I have some serious making-up to do."

Isabelle giggled. "What do you want to do first? Hold hands?"

"Let's start by calling for a pizza. But you're paying and I'm picking out the toppings."

"On second thought, let's start with this." In a moment of reckless abandon, Isabelle stretched up on tiptoes and kissed him squarely on the lips. "Now, what do you want on that pizza?"

THIRTY-ONE

*N*ate politely declined when the waitress tried to refill his coffee mug for the fifth time. No need to overwork his kidneys just because no one wanted to have breakfast with him. With so much to tell Nicki, he'd left several messages on her voice mail in her suite that they should have breakfast together. Here it was almost noon and still not a word. Good thing he went ahead and ordered the breakfast special or he might have starved to death.

Mr. Prescott was suspiciously absent from the concierge desk. Would a quick check at Oakbrook reveal Henry Prescott was also missing in action? What on earth was Nicki up to? And a better question might be why had he made her a partner at his agency? Today he could have used her expertise with databases as well as her woman's intuition. With Tony Markham in custody, Nate wanted to know every move the guy had made the day Danny died. In his deranged mind, Markham could have perceived Danny as a threat to a relationship with Isabelle. After last night, he proved himself capable of far more than stalking and perverse fantasies. He was capable of murder. Nate needed to secure conclusive evidence before more time elapsed.

"Mr. Price?" An attractive, middle-aged woman broke through

his fog. "My name is Mrs. Hern. I'm filling in for Mr. Prescott for an hour while he runs an errand. This message was left for you at the front desk." She handed him a sealed envelope.

"Thank you." Nate nodded, briefly wondering if he should have stood up. His mother's attempts to instill proper manners had left a vague imprint. He pulled out a sheet of stationery, embossed with the Carlton logo, and read:

> *Nate, I will be tied up today on at outing with Henry.*
> *We may be out very late tonight. Don't worry about me.*
> *I'm fine and will contact you when I get a chance.*
>
> *Your cousin and favorite employee, Nicki*

Nicki awake after the streetlights had turned on?

Not informing her cousin as to her whereabouts was one thing, but as her boss, shouldn't he be kept in the loop as to what she was doing?

Unsure whether to laugh or be irritated, Nate paid his check and strode out the front door for a head-clearing walk. The bright spring sunshine immediately started baking the back of his neck. Before he'd gone two blocks, Nate made the only choice that made any sense: He wouldn't let his pride stand in the way of finding Danny's killer. He punched in the detective's number to bring his ally up to date with yesterday's events.

"Chip? It's Nate. I think you should take a look at a Tony Markham for the Danny Andre homicide. That sicko broke into Isabelle's condo and tried to strangle her. He's been stalking her for weeks. Last night his violence escalated to a new level."

Marino issued his signature snide laugh. "I'm way ahead of you, old buddy. You don't think I got pals on the Germantown force? They gave me the heads-up right after they booked that pervert. But I'm glad you're keeping me in the loop. Sounds like you arrived in the nick of time. What, no white stallion to ride in on?"

"I rented one but couldn't figure out how to get him up on the balcony."

Marino snorted. "As much as I'd love to lock up Markham for the rest of his unnatural life, he ain't our man for the Andre murder."

Nate came to an abrupt stop, causing the sidewalk throng to detour around him. A few muttered comments as they passed. "What do you mean? I've seen him in action. He would have killed Isabelle if I hadn't gotten there."

"Yeah, I believe you. But that don't change the fact Markham had an iron-clad alibi for the weekend Danny died. He'd been arrested for voyeurism outside a college dorm at Ole Miss. Oxford Police held him forty-eight hours. Markham rigged a remote video camera to peek into windows. He claimed he was trying to catch a shot of a rare Western Kingbird, and filmed the girls by accident. Bird-watching—what kind of cockamamie story is that?"

Nate ignored the question. "What happened after the forty-eight hours?"

"Not one of the women would sign the complaint. They didn't want to be bothered, so Markham was released. And then he threatened to sue the police if they didn't remove any reference to the 'misunderstanding' from their database. Unfortunately, the period he was locked up covered the time Andre had been killed. Since then he got fired from his job, giving him more time to stalk innocent women. So I'm going to ask you nicely if you got anything *else* you want to share since this still is my case. Hold that thought, I gotta take this other call."

While Marino was gone, Nate tried to untangle something Isabelle had said. She told the officer who questioned her last night that she'd bought more time with Markham by saying what he wanted to hear. No doubt all women used the device to avoid difficult confrontations. Carlene Bradington said: *"I will always remember her brother as a kind man whose friendship I treasured during a difficult period."* Nate had never heard such a rehearsed delivery in his life. Was she putting up a smoke screen to hide her real feelings? *Friendship?* That wasn't how Tyrone Biggs described their relationship. *"What I'm telling you is that high-maintenance girlfriend had a nasty ex-husband, bigger than an ox. He came around one night and started trouble."* Who had Carlene been protecting— herself or her rich husband? Nate ducked under an awning to get out of the hot sun.

"You still there, Price?" Marino asked when he came back on the line.

"Yeah, I'm here. And I need to tell you about my trip to see Carlene Bradington. Isabelle asked me to deliver her condolences in person. During the visit something didn't sound right about her breakup with Danny."

"Let's not talk about this on the phone," Marino said after a brief hesitation. "Where can we meet?"

Twenty minutes later, the two former Mississippi State football players sat at a table in Kurtz's Deli. While Chip chomped into an Italian hoagie, Nate relayed everything he could remember about meeting the woman Danny had loved.

The detective listened without interruption. When Nate was finished, he set the rest of his sandwich down. "Sit tight. I can access police databanks from my car and make a few calls. Do you think Miss Andre will help us get inside the Bradington house?"

"Probably."

Chip stood. Before heading for the door, he said, "Call her to see if she'll meet us in Bartlett."

By the time he returned, Nate had paid the bill and boxed up Chip's leftovers. "Well?"

"Jackpot. Just like the little wife said, Ray Bradington played tight end for the Tennessee Titans. He'd been a big draft pick nine years ago. Plenty of talent, or so his coaches thought."

"How come I never heard of him?"

"Because he only played one season. Now he manages a fitness gym out in the suburbs. Despite his enormous salary and signing bonus, Ray failed to set the gridiron on fire. He also got into plenty of trouble while under contract. He broke somebody's jaw in a Beale Street bar. Then he almost killed a man a week later. Charges were dropped, no doubt after a serious exchange of money. But the Titan's owners ordered him to a therapist for anger management. Nobody can afford having a loose cannon on the field, especially since Ray averaged one unsportsmanlike conduct penalty per game. Eight months later, Bartlett police were called to his house for possible domestic assault. Ray had put sweet Carlene in the emergency room. This time the Titans cut him from the roster."

Nate's hands bunched into fists even though the adversary was miles away.

"I saw the hospital intake photos." Marino continued. "Man, that guy should be drawn and quartered for what he did to a woman half his size."

"Hard to understand why she stayed married to him," Nate said more to himself than the detective.

"She might have tried to get away, but he would find her and drag her home. Violence like that is unpredictable."

"You're right. Tell me what you want Isabelle and me to do."

"Do you think she would be willing to wear a wire?" Marino started texting a message.

"No, Chip. No. Isabelle has been through enough. I'll wear the wire. If Bradington is home, I'm sending Izzy out to the car. Like you said, a guy like that is unpredictable."

Marino stopped texting. "If the husband is home, what makes you think Carlene will even let you in the house? You may be the one sitting in the car, but a woman will usually invite in another woman. Why don't we let Miss Andre decide if she can do this?"

Nate wanted to make that decision for her, but knew he didn't have the right. Isabelle needed both Markham and Danny's killer behind bars if she was ever to find closure. "All right. I'll call Isabelle on the way to Bartlett. She might not want *any* part of this."

But Nate turned out to be dead wrong. Isabelle eagerly agreed and then beat them to the meeting spot half a mile from the Bradingtons' development. Isabelle jumped out of her car the moment Nate pulled up behind her. "What's the plan, Nate? Why is Detective Marino still sitting in the car?"

"Good afternoon, Miss Andre," Nate said with a smile.

Blushing, she leaned forward to kiss his cheek. "Good afternoon. Sorry, I got pretty excited after your call. Do you think the ex-husband killed my brother?" she asked, the color draining from her face.

"There's a good chance, but Marino says he needs your help to get inside the house. He's been on the phone trying to secure a search warrant, but apparently we don't have enough evidence for one. He's also waiting for a technician with a recording device. He wants you to wear a wire when we talk to Carlene."

Her eyes went wide. "Me?"

Nate slicked a hand through his hair. "I'm against it. I want to wear the wire, but Marino thinks Carlene will shut the door in my face. If she talks to anybody, it will be you."

"I'll do it."

"Hold on, Izzy. Carlene was legally separated when she met Danny, not divorced. Her husband has a hot temper. He's already put several men in the hospital during fights and has been abusive throughout their marriage. If Bradington is home, this could be dangerous. I would prefer that—"

Isabelle placed her hands on his chest. "No, Nate. I'm touched by your protectiveness, but I agree with Detective Marino. I have the best chance of getting Carlene to talk. I loved my brother. Please let me do this for him."

A white van pulled up behind Marino's sedan, drawing their attention. "That must be the technician. Let's go see if they're ready for me." She started to walk away, but Nate grabbed her hand.

"Fine, but you're not going in alone. We'll say I'm your grief counselor, or whatever explanation you like."

"My grief counselor?" Her magnificent cat eyes sparkled. "I guess it's a fitting role for my new *boyfriend*."

When Isabelle and Marino climbed into the back of the van, Nate checked his weapon and the extra clips of ammo in his pocket as though expecting a shootout with a drug lord. He remained within earshot of every one of Marino's instructions. He didn't like the plan one bit, but without an alternative, he had little choice in the matter.

When Isabelle was ready to go, Nate climbed into the passenger side of her Prius. Without a search warrant, Marino would have to remain outside the gate until Nate punched in 9-1-1, a number both he and Isabelle programed into speed dial.

At the guard shack, she leaned out the window and turned her luminous eyes up to the guard. "Isabelle Andre to see Mrs. Bradington," she said with a tearful hitch in her voice. "I'm not sure if she's expecting me or not. This gentleman is my spiritual advisor."

The guard paid Nate zero notice. "One moment, ma'am."

Through the window, Nate and Izzy could see him talking on the phone. Then, surprisingly, the gate lifted. Nate directed her to the Bradington home—a place that had been no safe haven for

Carlene. After she parked in the driveway, Isabelle climbed out and gazed at the luxurious mini mansion.

"Hard to imagine such a nasty man could live in such luxury."

"Money can buy all the good taste a person needs." Nate took hold of her arm. "You sure you're ready for this?"

"I'm positive. Now stop looking suspicious and start looking reassuring. You're my grief counselor, remember?" Izzy marched up the walk and rang the doorbell.

Carlene responded immediately but opened the door only a few inches. "Isabelle, I'm confused. Security said you were accompanied by your spiritual advisor. I've met Mr. Price, and he's no pastor."

Isabelle wrung her hands. "Nate was a good friend of Danny's. I couldn't get through this without him and his cousin."

"I'm sorry you're suffering." Carlene sounded contrite but the door didn't budge. "I remember the pain when my father died, but I can't help you. Perhaps I can pray for you." The massive door began to close.

"Please give me five minutes," Isabelle begged. "The musicians on Beale Street say Danny had a death wish—that he purposefully put himself in harm's way with dangerous people. Could you tell me about his emotional state the last time you saw him? Please, Carlene." Isabelle burst out crying, tears Nate knew were no act.

Carlene hesitated for an instant. "All right. I can spare a few minutes before my Pilates class. Come in." She ushered them into the impressive living room.

Not a single thing—not a magazine or new plant or forgotten coffee cup—was different from his first visit. Isabelle perched on the arm of a chair while Nate took a position near the window and switched on his recorder. The weight of the extra clips in his pocket and the weapon under his coat did little to mitigate his anxiety for Isabelle's safely.

"It has been a while since I last saw your brother. As I told Mr. Price, I ended our friendship when my husband and I decided to reconcile. Married women shouldn't keep single men as friends." Carlene issued a brittle laugh.

"Then maybe his friends were right. Danny was...suicidal." Isabelle's hand went to her throat.

Carlene shook her head. "No, that's not true. Danny's mental state was always upbeat, including the last time I saw him. He had a smile and kind word for everyone."

Izzy's tears returned. "You don't understand. I found a letter he wrote but never mailed. Danny was *in love with you*. He wanted to ask you to marry him. When you told him you didn't love him, that you thought of him as just a friend, it must have put him over the edge. I don't know how he managed it, but maybe he picked a horrible argument with someone. Some sort of suicidal confrontation because he'd made such a fool of himself." Isabelle covered her face and sobbed uncontrollably.

Nate moved to comfort her, but Carlene got there first. "No! You've got it all wrong, Isabelle." Carlene spoke in little more than a whisper, but her message was clear. "I *loved* your brother. Danny was the sweetest man I ever met, but Ray wouldn't let me go. If I divorced him for another man, Ray would make sure we never found happiness. Don't you understand? I had to break up with Danny, but love for my husband had nothing to do with it." Her words disintegrated into wrenching sobs.

"You're just as pathetic as that low-life turned out to be!" Ray Bradington thundered as he walked into the room, a man even larger than his stats conveyed. "You were working in a donut shop when I met you. This house, your designer clothes, and your six-hundred dollar shoes all came from me. But I've got bad news for you, Carly. You might as well have married that nobody sax player. According to my accountant, you'll soon be asking for your old job back at Donut Land." Ray's massive hand waved through the air. "Your perfect world is about to come crashing down. So why don't you take a hike with your crybaby pals? Here's an idea...you can all go out for donuts."

Carlene ran at Ray so fast Nate had no time to react. But if they wanted to end this, he had to give Bradington enough rope to hang himself.

"What did you do?" Carlene pounded on his chest with her fists.

Bradington grabbed her by both wrists. "You little fool. If you would have kept your mouth shut in the ER, we'd be sitting pretty right now. But you had to sneak around behind my back with that skinny musician. Why, because he's just so *sensitive*? I saw you in Jimmy's Downunder that night, hanging all over the guy, mesmerized as though Danny Andre was Satchmo come back from the dead."

Nate had heard and seen enough. "Let go of her, Bradington." He closed the gap between them.

Ray's hateful glare turned from his wife. "I don't know who you are, but I suggest you stay out of this. If you know what's good for you and your little friend."

"Forget about them. Talk to me, Ray!" Carlene screamed. "What did you do to Danny?"

Bradington refocused on the hundred pound woman in front of him. "Do you think I wanted that loser waiting for the next time we had a fight? I went to his dump of an apartment for a chat. I don't think you would've liked living there," he sneered. "I told him to find a new town to play his horn in or I would make him sorry. Mr. Valiant said he wasn't going anywhere, that he could wait until you'd had enough. I couldn't allow that. So I said I was going home to make *you* sorry instead." Bradington laughed. "That scrappy punk came at me swinging. He put up a pretty good fight for a while, but there's no talking sense to a *man in love*. Just for the record, I hadn't gone over there to kill the guy, only teach him a lesson."

"What about the heroin?" Isabelle demanded. "He died of a heroin overdose."

"Lucky break for me. I figured one of those lowlifes had junk hidden somewhere in that dump. Found it first place I looked—taped under the toilet tank lid. That took care of Andre waking up with a sore neck the next day."

"You're a monster!" Carlene struggled to break free from his hold.

"And you're a cheating wife!" He grabbed Carlene by the throat.

This time Nate reacted quickly. Pulling his gun from the holster, he leveled it at Bradington, a foot taller than Carlene. "Let go of her, Ray, or you're the one who'll be sorry."

Even though he'd been taught to turn the other cheek, every fiber in his being wanted to shoot Bradington. Nate cocked his weapon. "I'm not telling you again to let go of her."

"She's all yours." Bradington shoved Carlene toward Nate, throwing him off balance, and bolted from the room.

"Both of you get down on the floor and stay there!" Nate shouted, running through the doorway after him. He couldn't risk Bradington coming back with firepower. The guy had little to lose. But by the time Nate reached the garage, Bradington was peeling down the driveway.

In the distance he heard the sound of sirens for the second time in as many days. Detective Marino would be watching for Bradington's vehicle. The wife-beater and murderer wouldn't get away, and there would be no bribing victims to keep them quiet. Inside Ray and Carlene's three-car garage, surrounded by expensive toys and sports equipment, Nate inhaled a lungful of air. It was his first easy breath in a long while.

THIRTY-TWO

*C*rouching between the sofa and the wall, Isabelle couldn't remain hidden any longer. Nate had gone after Ray, a much larger man besides being quintessentially evil. Nate might be armed, but who says Bradington didn't have a gun in the garage? She'd already lost Danny to this psychopath for no other reason than Carlene fell in love with him. No way could she cower behind the sofa when Nate might be in danger.

"Stay here, Carlene," she said, stumbling to her feet. "Don't follow me."

"Where are you going? Nate told us to stay where we are!"

"And that's exactly what you will do. I wish I'd met you during the short time you and Danny were together. I would have loved seeing him…happy."

Isabelle ran into an empty kitchen, through a spotless utility room, and then into the garage containing an SUV, a small sports car, and an empty spot. Nate stood under the overhang, staring at the street as sirens grew louder.

"What happened? Is Ray gone?"

Nate grinned as he turned around. "He won't get far. I pressed 9-1-1 the moment he called us 'crybaby pals.' I don't even like donuts."

"Oh, Nate. I was worried Bradington had stabbed or shot you, and you're out here making jokes." She wrapped both arms around his waist and buried her face in his chest.

"*What*? You think I can't handle a two-hundred-pound ox when helpless females are depending on me?" Nate tipped up her chin. "Good thing I don't have much of an ego."

Isabelle didn't laugh at his joke. "Please don't take unnecessary chances, not on the job or anywhere else. I'm fond of you just as you are."

"*Fond* of me? I'm fond of flannel shirts and my Aunt Rose." His smile was slow in coming as they watched the arrival of the Shelby County Sheriff's Department and Detective Marino. "If you want to get something off your chest, you'd better hurry."

"I love you, Nate. I want to make that perfectly clear before we're rudely interrupted." Isabelle tightened her embrace.

"In that case you're in luck, Miss Andre. There was no expiration date on that offer of undying devotion in high school."

～

Nicki was the one who had devised their foolproof plan. Yet now she was having difficulty putting it into action. Henry's great-granddaughter, Antoinette, would bring Henry to the hotel around 2:00 a.m. Someone that young had no trouble staying awake, while Henry seldom slept more than a few hours each night, preferring instead to catnap during the day when the spirit moved him. Robert had been the most reluctant to participate because, as concierge, he had the most to lose. If they were caught, she would be asked to leave the hotel or maybe fined for malicious mischief. Henry would be sent back to the assistant living center with a stern reprimand. Hotel management would never risk negative PR by having a ninety-year-old man arrested. But the concierge might get fired, so Nicki was pleasantly surprised when Robert agreed. His exact words had been: "If you and Granddad insist on this ridiculous idea, I want to make sure security doesn't shoot first and ask questions later."

She and Henry weren't deterred by the threat of gunplay.

Robert planned to remain in his office after his shift to catch up on paperwork. He would keep Henry and Antoinette hidden until most of the hotel's patrons had gone to bed. Nicki was to review the details of their plan, drink a cup of chamomile tea, and sleep until her alarm went off at two o'clock. After all, she usually was in bed by 10:30, but tonight she wasn't the least bit sleepy.

Pacing the floor while reciting the poem found in Blake's keepsake box guaranteed she *wouldn't* be in top form when the occasion demanded precision. Nicki poured her third cup of herbal tea down the drain. It wasn't living up to the image of a bear dozing in an overstuffed chair. She'd just finished an entire bag of mustard pretzels and was eyeing a bag of cookies when someone knocked on her door. Every nerve in her body went on high alert.

"Are you still awake, *O'lette*?"

Only two people in the world called her that—an elderly woman who never left the New Orleans Garden District anymore…and her fiancé.

Nicki bolted across the room and yanked open the door. "*What* are you doing here?" She dragged him into the suite by his arm. "How did you get here so fast?"

Hunter produced his signature smile as he glanced around the room. "Thank goodness I'm not too late. I wasn't sure what time the mission would commence. Now, which question should I answer first, dear heart?"

"Take your pick." Nicki ran a hand through her tangled curls, self-conscious about her appearance.

"Stop. You look gorgeous, all flushed and frenzied." Grabbing her hand, he kissed the back of her fingers. "Regarding the what, it should be obvious. I was intrigued when I heard your plans and couldn't resist joining the expedition. Besides, I couldn't let my competition show me up with his courage and valor."

Nicki rolled her eyes. "Henry is older than my papaw, so your position as fiancé is not in jeopardy."

"Splendid. In that case I'm just here for the fun." Hunter ripped open the bag of cookies and popped one in his mouth.

"You do realize things could get dangerous."

"I'll be safe in the company of my favorite licensed PI."

"If we get caught, we could be arrested. The story might make the papers."

"No one knows the Galen name in Memphis. Nothing I do here will embarrass my family even if we spend the night in jail." He laughed with exasperating composure. "And we can call Nate to post bail. I would bet the ranch he's not part of your scheme."

"Of course not. That spoilsport would ruin everything. Nate doesn't even believe the jewels are still in the hotel."

"That boy is such a doubting Thomas." Hunter placed his hand above his heart. "I assure you that I'm a believer. Should I take a blood pact or drink cactus juice to prove my worthiness?"

"Not cactus, but maybe hemlock if you don't take this seriously." Scowling, Nicki shook her finger at him. "You didn't say how you got here so fast." She glanced at her watch. "I told you about our plan a little after seven, and now it's barely midnight."

"Never underestimate what a man in love can do…or the value of friends who own private planes. I talked a client into dropping me off in Memphis on his way to Denver. Because my investment advice made him tons of money last month, he happily accommodated the minor delay."

"And just like that you flew to Memphis?"

"With the woman of my dreams living in Tennessee, I keep

a suitcase by the door at all times." Hunter lifted her chin and kissed her nose.

Nicki shivered down to her toes. Not because the suite was too cold, but because no one had ever said such things before Hunter. Or made her feel so cherished. "Okay, Romeo, knock it off. You can stay if we talk business and no more mushy stuff."

Hunter straightened, clicked his heels, and then saluted. "Reporting for duty, Commander. What's our itinerary?"

"We rest until we rendezvous at o-three-hundred, but that's out of the question." Settling in a chair at the table, Nicki pointed at the opposite chair. "We have three hours to kill. First, I'll show you the electrical schematics for the fountain controls that I got from Robert, along with a map on how to find the mechanical room. Since you're here, you'll be in charge of turning off the water so I can investigate every nook and cranny without drowning."

"Do you think a Smithfield climbed into a fishpond to hide jewels under a plume of water?" Hunter's expression turned skeptical.

"I'm betting they turned off the fountain each night because decent folks kept decent hours, and the pond is only a foot deep. Hey, I thought you said you were a believer."

"Absolutely." He picked up the electrical schematics. "When I'm done memorizing these, I will bring you up to date on my mother's new ideas for our wedding reception. That should keep us awake nicely."

THIRTY-THREE

*P*recisely at the appointed hour, Nicki and Hunter met Antoinette and Henry in the courtyard. Not a creature was stirring in the hotel's grand lobby. Nicki introduced Hunter to Henry's great-granddaughter in a low voice.

"Pleased to meet ya," whispered Antoinette. "Dad said he can keep the security guards distracted for fifteen minutes but no more."

"Then let's stop jaw-boning and get to it." Henry released the brakes on his wheelchair and maneuvered himself forward with his heels.

"I'll head to the mechanical room to switch off the water," whispered Hunter. Clad from head-to-toe in black, including a knit skull cap, he looked like a cat burglar from a Peter Sellers movie.

Antoinette rolled Henry as close to the fountain as she could and pulled out her cell phone. She seemed content to catch up with texts while the others did whatever they were gathered to do.

Dressed in baggy shorts, a dark T-shirt, and flip-flops, Nicki sat on the low wall surrounding the fish pond. For a few minutes she listened to the traffic sounds on Third Street, a faraway television from some thoughtless guest, and the blood pounding in her ears. What if someone called the police? Hunter might make jokes, but he had already spent a night in jail for a crime he didn't commit, and she knew he didn't want to go back.

What if Henry suffered a heart attack from the excitement? Or more likely, what if she slipped on wet marble and broke her neck? How would a plaster cast or full-body traction look with her Lela Rose wedding dress?

Suddenly, the plume of water from the fountain stopped shooting into the air. Nicki had no more time to consider the consequences. Uttering a prayer, she stepped into the chilly water and waded toward its elaborate centerpiece. Robert would send Hunter a text message if security guards were headed in his direction or, if all went well, when the fountain could be turned on. The phone in Nicki's pocket would start vibrating if the guards resumed their rounds.

She had ten minutes at the most.

What on earth am I doing here? Inexplicably, Nicki was beset with a surge of practicality, paralyzing her in knee-deep water. She was a recent college graduate who had worked very hard to get her job at Price Investigations—a job she might forfeit if the hotel prosecuted her for trespassing or vandalism.

Ready to abandon her folly, Nicki locked eyes with Henry, a man who had witnessed decades of progress in his beloved hotel. Despite everything that had changed, they both felt the same excitement and drama that impelled the five original couples to play their game year after year. She winked at Hunter's chief competition and went to work.

Nicki moved around the fountain methodically as Henry aimed his flashlight into nooks and crannies. She ran her fingertips beneath edges and around trim pieces, stretching on tiptoes to reach decorative swirls and flourishes, while the final clue ran through her mind:

> *Remember to take your spare change*
> *When you look for Dorothy McGuire*
> *The king of the sea sees all*
> *So one promenade left*
> *A reach for the stars*
> *Then one sashay right,*
> *And a girl's best friend will be yours.*

According to Henry, Dorothy McGuire had starred in a film, *Three Coins in the Fountain*. Robert thought the reference to spare change confirmed the pond as the hunt's ground zero. Tourists loved to toss dimes and quarters into the water.

"Over here, Miss Price." Henry rolled his chair to the other side and shined his beam on a marble carving close to top. "That must be it—the king of the sea. The whale is the biggest fish in the ocean."

Nicki didn't bother to explain a whale was a mammal, not a fish. She was too busy climbing a slippery work of art. At any moment, she could break something or fall to her death—at least of embarrassment.

"Oh, dear me. Please get down from there before you kill yourself." Robert's panicky hiss nearly caused what he cautioned against.

Nicki grabbed a cornice to steady herself and peered over her shoulder. "Henry and I think we found something."

"The security guards are almost done with the chocolate cream torte I bought. They won't be shirking their duties much longer. Your time is up."

"Pay no attention to Bobby." Henry struggled to stand with the help of Antoinette. "We're very close now, Miss Price. I'm sure of it. Grab hold of that whale's head and turn it to the right."

Not considering how she would keep her balance, Nicki latched onto the king of the sea and gave it a twist.

At first it didn't budge. Then slowly, almost imperceptibly, it moved. She kept pushing as hard as she could until she had repositioned it ninety degrees to the left.

"Would you look at that?" Antoinette's exclamation echoed everyone's sentiments.

"Stay where you are, *O'lette*. I'm coming up to help." Hunter's slow drawl was a balm to her ears. He slipped off his Italian leather loafers and splashed through the water.

"Don't I look capable of lifting a whale's head toward the stars?" Nicki asked, giddy with excitement.

Hunter climbed to the spot where she perched. "Do you think I'll let you tell *our* grandchildren you did this alone? Not on your life. On the count of three, we'll lift together and turned this beast to the right. One…two…three."

After a moment of resistance, the piece of marble moved up an inch or two. Then with strength borne of sheer adrenaline, Nicki and Hunter shifted Moby Dick forty-five degrees to the right.

"What's happening, Miss Price?" asked Henry, his flashlight beam bouncing frantically around them. "I sure wish I could climb up there too!"

Speechless and motionless, Nicki and Hunter stared into a small, velvet-lined metal rectangle. When the whale reached for the stars, a tiny drawer hidden under a cornice opened. Inside were not one, but two matching letter openers. People Antoinette's age would probably not even recognize the ornate desk accessories from a bygone era, but enough stunning diamonds embellished the handles to make engagement rings for dozens of brides. And women of all ages knew about diamonds. Nicki carefully picked them up and tucked them into her pocket.

"Memphis PD!" A shout resonated over Nicki's shoulder. Simultaneously, every light in the grand lobby switched on. "Everyone freeze, except for the lunatics in the fountain. You two climb down slowly."

"Robert! What on earth is going on here?" asked a second voice, softer but no less piqued. "You're allowing guests to scale the hotel's priceless landmark as though it was the Matterhorn? It's three o'clock in the morning!"

"Would it be okay at three p.m.?" whispered Hunter.

"This will not end well," Nicki moaned.

"It may not, but don't think for a moment that my mother will let us postpone the wedding." Hunter climbed down to the water and lifted his hands in the air to assist her.

"I can explain what's going on, sir. Miss Price, Mr. Galen, this is Mr. Anderson, the hotel's general manager." Robert made introductions in a shaky but respectful tone.

"I recognized you from the portrait hanging on the second floor." Nicki sloshed toward the well-dressed man. "And I want you to know this is my fault. Mr. Prescott did *everything* to discourage me."

"Except for the obvious solution, Miss Price. He should have asked you to vacate the Carlton." Apparently, Mr. Anderson had little patience in the wee hours of the morning.

Henry thumped the arms of his wheelchair. "Shame on you. Your daddy, Edward Anderson Sr., would have let folks explain."

The general manager turned on his heel. "Henry, I didn't see you sitting there." He peered at the long-legged, short-skirted girl next to Henry's wheelchair. "And who are you?"

Antoinette looked up from her phone. "Just an innocent bystander taken prisoner by some crazy old people."

"Hey, I'm only twenty-six!" Nicki protested.

"Really? Then why do you hang out with my great-granddad?"

"Okay, enough!" Memphis's finest stepped front and center. "I gather these two are employees." He gestured at the Prescotts.

"Robert is our current concierge. Antoinette is his daughter. Henry is retired, but he worked here for more than fifty years." Anderson smiled at the former bellman.

"Time for you two wet rats to produce identification." The second patrolman spoke to Nicki and Hunter. "Then we're all going down to the station to sort this out."

"Wait a minute. I have an early class tomorrow." Antoinette sounded annoyed.

"Couldn't we settle this in my office?" said Mr. Anderson, perhaps mollified by the reference to his daddy. "Miss Price has been our guest for three weeks. And you must be her fiancé from New Orleans?"

"Hunter Galen, at your service, unless it involves controlling Nicki's behavior. Then I'm as helpless as anyone else." He handed his driver's license to the officer. "May I ask, sir, what dispatched you to the crime scene so promptly?"

"Somebody monkeying with the fountain controls triggered the silent alarm. Any breach of security automatically dispatches police and sends a text to Mr. Anderson's phone."

Hunter turned pale. "Sorry, my love," he whispered.

"Fortunately, I was in the vicinity for a fund-raiser," Mr. Anderson added.

"I need to see your ID now, miss." The second patrolman gestured toward Nicki.

"Sorry. The outfit didn't accommodate my wallet, but I can show you these." Nicki pulled the diamond letter openers from her pocket. "These are what we were searching for, not for ourselves, but for the rightful heirs. Henry and I just solved the Carlton's oldest mystery."

The two cops stared as the gems sparkled in the palm of her hand.

Mr. Anderson bent over to peruse them. "I thought those scavenger hunts were an urban legend, one that got better with each retelling."

"Those can't *possibly* be real diamonds," Antoinette concluded before returning to her social media updates.

"I would stake my life they are." Henry stomped on the metal foot rests of his chair.

"Okay, Mr. Anderson," said the first cop. "Are we arresting these two, three…four on trespassing charges, vandalism, and attempted theft? Or are we writing this up as a false alarm triggered during routine maintenance?"

"The hotel appreciates your prompt response, Officers, but I believe we'll settle this in-house." Anderson couldn't take his eyes off the letter openers. "May I, Miss Price?"

When Nicki handed him the prizes, he examined them as though they might disintegrate into dust. "Astonishing. Who would hide expensive jewels inside a fountain? We need to find the rightful owners."

"That would be Paul and Agnes Smithfield. They owned Smithfield Interiors, the company that designed and installed the fountain." Nicki pointed at the hotel's centerpiece. "But they have both passed on."

"Then the jewels belong to their heirs," said the hotel manager as the police headed for the door. "I want to hear each person's role in this, but not in the lobby."

"If it's all the same, I'm taking my great-granddad and going home." Antoinette eyed the exit.

"*Everyone*," Mr. Anderson ordered.

"Let me push Henry's chair," said Nicki. "There's something I need to ask him. I promise we'll be right there."

"What's on your mind, Miss Price?" asked Henry once the others had left. He was grinning as if he'd swallowed the proverbial canary.

"You knew where those diamonds were, or at least you had a strong suspicion. Since the Smithfields have passed on, why didn't you send your great-granddaughter to see if they were still there?

Antoinette is a sweet girl. She could've used the money for college or for her first house."

Henry shook his head. "I have several grandchildren, missy, and even more great-grand's. How could I favor one over the others? Besides, the jewels weren't mine to find. The hunt had to be finished, the mystery solved. That's why I needed a crack sleuth like you. You should do this for a living. You're pretty good at it. Now let's go get Robert's fat out of the fire. Good jobs like a concierge at a five-star hotel ain't easy to come by."

"We're on our way," she said. But unfortunately her cousin appeared at a most inopportune time.

"Nate! Um, what are you two doing here?" asked Nicki when he blocked her path to Mr. Anderson's office.

"According to my scanner, a sixty and sixty-three were underway at the Carlton Hotel."

Detective Marino scowled. "That's code for aggravated burglary and criminal trespass underway, in case you haven't gotten very far in the PI manual." His contempt for her hadn't mellowed much since their initial acquaintance.

"Nice to see you too, Detective. Shouldn't you be climbing back into your coffin? The sun is almost up."

"I hate to break up a reunion," said Henry, "but I really do need to explain everything that happened before my grandson gets fired." He advanced his wheelchair with his feet.

Marino took hold of the handles. "I'll take you since I'm dyin' to hear this explanation too. Nate, why don't you question your cousin alone?" He shot Nicki one final glare as he rolled Henry away.

Nate crossed his arms over his chest. "Unless you handed in your resignation in the last forty-eight hours, you'd better start talking."

Nicki tried to look innocent. "In a nutshell…we found a poem indicating they hid the diamonds in the fountain. But when Hunter turned off the water, he triggered the alarm. The cops came and caught us in the pond. Now Robert might get fired because he helped us." Nicki bit the inside of her jaw to keep from laughing.

"This isn't funny, Nicki. You might still get arrested."

"I know it isn't, but I'm so exhausted I'm slaphappy." She slumped onto a wrought iron chair. "What's new with you?"

"Where should I start?" Nate scrubbed his face with his hands. "Tony Markham broke into Izzy's condo and tried to strangle her, but I got there just in time. After I tracked down Danny's former girlfriend, Izzy and I went to talk to her. With Izzy wearing a wire and Detective Marino at the gate, Carlene's estranged husband admitted to murdering Danny in a jealous rage. That's about it for me."

Nick stared at him, speechless. "That skinny woman who came to his funeral?"

"One and the same."

"Markham has been arrested?"

"In jail without bond as we speak."

"And you and Izzy are back together?" she asked in a tiny voice. "Wow."

Nate rolled his eyes. "I've probably made PI history tying up both cases in the same day, yet *that's* what you're most impressed with?"

"Every time I look at Hunter, I remember the truly important things in life. That's what I want for you and Izzy." Nicki stood and hooked her arm through Nate's elbow. "Let's go talk to Mr. Anderson. If you verify that I actually work for you, I might not get kicked out of the hotel. After all, we are paid up through the weekend."

THIRTY-FOUR

*N*ate stared out the window of his room as rain pelted the city streets below. Huddled beneath umbrellas, a few brave tourists headed toward the restaurants and clubs on Beale Street. Maybe they were looking for good food, a cold beer, and some great Blues music on this Saturday night. Whatever they were searching for, Nate hoped they found it…because he certainly had.

He and Nicki came to town to help a friend in trouble—a man they thought had fallen between the cracks. Instead, they discovered that Danny Andre had lived an exemplary life of service. He had been helping others make a fresh start. In the end, his cruel and brutal death had nothing to do with his volunteer work or the bad neighborhood or a job on the fringe of society. A jealous love triangle—the last thing Nate would have guessed three weeks ago.

But solving Danny's murder wasn't the only thing lifting Nate's spirits on this dreary night. He'd been wrong about Isabelle Andre too. How could someone so not-his-type turn out to be everything he wanted in a woman? Funny what love could do when you gave it a chance.

Nate zipped his suitcase and checked his watch. He would

make their final night in the luxurious Carlton Hotel an evening to remember. These would be *his* dinner guests, not Hunter's. Nicki's fiancé had paid enough bills in Memphis. After all, he intended to take Nicki's advice about the important things in life. And his number one was milling by the door of Chez Francois when Nate reached the lobby.

"Just about everyone has arrived," said Isabelle, running to meet him. "We're waiting for Antoinette and Henry. They're riding together in the Oakbrook van."

Nate buzzed Isabelle's cheek with a kiss. "Where are Hunter and Nicki?"

Isabelle pointed at a bistro table near the fountain. "They're talking to Hunter's mom about some snafu with the Coast Guard. Apparently, maritime law requires a lifejacket for every guest at the reception."

"Not too many ships sink in the high seas of Lake Pontchartrain, but Mrs. Galen must learn that laws pertain even to her. Poor Nicki. She looks ready to scream." Nate waved at his cousin and then tapped on his watch.

"Good evening, Miss Andre. Hey, good buddy." Chip bowed to Isabelle and slapped him on the back. "I checked out the menu. Man, this restaurant will be way better than ribs and fries down the street. Thanks for the invite. Who's the gorgeous babe?" The detective eyed Antoinette as she approached with her parents and Henry.

"I'll introduce you at the table, but she's too young and way too feisty for you." Nate elbowed Chip in the ribs.

"Point taken. She sounds too much like your cousin." He smiled at Nicki across the courtyard.

"Your table is ready, Mr. Price," said the maître d'. Both he and Mr. Anderson were wearing tuxedos.

"Thank you. I believe we're all here," said Nate.

Mr. Anderson rubbed his palms together. "If I could have a few moments, Mr. Price, I have a special announcement to make."

"Of course. Take all the time you need. Why don't you lead the way?" Nate waited until everyone followed the maître d' and Anderson into the restaurant. Then he hollered to the couple still deep in conversation. "Hey, cousin, time to chow down."

Hunter waved an acknowledgment, slipped his phone into his pocket, and took Nicki's arm. But halfway across the court-yard a well-dressed woman with a massive bunch of flowers inter-sected their path.

"Now what?" Nate muttered to Isabelle.

"Why don't we give them another minute?" Izzy slipped her arm around his waist, a sensation he would never tire of.

While they watched from afar, Nicki's face crumpled with sor-row. "Uh-oh, this doesn't look good. Let's see if we can help."

"What's wrong, Nicki?" he asked when he reached her side.

"This is Mrs. Lansky, a nurse at Sunnybrook Care Center," said Nicki, sobbing. "Blake Koehler died last night. His condition began to deteriorate right after Henry and I visited him."

Nate couldn't remember exactly who Mr. Koehler was, but knew he had a role in the hunt for the jewels. "I'm so sorry, Nicki. Is there anything we can do?" It was a lame question, but nothing profound came to mind.

"Blake seemed to need closure, and Nicki and Henry helped him find it." The woman patted Nicki's arm. "Blake was happier that day than he had been in years."

"I will be sure to tell Henry that." Nicki dabbed her eyes with a handkerchief from the always helpful Hunter.

"Why don't you join us for dinner, ma'am?" said Nate. "Mr. Prescott is already inside, so you could tell him yourself. The more the merrier."

"Thank you, but my husband is waiting at home. I just wanted to give these to Miss Price. They're from Blake's family." She handed Nicki a bouquet of at least three dozen roses. "And Blake's box of mementos is to go to Mr. Prescott. I'll have it delivered to Oakbrook tomorrow. When Blake's family arrived to clean out his room, I told them about your visit. They made arrangements for the flowers and box of keepsakes then. They were so happy Blake enjoyed his final hours with an old friend."

Nicki looked ready to faint. "Thanks for telling me all this, Mrs. Lansky," she said between sniffles.

Hunter took charge. "Let me take these upstairs, sweetheart." To Nate he said, "I'll meet you inside the restaurant in a few minutes." He took the enormous bouquet from Nicki and smiled graciously at Mrs. Lansky. "A pleasure meeting you, ma'am." He headed toward the elevators.

"It was my pleasure to meet all of you." Mrs. Lansky wrapped Nicki in a hug and then headed toward the entrance.

"Dry your eyes, cousin," Nate said after she left. "You'll have plenty more to bawl about later."

"You're such a pain." Nicki accepted a hug from Izzy, but she stepped on his foot on their way to the table.

"Miss Price, over here." Henry called to her. "I saved you a seat. That young man will have the rest of his life with you."

"Nothing would please me more," Nicki said as she hurried to the spot next to Henry.

"I sure hope you'll stay by me," Nate whispered in Isabelle's ear.

"Absolutely I will. You seem to be a good man to have around." Isabelle squeezed his hand as they sat next to the Prescott family.

Nate extended his hand to Robert's wife. "Hi, I'm Nate Price. You must be Mrs. Prescott."

"I am, but please call me Crystal." She shook with a firm grip. "Thanks so much for the invitation. I've been dying to eat here, but once Robert gets home he refuses to come downtown again."

"I would be the same way, ma'am." Then Nate introduced Isabelle and Detective Marino.

"And this is our daughter, Antoinette, and my grandfather-in-law, Henry." Crystal beamed with pride.

Nate nodded at both. "I met Antoinette and Henry in Mr. Anderson's office yesterday. You must wish to pull my cousin's hair out by the roots. Robert could have lost his job because of her shenanigans."

"A little excitement is good for people. It keeps them young." Crystal smiled at her husband.

Robert straightened his tie and cleared his throat. "All's well that ends well. Don't you agree, Mr. Anderson?" He addressed the general manager.

"You're not kidding." Anderson bobbed his head energetically. "Both newspapers will run features on the famous Carlton jewels. It will be quite a story. The board of directors feels the publicity will keep us booked to capacity for months, if not years, to come. We're hoping the idea of annual getaways with friends will catch on." He turned toward the foot of the table. "Not that I like guests fiddling with fountain controls or climbing slippery works of art." Anderson shook his finger at Nicki. "You shall be closely watched if you ever return, Miss Price."

"If she does, sir, it will be as Mrs. Galen," said Hunter as he strode up to the table. "And I promise to not let her out of my sight." He took the empty chair next to the detective.

Marino lifted his glass of water. "I offer a toast to a very brave man."

"To Hunter and Nicki," said Nate, as everyone followed suit. He clicked his water goblet with Chip's. "Now, I believe Mr. Anderson has an announcement."

"I will be brief because appetizers on the house should arrive soon." Anderson rose to his feet. "Yesterday I called an emergency meeting of our board of directors. When I told them about the discovery, they unanimously voted to contact the heirs of the Smithfield estate. All assets not part of the corporation went to a granddaughter who lives in Illinois. I spoke with her today. Although she must consult with her attorney and tax advisor first, she wishes to sell the diamond letter openers and donate the proceeds to the Mid-South Food Bank here in Memphis."

The announcement received an enthusiastic round of applause.

"We could be talking millions," interjected Antoinette, clearly amazed by the largesse.

"Yes, most likely we are, Miss Prescott." Mr. Anderson smoothed down his tie. "But the Smithfields' heir was well aware of her grandparents' humanitarian nature."

"And she's probably *already* rolling in it." Marino directed his comment at Antoinette. Unfortunately, his deep voice carried across the table.

"I think it's rather generous, no matter what her financial circumstances are," said Nate, shaking his head at his former teammate.

"Hear, hear." Henry tapped his goblet with a fork as their first course arrived.

Anderson smiled as platters of chilled shrimp, oysters on the half shell, and caviar in pastry shells were devoured with effusive praise. For several minutes, Nate enjoyed the food, surrounded by old and new friends, and a brand-new love.

Then, midway through her plate of shrimp, Isabelle set down her fork. "Nate and I also have an announcement." She waited for everyone's attention. "First, I want to thank Detective Marino and the entire Memphis PD for solving my brother's murder."

Chip leaned back in his chair and enjoyed a round of soft applause. "Well, I did get some help from two concerned *visitors* from Mississippi." He looked from Nicki to Nate. "And I'm glad to see you two are getting along better these days." This time he looked at Isabelle.

"Very observant of you, Detective. That's probably why you're so good at your job," Isabelle said, blushing. "Nate has agreed to give me another chance after our rocky start. Next, although I haven't worked out all the details, I plan to move to back home. With Danny gone there's no one keeping me here, and Memphis holds too many bad memories after what I went through with Tony Markham."

"But there's no one left in Natchez with your parents gone." Nicki took a shell of caviar from the silver tray. "You should move to New Orleans where we live."

Isabelle waited as the waiter delivered a bottle of champagne for those who wished to partake. "I still have cousins and a few friends. Besides, Natchez is smaller and slower paced than New Orleans, and every town has houses to sell. Realty World even has an office there."

Around the table, everyone murmured agreement and words of encouragement. Everyone but Nicki, that is.

"How can two people date when one of them lives in New Orleans and the other in Mississippi?" Nicki didn't even try to hide her distress.

"That brings us to the rest of our announcement," said Nate, feeling Izzy's small hand slide into his. "I'm setting up a PI office in Natchez. I have plenty of family who'll make sure Izzy doesn't get lonely." While spatters of applause erupted, Nate locked eyes with his cousin.

"What about me? You hire and fire me all in the same year?" Nicki poured champagne into her glass even though imbibing was something she rarely did. "Is this because I stepped on the ME's toes?" She took a sip and glared at Chip.

The detective threw up his hands. "Don't blame this on me, sister. Your name never came up in my conversations with Nate."

"Perhaps you could discuss this tomorrow, my love." Hunter's melodic drawl floated across the room. "The waiter is ready to take our orders. And this is a night for celebration."

"I beg your pardon," Nicki said to the waiter. "I would like the most expensive entrée you've got." She lifted the menu to hide her face.

Nate gently pushed the menu away. "Order whatever you like, but I'm not firing you. You will be in charge of the New Orleans office. My secretary can continue to work for you in our current office, or maybe Hunter will make space in his building."

"Just think, Nicki. We can hang out whenever you come to Natchez for company meetings." Isabelle clapped her hands.

"No joke? I'll be in charge of Price Investigations in the Big Easy?" Nicki cracked her knuckles under the table.

Nate gave his order to the waiter and swiveled back to Nicki. "Consider this a promotion. No one's better at cyber-sleuthing than my cousin."

"You see, dear heart, a happy ending for one and all." Hunter winked from across the table.

"If Miss Price will be in charge, where can I put in my application? Together we make quite a team." Henry's comment triggered another round of applause.

Isabelle leaned close to his ear. "What a clever man you are."

"You have no idea, but you're about to find out." Nate squeezed her hand and then enjoyed the best meal of his life.

Everyone ate too much as they talked and laughed for hours. Henry entertained them with stories of the good old days. Detective Marino offered snippets of famous crimes of the fifties and sixties to match Henry's era. Mr. Anderson added historical trivia and vignettes about some of the hotel's famous guests. The meal lasted for hours. A few with an inch to spare even had dessert. Finally, one by one the guests thanked Nate profusely and left Chez Francois.

Long after the Prescotts had gone and Hunter and Nicki went up to their respective suites, Nate sipped the last of his coffee simply enjoying Isabelle by his side. Never before had he felt so sure about a person or the decision they had reached. "Are you happy, Miss Andre?"

She flung her silky hair back from her face. "I awarded you the dubious honor of calling me Izzy a while ago, so why the formal address?"

Nate gestured toward the ornate appointments of their private alcove. "A fancy restaurant like this seems to warrant proper titles."

"I suppose you're right. And to answer your question, Mr. Price, I say yes from the bottom of my heart. It's amazing how something good came from my brother's death. It was as though God didn't want me to be alone."

"Are you saying us getting together is some kind of miracle?" Nate gripped the edge of the table, feigning a hurt expression.

"Absolutely. I thought I'd scared you off for good."

"Love…and PI work…aren't for the faint of heart." Nate rose and offered Izzy his hand. "How about a walk before I send you home in a taxi? They say moonlight shining on Old Man River is a sight to behold."

DISCUSSION QUESTIONS

1. Despite her education and training, Nicki behaves badly at the medical examiner's office. What are the advantages and disadvantages of investigating a case in which you're personally connected?

2. Nate's meeting with Isabelle Andre opens an emotional wound. Why do high school rejections sting more than those later in life?

3. Nicki has always been an independent woman, especially on the job. Why doesn't she resent her fiancé's attempt to control her from afar?

4. Why is Nicki drawn to the retired bellman and the history of the Carlton Hotel?

5. The personality of the late Danny Andre is revealed throughout the story. Does your opinion of him change? How so?

6. Isabelle doesn't seem very likable at first. Why has she erected a wall around her heart?

7. The life of a blues musician can be difficult. What challenges did Danny face and yet, what was inherently irresistible?

8. What makes stalking a difficult crime to prevent, enforce, and prosecute?

9. The scavenger hunts of the 1950s would be impossible to duplicate today, even for the very rich. What has changed in the hospitality industry and in our society in general?

10. What valuable lessons does Nicki learn from the living participants of the Carlton scavenger hunts?

ABOUT THE AUTHOR

Mary Ellis is the bestselling author of a dozen novels set in the Amish community and several historical romances set during the Civil War. *Midnight on the Mississippi* and *What Happened on Beale Street* are the first books of a romantic suspense series, Secrets of the South.

Before "retiring" to write full-time, Mary taught school and worked as a sales rep for Hershey Chocolate. Her debut book, *A Widow's Hope*, was a finalist for a 2010 Carol Award. *Living in Harmony* won the 2012 Lime Award for Excellence in Amish Fiction, while *Love Comes to Paradise* won the 2013 Lime Award. Mary and her husband live in Ohio.

Mary can be found on the web at
www.maryellis.net
or
Look for Mary Ellis/Author on Facebook